Dangerous Solutions

Archeons, book 3

by James L. Steele

Nameless Volcanic World

The spacetime orb opened high in the troposphere, just below the volcanic plume. A giant flying reptile covered in dull yellow scales fading to black around his belly leaped through the opening, panicked at the lack of solid ground, and plummeted four hundred paces down toward the ash-covered surface. He tumbled head over tail, screaming in thirty different languages.

At last Norh remembered he had wings. As he flapped them violently, his body righted itself, his descent slowed, and with each stroke of his wings he rose two whole body-lengths up. Just below the clouds he stopped and hovered in place, turning to scan the landscape below.

Volcanoes were sprinkled about as far as Norh could see, most of them spewing toxic gasses. One in the distance seemed to be giving off a constant pyroclastic flow, engulfing so much of the land in boiling hot smoke and ash that Norh couldn't see beyond the cloud resting on the ground.

The angry mountain peaks stretched to the horizon, and Norh remembered they covered most of the planet. They didn't seem to be arranged in any particular pattern, not in a long line of mountains or in a ring around a tectonic plate. The entire world was just covered in them like warts. Norh remembered the crust of this world was thin, allowing the entire planet to heat up and magma to bubble up everywhere.

The frequent rain cleansed the atmosphere and kept it breathable. Otherwise this planet would be a toxic waste dump, just like Norh's garage when he was a kid, and his father bought a puppy but didn't housebreak it, so it shat all over the garage, and after a month without cleaning it up it was the nastiest place Norh could remember.

Norh tucked in his wings and flew over the mountain ranges, scanning the ground as he soared. Pockets of habitable areas existed in some of the valleys between the peaks, regions where lava flow occurred less frequently and life had a chance to take root. Norh was searching for one particular valley. He had no scent to guide him, so he used his eyes.

The mountain peaks didn't line up as Norh remembered. Nothing seemed familiar, and as Norh realized this he streamlined his body and flew faster and faster, scanning the ground as if he were mowing the lawn, back and forth, back and forth in straight lines.

"Where are they?" he roared in English. "The mountains moved. That's gotta be it. The mountains moved. I'm sure I opened the way directly over them—my calculations can't be off. No. No, the people must have moved to a different valley—but no, no, *that's* not right either. It's the only valley in sixty miles they can live in. The only life forms on this planet, and the only place they can live is that tiny valley. An entire ecosystem tucked between mountains of lava —"

Norh's mind kept wandering aloud as he mowed the air in hundred-mile-long strokes. His course took him through several plumes of ash and smoke, but he barely noticed. His scales insulated him from the intense heat, and he closed his eyes and relied on his Archeon senses to keep his course straight.

"—these poor people. Their bodies are so adapted to the heat and poison and the ash they can't live without it. Take them anywhere else, and they'll freeze to death. Horrible luck—not their fault, and it dooms them to live in this hell. How can God exist when things like this are happening all over the universe and nobody knows about it? I'm the only person alive who knows these people exist! But wait—wait—"

Norh did a Max Headroom double-take, shaking his wings, laughing at an imitation nobody was around to see.

"How did I find this planet in the first place? Oh, it's been so long I've forgotten all the years I spent on Kronia, thinking about the stars, watching them wobble, searching for the pattern of an unknown planet orbiting them. Yes. Yes, it took years to find them, but I did! I miss those days..."

Norh relaxed his rigid course and did a barrel roll. Suddenly he realized while performing a barrel roll, he could not be harmed, and now he flew in a straight line, imagining fighter jets and alien spacecraft shooting pixelated lasers at him. Norh flipped, dodged, and fired his own imaginary lasers back, adding his own sound effects. He launched a few nova bombs and cleared the screen, banking side to side in a lazy victory dance.

"Damn, Alex, that game is so much fun," Norh said. "I wish your mom would let you play it more. Hell, I wish she'd let *me* play it more. She doesn't want me to play it without you because you have homework and it'd be too distracting for me to play it while you're trying to work."

He flew into another cloud of poison gas and ash. Norh twirled around in it, shaping the clouds, blowing them backwards as he laughed, and then dove straight into the caldera.

As he hovered above the churning lava, Norh brought his hands up to his earholes, stuck his thumbs in them, and waved his hands at the lava. "Nah, nah, you can't hurt me!" He tried to give it a raspberry, but his lips didn't seem to move that way anymore.

The volcano spat a few chunks that splattered on Norh's underside.

"Is that all you got? As long as I'm here, you won't hurt these people!"

The lava pool bubbled and spat at him. Norh snorted and let himself drop in, submerging all the way. His eyes closed, and the lava wrapped him in a warm blanket. He spread his arms and legs and floated between the surface and the bottomless column of molten rock. When he was sure the elements had heard him, he righted himself, climbed up, and flew out of the lake and straight into the atmosphere, leaving a trail of lava behind him.

He did loops in the air, rolling and spinning. He'd forgotten how good it felt to fly, and he didn't want to waste a moment of it. He never wanted to take it for granted again, and he twisted and rolled every way he could.

Clouds of smoke and ash blew by. Norh huffed at them, flapped his wings, and pushed the smoke back where it came from, leaving his playground clear. He righted himself and soared over the deadly landscape, humming a tune he couldn't quite remember, but the word "Orabidoo" came to mind, and he flapped gently with the pace of the melody.

"Why haven't I bought one myself?" Norh said, thinking about the game again. "I can afford it, so why don't I have one?"

Suddenly he remembered where he was, and why. He flipped over and sped back the way he had come, chasing the magnetic field until it reached the right intensity. He had forgotten he could sense the planet's magnetism, and he remembered exactly how it felt over the habitable valley, and now he laughed at himself for wasting so many hours trying to find it by sight.

By this time he had flown halfway around the planet, but his new sense took him directly where he needed to be.

The daytime star had set on this side of the world, but the ground was alight in lava. Norh noticed a lava flow coming from one of the mountains, and his sense of the planet's magnetic field locked in place and told him he was in the right area.

"Shit!"

He brought his wings to his flanks and dove straight for it. He thought of the valley, of the villages, of the people inside it—people who had lived in this valley for a thousand years, intelligent but not quite self-aware.

And they were lonely. On a previous visit, Norh had scoured the planet for another sentient life form, hoping this would not become a lone species after all, but there was nothing alive on the world except for the people here in this one particular valley.

The lava flowed like ranch dressing. Norh would have preferred honey, or syrup—not flavored corn syrup, but real tree sap—that was the best. Norh craved pancakes. He promised to make some when he returned home, after he took care of this.

He hit the ground hard, aligned parallel to the flow, claws dug in. The flood of red-hot liquid smashed into him, but the Krone held his ground and pushed back. The lava yielded and pooled against him. He wanted to push the lava back up the mountainside, but it was too hot and thin to work.

"As soon as this is over," he shouted in a language he didn't know he knew, "I'm finding you a new valley! There has to be another one! There has to be some other place you can live on this world that isn't on fire!"

Even as he said it, he knew it was an empty promise. These people had to live in volcanic regions. Their bodies did not produce any heat of their own, and their skin was so thick and lungs so well-adapted that they were physically incapable of living anywhere without the searing heat and poison gasses.

The lava began to cool. When the weight of the molten rock became too much for him to hold, he began walking sideways down the mountain, and the lava moved down the slope with him, spreading out, cooling faster. Norh spread his wings and fanned it. The surface began to harden, and Norh kept walking, encouraging the liquid rock underneath to flow out.

Eventually, the flow finally stopped. He had tamed it. Norh turned around, expecting people to run up and thank him, but no one was there. Norh scented the air. He walked away from the basalt road he had just paved and into the valley where the village should be.

The entire valley was covered in fresh, volcanic rock. No scents anywhere. Norh was sure this valley was protected from all but the rarest lava flows, but it appeared this place had been covered many times. He realized his elevation was about six paces higher than he expected.

This valley had been full of life. Plants, animals, people—all coexisting here, surrounded by death and poison yet touched by none of it. Norh remembered it so clearly it didn't seem possible he was in the same place.

He wandered the valley, searching for a remnant of civilization, but the lava had destroyed all of it. His sense of magnetism confirmed the location, though his eyes still didn't believe it. He turned his head and neck up. The mountain peaks lined up with his memory now. A few new peaks had appeared since his last visit, which puzzled him.

Suddenly memories slammed back into his mind, and Norh dropped to his stomach, shuddering and wishing he had an aspirin, while also knowing aspirin would not affect his body anymore.

These people... Even with death and destruction surrounding them, they had still found a reason to fight amongst themselves. They were carnivores, and they ate the other animals that fed off the plants, so they began to fight over the hunting grounds. The valley itself was only three hundred square miles from end to end, and so narrow one could walk from one side to the other in just an hour.

Norh had thought they would learn to cooperate, but they never had. They'd just kept fighting. Norh had taken several of the most aggressive ones to the air with him, showing them how he saw the world, but it hadn't helped them gain any new perspective. All they cared about was their territory.

"Why didn't they see it?" Norh's wings unfolded over the ground. "Why did they keep fighting—why didn't they cooperate? If only I could have moved them somewhere else!"

Norh tried to cry, but he couldn't remember how. Wings hanging low did not seem to do justice to what had happened here, so he held his mouth open and gasped, trying to mourn them properly.

"Moving them wouldn't have mattered. They still would have fought. If only they saw the planet like I did. All those years... I'm so sorry."

Behind him, the volcanic flow resumed and began covering the valley in a new layer of rock.

Gaow

I

The raptors leaped through the portal, Deka scenting the air even before he touched the ground. He hadn't smelled this in so long, he'd begun to wonder if it had ever existed.

Relians.

More than a hundred of them. So many raptors and foxes just a few paces away Deka felt he was back on Rel again. They smelled real. *Solid.* Not impressions from the past, and certainly not panicking and running for their lives.

Many of them had noticed the portal and seen him and Rive step through. Shouts traveled across the shoreline, and the theropods and canines ran across the sand to meet their other theropod Archeon. Deka crossed necks and tapped claws with everyone as they crowded around to tell their stories. Deka had met most of them before; Rel's population had been huge, but there had been few complete strangers.

Many had felt their homeworld rumbling and had known something was wrong. Some had taken portals to the other side to see what was happening, and there they'd seen the antisphere ripping the planet apart and swallowing it in pieces. Most had been mesmerized by it, but these people had had the presence of mind to flee to the hub.

When the antisphere tore up more of the planet and portals began going out, they'd had no choice but to run through the nearest sphere.

Raptors had been separated from their foxes. They had been alone on their worlds for weeks or months. The foxes had begun to revert, and some had nearly sunk into their old ways permanently until Rive and Friend arrived.

"Rive brought me back," someone said.

"I chased the Gelleens so far away they had to rebuild the settlement somewhere else," said another. "Almost killed a few of them, but they were scared of me. I was scared."

All the foxes had similar stories, but they seemed to have raptors with them now—raptors who had lost their own foxes to the disaster.

"Rive brought you back?" Deka asked them.

The foxes flicked their ears, all agreeing, and Deka pointed at Rive.

"*Him?* He brought you back from the old ways?"

The foxes waved their tails, smiling and laughing.

"This raptor couldn't even keep his own fox from hunting, and he brought all of you back by *himself?*"

Rive looked down at his feet, rubbing his claws. His metallic claws clinked against his real claws, and it sounded distorted but also beautiful to hear another theropod laughing again.

Everyone had a story to tell, and Deka heard every one of them. Stories of survival and desperation, panic and devastation. Many had leaped through ways to planets decimated by the disaster, escaping the destruction on Rel only to find panic and death on the worlds they fled to.

No two had the same story, and as the planet's daytime star rose higher overhead, Deka took them all in. Some had been through nightmares even worse than the ones Deka had witnessed.

2

Gaow was a young planet that had yet to develop intelligent life, and most of the life that had emerged here still lived in the ocean. The animals were filter feeders, some passive drifters and others mobile, but competition had yet to arise among these forms of life. This harmony would remain until someone figured out how to take nutrients from someone else.

There was no competition among the species of plant life, either. With plenty of space for the large, leafy ferns and stalk-like trees to grow, they did not compete for light or nutrients. Their only challenge was the weather, which changed frequently and swung to extremes in temperature, wind speed, and precipitation.

The raptors had nothing to hunt, so the foxes had been the ones to go out into the water to catch the primitive life forms, each a strange mixture of both plant and animal components, representing life at the point where the genetic tree began to split.

The raptors could eat most of these creatures, but without the hunt, they were not very tasty, sustaining life but not the emotions. Most managed to derive amusement from watching their foxes hunt for them, and that at least gave the meat some flavor.

Deka and Rive sat on a small cliff overlooking the ocean, watching the foxes in the water and their raptors spectating from the shore. Even after all their time on this world, the raptors still smelled playfully jealous. A few reptiles had ventured out into the water, trying to swim just so they could hunt something. They stumbled and flailed while their foxes swam gracefully next to them.

"This was mine and Friend's private world," Rive said. His voice had a metallic sound which made him sound perpetually wounded and tired. "We loved it here. I used to spend days just staring into the water, watching the animals. Just thinking that for these few million years, everything is in harmony. Plants and animals keep to themselves, and nobody has to hunt or struggle to survive. Being witness to an ecosystem before the creatures develop means to steal nutrients from other creatures. Before predator and prey."

"Was it your idea to bring the the Relians here?"

Rive's gaze wandered back and forth across the shoreline. "I figured Friend sacrificed so many planets to whatever he was doing, so we should sacrifice our private world. It doesn't come close to making up for it, but this was the best place to leave them."

Deka turned to face the metal raptor. "What about you, Rive? What's your story of survival? Start from the part when you suddenly became able to bring foxes back from the old ways."

Rive rubbed his claws, still facing the ocean. "This..." He held up his grey arm. "The metal did something to me."

Rive felt his metallic arm with his real hand. His claws dragged over the frame, and he touched the seam between the metal and flesh.

"I know I was never much of a physical person," he continued. "Then the disaster happened. I saw the antisphere when it formed and started growing. I did the same thing Sonjaa did. I tried to help Friend calm down and stop thinking about... whatever it was. He couldn't, so he ran. There were too many people standing still and staring at it, and they slowed me down. Next thing I knew, my leg was gone. Then my arm. Then half my body. And Friend came back. He picked up what was left of me and carried me to the portal that led to the hub. I blacked out, but he told me the offworld portal collapsed as he was coming through. He was lucky he only lost his tail."

Rive gave off a scent of weariness, but with less skin, the scent was weak, and the added scent of the metal made him smell like some unknown species.

"When I woke up, this was the first thing I saw." Rive tapped a claw on his metal arm. "Friend had made a way to some uncontacted planet he called Reth. He told me the people there rebuilt me. My brain was still intact, and they kept it alive while they reassembled my body. Friend knew exactly what was missing and how it fit together, and he taught them."

Rive's body reminded Deka of the crystal people on Neben, with no visible joints, and the metal itself seemed to flex and move. Rive's arm was an articulate tube of solid grey matter formed into an exact mirror image of the real arm on his other side. There were no other parts connecting one to another. His arm was a single piece that behaved just as a real arm would, and the seam where the metal joined with skin was smooth and precise.

Deka reached over and grasped Rive's forearm. It was cold. Rive reached over with his real arm and touched his claws to Deka's.

"I know," Rive said. "I'm always cold now. Even daylight doesn't seem to warm me. These pieces don't feel part of me. There have been many days all I could think about was tearing the metal off."

Deka felt where the arm connected with the plate covering Rive's chest. It was so smooth Deka's Archeon sense of touch felt no molecule out of place. He had seen it deform like skin as Rive moved, but Deka could not feel any sign of distortion. Deka clanged on it, and it sounded as solid as it felt, but hollow.

"I don't know what happened to my internal organs. I know my heart is gone. I hear it beating, and it sounds like metal moving. Sometimes I wake up at night in a panic at the sound of it."

Deka studied Rive's legs, one mechanical, the other flesh and bone, both joining up to an artificial torso. "I don't see any joints in the limbs. How did they do this? What metal is this?"

"I'm not sure," said Rive. "I wanted to ask Friend, but as soon as I woke up, he told me to make a way offworld anywhere as fast as I could. He said he couldn't stop thinking about it, and he was afraid another antisphere was about to happen, and he couldn't concentrate on portals anymore. Our survival depended on me figuring out a way. I begged Friend to tell me how he did all of this, but either he couldn't, or he wouldn't. Now it makes more sense. He knew he would need me to make ways offworld."

Deka became transfixed by Rive's lower jaw, how it attached to his real skull, how the metal wrapped around his neck and joined with the torso. He looked as though he had been sculpted this way rather than salvaged.

"I wanted to meet the people of the planet we were on, but I never did, and Friend never told me much about them. I wasn't fast enough making a way to the next world. Later that day, he grabbed his head and screamed, and an antisphere swallowed the planet's star. It swallowed several planets in the solar system. He kept screaming that we were far enough away and it would never reach us, but it cut through part of the planet. By then I had made an offworld portal, and we left before it consumed everything."

Deka chirped, crying a little, his whole body quivering.

"I cry for them every day," Rive said. "I wish I had met them. Friend did tell me the metal is blended with other compounds to make it flex like muscle. This entire arm is actually one large muscle. My leg is the same way. My chest, my jaw... It feels remarkable. For a while I just took us to planets that were as far away from their parent stars as possible. I tried sending us back and forth between two worlds, hoping the equations in Friend's mind would reset and we wouldn't have to go anywhere or risk other planets, but if we went back to a place we had already been, the antisphere formed immediately. Whatever was happening, it was tied to his position in the universe, so I had to take us to different worlds. Sometimes I could make a new portal before Friend destroyed a world, sometimes not. Shortly after you caught up to us on Crexa, Friend said he saw it. He saw the universe as a whole. He saw the survivors, and he started telling me where to go. I listened to him, but..."

"That's when you started leaving a trail?"

Rive curled his neck. "I hoped you and Kylac were still following us, because I didn't know what to do. Then we found survivors. A single fox alone on one planet, a few raptors alone on another, six raptors and foxes on another world. Friend was right, and that scared me even more."

The fear coming off Rive was thick. The metallic sounds his body made were distracting—he didn't sound like a whirring, clanking machine the way Stephen's culture depicted them, but the metal hummed and sang on a molecular level as it contracted and bent.

"So that's another reason you didn't kill him," said Deka. "The survivors."

"Yes. He knew where to find them, and we brought them to safety after I helped the reverted foxes. I wasn't afraid of them anymore."

"That's hard to imagine."

"Deka, it was worse than that. All my life I wasn't just afraid. I saw it many times. Foxes reverting. My first instinct was never to fight and tame the fox, but to run away. When I was a hatchling, I was ashamed of myself. I hoped I would never have to do that to my fox. I was never sure if I could, and I was so relieved when Friend turned out to be stable." He stared down at the sand again. A raptor offshore slipped and fell in the water. Three foxes were helping her up. Rive continued. "The first time we met one of the refugees separated from her raptor, I almost ran away. She was faster, and she attacked me, but she couldn't hurt me. Even when she clawed my real body, it healed immediately."

"What do you mean?"

With his metallic hand, Rive grabbed the skin on his chest and ripped it away, exposing the bare muscle. Blood poured out of the wound, and Deka felt phantom pains in his chest.

Breaths later, the skin spread back over the muscle and sealed up. Nothing was left of the wound except for the blood running down his skin and metal. Deka met Rive's eyes again. The metal seemed to radiate cold now.

"He told me my flesh is infused with the metal, too. It knows what it's supposed to be, and it corrects any variation. But yes. It hurts. When I realized it did this, I chased down reverted foxes, lifted them up with one arm, and forced them to come back. It was incredible. I had to fight off hundreds of people to protect my fox, and it was easy. For the first time in my life, I wasn't afraid to be physical. I suddenly had desire to hunt. When I saw a reverted fox, I felt that urge to help a fox I had only ever heard about. I felt like a raptor."

Deka stared. Rive turned and met Deka's gaze for the first time since they left Rel's moon.

"Friend told me those people had rebuilt my body entirely out of this flexible metal, but he demanded they only rebuild the missing parts so I could still feel some warmth. He said the people of that planet lived their entire lives in this manner. Cold, unfeeling, separated from reality. If not for this skin, I would be completely numb, as they were. They liked the cold. Friend told me their brains process information faster at low temperatures."

Deka couldn't think of anything to say except: "*My God.*"

Rive tilted his head. "What language is that?"

"English."

He touched his claws. "Haven't heard of it."

"No... No."

Rive held up the flesh arm and looked it over. "Friend wanted me to have skin and blood because he planned to bring Rel back and give the survivors their home, and he wanted me to be able to live there again. I believed he could, so I watched him experiment, taking us offworld before the spheres consumed us. I tried to evacuate them, but as Friend neared what he called 'the solution,' there was less and less time. By then he'd begun experimenting with bringing worlds back from their own past."

"Hypsil?"

"I still don't know what went wrong there. He tried to restore a few other planets after he destroyed them. It was a nightmare."

"My God," Deka whispered, in English again.

Rive held his hands together, rubbing the claws just a little, but holding his head down in a sardonic smile. "I think I understand those words now."

"I wish Friend could bring planets back," said Deka. "Lone species or not, I would have liked to meet the people who helped you."

"So do I."

"Rive, I'm... I can't think of anything to say."

"You can tell me what happened to you and Kylac since the disaster. And who was that hairless creature Norh carried off?"

Deka turned to the ocean again, watching the foxes pull harmless animals from it. Some canines stood on the shore, feeding their raptors. Deka laughed a little at the sight and took a few deep breaths, deciding where to begin.

"His name is Stephen. A human. Lone species from a world called Earth. His first time offworld. Kylac and I ended up on his world by accident. He begged us to take him along and observe a few planets. We were just about to send him home from Kronia, but Norh volunteered to take care of him."

"Norh came with you for his sake?"

"Yes, and Stephen had no idea how incredibly special that was! I've been trying to get Norh to notice me for *years*, and here comes this furless primate who can't survive anywhere, earning Norh's attention without even trying."

"He didn't know?"

"He had no idea, and I didn't want to take out my anger on him. I was angry about a lot of things, though. I channeled it into finding Friend." Deka's voice dropped. "I hope Stephen is all right. I'm sure Norh took him somewhere on his own, but I wish he'd told us where. And now..."

Deka trailed off as he watched the foxes on the shore. They were so tame and calm. Deka thought of Kylac. He didn't want to imagine his fox any other way, but the longer they were separated, the more likely Kylac's animal instincts would rise to the surface, and Kylac would lose his higher mind. He was prone to it, and Deka shivered thinking about it.

"We made it offworld as the antisphere destroyed our planet," he continued. "Then Kylac and I spent a year traveling to planets in the contacted universe. We helped them recover after the portals went out." Deka tried to maintain an even voice, but thinking about everything that had happened reminded him he had no idea where to go now. "We found you shortly after we ended up on Earth. When we picked up your trail again, we cleaned up the messes your fox left behind. Planets torn in half. Atmospheres leaking into space. Entire species on the verge of extinction. And I kept meeting Sonjaa. Different body every time, different species. She died again and again in front of me, and I couldn't do a thing to stop it." Deka couldn't stop shaking, and now he couldn't breathe. "First I lost my planet. Then I lost my mate. Then I lost Chreeb. Now my fox! It never ends!"

Rive laid a hand on Deka's shoulder. The artificial arm felt cold, and Deka wanted to pull away, but he had a feeling no one had touched Rive in a very long time, so he ignored it as he cried.

"Chreeb didn't survive?" Rive asked.

"No, I talked to him for days, trying to help him wake up, but he was already brain dead."

"I'm sorry. He was a wonderful person. You always did adore the aquatics, and when you finally had a personal relationship with one, I thought you'd never leave Ixcy. I am so sorry he's gone. I am sorry about Sonjaa, and I wish I knew where Friend took your fox, but he did tell me where the rest of the survivors are. We should go to them and finish what we started."

"Without our foxes? Rive, they'll revert! Together they'll—they'll..." Deka couldn't finish.

Rive wrapped his neck around Deka's. The metal took Deka's heat, but the gesture calmed his nerves. He forgot about Kylac and Friend and Stephen and Norh for a moment. He stopped convulsing.

"I'm so tired," Deka said finally. "I have been moving nonstop since the disaster. I saw my mate die over and over. I saw entire civilizations end. Right now, all I want to do is curl up and sleep forever, but..." The touch of another theropod helped more than he thought it would. Deka caught his breath. "That won't help, will it? It won't bring my fox back. It won't bring Sonjaa back. You should make the ways, Rive. I can't keep portals open for very long."

Rive rubbed his neck against Deka's. The smooth, frigid metal contrasted with the warm scales. "Deka, I wish I could have told my past self to run as well."

Rive seemed less cold now, and Deka was glad. He imagined the metal raptor must feel twice as cold—without a body or his fox—as Deka felt without Kylac.

Juza

Two Relian canines spilled out of the portal together and landed on soft sand. Rocks lined this long beach, and the crashing waves split open large pods clinging to the rocks, making them bleed red.

Friend landed on top of Kylac and held him down as the portal closed. Kylac recognized the planet Juza, a temperate world with native people who stayed as far from the coast as possible. The bleeding rocks were quite toxic, which had made the ocean toxic as well. Everyone lived inland, where the water was fresh and there were no rock-clinging creatures that released poison into the water to keep predators away.

Friend lay snout to snout with him. Kylac threw the older fox off and rolled upright, looking down the beach, breathing in the noxious vapors coming from the ocean. Finally he turned back to Friend, who was sitting in the sand like a quadruped.

"How did you do that?" Kylac asked. "How did you open all those spheres at the same time?"

Suddenly Friend's scent was not in turmoil. "Something amazing is happening. I wanted to share it with you."

Kylac rose to his hind legs, looking in all directions. "Where's Rive? Where is Deka?"

"They both want me dead. I had to leave them behind."

Kylac whirled back to Friend. "What happened to Sonjaa?"

Friend stood up. "Kylac, imagine a square. It represents the universe. The portals you make—"

"We were on Rel!" Kylac shouted. "You brought Rel back from the past, and we were there to see it destroyed again!"

"Listen to me."

"You said you could bring back all the planets we lost. You were *wrong*! Why did I give you a chance? Why did I stop Deka from killing you?" He clutched his skull and clenched his teeth. "I should have known! You don't even know what you're talking about!"

Friend took a step closer to Kylac, reaching out to him. "I'm still figuring it out. You can help me."

Kylac stepped back. "You can't fix what you've done."

"We can help each other. Let me explain."

"No." Kylac took another step back. "I stopped Deka from killing you, but now I agree with him, and Rive isn't here." He fanned his claws and bared his teeth. "That leaves me."

He charged Friend. Friend snarled, meeting the younger fox head-on. Kylac bowled Friend over, and they rolled in the sand. A moment later, they separated and squared off three paces apart. Neither had a scratch on him.

"Kylac, I have a plan!"

Kylac snarled. "Is that what you kept telling Rive?"

"It's different now. You're here."

Kylac charged again. This time Friend grabbed Kylac and swung him around, but Kylac held on, clamping his muzzle on Friend's nose. Friend clawed Kylac down the side of his head, and they fell into one another, rolling in the sand again. Finally Friend pushed Kylac off and stood.

Kylac jumped to his feet. Blood ran down Friend's muzzle, and Kylac's head and chest also had open wounds.

Kylac was about to charge when he realized blood was starting to smell good. He held his breath. His ears folded, and he knelt, trying to hold himself together. He thought of Deka, trying to keep his scent in his memory. It wasn't working, though—Friend's scent still filled him with rage. He huddled into himself, trying to imagine breathing Deka's scent.

He felt a padded hand on his arm. Kylac threw it off and stumbled away, still shivering, still trying to force his mind not to take pleasure in blood scent. He stared at Friend. Blood dripped from the tailless fox's muzzle.

"I can't kill you without reverting," Kylac said. "Deka... has no idea where I am, does he?"

"No one does."

"If I revert, it may be years before he finds me, with the portals out. He may never be able to bring me back. He may have to kill me. Friend..."

"I can help you."

Kylac bared his teeth. "Stay away from me!"

"I'm not talking about sex! I have a theory."

Kylac snarled. His Archeon mind weighed the options between sparing other planets from destruction and reverting permanently, and he decided his life was worth the entire contacted universe. Kylac allowed scent anxiety take him—allowed his mind, at last, to take pleasure from the smell of blood—and charged Friend. They collided. Friend gripped Kylac by the shoulders as Kylac snapped his teeth at him.

Friend kneed Kylac in the stomach. Kylac yanked Friend down with him, howling and barking, pulling Friend close and clamping down on his arm as Friend snapped his jaws over Kylac's.

As they hit the sand, Friend shoved Kylac away and ran on two legs down the beach. Kylac rolled to all fours and pursued. His higher mind had shut down. Blood was now the only scent that made him calm and gave him any sense of pleasure, and he had to have more of it. Friend was wounded but still a threat, still inside his territory—Kylac's sense of territory extended as far as he could smell, and now he could not rest until Friend was either dead or bleeding so much the blood smell overrode his body scent.

Friend jumped on top of a half-buried boulder. Kylac didn't even notice that the ocean was red and giving off toxic fumes; all he could think about was extinguishing a scent in his territory. He sprang on top of the rock and followed Friend across it as a red wave crashed against it. Kylac landed in tide pools and slipped on wet surfaces.

Friend stopped at a ledge overlooking the ocean and turned to face the younger fox. Kylac panted, still snarling, his nose burning from the fumes. He approached Friend on all fours, teeth still bared, fur raised, Deka long forgotten.

Another red wave crashed against the rock. The fumes made Kylac dizzy. One of his hind legs failed to respond, slipping out from under him, but still Kylac stood on three legs, teeth bared.

A tiny flicker of conscious thought rose through the scent anxiety: Friend was holding his breath.

Kylac tried to turn around, but the world was spinning too fast. Another

leg gave out, and his snout hit the red-stained rock. Then a portal opened underneath him, and he fell through and landed on soft sand, in cleaner air. Another portal opened next to him, and Friend stepped through. Both spheres then winked shut.

Friend's scent was still in Kylac's territory. Kylac tried to snarl at him, but the world kept spinning, and he couldn't even raise himself upright. Kylac vomited. It did not clear his head. He heaved again as Friend knelt next to him.

"Imagine a square," Friend whispered in his ear. "It represents the entire universe. The portals you make are within that square, and you can travel anywhere inside it."

Kylac lay still as the world revolved around him, dry heaving and hating Friend's scent and wishing for more blood to calm him down. He didn't hear the older fox's words.

"Now imagine another square next to that. It represents one breath in the past. You can make a portal anywhere on that square as well."

Kylac panted.

"Imagine an infinite number of squares arranged in a straight line. They represent every finite division of time. The difficult part is isolating one particular square, because the square on which you stand is always different. Archeons are used to thinking of only their square, Kylac, where the universe is now, but it's possible to see where the universe has been. It's always moving. It's going somewhere. This means the universe exists somewhere."

Kylac hated Friend's voice, hated his scent in his nose. He would have given anything to be able to control his body so he could snuff that scent out and be at peace again. Kylac vomited again, though there wasn't much left to come up.

"The equations are the same for each square," Friend continued. "To cross the border..."

Friend started giving Kylac equations. The equations resembled ones that described the universe Kylac knew, but these had extra variables that included another dimension of travel.

As Friend spoke, Kylac had no choice but to listen. Gradually he began to hear Friend's words again, and to see the hidden dimension in the equations Friend gave him.

As his vision stopped spinning and his stomach settled, he began to ponder the equations instead of Friend's scent. The numbers came to life, chugging and cranking, one equation pushing another. The solution tantalized him; something new lay underneath all of it.

Kylac felt like an apprentice again, pondering the equations that defined the universe, letting them spin around and around in his mind but still unable to solve them. He remembered how it had been, sensing the solution so close—so perfect and so right—while the problem turned and aligned changed position in his mind until finally he had opened his first spacetime portal. It had led to empty space, but it had been a solution. He had glimpsed the universe as it truly was, and his mind had, for the very first time, crossed the barrier between what he perceived and what was real, and connected two points in spacetime to form a sphere he could travel through. It had been the most exhilarating feeling—enough to make Kylac go days without sex while he worked the equations out, becoming more precise day by day as he explored his ability and became an Archeon, able to hold these spheres open and allow people to travel light years and visit other planets instantly.

And now, here it was again, that feeling of sensing something beyond what he could smell, see, and touch, but on a deeper level. Friend's equations *worked*. Kylac sensed there must be a solution to them, and that when he had that solution, there would be a reward.

He sensed a solution. There had to be one, and a pleasant surprise waiting for him when he worked it out. A new perspective of the universe was taking shape as his mind worked out the equations. Each one returned results that another needed to continue, and his entire mind filled with a cluster of interlocking mathematical formulas. It always had been filled with equations anyway, back when he had maintained portals across the contacted universe, but that had been easy. Adding just these few variables changed everything, and his mind longed to work it out. The universe started to reveal itself as more than just a universe expanding into a mathematical void, but a *moving* one, traveling and spreading out, leaving a wake behind. The traditional Archeon equations assumed a stationary universe, but Friend's equations allowed for a universe in motion within another, larger structure, and now that Kylac became conscious of the motion, he could not ignore it anymore.

Something existed beyond the universe. A medium through which it traveled.

A Lake.

Kylac looked up and froze. An antisphere hung in the sky like a dark moon.

As Kylac watched, it grew. The sand began to ripple, and then, far in the distance, the ground began to heave upwards. Columns of rock, sand, and magma pulled away from the planet and toward the antisphere.

"Don't be afraid," Friend said.

Kylac pressed his hands to his temples, trying to stop the equations, but he had glimpsed something. He had reached beyond reality and felt a new connection, and his mind had to know what it was.

The antisphere kept growing. The entire planet cracked open. Kylac tried to stop the way from spinning, but the equations told him it wasn't spinning at all, which didn't make sense either.

The antisphere intersected the ground, tearing it into chunks. Kylac swore he could hear screams from distant people, an entire species crying in agony.

Friend was next to him now, pulling him to his feet, and Kylac leaned on him as he tried to stop everything, tried to clear his mind—but he wasn't sure where this new portal led, so he couldn't sense how to close it. It didn't seem to go anywhere, so it shouldn't be open at all, and therefore he couldn't close it because this way didn't exist—but it *did* exist, and it went somewhere, so he could close it, but he didn't know where it led, and therefore it didn't lead anywhere and thus did not exist—

Kylac clutched his head and screamed. Friend held him up as the planet shook and the antisphere ripped the landscape apart.

A regular portal opened up in front of them, and Friend nudged Kylac toward it. "Moving to a different world ends the equation in one location, but begins it on another. It's why Rive and I kept moving."

"Friend." Kylac said through his clenched teeth. "How do I stop it?"

Friend walked him to the portal. Kylac hung from his arm, mind reeling at what it was witnessing. In an instant they had stepped from a cool beach to a hot desert. Friend stopped, and the way closed behind them.

The equations stuttered. Kylac's mind became aware of his new location, and his Archeon sense of the environment readjusted and began the equations anew. Kylac sensed he had some time before they reached critical mass, and he collapsed into the sand, exhausted. Friend started to walk away, but Kylac reached out and grabbed him around the waist. He never wanted to let go of Friend again.

Friend knelt and held him. "You are now in a fragile state of mind, Kylac. Your mind is working the equations out. You won't be able to make normal ways until it does."

"I begged you not to tell me! I said I didn't want to know. Why did you do this to me?"

"Because you wanted to know what was happening. That's why you didn't kill me on Vico."

"I didn't kill you because Rive could have stopped me!"

"But you were curious." He rubbed noses with Kylac, licked him lightly. "Deka wanted to kill me, but you wanted to understand. This is what it means to know."

Kylac panted for a moment, still holding Friend. "I just destroyed that planet... I just... *Oh my God.*"

Friend's ears folded back and he tilted his head. "What did you say?"

"It's English. Stephen... I hope he's all right. Where are— Oh no! It's starting again! I can't think about anything else!"

"It won't stop until the gap between what you perceive and what you know closes. Until then, you will be without sleep and will barely be able to communicate. And yes, Kylac. You will be responsible for as many planets as it takes to figure this out."

Kylac shoved Friend away and stood hunched over, his claws and teeth bared, wanting to tear Friend apart for doing this to him. Then, in the tiny pause between equations, when his mind was slightly quieter for an instant, he realized something.

"You don't want me to get away. You crippled me so I can't make a portal of my own."

"You can make them, but it takes a lot of effort. I only succeeded in making one, and it was because Rive was in pieces. I am your only hope of controlling these equations. Listen to me, and you may only destroy thirty planets instead of fifty-six."

"Take me to Cham!" Kylac began to snarl, but sharp pain pierced his skull as the equations began to take over. "Take me back to Loam—maybe there's still enough atmosphere!"

"I saw the universe, Kylac. I saw it as a whole. Remember what Archeons have been saying for centuries? About how someday everyone will be an Archeon, and then the universe will change? This is enormous! Look."

Friend stood silently for a moment, and twenty portals opened simultaneously just above their heads, all leading to different worlds. Kylac lifted his muzzle to the sky, looking from one to the next. He recognized every world, and they were all millions of light years apart.

"I see the universe more clearly now," Friend said. I know there are exactly seventeen completely uninhabited worlds that happen to have an atmosphere we can breathe. It's not enough."

"Rive gave Vico an atmosphere. Do it for a few asteroids!"

"It takes time for an atmosphere to build up, even with a dozen portals spinning away. Time you won't have. What about temperature? Or food and water? You can't live without those."

"You can make ways instantly, Friend! That's not a problem for you!"

"We will as often as we can." The spheres over their heads silently winked away. "But there won't always be enough time. Sooner or later, we'll have to go to an inhabited planet, and you will destroy it."

Friend took a slow step toward the younger fox. "I know what you're going through, Kylac, and when you reach the end, you will thank me. Someday everyone will understand the universe in this way, and then we will look back on the deaths and realize the knowledge was worth it."

Kylac snarled, and then the equations became so loud in his mind he couldn't hear Friend speaking. He gasped, sat down, and tried to calm his mind.

Friend sat next to him, putting an arm around Kylac's shoulder. "We have to understand this. Fifty-six planets... I won't let them die for nothing, and neither will you."

Kylac looked at him. He tried not to breathe his scent, but he couldn't help it. He wanted to tear Friend's throat out... but he also knew Friend was his only chance of living through this.

"What about our raptors?" Kylac said. "The old ways."

Friend's stump of a tail wagged in amusement. "You're so confused you don't even realize what I just did. I brought you back from the old ways, Kylac. The *equations* brought you back. You don't need Deka. I don't need Rive."

"I'm prone to reverting, Friend. How many times has it happened to you?"

"I brought you back without a raptor. This confirms what I have been thinking for years. We are conscious creatures. We can control ourselves."

"You've never felt it before, have you? You're not prone to reverting. I am. Equations won't be enough. I *need* Deka—and you need Rive."

"I couldn't bring our raptors with us. You know Deka. He won't rest until he kills me. And Rive... He could barely open ways fast enough to keep up. He was scared of me. *He* wanted me dead, too. He just didn't have the courage to kill me. This is the only way you would listen to me." Friend held him tighter, shoulder to shoulder. "We will make this work."

Kylac clutched his head, digging his claws into his fur. The equations were still running, spinning, orbiting. Kylac loathed it already because these weren't normal equations. They would not work themselves out—Kylac had to manage every number, every result. He whimpered, begging them to stop and let him think. He couldn't even remember how to reply to Friend; the equations had taken over everything.

Friend held him. "It's normal, Kylac. You'll figure it out eventually."

Kylac wanted to snarl at him and make sure he never touched him again. For once, though, it wasn't the old ways sneaking up on him. It was a thought from his own desperate, civilized mind.

Unnamed Rainy World

Norh flew through the portal and held position five thousand feet above the ground, scanning the landscape for anything familiar.

He remembered these herbivores had crowded onto one little strip of land because it was the only place their food grew. Long ago they had fought over grazing territory, and now that they had achieved intelligence, they fought over land to grow their crops. It was the natural thing to happen to an intelligent species without a companion: no matter how intelligent they became, they would live to satisfy their animal nature.

Norh peered closely at the land far below, analyzing the visual spectrum from the infrared through the x-ray. A sound in the distance distracted him, and he turned his head toward it.

A thundercloud at the horizon. Lightning lit it from the inside, making a purple and blue web reaching from top to bottom, bottom to top, then back and forth.

It was time to convince these herbivores to cooperate, and he was willing to be the antagonist that brought them together. He had learned from his experience on the volcanic world, and he did not intend to make the same mistake twice.

Norh flew straight to the storm. The thunder grew louder, and the lightning scared him at first until Norh remembered it followed predictable patterns and should not intimidate him at all. Just in case, he did barrel rolls all the way up to the thunderhead.

He punctured the cloud. Electricity grabbed him, streaked along his scales, and branched off his tail, his claws, and his bone ridges. It was as if the cloud were a living organism responding to an invasion, and it attacked him from all sides. Norh halted and flapped in place. The lightning webbed him, striking him on the nose, claws, and all over his body, leaving harmlessly from the opposite side.

Norh flapped his wings and then folded them, streamlining himself to pick up speed. He flew in a tight circle inside the cloud, taking lightning bolts to his face. The electrons traveled down his scales and dripped off as he corkscrewed up the thunderhead, then down, then up, then back down.

The cloud condensed. The lightning became more intense, and Norh gritted his teeth against the wind. He closed his eyes and let his sense of electromagnetism tell him where he was in the cloud. The storm disturbed it, and for some reason Norh felt intimidated, but he remembered he had taken out bigger storms than this.

The thunderhead spun with him, some parts becoming more dense, but the rest of the clouds flung outwards. Norh broke his flight pattern and dove through the rest of the storm. The rain and hail pelting his hide seemed as if they should hurt, but he didn't feel a thing. The constant lightning washing over his entire body should have killed him—Norh's body reacted as though his life were in danger and this was an incredible thing he was trying to do—but he wasn't sure why he felt this way. There was nothing incredible about breaking up a thunderstorm. Every Krone could do it. Nonetheless, Norh felt powerful and invincible, while at the same time still feeling dumbfounded by the scale of his own actions.

Norh flew up and down the entire storm system so fast he overtook the sound of the rain hitting his own scales. Gradually the clouds separated. The lightning became less and less intense. The rain fell before the storm reached the herbivores' crops, and the hail ceased entirely.

At last Norh flew up and out of the storm and observed it from above. He had changed its course, cut wide swaths into the clouds, disturbed their collective motion, and now the clouds had begun to disband. When he heard no thunder and saw no lightening, he was satisfied.

He soared back to the herbivore territory, holding his mouth open and baring his teeth in joy. He wasn't sure why he was trying to spread his wings at the same time, but the gesture felt right, given the magnitude of what he had done. Even as he felt that sense of great victory, he also knew he had done nothing unique.

The Krone folded his wings to his sides and dove straight for the middle of the herbivore land. He still didn't see anyone, but once the people realized what he'd done, they would be waiting for him.

Back when these people had first begun farming instead of wandering and grazing, they'd started to make spear-like things out of the trees to guard their farming territory. Spears led to clubs. Clubs led to rake-like devices they held in their hands to simulate claws. Those led to explosive canisters that projected claw-like shrapnel. They had discovered all of these things before developing a written language, or theater, or any concept of astronomy. These people did not look up with wonder; instead, they faced one another and regarded each individual as a threat.

Norh would give them an enemy to band against, someone who threatened their very existence, who wasn't harmed by their weapons or moved by their cries for mercy. In time, he would give them a victory over that enemy, too, and, in doing so show them how to build each other up.

Norh crashed into the middle of a field. The waist-high plants they ate grew everywhere, untamed, which struck Norh as odd. He trampled the plants for hundreds of strides. He roared and snarled, issuing his challenge to anyone who could hear. As he stood there, he marveled at himself, as if he could see himself from their point of view. Norh felt huge, able to bend the entire planet to his will. He had broken up a thunderstorm, he had stopped a lava flow—he was indestructible.

Norh roared to the sky, commanding the herbivores to look at the horizon and witness what he had done. He had ended the rain, and now he dared them to do something about it.

Nobody came.

The plants blew lazily in the breeze, mocking him with leafy applause.

He walked around them, turning his head this way and that, eyes to the ground. The plants were not arranged in straight lines anymore. They grew wild, unclipped, uneaten. No shelters stood anywhere. He scented the ground, and sure enough, it was devoid of animal scent.

Norh spread his wings, rising two thousand paces in ten seconds. Then another two thousand feet. Then another, and another, until he came to the cloud line. He hovered in place and scanned the land from one side to the other. He saw creatures moving, but they were not the right shape, color, or stance to be the herbivores he sought.

Norh was sure he remembered sentient herbivores on this world. He lashed his tail and flew against the planet's rotation. He flew so fast the sun set and rose by his motion.

Again, Norh had a tremendous feeling of awe that he could do this, but he'd done it all the time on Kronia as an early morning stretch. Norh remembered a time when getting up in the morning for PT had been the most miserable part of his day, and all he'd ever managed to do were push-ups, flutter-kicks, and obstacle courses. Norh couldn't remember why he hadn't simply done a couple laps around the planet after waking up instead of physical training in the Army. It would have been far less miserable.

He surveyed the land again, but he still saw no intelligent herbivores. This puzzled him. He remembered being here just a few days ago, trying to push the species together and cooperate, and now he was at a loss trying to figure out where they could have gone in such a short amount of time.

Norh circled the planet twice in about twenty hours. He was aware of how long he'd been aloft, and this filled him with a strange sense of exhilaration, too. Norh was tired of that feeling. He tried to convince himself it wasn't a big deal, as any Krone could do it, but the feeling would not go away. It was as if his subconscious were coming back, and he didn't care for it at all.

He adjusted course and aimed his body straight for the slip of land the herbivores called their home. That he was able to calculate his exact position on the planet, determine where on the planet he needed to be, and aim straight for it from halfway around the world both astonished and bored him at the same time.

Hours later, he crashed to the ground, landing on all four feet, leaving skid trails for over a mile before he stopped. His nose picked up a scent here, and he followed it.

A bone stuck up from the soil. Norh approached it, sniffed it, and then reached into the soil and pulled the whole thing out. His hand held as much as a bulldozer, and he stared at his hand as the dirt fell out between his fingers, marveling at the sight. He reached down with another hand, grabbed another bulldozer of dirt, and let it fall in front of his eyes. His wings spread out and folded several times. Norh wasn't sure what a bulldozer was, but he had a feeling it served as a sense of scale.

He did nine handfuls in this way until he remembered the bone in his other hand. He examined it. A leg bone. From its shape, Norh could tell it had belonged to a biped, and the thickness betrayed it had once belonged to a female. The weight and density told him it had been an herbivore's bone. Again, Norh felt a rising sense of wonder that he could tell so much from just a sniff and a glance.

Norh suddenly realized he hadn't brushed his teeth in over a year. He didn't have a toothbrush, but he had a bone, and it might do the trick. He opened his mouth and started picking his teeth with it.

The taste of the bone triggered a memory so powerful he dropped the bone and fell to his stomach, unable to breathe, entire body writhing.

He remembered.

They had died more than six centuries ago. He had watched it happen. For years he had been their enemy, rushing in whenever they'd started to fight amongst themselves, but then they had begun to fight over something else. Instead of territory, they battled for females. They herded their own women, preventing them from learning language, treating them as currency.

Norh had watched helplessly, knowing where it would all end, and he waited patiently for several decades before it finally happened. The lesser males fought the more dominant ones. The dominant males responded by killing the females. This did not deter the others; they kept fighting.

Norh had mourned over their bodies for a year. Nobody but he would ever know they existed. Nobody would ever know any of their history had happened. How many other worlds were like this? Civilizations living and dying without so much as an outside witness? How many lives were wasted in such pointless struggles?

Now he lowered his head to the ground and cried for them all over again. It began to rain, and he allowed it to rain, wishing he could feel the coldness it had once inflicted on the people here—wishing he could feel the pain it caused. Norh despised being so insulated from the elements. Why was he immune to everything while so many other species were vulnerable? What did it mean? What was he supposed to do if not save the Lost?

Norh writhed and wept until the planet's daytime star set, cursing his invulnerability. Everyone needed it except him.

Palc

I

The metal raptor stepped out of the sphere first. Deka followed immediately after, checking the air. He smelled no airborne scents, so he lowered his neck and scented the soil.

"Nothing," Deka said. "Just as I remember."

Rive rubbed his claws. "That's why we didn't come here. Scents never last, even for canines."

"They would have stayed near the hub for as long as possible."

"And gone to the coast to make contact with the planet. Perhaps they were lucky and someone here understood their language."

Deka sat down. "You should make the way to the coast."

Rive sat as well, looking out over the desolate land.

Palc was home to two sentient aquatics, one a species of predatory fish, and the other a species of octopus-like people. No land animals. Life on this world had never left the ocean, probably due to the almost complete lack of dry land. What few landmasses did exist were so barren that scents disappeared into the soil instantly, leaving many off-worlders in a sensory void.

Deka was having a difficult time coping with it. The lack of anything to sense convinced his mind this place could not exist. He tried not to breathe too hard. He looked at Rive and breathed his scent instead, which helped relieve the anxiety. After a moment, he realized Rive was doing the same thing. Rive held his hands together, claws touching, and Deka knew what he was thinking. It felt so good to smell another Relian. Deka smiled back at him with his hands.

"Kylac wanted to come here right after the disaster," Deka said. "We went to other places instead. Hithe, Ixcy... We had to choose which worlds we'd visit. Which planets we would help, and which planets we wouldn't. Kylac and I were the only two Archeons in the contacted universe who could make offworld spheres for quite some time."

"I heard," Rive said. "I wish I could have been doing what you and your fox did. I only had time to evacuate one planet. Just one."

"It wasn't a happy life. Civilizations lived and died based on our choices. We saw so many places die because we went somewhere else. It made me wish we had never become so interconnected. That everyone hadn't relied on portal physics so much."

"The portals had never done anything like that before. If not for me and my fox, they never would have."

Deka tapped two claws together once in a sardonic laugh. "I know. It's nothing compared to what you went through. You had to help Friend destroy those worlds."

"At least you saved them. Especially Hithe." Rive rubbed his claws. His laughter sounded metallic and fake, but at least it was recognizable.

Deka laughed with him. "Kylac didn't want to go to Hithe. He knew I would be useless, and I was."

"So the people are all right? What of the causeways?"

"We brought the people back long enough to kill the active rock. They had planned to start rebuilding once the portals were open. They've probably had time to rebuild some of them by now. And they feel as good as ever."

Rive held his claws together, smiling wistfully. "I'd love to go back. I want to know if I can still feel the stone."

Deka bumped Rive's neck with his nose. "I'll take you there first chance we get."

They sat in silence for a while after that, thinking about Hithe and its gorgeous causeways designed for the pleasure of reptile species. Breaths later, a sphere opened, ocean and sand projected around its outer surface. He walked through and stood on the shore of a smooth beach. Nobody was around, but Deka did not intend to search every island for Relian survivors. He walked past Rive straight into the water, wading in until only his head poked above the surface.

Deka turned back to Rive. The grey and tan raptor stood on the beach, watching.

"Can you get wet?" Deka said.

"Water doesn't harm me, but it does make me colder. I'd rather not go in."

Deka bobbed his head from the neck. "I'll handle the people. You start working on ways to the next island."

Waves gently lapped the shore. The sea was always calm on this world. Moments later, Deka felt squishy skin wrapping around his arms, tail, and neck.

The Grett, a species with eight arms and a liquid-like body, preferred to be the ones who communicated with off-worlders. They spoke by making vibrations in the water, so they could sense Deka's voice with close contact.

Ten of them had wrapped themselves around various parts of Deka's body, four around his neck alone. Thankfully, they were careful not to squeeze too hard. To them, it was no issue, as their bodies were pliable enough that they could not be crushed. Their organs had no fixed positions, their brains were spread out across their entire bodies, and

even their eyes could migrate anywhere on the upper surface. They were practically living liquid, but thanks to their
companion species, they knew what it was like to be solid,
so they squeezed just tight enough to feel the vibrations in
Deka's larynx.

"Hello, everyone," Deka said. "Do you know Relian?"

They coiled up, vibrating against Deka. They were all
talking at once, and Deka separated the different vibrations
easily. One vibration he did not feel was their Archeon.

What happened? one asked.

Our Archeons died when the portals went out, another
said. *We haven't seen a single portal since.*

"Not one?"

No. Deka felt this from one of the Grett attached to his
tail. *Where is everyone? What happened?*

"I'm so sorry we didn't come here sooner. I can explain
what's happening, but please tell me where the Relians
are."

They squeezed him all at once, feeling the same emotion. Deka could tell it was terror.

When the portals collapsed, they were trapped here.

Not just Relians. A few others.

Thirty altogether.

Sixteen were from Rel.

Eight canines. Eight reptiles.

There was nothing for them to eat on land, and they
were scattered between the islands. We gathered them here
and began catching prey for them.

And then they started to wander.

And attack us.

Each other.

Anything.

Some curled up and never wanted to move again.

We asked them what was wrong, but nobody would
speak to us.

A few lunar cycles ago, they disappeared.

No one has seen them close to shore.

Some were so panicked their vibrations shook Deka's bones.

"Thank you," he said when they fell silent. "I must leave you for now, but I promise, as soon as Rive and I find the Relians and take them offworld, I'll come back and explain everything."

They began unwrapping from him, urging him to hurry, and then they swam off. He could still feel the remnants of their voices in him, as if they echoed within his skin.

Deka backed out of the water and stood on the beach. He took a few deep breaths.

"Deka?" Rive's voice. "What's wrong?"

Deka shuddered. The lack of scent here made him feel as though he were floating in a void. He walked a few paces inland and scented the area, but the land was so empty and barren he dropped to his knees and gagged as if he'd inhaled pure hydrogen.

Rive helped him up and walked at his side to keep him upright. After a few breaths, the shock passed, but the feeling lingered, and the land looked as empty as it smelled. Rolling hills, vast mountains in the distance, but not a single plant or animal. No fungi. No bacteria.

No life.

To Deka's mind, this place did not exist. Scent-based offworlders came here to experience it for themselves—something truly alien and terrifying. Stephen had had a difficult time on Eiae for the lack of light. Palc was a Relian's darkness.

"The Relians..." Deka said. "They went insane."

"The lack of scent?"

"Yes. They kept it under control by staying near the ocean, but it wouldn't have been enough. Eventually they would either fold into themselves, or lash out. They probably scattered around the land, trying to find some refuge from the emptiness. Does it affect you?"

Rive looked where Deka was staring, out across the barren soil. "Not as much as it used to. The people who rebuilt me made me in their image."

"What do you mean?"

"From what I know, they didn't have senses the way we do. They gave me a way to turn them off so I could be more like what they considered normal."

"Then you'll have to help me, Rive. I may lose my mind out here."

They were on the beach right now, exactly where the Grett had gathered the survivors. This place was vast and had all the familiar features of a landscape teeming with life. It did not seem possible for there to be none.

"Do you think they're alive?" Rive said. "I can't imagine anyone surviving here. If they fled the beach, they must be dead by now."

"There is a chance they found something on another beach.. We owe it to them to try."

"I am working on a way further inland."

"Good. I'll make another. We'll need them soon."

Deka covered his nostrils with a hand and took a deep breath through his mouth. It helped, but only a little.

The two theropods walked a hundred paces in silence, searching for a footprint, an imprint in the ground where someone had slept—any visual sign that the survivors might have come this way.

Deka tried to focus on Rive's scent to steady himself, but it was little comfort because it was also lifeless and metallic. Deka pressed closer to Rive.

"How often do you have to eat?" Deka asked finally, trying to distract himself with conversation.

"Once every six days," Rive said. "Never a full meal. I think I lost most of my stomach, too. Maybe all of it."

Deka shivered at the thought. The more he learned, the more terrifying his life sounded. He tried to think of something else to talk about. The longer he remained silent, the more his ears told him this place lacked sound as well as scent. Even their footsteps and Rive's metallic walking turned into a dull hush after a while.

"How did Friend know them? Did he make contact?"

"He didn't tell me, and he was so unstable I didn't dare ask."

The beach faded, and silence enveloped them. Deka had the sudden feeling that he could shout at the top of his lungs and his voice would never reach its destination. He shivered harder, looked around, saw the silence, smelled the lack of sights, heard the lack of scents. He stumbled to a halt, panting. His face and arms tingled from lack of oxygen. Somewhere in the haze of panic, he felt a touch on his arm.

"Deka, let's go back."

Deka shook his head and huffed. "I'm an Archeon. I can do this."

Deka was convulsing now, and Rive began guiding him back to the beach. Deka pulled away. "I can do this. I'm not going back. I'm fine! I can—!"

His whole body tingled, and his legs turned to gel. Rive held him up and walked him, sometimes dragging Deka as he rambled. Eventually Deka moaned as he gasped for air. He couldn't hear himself. His voice didn't seem to reach anyone, and Deka stopped walking altogether and lay curled up on the dirt.

Rive bent down and picked Deka up with his metal arm. Deka leaned on him, and Rive turned him around and began walking.

"Keep walking, Deka. I have you. I'm right here."

Deka stared at the ground and mumbled gibberish in multiple languages. He stumbled, but Rive caught him and kept walking him. He frequently went limp and kept repeating the same nonsense words over and over. Rive held him upright up and walked him.

"I'm taking you back. Nothing bad will happen to you. Don't panic..."

The next thing Deka knew was the sound of gentle waves lapping against the beach. He sat up slowly and then rolled to his stomach. Rive crouched beside him, watching him. Deka could barely smell him.

"What happened?" Deka rasped.

"Have you ever been here before?" Rive said.

Deka's mind cleared, and the memory returned bit by bit. "Once, before I was an Archeon. I heard it was a planet of aquatics, so I brought Kylac here. That's when I found out about the sensory void. Kylac took me inland; he wanted to experience that. I remember panicking. Kylac had to drag me back to the portal. Until I became an Archeon, I didn't remember any of it. After that, I stayed in the water, letting the Hagae carry me around." He laughed with his hands. "Some of the Grett wrapped around my neck, and I took them for a run on the beach. They had never felt running on the land before. I dashed up and down the beach with twenty of them around my neck. Feeling them laugh... That made the whole experience worth it. Kylac was better at handling a scentless planet than I was. I never went inland again until I became an Archeon. My Archeon senses helped me from then on. Now..."

"I think you should let me handle the Relians. Take the way back to Gaow and get some scents back in your head."

"Rive, I won't leave you. I can handle this."

"An Archeon, yes, but you're an injured Archeon, Deka. The disaster took a lot from you. It took something from all of us, one way or another. Wait here and work on a portal further inland. I'll search around here for now."

Deka was about to object, but then he looked out over the land again. His chest seized up just thinking about going back there. Still, he couldn't hide from it. He'd have to adjust. He faced Rive.

"All right. I'll make the way, and then I'll come with you."

Rive stood, his grey leg making metallic, singing sounds as it lifted his body. He turned and began walking inland.

"Don't lose your mind out there, too," Deka called after him.

Deka heard flesh and metal claws scraping together. He rubbed his claws, too, and watched Rive vanish over the hill, and then he began concentrating on a couple ways. There weren't many places these people could have gone to, but it was still a lot of land to search with the eyes alone. He tried to think of where they would most likely have gone.

He heard a splash in the water behind him. Several splashes.

"Deh-kah."

Deka's heartbeat sped up, and he slowly turned his head to the ocean.

A Haga floated in the water just a few paces out. Stephen would have said these predatory fish resembled sharks, and like those Earth fish, the Haga couldn't survive for any length of time out of the water. Yet this one remained on the surface, looking at Deka, speaking to him in Sonjaa's voice.

"I know you," she said.

Deka stood. Suddenly the world became full of scent. Hers.

"It's supposed to be over," he mumbled. "You're dead. I saw you die. It's *over*."

"What?" she said. She slipped beneath the waves for a few breaths, surfaced, and then spoke again. "I know your scale marks. I know your voice. I remember you."

Deka ran into the water. The shark swam in place, her head still above the gentle waves. Deka stopped when the water was up to his waist. He reached for the shark and embraced her.

2

Rive's mind adjusted to the lack of scent and taste, but e ven with only four senses active, this place was still disturbing. He walked far inland, glad to feel soil beneath one foot, but it was all the same dirt, the same rocks, and after a while his foot became numb to it.

When the wind blew, it felt empty. He was glad he couldn't smell how empty it was, or he would lose his mind as well. Rive wished he could have come here with Friend, could have made time to evacuate everyone. These people had needed help most of all, and he regretted it had come to this.

He walked a thousand paces inland, looking and listening. Palc was so quiet it seemed any sound he made would be heard all over the planet.

And then he saw something. Rive switched on his nose and breathed it as the wind passed over him. Blood, very old, and it barely had a scent, but it was theropod and canine mixed together. Rive approached it and scented it up close, a lone splotch of color in an otherwise monochrome landscape, and so dry it barely stood out at all. Rive calculated it to be fourteen days old.

He walked around it, searching for a trail, making wider and wider circles. The blood went nowhere. Finally Rive stood up straight and switched off his nose.

The smaller droplets of blood had been absorbed into the soil. Only this patch remained. The trail could have gone anywhere, but he remembered that a Relian's first instinct would be to move downwind of an attacker, so they had likely walked in separate directions, perpendicular to the wind.

Rive chose to go left. The constant wind against his face chilled his scales, and for a brief moment, his flesh and his metal felt unified. The metal and the flesh had different needs, and they were always fighting each other. One wanted heat, the other, cold. One wanted to feel the world, and the other wanted Rive to shut off his senses and live within himself. For just this instant, his body felt like a complete whole again.

Rive turned off his sense of touch and walked completely numb, with only sight and sound and the magnetic field to keep him grounded in reality. His Archeon sense of reality also kept his mind busy, but his senses still cried out for basic stimuli.

Eight hundred paces later, Rive finally saw it lying in the dirt. Rive ran, switching on all his senses as he neared. A Relian canine. Male. Ten paces away, he realized the fox was dead. With no bacteria here, the body had not decayed at all.

He walked up to the corpse. It had no scent—

Rive leaped away and shut off his nose. He fed his olfactory sense memories of death. Even the smell of death was preferable to the complete lack of scent. As soon as his mind calmed, he kept feeding it input from memory to fill the gap. When he felt steady again, he grabbed the fox by the neck with his metal arm and carried him.

Again he shut off his senses as he crossed the land, feeding himself memories to make the trip easier. Two thousand paces later, he saw exactly what he expected to see: a raptor lying on the ground.

The raptor lay facing Rive, still alive. He was curled into a tight ball, as if returning to the egg. As Rive stood over him, the raptor's nose took in Rive's scent, and he crawled toward him, reaching out. Rive stepped closer, crouching down, and the raptor's hand touched Rive's face. He rubbed Rive's scales, brought his hand back to his nose, and inhaled.

Life flowed into the raptor again. Color seemed to return to his scales, which were green and violet with blue swaths fading between the two layers. He raised his snout then and scented Rive up close, focusing on his skin and avoiding the metal parts.

"Can you speak?" Rive asked.

The raptor did not seem to hear him. From his scent, he was dehydrated and starved. Rive hoped he would survive being rescued.

3

Deka stood in the water so deep his face was almost under, but he had to be this far in to be close to her. Without limbs, she could not hold him, so Deka held her. She spoke Relian very well, which was incredible because Hagae vocal cords did not work well out of the water.

Sonjaa told Deka a story he already knew, but he let her tell it anyway because she needed to say it. She had always been drawn to the land. Even as a child she wondered what was on the land, and though plenty of people on Palc showed her what was on it, seeing it was not enough. She wanted to experience it.

When she swam through the portals to other oceans and saw worlds where life had left the sea, she wanted to know the people who lived on the surface. She spent years practicing making sounds audible above the waves, and she learned other languages.

In Haga culture, children choose their own names, and she chose Sonjaa, a name unpronounceable to everyone on Palc. She could not explain why she chose it, only that it felt like hers. She had spent her life traveling the oceans, speaking to every land creature she could find, learning language after language. She grew to enjoy the reptilian languages best. As different as they were, they all sounded so similar, and she sought them out on every world that had an ocean.

Then, as now, she had to surface to speak, dive, surface again, and continue the conversation. It frustrated her, especially during times like this, when she had a long story to tell but could only tell it one breath at a time, but she had learned to live with it. Deka did not even notice. He was just thrilled to hold her again.

When the disaster had hit and visitors had become trapped here, most had been afraid to step into the water, so consumed were they with scent deprivation. She had communicated with them from a distance, and with her help they had endured the land for much longer than anyone would have thought possible, but eventually the people had begun to wander aimlessly.

Deka felt her slimy scales, fascinated he could only move his hand in one direction, down her body; going up hurt him. "Tell me about your memories of being on dry land."

She was silent for a while before speaking. "How did you know I remember living on land?"

"I'll explain later. Tell me."

She slipped below the surface, swam for a few moments, came back into Deka's waiting arms, and then surfaced just enough to speak again.

She remembered Rel, and falling into a portal under her feet. She remembered a theropod with blue scales so dark they were almost black, with a red stripe running up his snout and over his back. She remembered biting his nose affectionately. She also remembered hunting for a fox, feeling grass and plants beneath her feet. She remembered killing with her claws instead of her mouth. At times the memories were so vivid she believed they must have been real.

When she let herself swim in the memories deep enough, she remembered hatching from an egg. She remembered having parents. She remembered being fed for a time, and then bonding with a Relian canine. Then she remembered going off on her own with this fox. Rupi was with child. Her breasts were just starting to show. She remembered feeding her, almost forcing her to eat more for the sake of the child.

She fell silent. "What next?" Deka asked.

"I saw you," she said quietly. "Many Relians. I was floating, and they were watching me. That is my last memory on Rel."

Deka held her tighter. "Sonjaa. You are about to die."

She slipped below the water but did not swim away. At last she surfaced again, listening.

Deka nuzzled her face with his snout. "Let me tell you my last memory of Rel."

As he spoke, a portal opened just up the shore, and Rive stepped through, practically dragging a live raptor behind him and carrying a dead fox. He studied Deka for a moment, was about to speak, but then closed his mouth. For the living raptor's part, he was barely aware of being back at the sea.

4

Eight bodies. One survivor so far. Rive had carried all of them back to the beach. He had been walking in all directions from the beach, and all of the bodies so far had been within five thousand paces. At first he'd assumed he wouldn't find anyone any farther out, but now he thought again. These people were mentally unstable, and there would be no logic to their actions. They would have walked headlong into a fire if it meant they could catch a scent.

Now Rive walked up to body number nine and switched on his sense of smell. Male. And dead. With a grim sigh, Rive shut the sense off again, picked up the body, and began calculating a way back to the beach.

The lack of sounds soon became overwhelming as well, and Rive shut off his ears. Now his entire body was numb, and it filled him with peace. Back when his body had been entirely flesh, he never would have regarded sensory deprivation as pleasant, but this was far better than the lack of scents and sounds and the numbingly similar tactile sensations. When Rive willfully shut his senses down, it felt soothing.

He wished he could shut his eyes off. He imagined it would feel so good to shut everything out for a while, especially here. Rive looked around, considering it. There was nothing to see, nothing would come by to harm him, and it would only be for a few breaths while he made the way. Still, he resisted. It would only distract him right now, and he did not want to lose the way to Gaow.

When he returned to the beach, Deka still stood in the water, talking to the Haga who had Sonjaa's voice, which should not be possible, since their two species had next to nothing in common. Rive did not disturb them. He had listened to the story Deka had told her, and knowing what happened on the other worlds had moved Rive as much as it moved her.

Rive lay the body with the other eight. Ten refugees accounted for. Only twenty more to go. When he checked on the only survivor, he found the reptile lying curled into himself, barely breathing, moving in slow motion, even with food just a claw's reach in front of him. The Grett and Haga had caught it for him, another species of shark covered in white scales that glowed in the dark to blind potential prey. Whitefish. The Haga had once hunted the Grett, but when they discovered the eight-armed creatures were intelligent, too, they began hunting the predators that hunted the Grett, and now the Whitefish were their prey and kept their distance from the Grett and Haga.

The half-eaten body of a whitefish lay against the survivor's nose. He had eaten, but his effort had been weak. Now he lay as if the scent of prey did not even reach him.

Rive glanced at the portal to the hub. The way to Gaow was in sight through it, and Rive wanted to take him there right away, but he was also afraid of the sensory overload of being suddenly surrounded by a hundred Relians all at once. In the survivor's weakened state, such a shock could kill him.

He listened to Deka and the Haga who smelled and sounded so much like Sonjaa. Seeing Deka in the water, as close to her as he could get, was not strange at all; Deka had always been fascinated by aquatic creatures. Hearing Sonjaa's voice coming out of this fish, however, *was* strange.

Rive left them alone and went back to the search. After just a few breaths, he switched off his ears and sense of touch. A few more breaths later, he shut his nose down and searched with only his eyes. He felt as though he were floating through space itself. Not a single plant or animal as far as he could see. Nothing to stop the wind.

The soil looked so fertile, so solid and stable, and yet lifeless. It made no sense to the eyes, and as Rive kept walking, the urge to shut his eyes off grew stronger. He began walking with his eyes closed for dozens of paces at a time. When he opened them again, he could not tell if he had moved at all.

He had never shut all his senses off at the same time before, but this seemed the perfect place to try. Rive closed his eyes again and kept walking. After counting thirty-one steps, he opened them again, looking around at the unchanged landscape. It would feel so good to not have to see it...

Rive walked faster. A moment later, he turned his ears and nose back on, forcing himself to endure it.

Finally he saw a break in the empty land and ran toward it. The wind carried the scent away from him, but he still caught a whiff of it in the otherwise vacant air.

Four raptors. Four foxes. Two more of other species.

Rive ran faster, going so fast his metal leg outpaced his real one, forcing him to slow down to balance his gait. It bothered him to realize he was capable of more, but his flesh held him back.

He reached the group and skidded to a stop. Everyone had curled into each other: raptor into fox, fox into raptor. They were breathing each other's scents, which probably helped, but it could not change the fact that they were trapped in an empty land surrounded by pure nothing as far as their minds were concerned.

So many were dead, and the living were barely responsive. He knelt among them and searched the universe for the beach. As he did, the urge to shut down overwhelmed him. Rive curled into himself, fell over on his side, and took refuge in the egg.

He let his nose shut off. Then his ears. Then his sense of touch. Then his tongue. Now for the eyes.

Rive wanted to. There was nothing to see anyway, so he had no reason not to.

Rive disliked how strong the urge had become. It felt dangerous, and he heeded that feeling by keeping his eyes open and forcing himself to look at the void. One by one, he switched his senses back on until he became part of reality again. In the back of his mind, something screamed to shut down.

Rive rolled over and stood. Only two of them were still alive, one raptor and her fox, each holding each other for their sanity and their lives. The other Relians had already died, each with their raptor or fox close by.

He opened the way, approached the surviving pair, and urged them to stand. No response. They were so absorbed in each other's scents they did not want to open themselves to anything else for fear of falling into the void that surrounded them.

Rive picked up the raptor, bringing her to her feet. Her fox followed automatically. They did not let go of each other, did not let their noses leave each other's bodies. He led them through the way, safely to the beach, and then went back for the rest of the bodies.

5

Deka climbed out of the water, carrying a large whitefish in his arms. It had teeth marks all over it, and it weighed about half what Deka weighed. He set it on the beach in front of the survivors, but they remained unresponsive. Deka smeared some of the fish's slime on his hand and rubbed it on their noses. They reacted in slow motion, moving their arms toward it and scenting the dead fish.

Deka placed one foot on the fish and ripped his killing claw down its body, tearing it open so the innards and fluids spilled out. The survivors reacted again, but dreamily.

Deka pulled off a piece of fish and fed it to the raptor who had lost his fox. The raptor slowly opened his mouth, extended his tongue, and tasted the fish.

"Eat," Deka said.

The raptor opened his mouth wide, took the food, and closed his mouth. He did not swallow right away. Fish was weak by Relian standards, but after all he had been through, it would be the strongest thing he had scented in as long as he could remember. After many breaths, he swallowed.

Deka held his claws together, pulled out another piece, and fed it to the canine. At first she was just as unresponsive, but she, too, drew closer toward the smell of fish. She took the piece, working it into her jaws painfully slowly. Deka then fed her raptor. She took the food easiest, though she, too, held it in her mouth a long time before swallowing.

Deka fed each of them until the fish was gone. By the end, they moved visibly faster.

"How are they?" Sonjaa called from the waves behind Deka.

"They improving, but they also won't recover until they leave this world."

"It really does disturb them, doesn't it? The barren land."

Deka heard her submerge. He waited a few breaths for her to surface again before answering. "It disturbs every scent-based species. Even sight- and sound-based people have a difficult time with the land on this planet. It's so alien to see no life on so much land."

"Why?"

"Imagine going to an ocean with no waves moving through it, where the water is perfectly still. Have you ever been to a place like that?"

"I have been to many oceans," she said. "The water is always moving."

"Almost always. I know aquatic species who live in water that can't move."

"But there's always life in the water. It makes waves."

"Go to Juza as soon as you can. The ocean has no life there. The water is poison, but you can survive for a few days before it affects you. It will be the closest you can get to what these people are going through."

She submerged, swam, and then surfaced again. "I understand."

A moment later a portal opened, and Rive stepped through, carrying two more bodies. Not Relians.

Deka stood. "I'm ready to join you."

"Stay here." Rive set the bodies on the ground next to the others. "Help the survivors recover, and keep them from wandering off. I can handle this planet better than you can. Besides..." He looked past Deka, at the shark just offshore, and rubbed his claws. "It would be rude to leave her alone."

Deka held his claws together, turning to her. Sonjaa submerged, swam under the waves, and surfaced again.

Rive walked back through the way, and then brought back five more bodies.

"Twenty-seven," said Deka. "Only three more. Could anyone else be alive?"

"I found these people four thousand paces inland. Much farther than I expected. Someone could still be alive. For once I'm thankful there aren't any trees or underbrush. Finding them by sight is easy when everything's so open. I'm going back through, hopefully for the last time."

"I hope so, too. I'm starting to feel uneasy again, even here."

Rive tilted his head. "Hold out for another half day. We'll be back on Gaow by then, with at least three Relians to bring back with us."

Deka touched his claws. Rive went back through the sphere, and Deka turned and looked out over the sea. He saw a pale glow under the waves in the distance, rapidly growing larger.

"Sonjaa..." Deka pointed at the horizon.

Sonjaa submerged to investigate. "More whitefish," she reported when she surfaced again. "They smelled the blood from the one I killed, and they're swarming."

"Aren't they a little close?"

"They always do this. As soon as they realize there's nothing in the water, they swim away."

Deka counted at least a hundred in the distance, but Sonjaa did not seem disturbed.

6

Rive struggled through the empty landscape, wanting to shut his eyes off more than ever. He felt every minute change in focus, every throb in every artery, every blink, every twitch of every muscle. All of it took conscious effort to control, and Rive stumbled many times. He disliked being so aware of his eyes working.

He had never felt this way before. He had been an Archeon for much of his life, and Archeons were always fully in tune with everything their minds did. It had never overwhelmed him before.

He kept himself somewhat calm by walking with his eyes closed for dozens or even hundreds of paces. That helped at first, but his eyes still wanted to hide from this place. His ears and nose and sense of touch had been hiding this whole time, but his eyes were scared and wanted to hide, too. Rive forced them to scan the land around him.

When the daytime star set, Rive walked in the dim light of the planet's twin moons. Now his eyes wanted to shut off more than ever. He was glad he could see just as well in the dark as most could see in the day.

The land only became emptier the further he walked. Rive became convinced this direction would yield no results, and he sat down to calculate a way back. The urge to shut everything down only became stronger when he held still. Now Rive's breathing ceased to be involuntary, and he breathed much harder than he needed to.

He turned all his senses on. He heard the silent land. He smelled the scentless planet. He touched the unliving soil. He tasted the stale wind. He felt the magnetic field of a world that led to nowhere, from nothing. The clutter of anti-stimuli seemed to silence the eyes' demands to shut down, and so Rive focused on that instead.

The way opened, and he walked through. He emerged at his last portal destination, walking into the wind. The featureless land offended his senses, and he did not want to breathe empty air. He let the way to the dead end close but kept the one to the beach open.

His ears dreaded the silence. His eyes feared the uniformity. His sense of touch loathed the sameness in the soil. Rive frequently stumbled and caught himself staring off into space. He often shook his head and body around to give himself some stimulation, but it was becoming less and less effective.

He walked a few thousand paces like this, and then stopped. The land was so uniform none of his senses could confirm he had moved from the portal at all. Only his Archeon training assured him he had moved, and he used this training to identify his place on the land and where his last portal was.

No sign of any people this way either. Rive created a way back and tried another direction now. He tried talking to himself, but it was his own voice inside his head. It reminded him his voice did not reach anyone, so it felt the same as not speaking at all.

He walked on in silence. He stumbled and threw himself around. Then he rolled on the ground a few times. He stood up, covered in dead dirt that did not even exist as far as his nose knew. Rive growled and kept walking through the darkness.

He could not allow his ears or sense of touch to rest. Step by step, he forced them to take in the disturbing reality—forced himself to face how empty the land was. He remembered that the environment bubbled with activity at the atomic level, and he thought about that. It helped his brain, but it did not help his body, which remained in full sensory panic to the point where even the metal seemed to be panicking as well.

Rive stumbled again and again, even though there was nothing to trip over. The ground was so uniform and dead that his feet kept expecting the ground to change at any instant, and walked as though it had. Rive growled at himself, at the ground, at the entire planet of Palc. The daytime star began to rise, and Rive was relieved for some extra visual stimulation from the contrast of light and dark.

Something cast a shadow in the distance.

Three shadows.

Rive ran toward them.

He stumbled frequently, hearing false sounds and smelling false scents. Rive shut those senses off and used only his eyes until he reached them. Two foxes, one raptor. One of the foxes was still breathing.

Rive chirped in delight and began making a way to the beach. He sat down in front of the fox, touching his nose to give him something new to sense. Rive rubbed his hand over the fox's fur and brought it to his own nose. Nothing had ever smelled so relieving.

His eyes shut off.

Rive gasped and tried to turn them back on, but he felt as if he were trying to stay awake after being active for two whole days. The body must sleep. The eyes must shut off.

He tried again. His vision came back cloudy and then faded to black again. Rive remained calm, stayed still, and tried to switch them on again. Gradually he realized he didn't know if he was still sitting upright or lying on the ground. He didn't know if the wind was blowing or not.

He had no way of knowing if the outside world still existed.

Rive relaxed. It felt as good as he imagined. He had no way of knowing if time moved. No world. No outside. All he knew was the inside of his own thoughts, and they were far less disturbing than anything happening to him out there.

Gradually, Rive became aware of something touching him.

Rive

He felt the presence of more people.

Rive

They were touching him, not in a literal sense, but Rive felt them close to him.

Rive

He didn't hear anything, but they were speaking his name.

7

Deka woke. The smell of the ocean was almost gone to him now, and the planet was becoming scentless again. He curled into himself, wishing he could shut off some of his senses.

It was dark, and he had hoped Rive would be back by now. Deka looked out over the water. His mate was still there. Deka could tell she was asleep because her movements were automatic and unthinking, allowing her to swim, and thus breathe, while sleeping.

Then Deka noticed the whitefish. The glowing swarm had come closer now, looking like a moon submerged under the calm water, and so bright he couldn't make out individuals.

Deka splashed into the water. "Sonjaa, wake up! Something's wrong!"

Her placid swimming ceased, and she turned toward Deka and surfaced. When Deka pointed to the fish, she submerged and then unhurriedly surfaced again.

"That's strange. They usually go away when they realize there's no prey. I'll scare them off."

"It doesn't matter. Just leave them alone."

"I can handle them. I've been hunting them all my life."

Deka ran deeper into the water. "Sonjaa, remember what I told you about the other versions of you? Just swim away. Get as far away from them as you can."

She rolled nonchalantly. "I'll be fine." And then she submerged.

"Sonjaa, please!"

She swam out to sea. Deka stood in the shallows, watching, wishing he could run out to her and help. A few dozen paces away, Deka saw the fish kicking up a frenzy in the water. He couldn't see Sonjaa anymore. Moments later, blood washed ashore. Whitefish blood and Haga blood mixed together. The swarm dispersed, the glowing, underwater moon whittling away until Deka saw nothing but dark waves approaching.

Deka didn't have the energy to scream anymore. He stood in the water until the star rose, and then he finally turned around and climbed out. He sat by the three survivors, trying to take in their scents, but nothing seemed to reach him. The sound of the ocean became silence. The smell of the water became silence. The sand itself became silence.

The next thing Deka knew, the star was setting again. At least a day had passed, and Deka had been in a waking sleep. The survivors had not moved at all; they were just as scent-deprived as he was.

Rive had not returned. Deka looked at the portal the metal raptor had left behind, which led to the middle of this void. He bared his teeth, pushed off the beach, and ran through.

Night had nearly fallen on this region of the planet. Rive's scent had not fallen into the dead ground yet, so it wasn't too late to follow. Deka ran, no longer caring about the need to conserve his energy.

The sameness of the ground played tricks with his feet. They expected the soil to change and told him to anticipate a hill, or a dip, or a rock, or a bush. When none came, Deka stumbled, snarling.

Deka ignored his nose and ears and scales. He ignored everything and thought of nothing but finding Rive. Every now and then he stopped and scented the ground to confirm he was still on his trail. The scent was weak now, almost gone, but enough of it remained for him to follow.

As the daytime star slipped beneath the horizon, Deka's thoughts turned to his mate. He wondered if he would watch it happen again and again until the day he died. How many Sonjaas were there whom he had not yet met? Would they all continue to die long after Deka was gone, or did they only die when he was around?

Sonjaa had been the first person absorbed by the antisphere. She had not been torn apart. It had taken her whole and intact. The antisphere was a way outside the universe, through time, and so she had been spread out across time itself.

His mind raced through the possibilities, but he wasn't used to thinking about time this way. He'd hoped her deaths would stop once they reached the source, but it seemed it was going to happen again and again, and Deka could do nothing about it.

Deka snarled as he raced across the empty land. He growled. He screeched. He would not accept it. He was an Archeon. He was a Relian reptile. He was not helpless. There had to be a way to stop this. Even if he could only save one of them, he was determined to take control, and that thought carried him across the scentless continent.

After a long time, he saw something. Deka ran faster, still thinking of Sonjaa, growling in determination. If he died out here, she might keep dying over and over forever, and he would not let that happen.

He neared the things on the ground, and Deka could smell them now. Two foxes, two raptors, and one of them was Rive. Not realizing how close he was, Deka ran right into Rive, kicking him hard. Deka's claws hit solid metal, and he stumbled around, holding his foot and screeching. After the pain calmed, he picked up Rive's neck and shook. He clawed him lightly on his scales, on his metal, rubbed his nose, rubbed his neck.

Rive's eyes opened, and he gasped, rolled to his feet, and stood hunched over, leaning on Deka.

"Rive, you've been gone for days!"

Rive turned slowly toward him, reminding him of the dreamy motions of the survivors he'd fed. "I have?"

"Two days. Did the land finally get to you?"

Rive shook himself a bit and then bent down to scent the refugees. Only the fox was still breathing, and barely.

"My senses shut down," Rive said. "I didn't tell them to. I didn't know it had been that long."

Deka curled his neck back, panting as the scentless land began closing in on him.

A portal opened to the beach. Deka's first instinct was to run through, but first he grabbed the living fox, hoisted him over his back, and carried him through the way. Rive dragged the other two through.

8

Twenty-six dead. Four survivors: two raptors and two foxes, awake and standing, feasting now on the whitefish. Their eyes were empty, and their scents fearful, but they were conscious and active again.

Deka and Rive sat side by side on the sand.

"I heard my name three times," Rive said. "Different voices saying it. That's when you brought me out of it."

"Whose voices?"

"I don't know." Rive sat for a while, quietly watching the survivors. Then he turned back to Deka. "You lost your mate again, didn't you?"

Deka stared out at the ocean. The currents had taken all the blood and death away long ago. "I should be used to it, but I never will be. That's the only thing that got me through that land. The anger that I lost her again, and I can't seem to help her. No matter what I do, she dies."

Rive faced the ocean again, breathing in the air off the water, enjoying the sensation of having scent without the simultaneous overwhelming desire to turn it off.

"Thank you for coming for me, Deka. I don't know what would have happened to me out there. Our last survivor definitely would have died."

"They would all have died if you hadn't found them to begin with."

Deka reached over and touched his claws to Rive's. It had been a long time since he'd shared a smile with another raptor.

"I'm so glad to be away from Friend," Rive said. "Now I can save lives instead of." He swallowed. "Watching everyone die."

Deka rubbed his claws gently against Rive's. "I'm glad to have you back, and to see you being physical for a change."

Rive scraped his claws against Deka's. The survivors looked normal now, their movements quick and easy, and wordlessly Rive and Deka came to the same conclusion. The refugees were ready for the sensory overload that was Gaow, and the remnants of Relian civilization. It was time to take them to the closest thing any Relian had now to a home.

Breek

I

Kylac lay on his side, trying to quiet the equations in his head. They would not stop leaping from one end of his brain to the other. He curled up and trembled, using the tremendous amount of nervous energy in his muscles to make himself tired. He had been doing so for days but had not slept at all in that time.

He was lethargic, but his body remained wide awake. Sometimes he forgot how to speak for entire days, the equations consumed so much of him. In the rare moments when words returned, Kylac had little to say.

Friend sat just an arm's reach across from him. He was always watching Kylac. Even when Friend was asleep, Kylac somehow felt Friend watching him. He hadn't said a word since Kylac destroyed Ince, that rocky world full of crater lakes instead of an ocean. Not a breath went by that Kylac didn't think about it. All the people he had hurt. All the people he had killed. That thought alone kept him awake. The equations sometimes felt like claws to the stomach after he had fallen.

A dense forest surrounded them, covering two entire continents. The trees funneled the rain directly into their trunks, keeping the ground bare and dry so competing plants could not sprout. There was no underbrush here, only tall trees and bare dirt. They were far from the nearest settlement.

Friend shifted and scented Kylac from a distance. "Can you speak?"

Kylac opened his mouth. His lips and throat moved, but nothing came out. The section of his brain that remembered things related to speech was instead full of ricocheting, orbiting numbers.

"Can you understand me?"

Kylac couldn't remember the gesture for yes. He was trapped in his own head, dodging numbers flying by—his mind guiding the result of one equation to the beginning of another hundreds of times in the span of a breath. Kylac thumped his tail against the ground. It was all he could do.

Friend regarded Kylac impassively. "It took me ninety-two Relian days to work past this part, when the equations are so overwhelming they take over completely. I was fortunate I could suspend them long enough to rebuild Rive. Once the emotion wore off, they took over again, and I was just as helpless as you are."

Kylac winced. His head hurt so much. Friend continued.

"Chaos, Kylac. It's one thing all species dislike. It's the one thing every species across the universe has in common. The mind hates chaos. The brain of every species takes its world and organizes it into something logical. It's the only way to survive, making sense of your surroundings. Whatever perception that allows a species to survive eventually becomes consciousness.

"Archeons learn to overcome this. To perceive reality as it *is*, not the way that was most efficient for survival, and I discovered an idea that acts like a disease on the mind. It's so disturbing, so perception-shattering, the mind can't rest until it figures it out. This is what you're going through now, Kylac. This new perception uproots everything not only your primitive mind taught you was true, but everything your Archeon training taught you as well. Your mind has to organize all of it."

Kylac winced again, not from the equations, but from Friend's voice. He wasn't saying anything Kylac didn't already know, and Kylac couldn't tell him to be quiet. He couldn't tell him anything. He couldn't even ignore his words.

"After the people of Reth rebuilt my raptor, and I told him to work on another way quickly, he began doing it automatically. I couldn't say very much to him either after that. The equations would not let me." Friend's ears folded back. Kylac hoped it was empathy and not pity. "I hope you don't have to go without sleep as long as I did."

Kylac wanted to snarl at him, claw his eyes out, rip his throat out... He lay limply, trapped in his own mind, aware of everything around him but unable to do anything about it. The numbers and equations had become claws in his muscles, holding him down.

"Your mind will eventually work it out. Then you'll be able to speak, and you can start trying to control the antispheres. But more important, you will begin to perceive the universe as spacetime moving through a Lake. Maybe with the two of us thinking about it together, we can figure out what the Lake is made of."

Kylac managed to blink a few times. He hoped to regain control of his limbs soon.

"The Lake," Friend said after a long pause. "You know it was actually Rive who gave me the idea? Rive was always thinking about things like this. He lived for theory, and I liked indulging him because he always had interesting ideas. He was never a normal raptor, but he was the one who suggested the universe itself must exist within some other medium, and it is moving somewhere, and that's what causes time. It would explain why gravity bends time, as this distortion represents slight changes in the velocity of the universe. That's as far as he went with the idea, but it made me think. On what is it moving? Where? Could this motion equal time? That's how it started. A single idea."

Kylac had much to say about that, but his words remained submerged.

"Many lone cultures have ancient traditions of forbidden thoughts. Ideas so powerful they could tear the universe apart. Certain words forbidden to speak, thoughts no one was supposed to have. Those are merely stories born of species' helplessness against nature, but if any idea could truly be forbidden, this is it, Kylac. Pondering where the universe really is, and where it's going. Pondering the Lake. Perhaps if someone perceives the Lake, it will cease to exist, or the nature of its reality will change. It happens to atomic particles. As soon as you observe one, its behavior changes. Imagine doing that to the medium on which the universe itself floats."

Kylac wanted to reach up and rip his vocal cords out.

"I've solved the equations. I can open an antisphere to any point on the Lake. I can stop it from spinning and keep it stable so it doesn't rip planets apart anymore. But I still don't understand why these equations work, or how to find anything in the Lake, and I still don't know what the Lake is made of. That's what I want. You will, too, once your mind solves the problem."

Kylac wanted to say so much. He wanted to sleep so badly. He wanted to move by himself, but he was paralyzed. Breathing was difficult. His heart struggled to remember how to beat.

Friend leaned forward, and his ears still folded backwards. "I wish I could help you. I always knew this was how Rive felt looking at me. Painfully worried, but neither of us knew what was going on. All he could do was keep a way in mind. He didn't know any uninhabited worlds to take me to. All he wanted to do was help me—and the one time I needed him, he could do nothing. It was agonizing for him."

Kylac growled.

Friend swiveled his ears toward the sound.

Kylac's growl finally turned into words. "The people! You killed! Suffered! More!"

Friend's scent did not become angry, but more compassionate. "I understand the agony you're in. Don't hold back."

Kylac tried to speak again, but the equations had fallen into the hole he had dug to get to his speech center.

"This is only the beginning," Friend said, softly. "I know you can handle this, and we will help each other understand it. Isn't it amazing? We're the first two people in the entire universe to perceive whatever is outside it, and just thinking about it changes reality. The conscious mind truly is the most astounding thing the universe ever produced." He paused. "In fact, I have been pondering a new idea. I know you have a lot on your mind, but I want you to consider this as well."

Kylac wanted to growl.

"There are other universes in the Lake," Friend whispered. "So much distance between them they almost never meet, but when they do, it creates a new universe. That's the beginning. What's the end? The conscious mind. When a universe's inhabitants are mature enough to perceive something beyond it, it changes reality and causes the universe to end."

Kylac stopped breathing.

"Now you're wondering why I would want to perceive it if I knew it would cause the universe to end. I don't really think it's that simple—it's just an idea—but I still want to test it. What is the Lake? If we can learn that, perhaps it would allow us to open ways to other universes. There *is* some logic to it. Our perception has been expanding for generations. First the environment was our reality. Then the planet. Then we became aware of the contacted universe. Now reality will expand to encompass other universes, and making ways to those places will only take as long as calculating a way to another planet does now. Other universes... just a day or two away. It's a natural progression. What if everyone has to go through this before they join the contacted multiverse? The process is painful, but think about what we will gain."

Kylac breathed again, and his heart started back up with a jolt. Chaos and anxiety filled his mind, and Friend's ideas only added more.

2

Friend had rolled Kylac over to his back to keep his body from becoming stiff. Kylac was grateful, as his neck had begun to hurt and he'd had no way to ask for help. Now he looked straight up at the bare trunks reaching to the sky all around him.

He thought about the three worlds he had destroyed. He remembered the exact population of each, and so far his own personal death toll was twelve thousand four hundred and sixteen. It wasn't easy to connect so many deaths to his own mind. As far as he felt, he had committed no action that led to their end. His mind had separated himself from their deaths, and he believed he could not be at fault because his teeth had not ended anyone's life. His claws had not drawn blood. Kylac wanted to force his mind to connect the two, but the equations still pinned him down.

He felt footsteps approaching. There was no wind, so Kylac couldn't smell who it was. He was sure it was a Dren, and the footsteps felt light, so it was probably young. He wanted to shout out to warn them away.

Moments later, a mammalian face came into view, covered in black and blue fur and a long, straw-like muzzle, similar to the anteaters on Stephen's world. The Dren had thick claws to break into the tree trunks, and they used the long snout to suck the sap directly from the tree.

The trees did not take this as a threat, and because of the Dren, they did not produce pollen or grow fruit. The male and female reproductive components were produced in the tree and then released into the sap. These components combined in the Dren's intestines with other components from other trees, and in this way the trees depended on the Dren to reproduce.

Kylac wondered what this young Dren was doing here so far from the others, since the nearest permanent settlement was hundreds of paces away. She was staring down at him, scenting him, licking him with her long tongue. Kylac couldn't even make his tail wag.

She smelled Kylac from face to crotch. Kylac wished he weren't so helpless so he could enjoy this, but she did not smell old enough to mate.

She suddenly looked up and scampered away. Their former Arodon predators were not fast, so the Dren had not developed speed as a defense, but they had developed ears so sensitive they could hear an Arodon slithering down a trunk fifty paces up.

All was silent for a while. Then Kylac smelled Friend. And something dead. Friend's muzzle came into view, and he gazed down on Kylac. He had blood on his mouth and chest. Kylac tried not to breathe it.

"Caught some food for us," Friend said, rolling Kylac to his side to face the kill.

It was an Arodon, male, and Friend had already gutted it. Kylac's heart stopped. His mouth moved, and he raised his neck. He dug inside his mind and finally found his speech again.

"You... killed an Arodon?"

Friend raised Kylac to a sitting position and sat down beside him, propping him upright. "There are no animals around here. The Arodon only eat animals that live on the plains, beyond the forest."

"You could've made a portal to the plains."

Friend wrapped an arm around Kylac. "I also wanted to bring you out of the trance."

Kylac threw Friend's arm off him, stood and walked a few paces away. He stopped and leaned on a tree, panting.

"You need to eat," Friend said.

"I won't eat him!"

"You haven't eaten in days."

"Then make a portal to some other world and catch us something else. Something that isn't self-aware! Or better yet, let's go to the Dren. Ask them to pull some sap for us. I don't think my stomach can handle meat."

"I wanted to kill something."

Kylac glared at Friend.

"I haven't hunted in over a year," Friend continued. "I needed to hunt."

Kylac growled. "Why him? You could have made a portal anywhere and killed something!"

"I wanted a challenge." Friend reached for the body and opened his mouth, but

Kylac growled and bared his teeth. Friend crouched, holding his claws out, and Kylac leaped at him, bowling him over. They fell and rolled, claws and teeth flashing. By the time they stopped, Kylac was on top of Friend, snarling at him. He had just enough presence of mind to realize what was happening, and he glanced down. Both were out of their sheaths. Kylac was about to sit on Friend before the anxiety rose past a point of no return, but Friend threw him off.

"I almost reverted!" Kylac said from his side. "I can't keep myself sane forever. You need help, too."

Friend was feeling a bleeding wound on his muzzle as he rose to his hind legs. "Raptors force us to have sex to calm our instincts. You experienced it yourself: the equations brought you back. We don't need sex to stay calm."

"Why did you kill that Arodon?"

"There's no food here. I had to hunt where I could."

The scent anxiety was starting to fade. Kylac stood up straight, glaring at the tailless fox, amazed they hadn't torn each other to pieces by now.

"You can take prey from anywhere. Why did you kill a sentient creature?"

Friend didn't answer at first. Kylac walked up behind him, held Friend's shoulder. Friend was panting. "I wanted to."

"Why not open a portal anywhere and take an animal?"

"They're all the same."

The equations still spun around, digging into Kylac's brain, but now a new connection formed among them. "All those people you killed... All those planets. Is that how you deal with the guilt? They're all just animals compared to you and what you can do?"

Friend held Kylac and licked his muzzle. "You'll understand soon."

Kylac bared his teeth. "I don't want to understand."

"Yes, you do."

Kylac snarled and dove for Friend's throat, clamping down until he tasted blood.

Kylac felt a portal opening just above his head. A sharp pain flared on his ear, and he yelped. Friend shoved him away, and he hit the ground hard, landing on his side. He reached up and felt his right ear. Part of it was missing, and warm blood soaked his fur. Friend loomed over him, panting through his nose.

A small portal opened on the ground between them. Kylac recognized the world as Moyn, and lying in the yellow grass was a chunk of thin flesh. It had stained quite a bit of the grass around it red.

"There's your ear," Friend said.

Kylac did not move.

The portal closed. Friend held Kylac in a cool, steady gaze. A new sphere opened over Kylac's hand, and Kylac froze. It opened to the same place on Moyn. His hand was now on the other planet, fingers resting on his severed ear.

"Take it."

Kylac wrapped his fingers around the bit of flesh and fur and withdrew his hand from the portal. It winked closed. Friend gently wrapped his fingers around Kylac's muzzle, and raised his snout up until they were eye-to-eye.

"I can open ways faster than you can kill me. Next time you try, remember you don't need your tail, or your hands, or your testicles to figure out the solution. Hunting was the one thing I was allowed to do without a raptor. I enjoyed it, I haven't done it since we lost Rel, and I want something of my former life back to remind me I didn't lose everything, too. I will hunt whatever I want, and you will eat whatever I kill."

Kylac said nothing. After a moment, Friend knelt down and began licking Kylac's wound. It stung, and all of a sudden the equations overwhelming Kylac's thoughts soothed him.

3

Kylac's bloody fragment of ear lay beside him. The Arodon lay splayed open and hollowed out. The meat of a sentient creature roiled in Kylac's stomach while equations roiled in his mind, and he had never felt more disgusted with himself in his life.

Friend was asleep. Kylac considered killing him while he slept, but he had to wonder if Friend had portals ready to go even now, at the first sign of trouble. Kylac shook his head and forced himself to give up on the idea. Kylac dreaded when his mind would open another antisphere. He dreaded the encroaching old ways. He whimpered, hugging himself.

He tried to think of a way offworld, but the equations blocked his thoughts. He could speak and move for now, and he hoped he would never forget how to do those things again, but there wasn't enough room in his head for portal calculations and whatever else his mind was working on at the same time. Instead he sat awake all through the night, watching Friend sleep, passively aware of his mind working on a problem that seemed to have no solution.

As dawn approached, Kylac smelled the young Dren again, and he looked over his shoulder. She stood between two tree trunks, keeping her distance. He turned all the way around and sat facing her.

It took him a moment to dig through the layers of numbers to find the Dren language, but eventually he was able to speak to her. "Hello. I'm Kylac."

"You ate him," she answered.

Kylac's ears folded against his head, and his right ear stabbed with pain at the movement. "Does Breek still have an Archeon?"

"No. He died when the portals closed."

Kylac's heart raced. He wanted to ask the child to find help, but he was afraid no one could get close enough to Friend to kill him. Besides, even if Friend were dead, that would not solve their biggest problem.

"I'm sorry," Kylac said, the words feeling hollow. "What's your name?"

"Tlee."

"Tlee... Please leave. Tell no one you were here. Hopefully we'll be gone soon, and nothing bad will happen."

She saw his ear then. "You're hurt. I can bring help."

Kylac imitated their gesture for *no* by tracing a left-oriented circle in the air with his muzzle. "Please, Tlee. Go, before he wakes up. He's dangerous. *I'm* dangerous. Never come here again."

She traced a right triangle in the air with her muzzle, their gesture for worry and concern. She hesitated, but then turned and padded away as fast as she could, which was only a brisk walk by Relian standards.

Kylac sat alone again, a pang in his chest matching the one in his ear. Even for just that moment, it had been nice to have someone to talk to. Someone who did not have lofty ideas about the universe. Someone he didn't fear.

"I wouldn't have hurt her," Friend grumbled into the silence.

Kylac did not turn to face him. "You killed an Arodon."

"I'm not hungry anymore."

Kylac growled. "Please, let's leave."

"If not this planet, it will just be another. You can't pick and choose. Not yet."

"Why aren't you evacuating them?"

Friend did not answer.

"Why aren't you evacuating them?" Kylac repeated.

Friend breathed.

"Friend, answer me! You can open ways instantly. Nobody has to die."

Friend sighed. "When you see the universe as a whole... Some things just don't matter as much as they used to."

"Even Rel? You seemed pretty concerned with bringing it back."

Friend spoke as if remembering something that had happened decades before. "Guilt consumed me then. I didn't understand what was happening. Now I see the larger implications of this. Nothing is broken. It's all part of the process. How many accidents happened with portals in Rel's early years? How many people died experimenting with them? This is normal. It's not something that needs to be fixed. We move on, and we discover."

Kylac sat quietly for a long time, and Friend's words became a new equation for him to ponder.

"What if you're wrong?" Kylac asked finally. "What if there's nothing in the Lake but us?"

"People said the same thing when portal physics was first discovered. We ignored the doubters then. We moved forward, and we joined the contacted universe. We will find out if I'm right soon enough."

Kylac had nothing to say to that. It seemed to be the end of conversation for all of eternity. Friend went back to sleep. Kylac sat in the darkness and listened to his faint breathing, jealous, angry, and exhausted.

4

The daytime star was rising, and Kylac wished he could see the sky. He hadn't slept, and he was tired beyond imagining, but he could not sleep. Kylac was convinced it would catch up to him eventually, and then the real suffering would begin.

More dread. It was on his mind a lot lately. He hoped Friend wouldn't be hungry again for a long time. He hoped he could keep himself together so this world wouldn't have to be the next casualty.

Kylac sat on the bare ground, facing Friend, thinking about the worlds they had lost and the people who had died for this. He tried to remember what he'd been taught about the early days of Rel's portal discovery. It took him a while to dredge up the memories from beneath the layers of numbers, but once he did, all of a sudden Friend's logic didn't seem so solid.

Yes, there had been accidents, and there had been deaths. Friend was right that this was the nature of experimentation, especially with untried concepts like this, but those pioneering Archeons of ancient times had not thought those deaths necessary. They had not considered anyone disposable, not even for the sake of discovering something as world-changing as portal physics.

Besides, those deaths had been measured on a scale of individuals. If it hadn't been for the constant background of equations in his mind, Kylac probably could have remembered each of their names. These were *planets* Friend was talking about. Entire civilizations. Kylac didn't care how big the discovery promised to be; it could not be worth that much. He refused to believe anyone in any other universe would have to discover it by sacrificing half their sentient life just to make the leap to other universes. And what next? Traveling to other Lakes? Entire universes sacrificed to make that leap? Where did it end?

And it still would not answer the biggest question: why does it exist?

Kylac's heart pounded, and his head hurt. The equations swirled faster now. Everything was almost ready to return. Kylac thought about Tlee. She didn't deserve to be sacrificed for something bigger. Nobody deserved this. Friend had made the choice for all of them. Kylac wished he could bite his own neck.

Or...

It was too late to help this planet, but Kylac realized there was a simple solution: he could let the antisphere tear himself apart. Malim had understood what was happening, and he had killed himself before he could hurt anyone else.

Kylac realized if he had any sense of responsibility, he would do the same.

Footsteps approached from behind. Kylac knew who they were without looking. He felt the tiny footsteps of Tlee, followed by about twenty others. He also felt slithering along the ground and down some of the tree trunks around him. All Kylac could think was that they would be fine so long as they didn't wake Friend.

"There they are," said Tlee.

"Relians," said an older voice.

"Canines with no reptiles," said a male voice.

"Is that... S'ny?" said another.

"The sleeping canine killed him," said Tlee sadly. "They both ate him."

Kylac wanted to speak up in his defense, but after everything he had done, the details did not seem to matter. They seemed more bewildered than angry at the death of one of their own.

"Kylac," said another voice. Kylac did not look back. "What is happening? Why did you kill S'ny?"

Kylac had a hard time remembering his words. It was several breaths before he finally spoke up. "Kill us. Please."

The natives remained still and quiet. Kylac now saw some serpents crawling down from the trees, slithering around himself and Friend. The Dren approached from behind, and Kylac felt them standing over him.

"We're dangerous," Kylac warned. His breaths were coming heavier now, trying to keep up with his racing heart. "If you don't kill us, your planet will be destroyed."

Silence. Then Kylac felt claws on the back of his neck. His nostrils flared, and he suppressed the self-preservation reflex.

"Please hurry," he said.

Another set of claws wrapped around Kylac's neck. Kylac kept his eyes open. One of the Arodons crawled over Friend's neck and began wrap around it.

"One of the Dren should use their claws on Friend," Kylac said, straining his voice to be as clear but quiet as possible. "Kill us as quickly as you can, or all of you will die."

The Arodon moved off Friend, and a Dren took his place, standing over Friend with her claws raised over his neck.

"What is happening?" a voice behind Kylac asked.

Kylac stared straight ahead. "Someday someone will explain, but trust me when I say you're better off not knowing. Please, just kill us. Now."

Kylac clenched his jaw and waited for it to be over.

One hundred portals opened all over the forest, ranging in size from Kylac's fist to as large as his head. Stationary, solid bubbles hovered between the ground and eye level, so close together they almost touched, the smaller portals filling the gaps between the larger ones. Before his vision was obscured, Kylac saw five of them intersecting the Dren standing over Friend. More portals had opened behind him. Kylac could not move without bumping into one.

A breath later, the spheres closed. Sickening thumps and splatters reached Kylac's ears as blood and bodies hit the ground behind him. The Dren standing over Friend was now just a few bones and half a face. The rest of her body was in twenty pieces on twenty different worlds separated by millions of light years. All that remained on Breek was the thin, twisting column of skin and bone that happened to fit between the spheres.

The Arodons on the ground around Friend had also been divided among multiple planets. Their bodies had enormous holes in them where portals had opened and then closed. Two of them were still breathing, but they were bleeding out so fast they were as good as gone.

Kylac rose to his feet and turned around as the entire group of thirty Arodons and Dren fell to the ground. Heads were missing. Legs, pieces of torsos, pieces of backbones. The holes leaked blood and organs. Many were moaning, trying to scream. Some of the trees had holes in them as well, leaking sap.

Friend stirred and sat up.

Kylac took off running through the trees, weaving between the trunks.

A portal opened a few paces ahead of him, and Friend stepped through. It closed just as Kylac skidded to a stop less than a pace from Friend's snout.

"Where are you going?"

Kylac ran past Friend and through the trees, following the scent of the group. They had come from the settlement, and if Kylac could reach it, maybe he could hide there.

Another portal opened up in Kylac's path ten strides ahead.

"You want to be like Malim?" Friend asked as he emerged. "Afraid of discovery? Afraid to be the first?"

Kylac veered away, dropping to all fours and tearing through the forest at full speed. Portals began opening all around him, all showing views of the same forest. Kylac weaved around them. The portals became more and more dense, and he had a difficult time dodging.

Ten spheres opened in front of him, and Kylac was moving too fast to avoid them. He ran right through one and into Friend's arms.

"Don't give up."

Kylac clawed him across the face and broke free, running straight ahead. He didn't see the portal open in front of him, and when he slipped through it, he came back out facing Friend again. Kylac looked around. Friend had surrounded him with spheres leading back to this spot.

"Don't let yourself become too agitated," Friend advised. "It only opens antispheres before you're ready to control them."

Kylac backed away, tucking his tail between his legs so it wouldn't wander into a sphere.

"Kylac, you're not afraid of me. You're afraid of yourself. I empathize, and when this is over, you'll understand the universe as I do. What's important right now is that you calm down. If you let yourself become too distracted, your mind will try to end the equations before it's ready, and you will destroy this world."

The remaining portals closed, leaving Kylac and Friend alone somewhere in the forest. Kylac backed away, panting, stumbling over his own feet. He took deep breaths, trying to bury the scents and images of the dead under the equations. He almost forgot how to speak. He backed into a tree ten paces away and stopped, staring at Friend.

"Friend..." He struggled to keep the words in his mind. "Do you remember how each species discovers portal physics?"

The other fox did not answer.

"By learning how to understand their companion species. It brings civilizations together. It doesn't destroy them!"

"This is more important than any planet. The math proves it. Don't be afraid of it."

"You're using portals to kill! Whatever's happening, it can only lead to more death!"

A portal opened in front of Kylac, and Friend's arm reached out, grabbed Kylac by the neck, and yanked him through. Kylac now stood nose to nose with Friend, the scruff of his neck in the older fox's grip. Kylac's knees became weak, and he forgot how to fight back.

"I have a new perspective," Friend whispered. Calm voice, screaming scent. "Rive and I always had new ideas, and people were tired of listening to us. They were comfortable with their view of the universe. Now I get to show them it's time to move on from all the old ideas."

"I will never let it happen!" Kylac snarled. "I will never be like you! I won't—I *won't*—I—I—" Kylac screamed.

Friend let go of him, and Kylac dropped to the ground, holding his head. The ground started to shake, and the distinctive sound of an antisphere pulling pieces of the planet apart traveled through air and soil.

Friend picked Kylac up. "Concentrate! Close it!"

Kylac couldn't remember how to speak. Again he was filled with the overwhelming feeling that this should not be happening. It was impossible—he could not close it, because it could not be open in the first place.

The ground heaved and crackled as columns rose from the very core of the planet, the sound echoing against the rim of the atmosphere. Trees in the distance uprooted and flung themselves downwards, and now they could see the Antisphere. It was only the top third, rising up from beneath the surface of the planet, swallowing everything. A sphere to nowhere.

No, Kylac realized. A sphere to the Lake. An empty area of the Lake where the universe was not. Where time was not. But something must be there, or Kylac could not make a way to it. Kylac tried to end it, but just seeing it made him panic.

Then Kylac remembered. He turned, slashed his claws across Friend's face, shoved his knee into his groin, then ran headlong toward the antisphere, following the trees as they vanished into it. The ground was shaking violently by now.

Kylac let his mind go. He let everything go. He was thrilled it was about to be over, and now he would find out what was on the other side. He would experience the Lake firsthand, and Friend would never know. That gave him some measure of satisfaction.

A sphere opened in front of him, a view of a vast field of flowering pink and white plants under a red star. Kylac tried to stop, but he was already moving too fast. He cursed in English and Relian as he ran through the portal and stumbled to a stop on this new planet. The place was familiar, but he could not think of the name.

The equations slowly began to reset. Kylac dropped to his knees and held his head.

Another sphere opened, and Friend limped through, bleeding from the muzzle.

"Don't try that again either."

"You can make me go through this, but I promise as soon as I figure it out, you're dead!"

"You won't kill me. Trust me. You won't."

Kylac smelled blood. Lots of blood, and it was starting to smell good. Kylac moaned and rolled to his stomach, burying his face in his arms and trying to remember Deka's scent.

Nameless Desert World

Norh lay in the sand, holding his throbbing head. The pain had spread to his entire body. Norh had never felt anything like this before—had barely felt pain at all during his life, and it scared him.

He lay in the dried-up lake bed, the same one he had dug over three centuries ago. It had once been filled with water, but now there was nothing left. As he clutched his skull, he muttered to himself.

"It already happened. It already happened. It already happened. I don't need to dig. They're all dead. They're all dead."

Four new riverbeds branched off from the lake bed, all of them dry. Norh had dug them over the past month, one right after the other. When he had arrived on this planet, he had been so sure the people here were still alive and needed his help. They had no companion to push their minds higher and lead to a new understanding of reality, so they had built their society around satisfying their animal nature. Norh wanted to help them.

They could not make portals to free themselves from the need to scavenge for water inside the plants, but he could make water plentiful so they would not have to. Norh dug a river. He had kept it up for weeks before he realized he wasn't sure where he was digging, so he soared high up to the clouds and examined the land. He found no water source to which he could dig, and no people to dig for.

Only then did he remember the fighting that had torn their society apart, treating females like plants to hoard and harvest, keeping everyone else away from the water as if it were theirs to control, repressing other members of their species just to protect their own individual existence. They wouldn't tolerate it. They fought the society. They fought the system. It had destroyed their species, and all Norh could do was watch.

Norh wasn't sure how he could have forgotten all of that, but it had happened three more times. Norh would go to sleep after mourning them, wake up believing the people were there, begin digging another riverbed, work on it for days, and then remember all over again.

He began working on a way off the planet, but before he could complete it, he forgot again. He began digging with single-minded purpose from the lakebed to some-where else. He didn't know where, only that water was far away, and if he could just reach it, he could save them.

He had dug more than halfway to his imaginary desti-nation when suddenly the memories of the final revolution flooded his brain, and he collapsed in grief, living them for the first time again. He had lost the portal, so he began mak-ing it again, and then he forgot everything and began dig-ging the riverbed.

Now Norh lay in the dry sand, brain trying to burst from his skull. He noticed some scales missing from his scalp, and he seemed to lack bone underneath them. This terrified him even more. How much had he forgotten? What else was there to remember? Right now he couldn't even remember how old he was, or tell the past from the present. His mind was a jumbled mess, his memories out of sequence. He clutched his head tighter.

"It's all in the past. It's all in the past. They're dead. It already happened. Stop digging. Remember the fighting. Don't dig."

His wings sprawled out in grief and fear as he worked on a way to the next world. He knew where he should go. The one place he went when he needed to get in touch with a friendly person. Norh had always treated his nephew as the son he never had, which was sure to scar the boy for life somehow, but Norh didn't care. Melissa and Alex were all he had now.

Norh told himself the story of this planet over and over as he held his head and cried for yet another civilization he could not save. Keeping the memory active seemed to help. He was terrified he would forget again and dig another river.

It wasn't the digging that scared him, or the wasted time. It was too easy to forget, and for the first time in his life, Norh wasn't sure about anything.

Genos

I

The sphere from Xeloc did not close as soon as Deka was through. Deka felt better knowing he had a fast way off the planet to a world that would kill the fungus, as this world was one place Relians were not supposed to visit for very long.

"You're sure Friend said Genos?" Deka asked.

Rive observed the benign-looking forest. "It was one of the first worlds he said he saw survivors."

"Did he happen to know why he thought they might be here?"

"He couldn't tell. Neither of us wanted to come here without a fast way back, plus the means to sanitize everyone, and I couldn't make that happen with what Friend was going through."

"I don't want to be here long either. Let's hurry and find them."

They began walking. Deka glanced over his shoulder, confirming Rive had kept the way to Xeloc open, and on that world he also held open a sphere to Selta. He turned back to Rive.

"I'm calculating a way of my own to Xeloc, just in case something goes wrong. I don't want to be here for the rest of my life."

"The Relians may already be," Rive said, neck sinking parallel with the ground. "That's another reason I never brought us here. It would have been too late even at the time. If nothing else, they deserve to know what happened."

Deka felt cold fear radiating from Rive.

Genos was a wet world. It never rained, rather a perpetual fog enveloped the biosphere. The plants and animals relied on it, and as Deka and Rive walked to the hub settlement, they spotted various animals that demonstrated adaptations to the mist.

A four-legged, hopping mammal had dimples all over its hairless body meant to catch the water that continuously accumulated on its skin so the fungus would not grow. It carried its drinking water with it everywhere it went. The mammal vanished into the thick fog as a white-furred primate dropped from a tree and stared up at Deka and Rive.

She looked at them, tilting her head, and then reached out to them. Deka squatted down and touched her between the ears. The primate chittered and squawked and jumped in circles, showing off her own adaptation: fur groomed in a way that channeled the water around to her back side where it dripped off her tail, which kept her fur dry and prevented the fungus from growing. A moment later, she leaped into the trees, disappearing through the fog.

"You shouldn't have touched her," Rive said.

Deka huffed through his nose. "We'll be infected no matter what we do."

Dozens of reptiles and mammals, birds and insects crawled over the wide path through the trees. One of the smaller mammals was sleeping on the path. It resembled a Relian canine, but these creatures had much thinner fur, and their skin secreted a toxic, antifungal substance. Both Rive and Deka paused to look at it. Though dozens of animals and insects passed it, none of them disturbed the tiny canine.

Rive walked up to Deka's flank, rubbed claws with him. Deka rubbed Rive's claws in return.

"You think this resemblance is striking?" Deka said. "You should see the canines on Earth."

Deka lowered his neck a little to scent the red canine. Disappointingly, it smelled nothing like a Relian, and he snorted to clear his nose. He straightened up, and they went on. After a few paces, Deka looked back at the sleeping animal, so small and serene amidst the flurry of movement on the path.

"I hope Kylac is all right," said the metal raptor. "I wish I'd been a better raptor. I might've been able to help more."

Deka couldn't think of a good reply, so they continued in silence. Walking became difficult with so many animals crossing the path in all directions, especially since most of the animals were more likely to stop and stare at them than to move out of their way. Deka and Rive stepped carefully, keeping their eyes on the path and always watching for movement.

Finally they came to a patch of forest with numerous rocks piled between the tree trunks. It was a thick forest with few leaves this far down the trunks, and no underbrush. With so many animals and people here, smaller ground-level plants had no chance to grow.

Animals walked and lay everywhere, just as they did on the path. Hopping and walking about, sleeping out in the open, some curled on top of other animals that weren't even the same species.

A bipedal reptile poked his head out of one of the piles of rocks. This Olmn had red scales at the front fading into a beautiful tint of white around its back. It had smelled the Relians, and now it was licking its nose, searching for other scents, probably smelling for their foxes. The Olmn did not have a true sense of smell, rather the nose served merely as a place on the snout where scent collected, to be tasted periodically.

The Olmn crouched outside of the rock pile, making calling noises that had no translation. Olmn and Jume crawled out of their rock piles as well, many from the same structures.

The Olmn with the red and white scales approached them. He appeared Relian in how he walked on his toes and held his arms curled in front of him, but his species stood more upright, closer to a human posture. Deka wished Stephen were here to meet him.

Six small birds were climbing over the reptile's body, their powerful talons digging into the flesh but never breaking the scales. The six birds continually grabbed individual scales, lifted them, puckered them between their flat beaks, and gnawed them clean.

Others in the settlement now came out of the rock piles and were stepping over and around the teeming animals. Many more bipedal reptiles appeared, and then some of the quadrupedal mammals as well. Deka thought back to Stephen, and how he would have understood these creatures. The Jume resembled Earth badgers the size of small bears, but with no claws, and every one of them covered in animals.

Four Jume came in sight, placing their giant paws between the animals as many more species crawled or hopped out of the houses, all turning their heads to see what was happening. The smaller animals twitched their noses, smelling them from afar.

The Jume were covered in brown fur that was perpetually growing. Tiny rodents crawled all over them, gnawing the Jumes' fur down so the birds could reach bare skin. The same birds that climbed over the Olmn also perched and clung to each member of the Jume, pecking systematically at their skin.

Deka and Rive remembered how all the other animals' lives intersected with those of the birds and rodents. Some of the other species cleaned the birds while they slept, preening their feathers for tiny microbes. Others collected stray pieces of fur from the Jume that the rodents failed to eat. Others kept water from accumulating on other animals. Each animal did something for another to help them survive, and they were all here, living together, with the Jume and the Olmn at the center of it all.

Deka's neck began to feel itchy. The fungus had already taken hold on his skin. The skin on Rive's leg also started to itch. They looked at each other. Deka took Rive's hand and rubbed claws with him.

Less than a breath later, birds about the size of their hands landed on them. Their talons sank deep into the skin, allowing them to hold on no matter what the angle, but they never drew blood. One of them grabbed a few scales on Deka, tugged them up, and mouthed them. Deka rubbed claws with Rive as a bird mouthed the real scales on the metal raptor's chest.

The locals called them *companion birds* for good reason.

The Olmn with red and white skin and six of these birds walking over him stopped less than a pace away from the Relians. "Are you Archeons?"

"We are," Rive answered, wincing from the birds' ministrations. "We heard Relian survivors are on this planet. Do you know where they are?"

"I know where they went. What happened to the portals?"

Deka squeezed Rive's hand and let go. It was the metal raptor's turn to explain. As he did, Deka backed up, scenting the air. So many animals were here even Deka had to think consciously to sort them out. He wished Kylac were here. He could have done it instantly, and probably found the Relians already.

More companion birds landed on Deka. At one point he counted eleven pairs of sharp feet digging into his scales, eleven beaks mouthing him, eating the fungus. Deka tried not to wince, as he was in fact quite thankful they were there. Right now, they were the only thing keeping the fungus from eating him alive.

The moist biosphere of Genos supported a species of fungus that fed on flesh, and it covered everything from the tropics to the tundra. Deka looked over the group of Jume, pondering that their fur was not naturally short. They had never evolved a growth limit, as the canines of Rel had. A species of rodent ate the fur, which kept it trimmed, and that allowed the tiny companion birds to reach the skin.

Deka grumbled as one of the birds moved from his outer thigh to his inner thigh and began tugging at the sensitive skin. The painful, wonderful birds. Their bodies were immune to the fungus's flesh-eating appetite because they ate the fungus, processed its compounds, and secreted a chemical the fungus did not like.

Every species of animal here had developed some way to deal with the fungus. Some deflected moisture so it could not grow; others grew thick feathers or fur so it would grow on that and not on the skin.

Most, such as the Jume and the Olmn, relied on some other animal to deal with the fungus for them. The Olmn had never evolved a defense against it because the birds kept them clean. The Jume had never developed fur that stopped growing because the rodents trimmed it for them, and the birds kept the fungus under control.

Deka screeched as the birds began picking at his slit. He wanted to reach down there and chomp his teeth at them, but Deka leaned on a tree and endured the discomfort. It was either that, or let his flesh rot.

Rive was telling them what happened to Crexa. Deka had heard the story many times, on many different worlds—all the places they'd been, all the good Deka had done, all the pain Rive endured watching Friend go through something he did not understand.

A new companion bird landed on his snout, and Deka snorted, counting twenty tiny beaks mouthing him now. He was aware of some of the Jume and Olmn watching him now, laughing at him as another offworlder not used to the birds.

He promised not to be here more than a day, but not because of the birds. Deka could live with the birds doing this to him after a while. He had done it before, years ago, when he and Kylac had visited.

He feared the survival mechanism the fungus had. The Olmn, the Jume, and many species on Genos lacked a critical hormone which, in most other species, allowed their bodies to maintain temperature and metabolism. The inhabitants of Genos never evolved such a chemical because the fungus produced it for them. As it ate the skin, it secreted this hormone as a waste product.

Offworlders had to be careful about remaining on Genos too long. The longer the fungus fed on the skin, the more the organ that produced the hormone atrophied, and eventually the body would assume that organ was a cancerous growth and destroy it. Offworlders with compatible skin could become dependent on the fungus in only a quarter of a year.

All offworlders knew the importance of killing the fungus before venturing to other worlds, so no portals led to Genos from moist planets, or worlds whose people had vulnerable skin. Archeons arranged portals so that one had to go to and leave Genos by way of some relatively inhospitable worlds first. The only direct ways Archeons maintained to other worlds were those that led to deep ocean. The spores did not sink, so maintaining spheres for the aquatics to visit the ocean was safe.

While this world was a beautiful example of unconscious nature coexisting with conscious creatures, Deka did not want his freedom as an Archeon curtailed by a little fungus. As soon as they found the Relians, they would return to Xeloc, take a plunge in the mildly acidic ocean to disinfect their skin, and then travel to Selta for an emergency checkup, taking the Relians with them.

If it wasn't already too late.

Deka watched Rive. The metal raptor must have switched off his sense of touch, for he did not even flinch as the birds clambered over him, and Deka envied Rive that ability. Rive was just finishing the part where they lost their foxes on one of the moons of Rel when the Olmn who had greeted them spoke up.

"Our Archeons died in the first disaster. Each region has been isolated. We've been forced to return to the old ways."

Deka flinched at the words. They did not mean the same thing here as they did on Rel, but the separation anxiety surged again, and only the distraction of the birds poking and prying at his scales kept his fear and grief under control.

"Relians did come here, but they were from the second disaster. They had fled to Genzin, and from there to Horos. They were then forced to come here."

Deka knew Horos, one of the intermediate worlds to Genos full of plants that emitted noxious chemicals into the air instead of pollen. The chemicals killed the fungus, but the Relians would not have been able to stay there. They must have poured into the nearest portal they'd found, just before the contacted universe closed.

"Where are they now?" Deka asked, still leaning on the tree, his entire body involved in enduring the beaks and talons of the tiny birds covering him.

"They left the hub a while ago to settle in the acclimation areas."

The acclimation villages were regions where the people of Genos went to acclimate themselves to environments with little to no fungus. Those who wanted to travel off-world used them frequently. The exercise was similar to a Relian living in high altitudes to help the body become used to atmospheres containing less oxygen.

There were six villages in those regions. Deka glanced at Rive. "I'll go to the three nearest. You take the three farthest."

Rive bobbed his head and turned back to the people of Genos. "Have you heard from any other regions about what's happened to them?"

"We have received news from many areas," said one of the Jume, "but none on the Relians."

"Will you keep the portals open?" someone else asked.

Deka looked at Rive. A new bird landed on the metal raptor's snout, but he didn't seem to notice.

"I can establish a permanent way once we know it's safe," Rive said. "Where should it go?"

Rive could still be an Archeon, linking planets and communities together all over the contacted universe, and Deka was trapped only making ways for himself. Deka ached with jealousy seeing another Archeon who survived the disaster still able to hold portals open for months or years at a time, but he was also glad the disaster had not taken that from Rive, too. Rive had lost half his body to the disaster, but at least his mind was still unaffected. Deka tried to hold his claws together in a smile, but several birds were cleaning his hands, and he didn't want to interrupt them.

Holding back a grunt of discomfort, he began calculating the way to the first village.

2

Rive concentrated, the equations concluded smoothly, and the way opened. He walked up to the sphere, glancing to the side at Deka. The blue and red raptor still winced as the birds climbed over him.

"You're lucky you don't have to endure this." Deka said.

Rive clicked his claws. "Actually I haven't turned my sense of touch off."

"What? How?"

"The birds *want* to touch me. I want to feel every little movement."

"The fungus is itchy, birds and insects are crawling on me. I wish I could turn off some senses."

"People don't avoid touching you. I envy that."

He turned and walked through the way. His first destination was a settlement near the mountains. A few tricks of land formation all but canceled out the wind, the trees were much sparser, and the air was drier, so the fungus was thin.

The animals had adapted for this environment, and they tended to have much more benign ways to deal with the fungus. Rive stepped away from the portal and walked down the path through the thin trees. More than thirty animals sat in his path. One of the furry, burrowing mammals was grooming himself, his saliva a mild poison that inhibited the growth of the fungus. This was not enough to kill it, but it slowed the growth enough to prevent his skin from rotting. Various flying insects and scurrying rodents crawled over this burrowing mammal as he groomed, smearing some of the sticky saliva on themselves in the process, inhibiting the fungus on their own bodies.

A large, pink bird sat on the ground next to this mammal. It was bald, unable to fly, and until its feathers grew back, it was helpless. Various beetles and wasp-like insects crawled on the bird, covering it from beak to foot. These insects were found only in this region, as fewer companion birds lived in the higher latitudes where the fungus grew thin, which made room for other species to fill the niche. This bald bird was not immune to the fungus. It shed its feathers four times a year, when enough of the fungus accumulated on them. The insects that crawled on it ate the fungus now, keeping it safe during its vulnerable days.

For the Jume and the Olmn, this region was the Genos equivalent of living on the edge, with so little of the fungus to generate the chemicals they needed to survive. For any Relians, though, it would have been an ideal place to stay.

As Rive walked down the path, he looked at the rodents and canines and felines and birds and insects. They stared at him and yawned. None of them had an instinct to run away. Predators had not evolved on this planet since the appearance of the fungus. It was the common enemy to all life here, and all life grew up around defending itself against it. Evolution rewarded cooperation on this planet, not competition, so while life united to survive the fungus, it also came to rely on it. Rive wished he could stay longer to witness this in more detail.

The companion birds were still climbing him and nibbling his skin. A couple pecked at his metal parts before giving up. Rive rubbed his claws. He owed these humble creatures his life. He decided to keep his sense of touch on so he would not forget the birds.

The path before him opened into a large, empty field. Rocks had been piled into houses, but here there were no trees forcing everyone to be close, so the rock piles were spread much farther apart.

A small family of rodents emerged from one of the houses, each with a tuft of fur in its mouth. They scampered off and crawled into a hole in the ground. Insects crawled into and out of the houses, and birds landed at the entrances and hopped inside.

Rive scented the air and the ground. Relians were here, and their scents came from the farthest side of the settlement. He guessed they would be as far away from any trees or people as they could be. He made his way through the settlement, carefully stepping over the animals and trying not to wince as new birds landed on him and probed him for food.

A few moments later, insects joined the birds, and Rive felt them crawling up his feet, over the seams between the metal and the flesh, gnawing him with tiny pincers. The sensation of a thousand tiny feet all over his skin was enough to make him laugh.

Halfway through the village, he wondered where the people were until he heard shouts coming from the other side of the clearing. Far in the distance, the trees resumed, and the forest thickened just a little. A large group of Jume and Olmn had gathered out there. Rive stepped over the sleeping animals with insects and rodents crawling over them. He stepped over reptiles warming themselves in the open as their scales popped off ten at a time, and a flurry of rodents, insects, and birds scrambled to retrieve the fungus-saturated pieces.

The metal was agitated. Rive hesitated for one step as his mind processed the sensation. He was sure it came from the metal and not himself. It didn't like all these feet crawling over him. It didn't like the feeling of fungus clinging to him.

Rive hadn't noticed until now that so many sensations began to annoy him, but he could feel the fungus on his scales. It made him feel powdery and slick at the same time.

The birds and insects ate the feeling off his scales, but it always returned.

Rive held his metal arm in front of his muzzle. Insects swarmed over its entire length. The companion birds avoided his metal parts, but the insects loved it there because they did not have to compete with the birds for food.

The metal hated it.

Shoving the feeling aside, Rive maneuvered through the animals and approached the gathering. He counted sixty people here, with Relian scent among them. Rive's heart sank a little.

As he approached the back of the group, his ears picked out the distinct sound of Relians speaking the Genos language with an accent. He stood at the edge, trying to see over an Olmn's shoulders. Her body was covered in insects, rodents, and a few companion birds. Everyone's body was covered.

He could barely see the raptor and the fox between the Jume and Olm. People were handing them various animals, and the Relians were taking the animals, licking their skin or fur or scales, and then passing them around. The animals in everyone's hands looked confused but relaxed. Rive backed away a few steps and sat down.

The people of Genos had a celebration every time an offworlder joined them, especially a predator species. It involved meeting all the local species and licking each one's skin as an act of commitment. It showed that the offworlder was not afraid of the fungus anymore. For the raptor, it would be an even bigger commitment, as the raptor now had to commit to eating only insects, and giving up hunting was one thing most could never bear.

Rive hung his head, wishing he had come to this planet first. It was just as Deka described: always some other planet that needed help more. Always somewhere else they needed to be, and civilizations lived and died by their decisions. He realized it was only a taste of what Deka and Ky-lac had been through because of him and his fox.

The celebration separated enough for Rive to see the Relians in the middle of the crowd. The raptor had black and green scales, and she held one of the tiny reptiles in her hands. The reptile was covered in insects, and she held it up to her snout, licked the insects off and chewed them. Rive smelled no reluctance or disgust or remorse, and he held his claws together, relieved. Her fox had fur so short she was nearly bald thanks to the local rodents chewing it down.

The raptor saw Rive, passed the animal off to someone else, and nudged her fox, who turned to him as well. One by one the Genos noticed Rive, and the ceremony moved to include him. They gathered around him, asking question after question. Where the portals went, and how he got here, and why he smelled like metal, and what was this stuff on his skin. As hard as some of the memories were, Rive never tired of telling the story of the disaster. Every-one deserved to know what happened to their Archeons, and that he had been part of it.

The daytime star had set by the time Rive finished. His presence effectively ended the ceremony, and the people began to part ways. Some stayed and offered their suggestions for where the offworld portal Rive promised should lead.

Soon all that remained were the three Relians and the animals. Rive approached them, embracing the fox first.

"It's good to meet another Relian," said the fox. "I'm Sirna."

When the fox he pulled away, the raptor touched her neck to Rive's. "I'm Nelt—and you are cold!"

Rive took a step back, regarding them. They were still Relians, but they smelled more like the fungus than reptile and canine now.

"It is my body now," Rive said. "I wish I knew more about it, but I'm grateful to be alive."

"So are we," said Sirna, waving the tip of her tail. "When Genzin was destroyed, we fled through a portal that led to some world with bad air. We ran for another portal just before everything collapsed, and we ended up here."

"Nobody knew what was happening," continued Nelt. "The Genos were more confused than we were."

"I presume you came here to delay assimilation as long as possible."

Nelt bobbed from the waist. "After a while, we realized the portals weren't coming back, so we planned for the worst. We hoped the drier air would delay it."

"Not long enough," Rive said. "Deka and I have been visiting other planets, trying to retrieve everyone we can. I am sorry we didn't come sooner."

Nelt took Rive's flesh and bone hand in hers and rubbed her claws against his. Sirna's tail waved.

"Come with us," Nelt said.

They led Rive up the field of complacent animals, to where the ceremony had been before Rive intruded. They stopped at the small house.

"This was our home," Sirna said. "When we first arrived, we did everything we could to separate ourselves from the people. We didn't want to be here for the rest of our lives."

"As of today, we don't live here anymore," Nelt said. "The longer we stayed, the less we wanted to be apart from these people. I had a difficult time giving up hunting, though. So many years I hunted for Sirna, and I loved the challenge—especially hunting other predators. The bigger the better. The longer the claws, the more I liked it." She clicked her claws.

They turned and led Rive into the settlement. The houses were all shared by the community, with none of them belonging to any one person in particular.

"I hated the thought of giving up meat," Nelt continued. "I'd heard stories about this place, and I couldn't wait to leave."

Bipedal, toothless reptiles walked from house to house, birds and insects following them, and other animals following the birds. Jume walked about, rodents eating their fur and sometimes dropping pieces as they passed. Other animals trailed after them, snatching up the scraps and scurrying away.

"Then Genos reached out to us," Nelt said.

"Just look at these animals," said Sirna. "Where else in the contacted universe can you meet the animals like this? I'm so used to everything running away."

Rive looked at both of them. Birds and insects covered them in constant movement, and other animals were always behind them to clean up any leftovers that fell as they walked. Even those animals had companions to clean the fungus off them. Each individual became an ecosystem, impossible to separate from the web of interdependent creatures.

"On Rel, the animals were afraid of us," Sirna continued. "But here."

"We live with them," Nelt finished. "And the Jume and the Olmn, they've been so good to us. The Olmn taught me how to survive on the insects."

"She grew to like it," said Sirna. "I never thought she would give up hunting for anything."

"I don't even miss it," said Nelt. "Our bodies became dependent on the fungus a long time ago. We just didn't want to admit it. But then we decided to commit. We're locals now."

They stopped at another house, and Nelt went in and returned a moment later with an Olmn by her side. He had white scales with only a few flecks of green. His scent resembled Nelt's, and Nelt's scent had hints of hers within it.

Rive held his claws together. "You committed to more than just the planet."

"She waited long enough," said the Olmn, "but she finally did." The Olmn took Rive's hand and rubbed his claws with his fingers. He had no claws himself, but the gesture was correct, and he had obviously had much practice. "I am Yeel."

"Nice to share a smile with you," Rive said. He faced Sirna. "And have you found a way to fit in?"

Sirna's tail waved. "I'm never without! These people know what a fox needs. I don't mind it here now. With the portals gone, it's been boring sometimes, but they say you're going to make a new one. When?"

"As soon as we deal with my fox," said Rive. "Once we know it's safe to connect the contacted universe together again, the Archeons will start making new ways. I am so sorry we couldn't come sooner, but I am grateful you're both happy."

"They weren't always," said Yeel. He let go of Rive's hand. "But now she is not afraid of the fungus. Once she stopped living in fear, she began to laugh again."

Rive held his claws together. "Not every offworlder enjoys this, especially the carnivores. Most Relian theropods can't give up hunting, and many foxes don't enjoy living off the plants exclusively. I sometimes wondered if I could live in a place like this. I never enjoyed hunting."

Nelt blinked and curled her neck backwards. "You didn't?"

Rive rubbed his claws faster. "No. I never had a hunting preference. I didn't even have a mate on Rel."

"No mate, and didn't like hunting?" Nelt cocked her head at him. "Are you sure you're a raptor?"

"I was never a typical Relian, but my fox enjoyed hunting. He was the only thing keeping me from committing to a planet like this."

"Will you be going to the other settlements where the fungus is light?" Sirna asked. "We've been talking about going there ourselves to find out what the other Relians have decided. We split up so the fungus wouldn't spread between us, and we haven't met them since. I'd like to know if they want to stay, too, and then maybe we could all be together."

Rive rubbed his claws. "I'm working on the way right now. I'll keep it open for a while so everyone has a chance to contact the other settlements."

"Thank you," said Nelt, touching her neck to his again, without flinching this time. "And thank you for coming. I worried we'd live here the rest of our lives never knowing what happened to Rel and Genzin."

Rive sat on a rare place on the ground where an animal was not. "I wish I could say the danger has passed."

Nelt and Sirna settled down in front of him, with Yeel next to Nelt.

"You mentioned your fox," said Nelt. "Where is he?"

Rive opened his mouth and nothing came out. He just realized his sense of touch had switched off. He hadn't felt the insects or the birds since the ceremony, but he had not told his mind to switch it off. Rive turned it back on, relieved to discover he still could. The metal seemed to vibrate with displeasure, especially from the insects crawling on it.

Rive shuddered, both from the physical sensation and the truth he had to tell. "His name is Friend."

"The Archeon?" said Sirna.

"Yes. He is my fox."

3

Deka disliked this place. The air was thin, the trees were thin, the animals were sparse. Living this high up was risky, even to the Genos, the same as living on the frontier. Few ventured here, and the ones who did tended to be those who wanted to stay offworld for a while.

The companion birds tugged at his scales. Deka took some comfort in knowing many of them would fly away soon, once they realized Deka wasn't accumulating so much fungus anymore. Deka felt insects crawling up his legs. In moments they were all over his body.

He walked through the trees, their trunks spaced so far apart this could barely be called a forest. He passed a few shelters, and Jume and Olmn came out, scenting him from a distance as they ran up to him. In no time he'd drawn a large audience, and Deka told them the story of the disasters.

"I'm here for the Relians," he finished. "Do you know where they are?"

The people pointed him to a place far outside the settlement and told him to look for a cave. Deka allowed himself cautious hope. The fungus would be thinner still if they went deep enough, and if the cave was dry.

Deka trotted away from the crowd, hopping over animals and moving as quickly as he dared. His companion birds fluttered and squawked as they flew after him, as if telling him to slow down.

He followed old fox scent between the sparse trees. Animals stared at him as he ran up to them, but none made any motion to run away, and Deka marveled at the lack of fear response. Life on this planet cooperated. Everyone feared only the fungus.

"Deka!" a voice shouted, in slightly accented Relian. "Deka, I know you!"

He slowed to a stop. A Jume was following him about twenty paces back. The four-legged, bear-sized badger was crawling with rodents chewing her white fur and insects swarming over her exposed skin. He didn't recognize the body, but he knew that voice. "Sonjaa."

She caught up to Deka, breathless. "You know me? You really know me?"

Deka held his hands together, rubbing his claws in a smile. "Have you often dreamed of being a raptor? Do you have clear memories of living offworld, with a Relian reptile, traveling to other worlds and learning their languages?"

"So... Something's not wrong with me? Are the memories real?"

Deka hesitated, and then reached down and touched her face, tracing his claws over her fur. "Is Sonjaa your name?"

"I've been calling myself that for so long everyone else calls me by that name. Deka, is it true? These things I remember... Did they really happen to me?"

Deka crouched and embraced her, and she wrapped an arm around Deka's neck, breathing in his scent. The insects migrated between them, and some of the rodents on her body hopped onto Deka and began sniffing around. A few of them puckered a few scales between their paws and nibbled.

"Relian scent has always been so enticing," she said, "but I haven't met many of them who would let me touch them."

Deka fell silent for a few breaths. When he was sure of what he felt, he spoke. "Every time I meet you, it's as if you were never gone. Everything you remember is real."

"So I am a Relian," she breathed. "Deka, wherever you're going, let me come with you."

Deka released her and looked her in the eye. "Sonjaa, you know that can't happen. Your body needs the fungus to survive."

"I'm a Relian. I'll adjust, and I'm sure the Selts can help. I don't want to be away from you anymore. As soon as I caught your scent, I knew it was you." She rested her paw on his claws. "Whenever I thought about you, it was always as a memory, not a wish. I knew you were real, and now you're here. Please let me come with you."

Deka closed his eyes and took a breath. "Your last memory of Rel. What is it?"

"My last...?" She thought. "I remember people were looking up at me, and I was spinning around. And that's it."

"You were caught in the antisphere that destroyed Rel, and ever since then I've met you on almost every planet I visit. A Krone had your memories. A theropod on Xce had your scent. Each one of them has been drawn to me and every person I've met who had your scent and your memories has died."

The Jume glared at Deka.

He embraced her again, rubbing his neck along her upper back. "Please don't think I'm turning you away. I want you with me, but I don't want you to die." His words stuttered with light chirps of grief. "I've tried to prevent it, but I can't protect you. I can't stop it, and I have no idea what to do about it."

He held her for a long time. Neither said a word. Her scent filled him with a mix of joy, dread, grief, reunion, and pain.

"It's your choice," Deka finished. "If you want to live, go back to the village. If you stay with me, I promise you will die."

She ended the embrace and rose halfway off the ground, raising her head to Deka's eye level. "I'm coming with you."

Deka took a deep breath, enjoying being able to breathe her scent again, for however long she would be here. "All right, but when you have the choice, choose life."

"What do you mean?"

Deka turned and followed the trail of old fox scent further into the forest. Sonjaa walked at his side.

"You died trying to help Friend close the antisphere," Deka explained. "You will have a choice soon, whether to risk your life and help, or save yourself. I promise, you cannot help. This time, save yourself."

"I don't understand."

"I hope you will, when you have to." He nudged her flank with the side of his muzzle. "I'm going to find the Relians. If they want to leave, and if they're able to leave, I'll take them to Xeloc to kill the fungus, and then to Selta."

"No matter where you go, I will come with you."

Deka didn't bother to correct her. It was enough to hear her voice.

They walked side by side through the woods for some time, always careful to avoid the animals in their path. Sonjaa paused to eat a piece of fruit that had fallen from one of the trees. She ran and caught up to Deka, looking up at the insects and rodents crawling over his skin.

"Why are they on you? You have no fur, and they can smell you're a reptile."

"My scent is probably confusing. They can smell we're together, so they assume we must be the same species."

She chittered. "That's funny. They think you're a mammal."

Deka walked hip to hip with her. "Eventually they'll give up and migrate back to you."

His Archeon senses told him exactly how many feet were crawling over him, how much pressure each one exerted, the amount of friction and grip needed to keep them from slipping off while upside down, and much more. He wished for a subconscious again so he could ignore all of that information and focus on Sonjaa. They had so little time he didn't want to waste even a portion of his thoughts on anything but her.

They reached the cave mouth. Deka bent down and scented the ground. The fox scent was old, and he didn't smell raptor anywhere. Deka's toe claws rose.

Sonjaa tensed beside him. "What's wrong?"

"I smell fox but not raptor." Deka looked around. "You're not in danger, but stay out here unless you want to see something disturbing."

"Like what?"

"If I'm right, we have a fox without a raptor down there."

Deka stalked toward the cave mouth. The scent coming from inside was stale and moist and full of death. Deka listened a moment and then went inside. Sonjaa followed, her body posture looking far too relaxed. Animals here did not fight each other for survival, so she had no defensive or cautious stance.

Deka walked down a shallow slope and through a long tunnel. The light quickly faded to black, and the canine scent grew stronger. He stepped in water, and at the sound something shifted at the other end of the cave. Deka didn't wait for it to attack him; he tore through the tunnel, his toe claws slicing the water.

The tunnel opened into a small chamber, much of it covered in a shallow pool. A fox jumped on him and sank his muzzle into his neck, snarling and thrashing. The raptor swung around, grabbed the fox by the neck, and ripped him off. The fox landed in the water, rising to all fours to bare his teeth at Deka.

Half the fox's skin had rotted away. Most of his face had been eaten down to the bone, and much of his inner chest was exposed, as was the skin under the arms. Parts of his legs were missing. His fur had been stripped in some places, and the fungus had grown so thick on his body that the normally pink skin had become webbed and powdery.

The fox coiled up, about to lunge, but Deka jumped onto him, sank his killing claws into the fox's already open chest cavity, and swiped down. The fox howled. Deka lay on top of him and held his neck down with his mouth.

The fox reached around, scraped Deka with his claws, digging at his scales. Deka ignored it, forced the fox to breathe his scent. The fox continued snarling and howling. He sank his teeth into Deka's shoulder and thrashed his head.

Deka clamped down on the fox's neck and jumped away, taking the fox's throat with him. The fox gagged and choked as the water filled his body cavity up, now entering through the throat as well as the torso. Breaths later, the fox stopped making noise, and all movement ceased. Deka opened his mouth and let the fox's neck fall into the water.

He turned then to face Sonjaa, who was standing at the tunnel entrance, staring at the canine.

He nuzzled her. "Have you ever seen predation? Or defense?"

"On other worlds, but ne... never here." She stammered, unable to take her eyes off the half-eaten canine. "I knew that fox."

"Didn't anyone check up on them?"

"They made it clear they did not want to stay on Genos. We let them be."

Deka looked around. In the only dry corner of the cave lay a decaying body of a raptor, covered in fungus which had eaten the body down to the bone. The only flesh left on it clung to the torso and legs.

Deka pieced it together. "They took refuge in a cave, trying to escape the fungus. They didn't let the insects or rodents come with them. The cave is far too moist. Raptor died first, left his fox to revert."

His voice choked on the last word, and he turned away, heading back up into the tunnel. Sonjaa turned and followed as Deka ascended.

"What happened to him?" she asked. "Why couldn't he speak?"

Deka stared ahead, eager to return to the light and fresh air and rodents and insects crawling all over him. "That's what a fox is without a raptor."

"But why?"

Deka took a few strained breaths through his nose before answering. "Primitive foxes survived by keeping other scents away from them. Even other foxes. Without raptors to help them keep their instincts calm, that's what they become again. It's actually a good thing nobody went to the cave. They would have been killed."

"Can a fox come back from that?"

Deka stumbled, kept walking. "If it's not too late."

"Deka, what's wrong?"

He stumbled, tripped, caught himself against the wall.

"It's my fox. Every day that passes is another day Kylac is without a raptor. Every day, he gets closer to becoming *that*."

She pressed against him, holding him up as they walked out of the tunnel together.

"I think I remember him. He's smarter than that fox down there."

"Much smarter, but that won't make any difference. Too long, and he'll become just as mindless. Living to satisfy his instincts." Deka's voice broke again. "Too long, and he'll be beyond my help."

The light brightened, and they emerged from the cave. Instantly insects found Deka and began searching his scales. The rodents leaped from Deka's body to Sonjaa's and finally found the fur they were looking for.

Deka walked a few paces from the cave and sat down, staring at the ground, unable to get the fox's animal-like scent out of his mind. Sonjaa sat next to him, her thin fur brushing Deka's thigh. Insects and rodents traveled back and forth between them.

At last Deka stood. "I'm making the way to the next acclimation village. Did you still want to come with me?"

"I will follow you anywhere," she said, rising, and this time, Deka believed her.

4

Rive led the way through the thin forest, with Nelt and Yeel behind him and Sirna bringing up the rear, each of them crawling with insects and birds, plus a few rodents nibbling on Sirna's fur.

The forest barely existed on the lee side of this mountain range. The soil was still alive, and animals were everywhere, all adapted to this environment. This was a place where the moisture in one's eyes was the only moisture in sight. The trees and vegetation hoarded it, mixing it with toxic chemicals so animals and other plants wouldn't be able to tap it. Only those people of Genos who intended to survive offworld for days at a time would ever try to live here, as the fungus grew so thin it barely produced any hormones at all.

They had passed a few houses, all of them standing alone and empty. Other than the animals, there was no sign of life.

"Why didn't you all come here?" Rive asked.

"No food. Very little water," said Sirna.

"So you split up to keep contact at a minimum?"

"We agreed it was the safest plan," said Nelt. "The fungus was on us already, but we figured if we split up, it might not spread as fast. Some favored one region, others wanted another. One pair came this way."

"Jolete and Mersa," said Sirna. "Would have taken them sixty days to reach it from the hub."

"They feared the fungus that much?" said Yeel.

"Everyone did," said Sirna. "It's a beautiful planet, but nobody wanted to be here forever. Now it doesn't matter. Rel is gone, so we have to make new lives anyway."

"How does anyone survive here?" said Yeel. "I'm beginning to feel ill."

"You've never been to the frontier?" Rive asked.

He smacked his lips and licked his nose, groping for moisture. "There's no food, no water, no fungus. I haven't left Genos, so I never had a reason to come to these villages."

"They could have found water underground," said Rive. "They could have even hunted out here, where nobody would see them."

"Hunt?" said Yeel, stumbling and licking his nose again and again. "You mean consuming the animals like fruit? They would do that here, to animals that don't know to fight back or run away?"

"If this raptor didn't want to give up hunting, I can understand why she'd want to come here," said Rive.

"To be unable to survive except by taking the life of another..." Yeel shuddered.

"You seem surprised," Rive said. "I thought you would be used to predators." He glanced at Nelt, who was holding her hands together and rubbing her claws in a coy smile.

"Actually, Nelt is the first predator I ever met," said Yeel.

Rive stopped and looked back. The others stopped with him, eyes on Rive.

"The *first?*"

"I know about them," Yeel said, "but she was the first."

Rive blinked.

Nelt stood close to Yeel. "I'm just that good at catching defenseless lizards." She clicked her claws a few times.

The predator humor seemed to fly right over Yeel's head. He leaned on her and continued. "I have been learning about predator/prey relationships on other planets since I hatched. I had planned to start conditioning myself so I could go offworld and witness it, but before I was ready, the portals closed."

"Then he got busy with other research," said Sirna, waving her tail.

Nelt held an arm around Yeel. "I figured since he couldn't go to other worlds to meet predators, I'd bring one to him."

Rive rubbed his claws. Seeing a flat-footed lizard and a theropod together emphasized the differences between them. He glanced at Nelt's hands. "You should show him what those claws can do."

"I have," she said, swiping her mate down his flank. He winced, scent giving off amusement.

Rive held his hands together in a smile and led them onward. At one point he stepped over a snake covered head to tail in a colony of insects. He paused to watch as the insects passed over it. The snake opened its mouth, and more insects crawled off and out of its body, taking dull scales, broken teeth, and indigestible food particles with them. In return, they left the snake tiny water droplets in its digestive system which they'd brought up from underground, and as the insect colony disappeared underground, the snake crawled away, clean and fungus-free for another few days. Rive rubbed his claws together and walked on.

In time the Relian scent became stronger, and then a structure came into view. Rive trotted faster, leaving the other three behind. They had stopped and were panting, but it wasn't hot. Rive glanced back at them and noticed the birds were gone, as well as the insects and mammals. Rive didn't feel anything crawling on himself either. He made sure his sense of touch was still turned on.

Rive approached the house alone, keeping all his senses on and alert.

"Hello!" he called out. "My name is Rive. I'm an Archeon. I'm here to take you home."

Several breaths went by in complete silence. He was beginning to have flashbacks to Palc as he approached the piled rocks. Then the scent of death struck him. Not Relian death, thankfully, but a scent coming from the other side of the house. He took in a few more breaths and shuddered, glad the others hadn't accompanied him. At last he stretched his neck through the door and looked inside.

A raptor and a fox lay on a pile of dried sticks. They were both so thin Rive could see the bones in their legs. The fox's fur had fallen out in patches, and the raptor's scales were dirty and cloudy, as if she hadn't shed in years. Rive went to the raptor and shook her shoulder gently.

"Jolete. Mersa. I'm here to take you home."

They stirred in slow motion. Jolete, the raptor, mumbled something. Her fox, Mersa, raised an arm and pushed against the ground, raising her torso halfway off the makeshift bedding.

"Whanan ksslal murahn nnnnnn," said the fox.

Rive approached her slowly, scenting her breath. He huffed and then reached under her with his metal arm and lifted her to her feet. Still muttering, she did not seem to notice.

Rive tried to lift the raptor the same way, but she was limp and immobile. Rive could have lifted her, but trying to carry both at once risked hurting them. Rive left Jolete for the moment and walked the fox out of the house. Holding her with his metal arm was easy, but she would not move on her own. Finally Rive picked her up, disturbed by how light she was, and carried her to the waiting group.

"Is she all right?" Sirna asked.

"She's alive," said Rive.

He gently set the fox down. Sirna knelt and held the fox's head as she struggled to breathe. Rive turned and walked back toward the house. Plantigrade footsteps followed him, and he caught Yeel's scent.

"Do you need help?"

Rive glanced at him and held his claws together as they walked side by side. "You matured just this year, didn't you?"

Yeel's scent was very young, and the laughter in his scent equally so. "I did."

"A little young to take a mate. Especially an off-worlder."

Yeel's tongue was danging from his mouth, desperate for moisture and scents. "I know, but... but..."

"There's just something about her?" Rive held his claws together.

"Exactly," Yeel said. "She's a musician, you know. Has a wonderful voice. I sing as well. That's how we met. We taught each other songs."

"And Nelt has never hunted on this planet?"

Yeel seemed to take that as an accusation. "Never! She likes eating insects. I know it's strange, but it's true." He involuntarily licked his nose, and his attention snapped forward. "What is that taste?"

They had reached the door to the house. Rive placed his metal hand on Yeel's back. "Do you want to know what a predator does?"

"I know what predators do," he said. "They eat others to survive."

"You must have wanted to see it, since you were about to begin the process to go offworld. If you still want to, walk behind the house."

Yeel whipped his tongue back inside his snout. "What's over there?"

"Take a look. I can handle the Relian."

Yeel glanced at Rive and then walked past the metal raptor and around the house, not a hint of caution or suspicion in his step. Most species would move hesitantly into the unknown, but the people of Genos were just like the animals.

Rive watched him go and then went back inside the house. Jolete, the raptor, still lay limp and only semiconscious, and he picked her up in both arms and carried her to the waiting group. He laid Jolete next to her fox, who was beginning to show signs of coherence again.

"Where's Yeel?" Nelt asked.

"Behind the house. I told him he should look. Give him a few breaths, and then go to him."

"Why? What's behind the house?"

"Everything he thought he knew about predators."

The emaciated fox sat up. She was breathing normally again, and her gaze was focused as she turned to Rive. "Rive? Is that you?"

Rive bumped his snout with hers

She closed her eyes, joy and relief in her scent. "Finally... We're going home."

Beside her, the raptor painfully raised her head. "You came for us..." Each word was an effort, and she sank back to the ground. "We did it. We lived."

Rive waited for the fungus to do its work. When they seemed coherent enough to answer questions, he asked. "How did you survive out here for so long?"

"I dug for water," said Mersa, the fox. "I had to keep digging new wells. They kept going dry. The ones that didn't… The fungus grew on the water, so we couldn't drink it."

"I hunted," Jolete said, "when I could. Animals were hard to find. Sometimes we'd live for days on a few bites apiece."

"Some days we just stayed by the well," Mersa added. "We did nothing but drink. Saved energy."

Rive scented their breaths as they spoke, checking their health. "Was anyone else here?"

"No," Mersa said. "When the portals didn't come back, everyone returned to the towns. There was no reason to stay. We had the whole place to ourselves."

"Which was good," said Jolete. "I didn't want the Genos to see us like this."

As thin as they were, they smelled healthy again now. Rive knew what that meant, and there was no point delaying the inevitable. He looked at each of them in turn as he spoke.

"Jolete. Mersa. I'm sorry to tell you this. You're both dependent on the fungus now."

The two survivors went blank.

"No…" said Jolete. "We escaped it. We went hungry and thirsty. We came here so it wouldn't take us."

"The fungus is still here," said Rive. "It's not thick enough for the Genos to live here, but it's been on you the whole time."

"How do you know we're dependent on it?" Jolete snapped. "How can you know that?"

"Both of you were incoherent when I arrived, but when I carried you here, you came back to life. There's no better proof." He swallowed, feeling how hollow his words sounded. "I'm sorry."

Mersa looked down at herself. "But our skin didn't rot."

"It has," said Rive. "Not enough to eat you alive, but enough to make you lose a lot of fur and scales. Nothing has been around to eat it."

They smelled as if they wanted to snarl at him but lacked the muscle power to do it. They glared at Rive, then at each other, both shaking about to speak, cry, or reach critical mass. Eventually, they dreamily reached out and curled into one another, and they lay still in each other's embrace.

Rive stood and began walking back to the house. Nelt joined him.

Her voice was quiet. "Did you have to tell them now?"

"They need time to think about what they want to do. There is a chance the Selts can restore the gland, but they are likely to die trying to free themselves of the fungus."

"The Selts can fix anything."

"Even the Selts can't restore an organ that failed years ago. There might be too much damage."

"But there's a chance."

"Yes. Always a chance." He couldn't bear to kill hope.

Nelt looked back at the others. "Sirna is comforting them."

"I'm glad someone can. I still wish I had come sooner."

They walked a few paces in silence.

"If it makes you feel better, Rive, I'm not sorry."

Rive took her hand with his metal hand and touched his false claws to her real ones. She seemed surprised by the wrong feeling and odd sound, but she did not recoil. For a brief instant, Rive felt warm again.

They had reached the house now, and Rive peeked around the side. Yeel was kneeling at the rear of the structure, facing the distance behind it.

Nelt ran to his side, but he did not react to her touch. Rive approached them and looked out across the dry expanse, confirming with his eyes what his nose had already told him he would find.

Only a few sparse trees stood between them and the horizon, and as far as they could see lay skeletons of small animals. Birds, lizards, mammals, most no bigger than a fox's head, splayed open, emptied of their insides. Jolete and Mersa had not eaten the skin, and all the skeletons were clad in grey threads of pure fungus, cocooning the bodies so that only the bones protruded.

Holes dotted the ground, Mersa's attempts to dig for water. Rive scented one from a distance. Dry, but dead, fungus odor came from it.

Rive looked down at Yeel. The Olmn looked and smelled as if his mind had gone numb. He was still on his knees, gazing off into space. Nelt crouched next to him, rubbing him with her claws, lightly mouthing his muzzle with her teeth.

Rive's hands sank. Yeel had to see it eventually, and it may as well be on his own planet.

"We need to leave," Rive said.

Yeel did not move.

"You could go into a coma if you stay here too long."

Yeel flinched and licked the tip of his snout.

Rive reached down with his metal arm and lifted Yeel up. Nelt took his other side, and together they turned him around and walked him back to the survivors.

"Nelt," Yeel's voice was slow and breathless as he turned to his mate. "Did... you ever do that?"

Nelt met his eyes. "Every three days. I took down animals a hundred times that size. I loved it."

"You... You enjoy killing?"

"I used to, but now I'm on a world without predators or prey, and it's so beautiful I don't want to ruin it."

Yeel leaned over and rubbed his muzzle against hers. Rive couldn't rub his claws together, so he rubbed them against Yeel's arm instead.

5

Deka and Sonjaa stepped up to a pile of stones in the middle of a dense settlement. They had been through the frontier region further down the path but found only old Relian scent leading back here, where the fungus grew as thick as ever, to the delight of their companion birds, insects, and rodents.

Deka followed his nose to one particular structure within the dense forest. It was nighttime here, and a group of Jume, Olmn, various animals, and two Relians slept next to and on top of one another. Some of the nocturnal creatures fed on the fungus while the companion birds slept, and these lizards and rodents and insects were the only things moving about inside the house.

Deka rubbed his claws, and Sonjaa grabbed his hand and rubbed her fingers against his claws. Deka glanced at her, and they backed silently out of the house.

"I'm too late," Deka said.

"They smell happy," said Sonjaa, still holding Deka's hand, sharing a smile with him.

"They do," Deka admitted. "I don't want to wake them, but I'd like to hear their story."

Sonjaa regarded him. "Would you assimilate?"

"No. This is a beautiful planet, but I wouldn't want to stay here forever. I like being able to go anywhere."

"I wish I could. All my life I've wanted to live longer than a few days offworld. I wanted to run with the predators. It always felt like my place. The most I could do was learn their languages."

Deka took a deep breath. "Let's wake them. Hear what they've decided."

He went back into the house and reached down to shake the raptor. Sonjaa followed him, stepped over a few sleeping animals, and nudged the fox. The Relians stirred and looked up, but they were not startled. Their fight or flight instinct had atrophied.

The raptor caught Deka's scent and rolled to his feet, grabbing his fox and pulling him up as well. Both Relians smelled like the fungus, and they did not even seem to notice the nocturnal lizards and insects crawling on them.

"Deka!" said the raptor as loud as he could without waking the others. "You're here! Finally!"

"What happened to the portals?" said the fox.

Deka and Sonjaa motioned them out of the house, where they could talk. Once outside, each made space for their feet between the sleeping birds and furry animals and stood close enough to reach each other's claws.

"Good to find you well, Ketrik," Deka said to the fox. "Same for you, Osis. This is Sonjaa, my mate."

They turned and faced her.

"Why do you smell like a raptor?" Osis said.

Deka rubbed his claws. "Because she is one, but that's a long story."

Ketrik's ears flicked back and forth, and then he turned to Deka. "I'm so glad to catch Relian scent again."

Osis took Deka's hand and rubbed his claws. Deka smiled with Osis.

"I'll explain what happened later," Deka said. "I think I already know the answer, but... Did you commit?"

Ketrik wagged his tail. "The fungus took us a long time ago."

"Leaving the acclimating houses was the only way to find food," said Osis, "and if there's any water, the fungus grows on it instantly. We couldn't delay it."

"This is our home now," resumed the fox. "And now I can't even remember why we were afraid of it. This is a wonderful place to live. Osis went local."

"You took a mate?" Deka said.

"Several of them. There's no Relian civilization anymore, so why not become a fox?"

Deka and Osis shared an uncomfortable laugh.

"And Ketrik became a raptor," Osis went on. "He's been with this one Olmn a lot lately. Hasn't been with anyone else hardly at all."

"This place does something to you," said the fox. "And I like it. It's been fun, learning how to live."

Deka expected to find Relians in grief for being trapped here for the rest of their lives. Knowing they had found a way to be happy made him feel better. He released Osis' hand and held his own hands together, smiling at the Relians.

"Where is your fox?" Osis asked.

"It's a long story. I'm fortunate enough to have my mate still."

Osis' eyes darted from Deka to Sonjaa.

"Another long story," Deka added. "I'll tell you on the way, if you want to come with us."

"Where?" Ketrik asked.

"We're gathering the Relians at the hub. It's everyone's chance to try to leave Genos if they want. First an intermediate world to kill the fungus, and then to Selta to try to restore the gland that makes the hormones."

Osis curled his neck back. "The other Relians—how are they?"

"Two are dead. I hope Rive is doing better than I am. I have one more place to visit, and then we return to the hub."

Osis and Ketrik looked at each other, then at Deka and Sonjaa.

"We'd like to meet the others again," said Ketrik.

"I thought you would. The portal is near the acclimating houses. Follow me." Deka led them through the trees, preparing to tell his story—and Sonjaa's—once again.

6

Yeel's eyes were as empty as his scent. Nelt sat right up against him, touching him as only a Relian would touch a mate, but it did not seem to help.

Just a few paces in front of them, Jolete and Mersa were devouring a few rodents. Rive had taken Yeel to witness the miniature hunt, and everything had happened right in front of him: the chase, the kill, and now the consumption. Bones crunched, blood flowed, flesh disappeared down gullets, tongues licked lips. Now, with the prey gone, Jolete and Mersa were cleaning each other off. The raptor had been the one who had chased and caught the prey, and now she raised her neck so her fox could clean blood and fur from her scales.

Sirna watched Yeel and Nelt, smelling of concern and agitation.

Rive leaned closer to Yeel's earhole, speaking quietly but firmly. "That is how it is done."

Yeel was still far, far away. "I..."

Nelt had her arm around Yeel's back, and she raised her hand to his neck, rubbing it with her claws. "That is everything you learned about. That is how predators survive."

Yeel was breathing deep, tasting his nose frequently. "I cannot imagine you... *you...*"

Rive ran his claws up and down Yeel's back. "This is the difference between knowing about predators and witnessing it. Many species are not like you. They can't live on plants. They have to eat other creatures."

Jolete and Mersa had finished grooming each other, and now they returned to the waiting group. They had much more life in their steps now, though they were still sickeningly thin.

"Eating other creatures to live," Yeel whispered.

"Now you understand?" Nelt said. "Everything I told you? Does it make sense now?"

Yeel finally turned away from the survivors and faced his raptor. "I see it, but I don't understand. What is happening?"

"Life consuming other life," said Rive. "It is how life evolved on most worlds. When the portals open up again, you should witness more of it."

Yeel had not looked away from his mate.

"I gave it up," Nelt said. "I *want* to live here, so I gave it up, and I don't miss it anymore."

"Why would anyone want to keep it?" said Yeel. "It is..."

"Your language doesn't even have a word for it," Rive said. "You do not experience these impulses."

"I want to understand," Yeel said. "You feel this all the time?"

"Not since I came to Genos," Nelt said. "I haven't hunted here, not even before I decided to stay. I chose not to hunt because I didn't want to disturb the people. I wanted to be part of the beauty instead of destroying it. So did Sirna. We may be predators, but we can control ourselves."

Yeel didn't take his eyes off Nelt. If Yeel had been any other species, he would have reeked of fear, but Yeel's scent held no trace of it. Evolution had left a gaping hole in his instincts where fight or flight should have been. Rive leaned even closer and took in the scent, fascinated by it.

Eventually, the young Olmn leaned forward and rubbed his snout with her. She helped him to his feet, and Rive turned away from them. He let the equations conclude and then opened a new sphere to the final acclimating village.

Rive stepped through the way first and scented the land on the other side. Nelt, Sirna, and Yeel followed him.

Yeel still smelled empty, but quickly that emptiness was filling back up with affection. Rive held his claws together. Yeel had quite a journey ahead of himself, discovering all his mate's emotions and reflexes and history. Rive envied Yeel in a way, so young and mated to someone so different.

This area was full of sparse stone shelters, but all were empty. This was supposed to be one of the regions the Genos went to acclimate themselves to environments with little to no fungus, but it seemed something had changed, for fungus grew everywhere, and thick. Rive felt it collecting on his scales already.

Insects crawled up his legs and began eating. Their timing was perfect; Rive had just begun to feel dirty from all the fungus spores building up and sprouting on his scales. The companion birds were a great comfort. Twenty landed on his real skin as a few thousand insects crawled on the metal. Rive spread his arms and legs and let them feast.

His eyes shut off.

Rive stood still and kept his breathing regular. His sense of hearing flickered, and so did his sense of touch. His sense of electrical fields wavered, and he suddenly couldn't tell which way was up.

He concentrated and managed to turn one eye back on. His vision was hazy, but he could make out Yeel and Nelt and Sirna and the two thin Relians looking down on him, moving their mouths.

He didn't know when he had fallen. Rive focused on his ears, trying to switch one of them on, but nothing happened. His vision flickered for a few breaths, and then it cut off. Rive floated alone.

Rive had the feeling of someone touching him. Not insect or companion bird or fungus, but something.

He ignored it as simply his mind creating input to sense, so it would not lose its grip on reality. The sensation persisted, though, pressing in on him tighter and tighter, as if an entire civilization were standing next to him, trying to touch him all at once.

Rive

This time Rive was ready. He directed his mind to think of an answer. I am here.

Rive

Yes.

Nothing this time. Rive waited. He waited a long time. Gradually a feeling built up inside of him and bubbled to the surface as a thought that did not come from his own mind.

Rive felt relief. The feeling had its roots in the constant sensory input. The companion birds and insects had been too much. The scents... too much. Relief was better. No senses. No outside world.

The raptor became aware these were not his ideas.

Where are you?

A mood came to him, not a voice but a consensus. It made Rive feel cold. It stole his heat, though it did not want to.

The metal

The consensus returned heat to Rive's mind and stood closer to him.

7

Deka stepped through the portal and stood just outside the hub settlement. Sonjaa followed, then Osis and Ketrik, and then another raptor, very thin from living on the edge of the life-supporting zone for so long.

The new arrival was their last survivor, from the final acclimating village, a lone raptor. The only words he had spoken were the words he'd said when Deka introduced himself: "Take me home."

Deka didn't know his name. He didn't ask where his fox was. Deka had already guessed what must have happened, and it was one of those times he wished he weren't so good at finding and connecting details. He respected the raptor's silence and did not ask anything further of him.

They settled down on the ground, and Deka addressed them all. "We'll wait here for Rive. I'm sure he won't be long."

It was dark now, and most of the animals around them were asleep. The ones who weren't asleep groomed or fed on the fungus that grew on the sleeping animals. The companion birds had also settled onto branches and rocks and bare spots of ground, necks curled backwards into their plumage. Serpents and rodents took over the job of cleaning Deka's scales. He thought he would be used to it by now, but it still irritated him.

When he woke with the daylight, there was still no Rive. Deka had a feeling he should never have left the metal raptor alone. He began calculating a way to the last region he would have visited.

Sonjaa rose from his side and nuzzled his snout. She held his hand, shared a smile, and lightly nipped him on the nose. Her teeth would never break the skin, but the gesture still made Deka forget she was not a reptile. He nipped her in return.

Sonjaa tipped her head at the silent raptor nearby. "What's wrong with him?" she asked quietly.

Deka sighed and rolled to a sitting position. "Outside the shelter, I smelled old blood. Canine. The raptor still smelled of it, too. His fox ran off, probably too hungry to care about the fungus anymore, and he reverted to the old ways in the wilderness. Our raptor couldn't bring him back. He had to eat his fox to survive."

Sonjaa was breathless. "How do you know?"

"Signs, scents, disturbances of the environment. An Archeon learns how to take in all that information."

Sonjaa turned to the silent theropod and dropped to her stomach, head between her paws.

"He knows he didn't have to do it," Deka continued. "All they had to do was choose to live with the Genos, and they would have survived. Now he depends on the fungus anyway, and he has no fox, so it was all for nothing. Do not speak to him until he is ready to speak."

"I wouldn't know what to say."

"He knows he made bad choices. He will let the Selts try to restore him. If he lives, he will move on. If he dies, he won't mind."

"These Selts... Can they do anything for me? Can they help me live offworld?"

Deka looked down at the ground, at one of the sleeping companion birds right under him. It slept without any fear of harm. Deka contemplated how easy it would be to take advantage of that. Easy meals were all around him, but he did not want to disturb this place. After a moment, he looked back up at Sonjaa.

"You never had a gland that produced those hormones, Sonjaa. You can't live without the fungus."

"I want to go with you."

"I want you to come, but there's a crowd here, and I'm sure there will be one where Rive is, too. When it's time to make a choice, remember that you will fail."

"What choice? Fail at what?"

"I don't know, but you'll choose to do something. Something you feel strongly about. You will fail, and you will die, so please, choose life. *Your* life."

Deka concluded the equations, and a sphere opened in front of them. Deka stood. Sonjaa rose to all fours and looked up at him.

Deka held her gaze. "I'm checking in on Rive. Please remember what I said."

"I will."

Deka stepped through, Sonjaa at his side, head held high and confident. The fungus spores in the air didn't feel as thick as at the hub, but there were enough for the birds to eat as they landed on Deka and Sonjaa.

Deka smelled Relians nearby and ran through the trees. Piles of dead animals littered the ground, their skeletons wrapped in fungus, the scent of old blood everywhere.

The Relian scent grew stronger. He saw a group of them through the trees, and Deka called out.

"Rive? Rive, are you there?"

Everyone faced him. They smelled agitated and terrified, all except the solitary Olmn among them. Deka caught up and saw what they had gathered around.

Rive lay motionless on the ground under a pile of tiny birds and crawling insects.

"He just collapsed," said the thin fox. Deka winced when he saw her.

"Are you Deka?" said the healthy-smelling raptor. She smelled like the Olmn, and he smelled like her.

"Yes." Deka crouched by Rive. "How long has he been out?"

"All night," said the thin raptor. "His portals closed, too. We've been trapped here."

"What's wrong with him?" said the raptor who smelled like the Olmn.

Deka shook Rive gently, then more forcefully, but Rive remained limp. "I don't know. Last time I brought him out of it, but it's not working now. Are any other Relians here?"

"I smell a fox somewhere," said the healthy fox, "but I haven't found him. And he doesn't smell right."

Deka turned to the two healthy Relians. "Help me carry him."

They lifted with their legs and held Rive between the three of them, Deka at the front and the other two holding the metal raptor's legs. The Olmn walked between them and supported the middle. Even the two malnourished Relians ran to either side and helped hold Rive up as well. Deka steered them toward the portal. He was close to his limit for how long he could hold one open, so he tried to move them faster.

Sonjaa trotted to Deka's side.

"I wish I could help."

"No need," Deka said softly. "Just remember your promise."

They walked for a few paces, and then the scent hit them. Everyone jerked to a halt. The fox scent was strong and sharp, and now they could hear snarling.
Deka bent at the knees, and everyone followed his lead and lowered Rive to the ground. As soon as he was down, a fox appeared in the distance, stalking on all fours between the trees, his fur matted with blood.

Deka crouched and spread his claws. The fox howled and charged him headlong. Deka rushed forward, colliding with the fox and bowling him over. He slashed the fox across the snout and chest a few times, and then lay on him, pressing him against the ground and forcing him to breathe his scent.

The fox snarled and thrashed, trying to worm out of Deka's grip. He got one leg free and scraped Deka's stomach. The fox pushed Deka over just enough to escape, and Deka rolled to his feet. The birds covering Deka held on for their lives, and Deka wished they had a flight reflex. Other companion birds flew around them, trying to land on them, but Deka and the fox were moving too fast.

The fox scented the others then and charged past Deka. Deka tried to catch him, but his claws only scraped the reverted fox across the shoulder. The fox slipped by, heading straight toward the Olmn. Deka saw that the Olmn wasn't moving. Just like all the other animals here, it simply never entered his mind that someone running toward him might intend to harm him. He stood still, staring with open curiosity.

The healthy raptor jumped in front of the Olmn, mouth open and claws spread. The canine did not slow down, and he slammed into her. The raptor caught the fox, raised her claws, and slashed the canine across the chest. Then she kicked him down to the ground and jumped on him, holding him down.

Deka slid to a stop, kneeling by the fox's head. The fox clawed at the raptor's legs, howling and thrashing. She pricked her killing claws into him, not very deep, but enough to get his attention.

Deka covered the fox's mouth with a hand.

"Come back," he said, his tone even and soothing. "Remember. You are not this. Remember who you are. Remember who you are."

The fox continued thrashing and snarling and trying to bite Deka's hand and claw the other raptor's legs.

"Come back to us. Remember."

The fox struggled less and less as time passed. The raptor on top of the fox withdrew her killing claws from him and lay on the fox instead.

"Remember," she said.

Many more breaths passed. By now the others had left Rive's side and gathered around the reverted fox, including the Olmn, whose scent was so young. Deka tapped his claws together and faced the raptor on top of the fox.

"You raided the nest for that one," he said, in Relian.

She brushed her claws against his. "You would have, too, if you'd heard him sing."

More breaths passed. The fox was much calmer now, and Deka released his hold on him. There was thought behind the eyes, and the fox's scent was full again.

"What's your name?" Deka asked.

The fox whimpered. "I am... Folv."

"I'm Deka, and I'm here to take you home. Where is your raptor?"

The fox couldn't stop whimpering and whining. The female raptor got up off him and stepped back. They let the fox cry.

8

The surviving Relians mingled with the Genos. There was no point denying it anymore. They had all become dependent on the fungus.

Folv and the silent raptor sat close. The raptor's instinct had driven him to take possession of this lone fox. Deka had hoped it would happen, and he was relieved. They seemed to have renewed one another's reason to live.

Jolete and Mersa had little to say to anyone. Mersa's ears were back, and Jolete's muzzle was down. All the suffering they had endured, and it had been for nothing.

Osis and Ketrik were trying to engage them, but the two thin Relians spoke only a few words in reply. Nelt and Sirna had much to tell everyone, but their happy words only seemed to depress the Relians who had not fared so well on this planet.

At last Yeel stood and began to sing. As the Olmn's song wound around them, it diluted the remorse. For Deka, it replaced the grief with somber satisfaction. It was over. They were leaving at last, and everyone finally knew what happened. Jolete rubbed her claws. Mersa's tail wagged for the first time. Even the silent raptor held his hands together during the music. Folv embraced the silent raptor tighter and licked his snout.

Deka took Sonjaa's hand. "Nelt was right. Yeel has a good voice."

Nelt joined her mate at his side, and they sang together. Their voices merged perfectly, weaving in and out of phase and tone. Even to Relian ears, they were beautiful.

Something shifted behind Deka. He turned. Rive was awake. Deka rose, letting go of Sonjaa's hand, and leaned over the metal and flesh raptor.

"Rive, it's all right. You're back on the hub. Everyone is here."

Rive smelled terrified, and Deka was glad to smell that again. It seemed healthy.

Rive rose slowly to his feet.

"How long was I gone?"

"Two days."

"Days?"

Rive turned his muzzle to the ground and took a few deep breaths. "I lost the ways."

"I'm just breaths away from Xeloc. We'll have to wait there long enough for one of us to make a way to Selta. We have four Relians who want to leave, and four who want to stay."

Rive touched his metal arm, feeling all the way up to his shoulder, his neck, and then his lower jaw. The insects crawling on him migrated to his real hand, trying to stay out of the way of the companion birds also nibbling on him.

"I'm not sure what happened. Words..." Rive shook his head. "I can't think how to describe it."

"Think about it." Deka rose to his feet. He reached out and swiped his claws down Rive's metal flank. "I need to know if I can leave you alone ever again."

Rive took Deka's hand and rubbed claws with him. "Thank you for rescuing me."

The equations concluded, and a sphere opened to a view of Xeloc's mildly acidic atmosphere and ocean.

Deka raised his voice to address the group. "Everyone, now is the time to choose. I can't keep the way open for very long. Anyone who wants to take a chance and let the Selts try to restore you, step through. We'll decontaminate there first, and then we'll go on to Selta."

The Relians stood. Osis and Ketrik embraced the other four, as if for the last time. The others painfully returned the gestures and faced the portal. The silent raptor was the first to walk through, followed immediately by his new fox. Then Jolete and Mersa walked through.

Deka and Rive touched claws with the four remaining Relians on the way to the portal.

"Keep Yeel safe from predators," Deka said to Nelt.

Nelt leaned against her mate. "As soon as the portals open, I'll take him to meet more."

Deka took Yeel's hand and rubbed his claws against the Olmn's fingers. "Learn how to fear her. It's healthy."

He returned the gesture, smiling with his scent. "I'm eager to be taught."

Deka then turned to Sonjaa. She stood a few paces away, and he closed the gap between them.

Deka lowered his neck to be at her eye level. "I'm so glad you came with me, Sonjaa, but now you can't follow."

"I understand."

"But you lived! You have no idea how much that means to me."

"You have no idea what this has meant to me," she replied. "When I'm with you, I finally feel like myself. I feel real." She hesitated. "You will come back?"

"I promise." Deka took her hand, stroked her fingers with his claws. "And I'm an Archeon, so I can't forget my promises." He looked around at the rodents and lizards and birds everywhere. The grooming of the birds on his scales now felt life-giving instead of irritating. "Maybe this place isn't so terrifying. It does have a certain beauty to it. I would commit to it for your sake, Sonjaa. I think I could learn to enjoy it here. I'll return soon."

Deka turned and approached the portal. The Relians were beating at Rive's scales, encouraging the birds and insects to leave him. The birds flapped overhead, waiting for them to stop so they could land again, but the Relians didn't give them a chance. When his body was finally bare, Rive ran through.

Deka submitted to the same beating. Once he too was free of birds and insects, he walked through the way, stopping a few paces ahead on the other side. Closing his eyes, he savored the feeling of the fungus shriveling and dying and falling away like old scales. He let the portal slip away.

Behind him, the Relians screamed. Deka's eyes flew open and he turned to see Sonjaa lying on the ground, sliced in half through the torso. Half of her was here on Xeloc, and the other half was back on Genos.

She managed to look up at him. "Deka, help me!"

The Relians formed a thick mass of fur and scales, pressing against her, trying to stop the bleeding and hold what remained of her entrails inside her.

"Deka, what's happening?!"

Deka did not even try to run toward her. He turned away and closed his eyes again.

"Friend! Rive! Help me, please! Someone! Help!"

Deka turned away and looked out over the ocean. He breathed the acidic air. He lowered himself to his stomach and closed his eyes, hoping Rive was calculating the way to Selta. He didn't want to stay here long either.

Suum

Kylac was on his hands and knees in the orange-colored grass.

"Please no, not here, not this planet, please no..."

"You can close it!" Friend was standing just behind Kylac. "It's just a portal. Nothing different about it except where it leads. Close it the same way."

Kylac had tried many times to close the antispheres after his mind opened one, and so far they had lost six planets.

"Not again, please stop, please!"

It felt like the instant before vomiting, when the muscles are only threatening to contract. Kylac had been dealing with this feeling every moment for days, always on the edge of opening an antisphere, and it would not let him rest. He would rather be vomiting, or feeling on the verge of it for days at a time. It would have been easier to deal with than this, knowing entire worlds were at stake if he did not resist.

An antisphere hung thirty paces away from Kylac. It had started as a clawtip, and now it had expanded to the size of a Relian canine. Kylac sensed he was making progress, for on the previous worlds the sphere doubled in size every breath and a half. Now on Suum, where the plants had not evolved photosynthesis, Kylac had figured out how to slow the antispheres once they had opened, and he sensed he was close to reversing the equations and closing the hole.

The ground trembled. The land under and around the portal began to buckle and heave. Kylac had not figured out how to stop the portal from spinning and drawing things into it, so he desperately tried to stop the antisphere entirely. He stared at it, forcing his mind to look at the emptiness that lay beyond. In the end, that was what made the whole situation so terrifying. He was opening portals to nowhere, and yet these portals lead somewhere. He wanted to perceive it, and he did not want to perceive it. He had to know what it was, and yet his mind recoiled from it.

"You're almost there." For once Friend's voice was a comfort. "Run the equations the other way. Don't be afraid of what's on the other side. Force your mind to take it in, and you'll control it!"

Kylac hung his head, closing his eyes as if it could provide any relief. His ears folded back, and his tail hid between his legs. The equations in his mind had a conclusion and a logical order, and they formed tidy, intricate patterns when solved, and Kylac loved that feeling, but instead of revealing an orderly universe in which he could travel anywhere at any time, one of these antispheres opened up. Chaos. Nowhere. Disorder. The solution was correct, but the results were always wrong.

He raised his head and looked again at the sphere to nowhere, which the equations told him must lead everywhere, which made no sense—and yet here it was. Everywhere and nowhere at the same time.

Kylac reached into his thoughts, grabbed one of the equations, and tried running it backwards. He had tried this before, but every time the whole thing spun out of control. This time he was determined to keep the equations in a structure, working together instead of flying around in his head anywhere they pleased.

The other equations began spinning in reverse. Kylac held each one up in turn, inserting numbers where needed, removing numbers when not needed, putting one equation on hold while it waited for results from another. The lattice of rotating equations Kylac built in his mind was shaky at first, but it held. The sphere's growth slowed.

"Good! Good! Keep it up!"

Kylac looked from calculation to calculation, checking in on them. He had never worked so hard to maintain equations before, even when he was an apprentice. He knew these equations very well by now, how they behaved, what they needed, what would send one spinning out of control, and what would lull it into peaceful coexistence with the others. This was an order of magnitude more complicated than the portal physics he had learned before.

He gave each equation the attention it deserved. He knew most of their likes and dislikes, their metaphorical cares and woes, and he catered to each of their individual needs. The equations stayed in their orderly lineup as they ran the numbers backwards. The antisphere began to contract.

"That's it! You're almost there!"

The equations stood as an enormous tower inside his mind, and Kylac was the only support beam holding the whole thing up. It was his duty to run to each point of the tower, support that side, then move to the next place, and the next, thousands of times a breath, becoming every support at the same time.

Kylac kept the equations moving. Some returned results, and Kylac fed those numbers into the other equations, spun them, and held the idle ones up so they wouldn't start running random numbers on their own. Kylac had learned how to prevent that a few planets back, and his head had been less crowded since.

Every equation returned a result.

The ground stilled. The antisphere winked shut.

Kylac collapsed to his side. He let go of the equations for less than a breath, but the structure in his mind stayed steady. The equations stayed in formation, idle, but not happy. He felt a few of them growing restless already, tempting him to plug random numbers into them and try to run them again until they made sense. Kylac held them still.

Friend dropped to Kylac's side, embracing him with his whole body.

"I knew you could do it, and you're learning so fast! It took me forty-eight worlds to figure out how to close an antisphere. You did it in thirteen."

Friend's scent was repulsive. Kylac had the nagging desire to keep that scent away from him, but he resisted. In that moment while his mind was distracted, some of the equations started up, using random information, and the enormous machine of interlocking formulas in his mind began to chug again. Kylac's mind was too occupied keeping them in orderly positions to stop them from working. Kylac moaned and curled into himself.

"I know." Friend licked the inside of Kylac's remaining ear. "They won't stop until every possibility has been calculated, but then you won't have to work to keep them in order. Everything will know its place and will never wander off again."

Kylac felt suffocated by Friend's scent. Too much, too close, too hard to keep his fur from bristling.

"Friend... Take us to Gaow. It's safe now. I think I can go there without destroying it. We need raptors around us."

"They will kill us on scent."

"You don't know that."

"Rive would have taken Deka to meet them. Your raptor will have turned our entire civilization against us."

"He wouldn't do that. Not without trying to bring us back. But even if they are against us, you can take us off-world instantly. There's no risk. Let's just go"

"We don't need them."

"Friend... Can't you feel it? I'm starting to hate your scent. Right now I'm fantasizing chasing you away. As far away as possible. Bleeding. I can't stand having you close to me. It's the old ways."

"If you haven't reverted by now, you never will."

"Equations aren't enough. I'm starting to panic. Please take us to Gaow."

Friend snarled and shoved Kylac away, rolling to his feet and walking a few paces off. "I have seen beyond the universe! I will not go back to the raptors to keep me docile and submissive!"

Kylac rolled over to face him. He could only see his back. "We need them."

"Maybe instead of relying on them for our sanity for generations we should have been working on building ourselves up to handle the old ways without them."

"They tried that. Our instincts are too strong."

"They tried centuries ago. It's time for another attempt." Friend straightened up and took in the scents of a field of orange grass that stretched from horizon to horizon. Over the hills to their left lay this world's hub, currently inhabited by about seven hundred people. The gentle breeze washed their collective scent over the two foxes.

"We used to be independent, Kylac. It's how we survived. The raptors forced us to be something else. And after seeing the universe as a whole, I have to wonder why we let them."

"Friend, what happened to you? This isn't like you."

"Years."

"Of what?"

Friend stared off into space for a while. Kylac continued.

"The Friend I've known since I was little always had his mind on some big idea. You loved talking to Rive about these things. You two never stopped. You practically lived in the quantum world. That was pretty much all you did together. Never talked about anything real. Always ideas. What happened? Didn't you enjoy being with Rive?"

"He was a good raptor, but why do I need him? Why do I *think* I need him? I don't. Foxes are supposed to be independent. We should use our instincts, not divert them into something as useless as sex. How many years of my life did I have to waste doing that?"

Kylac rose to his hind legs. The numbers still ran in the foreground, but now that they had organized themselves into a structure instead of flying around in all directions, he could think again.

The tailless fox turned to Kylac. His ear flicked. "I told you. When you see the universe as a whole, some things just don't matter anymore."

A small antisphere opened between them. Kylac crouched and searched his mind for the conclusion. He was prepared to run the entire apparatus in reverse again, but as he looked into this antisphere, he realized he was not connected to it. Friend's eyes swam in it instead.

"Look at it," Friend said. "That is the Lake. This reaches back to the past about six days ago, slightly to the side of the path the universe is moving along. We can't perceive it any other way except through mathematics." He sighed blissfully. "This is *real*. It's wonderful, and I didn't need a raptor around to make sure I stay calm and don't hurt anyone."

"You needed a raptor to make offworld portals for you."

Friend approached the antisphere, never taking his eyes off it. "Rive never knew what to do with a fox who reverted. He would never have known what to do with me if I had. He couldn't even hunt for me, Kylac. I had to do it. I had to keep myself under control, and when the antispheres began appearing, I had to figure it out on my own. I've never needed a raptor. I never wanted one. I can admit that now."

"We need a raptor's scent to calm us down," Kylac said. "Without it, the old ways will rise."

"Now is a good time to learn how to control them yourself."

"Friend, you were never prone to reverting. I am. If it were that easy, no fox would ever revert. I know. I've tried to keep it from happening, but Deka is the only one who can help me keep my higher mind from sinking."

Friend was now circling the antisphere, looking it up and down. "We've come this far without raptors, and look what we have discovered. A little discipline and self-control is all you need. We're just too used to the them doing it for us."

Kylac's tail waived. "And what do you suppose a fox who could control himself would be like? What were we before the raptors tamed us? We were territorial. We killed every scent around us to protect ourselves. We didn't care who we killed to survive. As long as we lived, that's all that mattered." Kylac's voice turned cold. "Just like you."

Friend's gaze hardened. The antisphere closed, and Friend turned to glare at Kylac. "This is not survival. This is discovery."

"All that matters is your discovery. Doesn't matter who has to die for it, so long as you are satisfied. Imagine if every Relian canine were like you."

"Kylac—"

"An entire universe full of foxes wiping out planets to satisfy their curiosity. Scent anxiety in a different form. The raptors kept us from becoming that. That's why we let them tame us—we know what we would be without them!"

All of a sudden, Friend's scent wasn't far away enough.

"And for centuries we were afraid of ourselves," said Friend. "Afraid of what we would become without the raptors. I had the courage to find out. Do you?"

Kylac's single ear folded back. "I've been on that other side more than you have, and I hate what I become. It's been happening this whole time. The equations... They're not calming my scent anxiety, Friend. They're forcing me to be conscious while I revert."

"And if you could take control of yourself while you revert? With a conscious mind behind the old ways, what would you be? What could you do?"

Kylac's ears wanted to fold back even more, and his missing ear hurt from the strain. "I would be free to destroy entire planets to calm my scent anxiety. What next, Friend? Entire universes?"

Friend did not answer.

"This is what our ancestors warned us about! They said without the raptor, the fox would become cancer that consumed the entire universe, and you're living proof of it."

"I'm living proof of what we can achieve without them holding us back. Encouraging us to waste time having sex when we could have been learning to control ourselves."

Kylac turned away from Friend, let himself fall over, and closed his eyes. "Stop talking. I'm tired of hearing your voice. I'm so tired... Why can't I sleep yet? Don't I have enough control?"

"You have organized the equations in your mind, and you are familiar with what each equation requires. Now it is only a matter of solving them when you want to solve them. Then you will have to reconcile the portal physics you already know with this new system. Once you do that, you will sleep."

Kylac groaned. Friend's voice was irritating and his scent repulsive. All his problems would be solved if Friend were dead—if that scent were snuffed out and far away. Kylac opened his eyes and looked at him. The older fox was still giving Kylac the hard stare.

Kylac curled up, whimpering. For the first time in his life, a person's scent did not go straight to his sheath. He missed the association Deka had built up in his mind. Now the equations had taken over, and it did not feel good at all.

"Don't think about Deka," Friend said. "After you solve the equations, you'll understand why you don't need him. How he was holding you back. How you wanted to get away from him your whole life, but you stayed because it was expected of you, and you believed what everyone told you, that you're dangerous and you need him to stay sane. How your entire civilization was designed to hold you down."

Kylac clenched his teeth. His words came out in English. "Friend, shut your *fucking* muzzle!"

At last Friend was quiet for a moment. Kylac lay still, wishing he could sleep, wishing he could think about something besides the massive structure of equations he had built in his mind.

"If you want me to understand you," Friend said, "you need to keep talking."

Kylac rolled back over and faced him. "Fuck you shit bitch I hope you fucking choke on your own puke go to fucking hell you piece of shit motherfucker bastard cunt asshole up yours dickwad piss the fuck off you son of a fucking bitch!"

All was silent for a few beats. The wind didn't even shake the grass. Then Friend responded in English. "This language seems to be based on imagery, so it's a visual species... Apparently with a lot of anger directed at everything except itself, so it belongs to an uncontacted species. Was this the language of that hairless creature Norh carried off?"

"His name is Stephen," Kylac said, still speaking English. "I hope he's all right. I hope Norh got him off Rel in time. He must have; he knew the disaster was coming. All Stephen wanted to do was learn about the universe, find out what's out there. Instead, we had to show him aftermath of the disasters you caused!"

"Will you stop going back to that and think forward for once in your cock-obsessed life!"

"Go fuck yourself," Kylac muttered.

"That you can only say these things in an alien language tells me you are thinking differently for the first time. This is what new perspective feels like, Kylac. This! Not the perspective the raptors want us to have! They don't want us to have any power over our lives! They're afraid of us."

Kylac sat up. "They have good reason to be! You've murdered millions of people, and you don't even care! I hope hell exists and you're the only one there!"

"Calm down, Kylac, or you'll lose the equations."

Kylac stood, claws spread. "Now who's holding me back? Now who's trying to keep me sane?"

Friend remained upright and relaxed. "I'm giving you perfectly logical reasons not to be angry, but you keep finding ways to make yourself angry. Do you want to destroy this planet?"

Kylac snarled. "Your voice is pissing me off! Your scent makes me sick! I haven't stopped feeling reverted since Juza. I *hate* feeling this way, and if you'd ever reverted before, you'd know what it feels like, and you'd be so scared you'd run out of shit!"

"You're controlling antispheres now, Kylac. You can control yourself, too."

With a wordless cry, Kylac charged the other canine. He expected a portal to open in front of him that would send him offworld, or drop him behind Friend, but nothing appeared. Instead, Friend crouched into attack stance and snarled back.

They met in a flurry of teeth and claws. Blood flew from Kylac's muzzle. Blood was on Kylac's hands. Smelling Friend's blood on his claws felt enormously satisfying. A wounded scent was a weak scent, and a weak scent could not harm him. Kylac swiped and bit and kicked.

By the time the two foxes separated, both were covered in blood, each other's and their own. Seeing a fox's muzzle curled up in a snarl excited Kylac as he had never been before.

Friend lunged at Kylac, going for the throat, but Kylac was ready for him as they grappled and bit and clawed each other again. Blood and fur flew, and then they separated, this time ten paces apart, and squared off again.

Kylac felt the equations wobbling. It was like being caught in a cloudburst, and he lowered his attack stance and sank to the orange grass, breathing regularly, trying to keep the equations calm, never taking his eyes off Friend. After a moment, the tailless fox also sat, his face still curled into a snarl.

Kylac had just enough presence of mind to realize what had happened, and that he had come out of it only because of the tower of equations. It had threatened to topple and take all his progress with it. His mind had refused to let that happen. It alone had prevented Kylac from descending into the old ways.

Friend's ears bloomed, and he spoke in Relian as he licked a gash on his arm. "The equations are still keeping us from reverting. Now do you believe me? We don't need raptors."

Kylac's words were barely articulate through his clenched teeth. "Why is that so important to you?"

"Because we can finally break free. New universes await us out there, and we can explore them ourselves without reptiles forcing us to be obsessed with sex."

Kylac growled low. He hated that voice, and the scent was beginning to disgust him again. "With Deka, I was calm. I felt peace. The equations... They just force me to be awake while I'm anxious all the time."

"Amazing to think about, isn't it? We can perceive the universe as it really is, but this whole time we've refused to perceive ourselves for what we really are."

"I would rather die in the old ways than live to become you."

"This is what we're meant to be, body and mind, capable of anything."

"Fuck off," Kylac said in English.

Friend responded in Relian. "Not long before you reach the solution."

A hundred tiny antispheres opened up all around Kylac, filling the air between him and Friend with tiny portals to nowhere. Kylac dared not move a muscle for fear of losing another ear, or a finger, or part of his sheath.

He had no choice but to look into the void. The Lake. The place where the universe rested. It wasn't space, it wasn't time, it wasn't anything he knew. The equations told him it was both nothing and something at the same time, which was impossible, and yet it existed, and somehow their universe depended on it.

The antispheres closed all at once. The orange grass was gone, bare dirt in its place. Every plant as far as he could see was gone except for the patch of grass Friend was standing over. Kylac turned to Friend, ears folded back, glaring at him.

"Did you just...?"

"I opened a few hundred ways around us."

The breeze blew with less resistance now. The air coming from over the hills reeked of blood.

"The people at the hub. You killed them too!"

"It smells better without all those scents around. I'm getting faster at calculating the antispheres. They really are just ways." Friend took in a slow breath and sighed contentedly. "It feels so good to be myself. To do *something* myself. This belongs to us, Kylac. It's ours." He sat down on the only patch of grass in sight. "All my life, people have been telling me to be afraid of the old ways. To be afraid of what I am. To be ashamed of it. Now we're proving that we don't need to be. We can embrace our old ways and allow them to be part of us instead of letting their fear and shame turn us into something else."

Kylac scented the air. It did smell better now. No people nearby. No strange plants. Nothing around to threaten him. He breathed easier.

Friend's voice sounded oddly soothing now. "You will not revert, Kylac. Instead, you will become what you are supposed to be. You will not only know the universe as it is, you will know yourself for what you are. Embrace both, and you will be alive for the first time. Imagine all the new discoveries that await us."

Kylac stared out over the horizon, thinking of the hundreds of people who used to be over there. They were now scattered across the Lake in tiny pieces. Kylac bared his teeth, trying to force himself to feel misery and disgust, but only able to feel comfort and peace.

Earth

Mt. Everest was a beautiful sight from a distance, but the view from it was rather disappointing. After all the hype, Norh assumed he would feel a sense of euphoria from standing at the top of the world, but it looked far more impressive from the air, where he could see the entire mountain range and the whole subcontinent. Still, a part of him did appreciate the thrill of being here, the highest mountain above sea level on the planet.

Norh reflected that the scenery would be far better if there weren't all these people trying to be on the summit, too. He turned and looked down his flank. Two people were standing there, wearing breathing masks and thick clothes. Norh couldn't see their eyes or read their facial expressions, but they seemed to be anxiously waiting their turn.

Norh sighed. He figured five minutes was all he should indulge himself. He spread his wings and took to the air. He decided not to fly east, as all that was over there was ocean, and he wanted to see the sights on his way home. He'd never had a chance to see much of Earth, and now seemed like a good opportunity, so Norh flew west.

As the Sahara appeared, Norh had an idea. He laughed with his wings and dove to the ground. He embraced the sand with his arms and legs and dug four trenches spread out over fifty miles. When he closed the last circle, he took off, leaving behind a fifty-mile-wide smiley face. It would probably only be there a day or two, but that should be enough time for a satellite to find it. He couldn't wait to see the news broadcast.

He took a detour north and cut across Europe. Rome was pretty in a falling-apart kind of way. After circling it twice and admiring how confusing the streets looked from the air, he veered to the left and cut across France, another old-world beautiful place. The Eiffel tower didn't look nearly as romantic as he imagined—just a lampstand coming out of the ground. A part of him made him feel it was a beautiful lampstand nonetheless.

Over the Atlantic Ocean, the headache became worse. It made his wings flap out of synchronization from time to time, but he only lost a few meters in altitude before he found rhythm again.

He noticed a passenger plane to his right. Norh waved to it, and it occurred to him that he lacked a flight ID and should probably choose one in case someone called him, or sent jets to intercept him. He decided on Golf Mike Oscar Victor Juliet, and was ready to address anyone who flew by.

Finally the east coast of the United States rose up over the horizon and passed under him. He flew over Delaware, and from there Philadelphia was just a slight turn to the right. Norh veered and began his descent through the clouds.

His aim was perfect. No adjustments. No corrections. He descended in a straight line from the upper atmosphere and landed in her front yard. Though he didn't look at the sun directly, he knew where it was in the sky, and that it was seven in the morning. He had timed his arrival perfectly to catch her before she left for work.

Folding his wings, Norh walked up to the door and rang the bell. A minute later, the door opened, and a puzzled woman dressed in a green, button-down blouse and white slacks stood in the frame.

"Melissa!"

The woman at the door stared.

"You wouldn't believe where I've been! My God, there's so much to tell you! Did I miss Alex? Is he at school? Oh, of course he is... Well, I could have been here in time to see him, but I had to swing by France first. Always wanted to see the place. I passed some waterfalls, too, but I would have missed you if I had stopped to see them. Plenty of time for those later."

The woman was still staring.

"I'm sorry for dropping by without calling first, but this is too important. Tell the office you can't be there today. We'll go to the park, and I'll tell you everything."

Norh became aware of sounds around him, and he swung his neck around and peered over his shoulder. People were standing at their doors and their cars, staring up at him. Norh gave them a friendly wave and then turned back to Melissa. Her scent had changed from mindless bewilderment to piss-your-pants terror.

"What's wrong, Melissa?"

Finally she opened her mouth and gasped. She slammed the door, and Norh heard the distinct sound of footsteps running into the house. The footsteps paused, and then Norh heard the sound of a phone dialing.

A shot rang out, and Norh felt a poke on his flank. He turned to see a man in a business suit pointing a handgun at him. The man pulled the trigger again, his hand jerking with the recoil, and Norh felt another poke, on his shoulder this time. Norh noticed other people in his peripheral vision pulling guns out, some of them very big.

Norh spread his wings. "God damn it, I hate Philly!" He flapped and rose to the air. More shots fired, but none hit him. In seconds he was above the clouds and flying east. "How has she lived here all these years?"

The headache was awful. He had hoped his sister would give him a place to rest, and he had no backup plan in case she called the police, or the media, or the government, or whoever people called when a member of the family showed up at their door unannounced.

Norh tried to wrap his head around what had just happened. Why had she screamed like that? He'd been over to see her many times—Alex was the only reason he took vacation at all. And her neighbors. They had seen him plenty of times before and never pulled guns on him. The world had gone insane.

He was out over the Atlantic, nowhere to go, no family to crash with. He flew casually, banking left and right humming a tune. Then Norh realized something. He streamlined his body and picked up speed.

He had failed to save those civilizations on uncontacted planets, but there was something he could do here to help. Norh checked his sense of the planet's magnetic field, adjusted his heading, and flew straight for Germany. In just a couple hours, the pastoral landscape that comprised most of the country lay beneath him. It was so old-world beautiful, and Norh remarked that things really were like that. Nothing like it in America, where everything was fake, trying to imitate someone else's style. He flew straight for the capital, gritting his teeth.

"Hold on, Berlin! I'm coming! It's time to tear down that wall!"

Norh had never been to Berlin before, so at first he wasn't sure what he was looking at, but he knew what to look for. Entire nations of the world couldn't do what he was about to do, and the country needed him.

He flew low, just a thousand feet over the buildings, searching for the divide. Norh loathed the pollution, but he endured it for their sake. He flew back and forth over the city, scanning it once, twice, three times. Norh began to doubt his eyes. He was sure he remembered a wall enclosing half the city.

A pair of jets buzzed either side of Norh at almost the same time, kicking the wind and making Norh bank side to side.

"What the hell?" he called to the passing jets. "I'm not a red balloon! Leave me alone!"

He swung his tail, steering himself back on course. The longer he searched, the more sure he was that the Russians had torn down the wall and replaced it with some kind of magnetic force field. Norh folded his wings and dove into the city.

He landed hard on the pavement, exactly where one of the checkpoints would have been. People on the streets screamed and ran. People in squished little European cars climbed out and stared at him. Norh didn't understand why everyone fled. Nobody on the street had ever fled from him before whenever he landed.

Norh stood on all fours where the wall should have been. He saw no wall and felt no force field. Cars and people moved freely from one side of the city to the other.

His head throbbed, and Norh clenched his eyes shut. He kept hearing people shouting at him, and he wanted to stay a few minutes longer and learn the language, but the pain kept growing, and he knew of only one place to go to relieve it.

Norh spread his wings and took off toward Everest again. He hoped the cold would soothe his head, but at the same time he remembered the cold would not reach him. He began making a new way, growling and cursing as the pain increased.

Genkai

I

Rive's sphere did not close behind them. He and Deka stood on a world orbiting two stars. The complex orbits this planet followed yielded unstable and volatile climates. For one century it was hot, then frigid for the next hundred years, then rainy and warm for another fifty years. As a result, the life that inhabited this world was as cyclic as the climate.

Right now Genkai existed in a temperate phase, the plants plentiful and thriving. These plants had massive root systems and were able to lie dormant when the climate turned bad and then emerge again when the climate became favorable.

The people of Genkai had seen Rive and Deka emerge, and now some of them flocked to meet them. Soon the two raptors were surrounded by tiny, hopping mammals and flightless birds as big as Deka's head.

"Where is everyone?" said one of the mammals.

"Where are the portals?" said one of the birds.

Deka rubbed his claws. He felt guilty being amused by the sight of tiny animals speaking to him, but it was hard to resist.

Rive told the old story again, leaving out no details. As he did, Deka scented the air and walked away, hoping the Relians they searched for would be at the hub. He caught a single scent, theropod, and followed his nose through the thin trees.

These animals resembled smaller versions of the Tesha, the telepathic rodents on S'rin. Stephen would have said they resembled rabbits, ears and all, and they ran past Deka side by side with chicken-like creatures, some flapping their wings, trying to pick up speed, an instinct of their hosts they could not shake. Most did not even pause to look at him as they funneled into the hub. Deka clicked his claws and followed the scent deeper into the forest.

The animals here had not developed intelligence. Instead, the pathogens that infected those animals had. Two different species of virus, but unlike most viruses, these happened to survive by allowing the host cell to live. Each cell only replicated enough copies of itself to replace destroyed viruses, so the animal was never harmed. These viruses grew and reproduced within their host animals, evolving independently of the hosts, but still dependent on them.

Eventually a kind of intelligence had emerged, with the mind spread out across many individual units, learning how their hosts' bodies worked. The viruses learned how to infect every cell in the animal's body and use it to store memory and control movement and metabolism.

When the host died, the viruses moved to a new one. In this way, each body was a colony of viruses comprising an individual, with continuous memories going back hundreds or thousands of years.

Each individual of Genkai was comprised of billions of viral particles, making these tiny animals the vessels of a grand civilization. Currently, the two species of virus inhabited the birds and the small mammals. In other climate phases, they would inhabit the sea-dwelling mammals and the tree-climbing primates, or furred reptiles and marsupials.

They had had so much confusion to overcome, not knowing exactly what they were. For generations they thought they were the animals, and had created numerous myths to explain why they felt compelled to switch bodies every so often, and how they handled a new set of instincts upon each transition; why some could only inhabit mammals and others could only inhabit reptiles and birds. Then when the two species met, they had eventually figured out that they were another life form infecting these animals. The trauma had been incredible, as Deka had heard, but out of that discovery emerged portal physics, and some fascinating mythology, which they still retold to others.

Sentient pathogens were quite rare in the contacted universe, and Deka found it amusing to talk to sentient creatures whose body language and voice never matched their spoken words. The virus that infected reptile and avian species took on the mannerisms of its hosts, and these behaviors were automatic. The chicken-like creatures would preen and cluck and roost while having conversations about the nature of the universe. The virus that infected mammal and marsupial species also took on its host's voice and mannerisms. The rabbit-like creatures would graze and cuddle up to one another in large groups while contemplating portal physics. The disconnect between the mind and the body made visits to Genkai fascinating on so many levels.

Deka's good mood vanished as he looked ahead. He recognized the shape of a broken negative sphere as wide as a Relian reptile, hovering just a pace off the ground, but only one shattered piece remained in place, forming a convex, opaque lens.

A raptor sat about twenty paces in front of it. Her scent was empty, and her breath was shallow, as if she were sleeping.

Deka paused and gazed into the lens. He saw nothing through it, not just empty space, but absolute nothingness. Yet this thing led somewhere.

Deka turned away and approached the Relian sitting before it.

"Hello."

Now that he was up close to her, he recognized her scent. They had met before, and though he didn't know her well, he remembered her name.

"Emmi? I'm here to take you home."

She did not move. Deka was not even sure she'd heard him. He placed his hand on the back of her neck and tried again.

"Emmi?"

He could not feel her scales. His hand did not touch her, and it reminded him of his last time on Rel, being right next to the Sonjaa of the past and yet she could not perceive him. Deka slowly withdrew his hand and faced the negative lens. To stare at it was to fall endlessly into the very hopelessness all self-aware creatures tried to ignore: the possibility that life is meaningless, and they are all powerless to do anything about it. Deka felt it, too, and more. The longer he stood here, the more he wanted to lie down and stare forever because there was simply nothing else worth doing.

Moments later, Rive crunched through the underbrush and stood a few paces behind Emmi. "The Genkai told me what happened," he said. "She's been here since the first disaster. She won't talk, eat, or sleep."

Deka tore his eyes away from the abyss and faced the metal raptor. "What about their Archeons?"

Rive's hands sagged. "All four are still unconscious."

"After all this time? Haven't they found new hosts?"

"The problem isn't in the body. It's the mind."

"All four..."

"It's likely too many particles were damaged. The planet has been isolated, and nobody is around who can examine the Archeons in more depth. I told them we would help with that while we're here. We can establish contact with the other regions." Rive turned to Emmi. "They tried to care for her, but she doesn't respond. And they told me she does something else."

As if hearing a command, Emmi stood up, never taking her eyes off the lens, and walked straight ahead. She stepped into the nothingness and disappeared.

Deka crouched, tail up, toe claws raised.

Rive's neck had curled backwards. "They weren't joking."

"Why did she do that? Where did she go?"

"They said she will be back soon."

"*Back?* How can she come back?"

"She will return suddenly and do the whole thing again. It happens over and over, many times per day." Rive held two claws together in a grim smile. "Needless to say, the Genkai do not come near here anymore."

Toe claws still raised, Deka walked around the lens. It was a two-dimensional section of a sphere. Looking at it directly seemed to form an opening to a vast expanse of space and time. Looking at it edgewise, it was so thin it disappeared. The dimension of depth collapsed when looking at it from multiple angles, so it always appeared flat. It reminded Deka of Stephen's old glasses, if they were opaque and gave off feelings of dread and sadness.

"Do you have any idea what these things are?" Deka asked.

"Friend said they were sections of spacetime that stopped moving with the rest of the universe."

"Kylac had the same idea. Did Friend figure out how they formed?"

"He didn't say. With the things he was doing, anything could happen. Even he could not predict the consequences."

"Kylac suggested it could have been a result of an antisphere colliding with a normal way."

"Possibly, but his guess is as good as mine."

"As good as Friend's, too," Deka grumbled.

Deka had circled the whole thing. It was difficult to make out because no matter which angle he looked at it, it lacked depth. He glanced at the ground below and saw it cast no shadow. Deka shivered and joined Rive at his side. The metal raptor was gazing into the negative lens, and Deka stared with him.

"I hoped I would never have to look at something like this again," Rive said. "Broken spheres. Antispheres. They lead to the same place."

"They have that effect on everyone."

"Friend told me it's a taste of what he sees every day. That most people can't handle seeing beyond the universe. He said it's because we are looking at something outside our comprehension."

The negative lens stared back at them.

"The view swallows the senses," Rive continued. "Scent, sight, touch—all of them. The mind somehow knows what it is looking at. That this really is nothing."

"But it can't be nothing. We're looking at something."

"Friend said that was the essence of what he was calculating. The reason he couldn't control the equations. The reason he had to destroy more than fifty planets before he figured it out."

"Figured what out?"

"He never told me. Or maybe he couldn't. But this is what he saw. This is the reason for the disasters. One Relian canine trying to understand the view."

They gazed outside their universe for a while. The longer they looked, the more depressed and agitated Deka felt.

"We should go," Rive said.

Deka clenched his jaw and sat down, facing away from the lens. "I want to be here when she comes back."

Rive moved as if about to object, but then he sat down as well. Deka kept his eyes on the spot where Emmi had been. He hoped they would not have to wait much longer. Already he was beginning to feel that all was hopeless and he should give up. He couldn't stop thinking about Kylac, how his fox would surely have reverted by now, beyond all return, and though he may save his culture from extinction, if he ever met his fox again, Deka would have to kill him. It was times like these Deka regretted becoming an Archeon. Right now, he wished he still had a subconscious so he could bury these thoughts, but his mind forced him to ponder the possibility at the same time as he held out hope that Kylac's animal nature would not have taken over his mind permanently. He focused on the ground where Emmi had been, and he waited.

He looked back at Rive. The other raptor's scent told Deka he was also fighting something. Many breaths passed, and Rive grew more and more agitated. Finally Deka spoke.

"What's wrong?"

Rive's voice was tight. "I think I'm shutting down again. The negative lens..."

"This thing would make anyone shut down. Remember on Rel, how many people just stared at the antisphere as it came closer?"

His metal arm twitched. It then bent in a way it was not supposed to. "This is different." His lower jaw deformed in random places a few times, and he tried to speak through it. "Some...thing doesn't... want me to perceive this." The metal returned to its expected shape, but now the claws on his metal hand were starting to melt and flow back up his arm, as if attempting to escape. "My senses are trying to switch off, and I can't fight it."

Deka whimpered and went to the metal raptor's side. "Shut down, Rive."

He looked over at Deka, twitching, reeking of fear. "I have portals to make. If I do, I don't know when I'll wake up. I might never come back."

"I'll be here. You need to find out what's going on."

Rive shuddered as the metal wrapping around his neck lost its reflective sheen and began to melt. It appeared to be trying to flow away from the negative lens. It looked as if Rive's flesh was the only thing holding all of it in place.

Rive reached up with his real hand and wove his fingers with Deka's, rubbing claws. "I wish... I could be more help."

"Help yourself," Deka said. "I won't leave without you."

Rive looked away. All at once, his eyes went blank, and then his scent seemed to cut off as well. Deka held Rive and guided him to the ground, laying him gently in a comfortable position.

He stood then and turned around. Emmi was back, sitting in the exact same place. Deka felt a chill. He walked up to her and touched her shoulder again. He still couldn't feel her scales.

Deka pushed her. His hand did not move her. He pushed harder, then braced himself and threw his whole body into it. With all his strength, he could not budge her. He dug his claws into her and swiped down her arm as hard as he could. His claws did not reach her scales.

Deka sat next to her, keening softly, feeling her face, wishing she were still behind those eyes. Then a familiar scent hit his nose, and he turned away from Emmi and looked through the trees. A burrowing mammal sat by a tree, watching him.

Deka sighed. "It's all right, Sonjaa."

The rabbit hopped all the way up to Deka and then rose to her hind legs, paws together and nose twitching. She spoke in accented Relian. "You... you do know me?"

Deka closed his eyes. "Yes. I do."

2

This time Rive didn't care if he was out for a entire year. He had been hiding from this feeling just under the surface of his mind for too long. Whatever it was, he was ready to face it.

He existed nowhere. He had no body, no limbs, no eyes or ears or sense of the electromagnetic field. And yet he felt people close to him, pushing up against him, squeezing him.

Rive's mood changed.

This was better, he felt. The outside world was such a burden to sense.

Talk to me.

He waited for a response. None came immediately, but he began to feel different as the many presences jostled against him. Then he began to see something. A landscape, but he did not recognize it. Quickly another sense hit him. Scent. He smelled the planet, and now he recognized it as the same world on which he had acquired his new body.

He looked down but saw nothing. He was not a body. None of this was real. His sense of touch was gone, replaced by the crushing feeling of people standing against him.

I know where I am. What is happening?

The view changed. Suddenly the planet became molten, and his vision hovered over a lake of lava. The land smelled of sulfur, nickel, iron, and hundreds of other metallic elements.

He descended into the lava. The metallic scents flooded him, and now his vision zoomed in on the metal itself. He saw its elements, and he recognized the atoms for iron and gold and silver and many others.

A feeling rose up in him that these were not how atoms actually appeared. This was merely how Rive perceived them while making connections between points in the universe. Right now he was staring at elements he had never seen before.

Rive felt his metal.

He saw the new elements. The metal made itself known.

The elements were moving in the lava, combining, separating, recombining. They formed large chains, and the chains became sheets, and then he realized what he was looking at. These metallic elements were not molten in this ocean of lava. They were still solid, and the lava gathered them into clumps.

His vision changed. He received a feeling that vast amounts of time had passed. The lava was still everywhere, but now there were entire mountains of this metal, the storm clouds overhead constantly bombarding them with lightning. The presences squeezed Rive harder, tickling him with feelings of nostalgia.

His view moved closer to the mountains and then plunged into them, revealing a new reality of swirling sensations and geometric patterns built on top of electric impulses. Rive did not understand any of it because there were no visual, audio, or other sensory cues. Quickly his view pulled outside the mountain, more time passed, and he saw pieces of the metal mountains breaking off. They formed insect-like bodies that moved about on their own, sensing the world, trying to understand it.

Hundreds of them. Thousands. Metal explorers moving around the planet, observing the animals struggling for survival against the elements. They studied these animals, and they determined their fragile anatomy meant they had to run from everything. If a lava flow came, they had to avoid it. This concept alone consumed the metal mountains and their explorers for years.

Rive had the feeling that more time passed. As an intermission, a feeling rose up in him that it had taken them since the first disaster to piece together this presentation, to tell this story in a way that he could understand. They had tried to communicate with him before, but Rive could not perceive their language as they thought.

Now he saw Friend. The fox was touching one of the metal mountains.

Then he was surrounded by the metal explorers.

Next, Friend lay on the ground, asleep. One of the metal explorers melted and flowed into his mouth. Rive's vision changed, and he became aware of the metal exploring Relian anatomy, from the digestive system to the brain itself. The metal figured out that the brain was where biological creatures kept their thoughts, and they deduced Rive would be the same way.

Rive idly wondered where he had been when Friend came here, why Friend hadn't invited him along, and how his fox had found this planet in the first place.

Again he received the feeling of passing time. Volcanoes erupted, sulfur rained down on the planet, and more lightning struck the mountains. Friend and the metal managed to figure out basic communication.

Now Rive felt some of Friend's thoughts: this place had become a private world of his own, in addition to the one he shared with Rive. Friend knew he was going against the rule of lone species, but he could not resist learning more about this one, as there was nothing like this in the whole contacted universe.

More time passed, and now Friend returned, dragging the mutilated body of a Relian reptile with him.

The metallic explorers gathered around them. Friend allowed one of them to melt into him, and he was able to ask them to do something: to rebuild this raptor as a metal explorer.

Vision and scent switched off, leaving Rive in a void again. All he felt were the people pressing up against him. Rive tried to embrace them. He felt a flowing sensation all over himself in return.

3

Deka couldn't stop laughing, but thankfully this version of Sonjaa didn't seem to recognize the gesture. He was talking to a burrowing mammal as though she were his mate. She had her voice, and her scent, so his mind told him this was Sonjaa, and yet she was only as large as his foot. The disconnect felt ridiculous, but it also felt good to laugh again, here by the void.

He lay on his back, the little mammal lying on his stomach, nose to nose with him. As Deka told the story of Sonjaa's many incarnations, Emmi stood up yet again and strolled into the negative lens. She always reappeared when Deka and Sonjaa weren't watching, and then, after many breaths of sitting and waiting, she would rise to her feet again and walk into the broken sphere. Each time, she strolled casually and apparently without fear toward the lens, closer and closer, and then slipped inside and disappeared.

"Now I remember why no one ever comes here," Sonjaa said, after they had watched this a few times. She turned to Deka. "Why are you here?"

"We came to find survivors."

Sonjaa looked back at the sitting raptor. "What happened to her?"

"I have an idea, but I don't like it."

"Please tell me. We've been trying to figure it out since our Archeons fell asleep."

Deka sighed and faced Emmi, who sat motionless in front of it. He counted six hundred and three breaths from her appearance to her vanishing.

"She's an impression of someone who is now dead. Maybe on Rel she willfully walked into the antisphere and was lucky not to be torn apart. Or she walked into a normal sphere to try to escape it at the same time that the antisphere collided with the portal. Either way, it left this here. An imprint of her last moment."

Sonjaa watched her. "Is she aware of what's happening? How can we make it stop?"

"I wish I knew."

Emmi stood and walked the twenty paces straight into the lens. No matter how many times it happened, it did not become easier to watch.

Deka turned back to Sonjaa. "Do you remember what I told you? About the other versions of you I met?"

She scratched an ear with her hind leg, which made her other paw thump Deka's chest. "I was listening. It doesn't make me feel any better, knowing I'm not unique."

"Oh, but you are." Deka nuzzled her tiny pink nose. "Every version of you I meet is different. You've all had your own lives, but you also have much in common. Memories of me, an affection for reptilian species, your love of languages." He paused, stared at her minuscule face. She smelled as large as a theropod, and her voice sounded too big for her body. He finished softly. "And your death."

She groomed her ears with her forepaws. "All those other Sonjaas must have been stupid. I won't do anything like that. I promise."

Deka grabbed her by the scruff of the neck and lifted her over his face. "Sonjaa, please listen to me."

She squirmed and kicked her hind legs in Deka's hand. "Ah! Fine, fine, I'm listening!"

"You are Emmi."

She stopped squirming and dangled limply, staring at him, ears back.

"The first Sonjaa died trying to do something brave," Deka went on. "She failed, and now she's trapped in a loop, repeating the same actions over and over. Soon you'll have a similar choice. You will want to do something, you will fail, and you will die. Choose life."

The rabbit in his hand gazed down at him, nose twitching. After a few breaths of reflection, her ears rose and danced side to side in a gesture of acknowledgment. Deka lowered her to his stomach and released her again, amused by having a warm, fluffy body resting on his stomach.

"All right," Deka said. "So tell me about you. Tell me your story."

She sat on her haunches, staring up at him. "Promise you won't laugh."

"How about I laugh constantly, but you won't be able to tell?"

"Fair enough."

4

Rive was still aware of the people. They were so cold. No matter how warm they were, heat did not seem to reach them. In time he realized they did not even know what heat was. So many ideas such as heat, respiration, lust, and fear.

They were still trying to understand these things when Friend arrived.

Then, when they had a chance to leave their planet and explore the world outside their perception, they took it.

Rive received the feeling that the metal did not enjoy sensing the outside world. It preferred *this*.

His mind switched to a new world, one comprised of connections—a conscious mind made of metal that was as large as a mountain range, trillions of individuals in constant contact. So many minds linked together created a new reality. One without pain, hunger, action, sound, or survival. Only thought existed here, and in that thought, any reality they preferred. This was their reality. It had no visual cues, no audio or physical sensation. It was a reality they had created together. It was their language.

Rive had no way to comprehend these sensations. They had no parallel to his own senses, and he began to feel this network of signals and thoughts pulling him apart. He begged them to send him back to the void. Finally, the metal released him, and he existed in blackness again, though the metal felt sorry leaving him out of their multitude.

Multitude?

Rive had a feeling the mountain range was inside him. He was aware once more of the presences pushing against him. He looked down, and now he had a body again. The metal felt tighter now, hugging him, reminding him it was here.

Rive floated in the void for a long time, thinking about nothing, letting everything sink in. Then he requested to be brought back in, to their world of pure thought and mental connection.

They told him to be patient. They were still learning his anatomy. They had only begun to learn Friend's, and his was completely different, but they wanted to learn.

As uncomfortable as it was, Rive wanted to perceive their reality.

5

Sonjaa's viral lineage reached back eight hundred and forty Genkai years, comprising seven hundred and ninety-seven animal bodies. She had been there before the discovery of portal physics. She had witnessed both viral species leave their world for the first time.

Sonjaa had predicted they would one day visit a planet of theropods and canines, and when that day came, she was among the first to visit them. Sonjaa had dreamed of being mated to a Relian. She told people the stories for centuries, about how large she saw herself, and always with a red-furred canine nearby. As the centuries passed and they learned more about other cultures, the visions made more and more sense.

Sonjaa had lived on Rel for over a century, had developed relationships with many of the people there, but had found no one who matched the scent in her mind. Eventually she had given up the search and traveled to other planets. Fascinated by their unique languages, she had learned them all. She happened to be back here on Genkai when the disaster struck. Now she had finally found the scent she had been searching for since her first life began.

As Sonjaa told her story, Emmi walked into the lens fifteen times, always reappearing when they were not watching. Sometimes this distracted Sonjaa, and she would stop speaking long enough to watch the raptor disappear before resuming her story.

Deka lay on his side, facing away from the lens. The mammal that was Sonjaa sat on his shoulder, looking down the side of his muzzle. Deka was still hung up on the first thing she had said.

"You are eight hundred and forty years old?"

"Yes."

"But the disaster was little more than a year ago. How is this possible?"

She thumped him with a foot. "I hoped you could tell me. I didn't even have names for the creatures I remembered for several hundred years. Then we discovered portal physics and joined the contacted universe. We found Rel, and everyone understood what I'd been trying to tell them."

"Until now, the version of you I met on Kronia was the oldest."

She snuggled against him, closing her eyes. "Deka, I remember sharing kills with you. None of the mammals I can inhabit are as large or strong as a Relian theropod, so the memories were always exhilarating. When I went off-world, I tried to move myself into the bodies of larger mammals."

"How did it work out?"

"I couldn't take over. I couldn't live there. Only the mammals on Genkai are receptive to me, but I tried. I wanted to run with the Relians and help them take down prey. I wanted to feed a fox. Eight hundred years is a long time to live like that. To want to be able to do something, but all you can do is watch."

He reached up with one hand and rubbed her tiny head with his fingertip. His claw alone was half as long as her body. "Can you describe what it's like to move yourself from one animal to another? It sounds remarkable."

She leaned into his touch and began telling him. Deka sighed. He considered snatching her up and carrying her little body somewhere far away where nothing would harm her, but he glanced at Rive, and then he looked at the lens. The longer Sonjaa talked, and the longer he looked, the more the lens seemed to be reaching out to Sonjaa, as if to take back what was not supposed to be here.

6

Rive had no idea how long he had been part of the Multitude. Their world was so different from his that his mind scrambled to find some parallel—any parallel—to keep himself grounded in reality.

When he found none, his mind created metaphors. He imagined himself tangled up in a giant arachnid web made of neural activity. He imagined jumping through mountains made of electricity, and every individual living inside it had a different color and frequency. He imagined flying like a Krone through a thunderstorm, clouds shooting him with energy, and the energy was not just language, but reality.

The Multitude extinguished these visions as soon as they appeared, forcing Rive to perceive their reality as it was. Eventually, his mind began to adjust.

Their reality was theirs alone. It had no solid form but changed and moved according to each individual's whims and desires. Reality itself was their language, and Rive slowly began to perceive the patterns. Finally he sensed complete sentences instead of just moods.

Then something invaded this realty, warping it, pulling it apart. Rive recognized it instantly. It was sound. Deka's voice. He was talking to someone.

An instant later, another new sense invaded this perfect world of thought. Scent. Rive recognized Deka's, and he also recognized Sonjaa's. Rive's reality twisted around him as he comprehended these senses, which disturbed the others around him, and so on around the collective universe.

His outside senses switched off again. Reality restored itself, and peace washed over him. He had the feeling this was only a taste of what the Multitude endured every day at the mercy of Rive's senses taking in the physical world.

Rive was now part of them instead of separate from them, still learning their language, but much more comfortable now. He knew, now, how to change reality to express himself, but he found that much of what he had to say did not apply to them. This was an noncompatible species, unable to comprehend how he lived. They could not understand primal urges based in the body like hunger, fear, and lust. They could not understand a reality that did not change with their thoughts. Perceiving such a place at all had been terrifying to them, and they had only just begun to explore it when Friend had visited.

Suddenly Rive felt sorry for them. An entire universe existed beyond what they knew, and they had no capacity to understand it. Now they understood that an entire universe beyond *that* universe existed, which they also could not hope to understand. Rive wanted to explain it all, but his explanation had no parallel in their language.

They were at an impasse. Rive floated in their reality a while longer. After half an eternity of changing his reality and clumsily making himself known, a thought emerged that consumed everyone, including Rive.

Go back

7

Deka lay on his side, hands curled together in riotous laughter. Sonjaa braced herself on his shoulder, telling Deka about her memories of laying eggs. He had been there, had watched it happen, but Sonjaa had never talked about how female theropods of the planet Rel did not feel very much during sex. Everyone joked about it, including Sonjaa—how instinct compelled them to couple, only to be disappointed. The act of sex fulfilled a need to be close to someone, and for many, that was more than enough, but the physical pleasure came from laying eggs. Raptors even had ways of tricking the body into laying a clutch of unfertilized eggs, simply for pleasure, and Sonjaa had never told Deka that she had done it several times before meeting him. It was something every mother taught her daughter, and she described in great detail how it was done, and how it felt to spend an entire day laying a clutch, mind delirious in bliss, and that she didn't need him to experience it.

When she'd had their clutch, Deka had held her hands as Sonjaa climaxed for hours. It had never felt that good in any of her Genkai bodies, and she had spent almost a millennium trying to find a way to make it feel as good as she remembered from her Relian life. Now she began telling him about all the ways she had tried to equal that level of ecstasy. She had been very creative, and hearing about her incredible sex life over the centuries made Deka's arms hurt from laughing so much. He couldn't remember the last time he had laughed like this.

Meanwhile, Emmi stood up, strolled into the lens, reappeared, stood up, strolled to the lens, reappeared...

Sonjaa glanced at Emmi from time to time. She had just reached the part of the story where she had persuaded a Yimidrin male to try to penetrate her when Emmi reappeared again. Sonjaa trailed off and stared at the statue-like raptor.

"Well don't stop now," Deka said, hands resting in a contented smile.

"Is she always doing that, or is it only when I'm watching?"

"It seems that way, doesn't it? As if she only loops when someone is watching. It's probably tricking your mind into believing you are causing it to happen."

Sonjaa watched for a while. "Why hasn't anyone tried to help her?"

He caught a change in her scent. "Sonjaa..."

"Someone should stop her."

"She's an impression. It's already done. You can't undo it."

"What if you're wrong? What if there's a way to help her but nobody's tried?"

He saw the determination in her eyes, and his heart sank. "Sonjaa, remember what I said. You're in the loop, too. Don't let it repeat. Please. You have the choice."

"I can reach her!" She hopped off Deka's shoulder and over to the raptor. As soon as Sonjaa neared, Emmi rose and began walking to the lens.

Deka opened his mouth to shout, but only a breath came out.

Sonjaa hopped alongside Emmi. Deka raised his head. Relians appeared all around him, staring blankly ahead, as if their conscious minds had fallen into the abyss before their bodies. Deka noticed them, but it didn't matter. He had not planned to run after her.

Sonjaa and Emmi passed through the lens together. As soon as they were gone, the Relian impressions disappeared. Deka closed his eyes and let his head drop back to the dirt. He didn't want to cry. Instead he thought about his mate trying to couple with everyone she could, every shape and size, chasing that feeling of laying eggs she remembered so well. He clasped his hands and tried to laugh.

When he opened his eyes again, Emmi was sitting in front of the lens again.

8

Deka raised his head and scented around. He was in the trees, Rive unconscious beside him. Deka had dragged him here, far away from the lens. He could not bear to be near that thing anymore.

Little mammals and flightless birds surrounded them, sleeping on and against them. Deka noticed everyone slept only on the skin parts of Rive. He rubbed his claws as he lowered his head back into the neck-shaped gap in the flock.

He had been here for six days, waiting for Rive to wake up. He had made portals to other parts of Genkai and brought more experienced physicians here. They had examined their Archeons and were working on helping them regain consciousness. Deka had the way back to Gaow in mind, but there was no reason to leave immediately. Despite what had happened at the lens, this was still such a pleasant place, and the people here were as old as the contacted universe, so they had been fascinating to speak with. They remembered their world before portal physics, something not many cultures could claim. Deka was especially interested to hear about life on Rel hundreds of years ago. The stories these people told kept him thinking for days.

Deka felt movement beside him. Rive was awake at last, and this time he did not smell scared, as he had every other time he'd shut down and fallen into the sensory void, as he called it.

Deka rolled over slowly, giving the animals time to run and hop away. As soon as he settled again, the people of Genkai returned and nested on top of and around him. Deka held his claws together. As old as they were, and as advanced as their minds had become, the Genkai still had to appease the animal nature of their hosts. It was both amusing and beautiful.

Rive had just now noticed where he was, and that he was covered as well. He laughed with his claws and then took a deep, slow breath, as if seeing the world for the first time. "Deka, I understand now." He held his metallic arm up to his eyes, turned it around, and flexed his fingers. "The people who rebuilt me... They're still alive."

As Rive spoke, a dozen more hopping balls of fluff and birds landed and snuggled up to Deka.

"They had just begun to explore their planet when Friend showed them there was a whole universe out there. They wanted to explore that, too. They had a chance to send an explorer to other planets. That's what this is. That's what I am."

He showed Deka his metal arm, tapping his claws against it.

"They *are* the metal. They've been trying to communicate with me since the disaster. Finally they figured out how to show me what happened. They don't live in the real world. They create their own reality with their thoughts. They knew nothing of the physical world until recently. Perceiving it terrifies them because they can't change it. To them, it's inconceivable for reality to affect them. So they shut me down whenever they can't handle the sensory input. They want to go home."

"Did you tell them what happened to home?"

"I tried, but they don't understand."

Deka stretched, reveling in the feeling of fur and feathers nuzzling him.

"I have the way to Gaow in mind. Let's find something to eat."

Rive couldn't stop looking at his arm. "And then I'm taking them back."

Ashen

Kylac leaned on Friend as they walked through the sphere together, his fur standing on end from ear to tail. Moments after they were through, the way closed, leaving them standing in a wide-open grassland. Kylac was screaming.

Fifteen bipedal canines raised their heads from the carcass of a massive reptile, eyeing them with curiosity. In his head Kylac was shouting that it should have worked. He was sure he had found the solution, and it should have worked, but the antisphere had continued growing and growing, and no matter how hard he'd tried, he hadn't been able to stop it. He had begun to think he'd lost the structure the formulas had formed, or that he had built the wrong structure and now had to start over again.

So Kylac came to Ashen screaming, deliriously tired, and furious with himself. Given how long he had been working on the problem, he thought he should have figured it out by now, and he hated himself for taking so long.

Friend lowered Kylac to his hands and knees. Friend knelt next to him, still holding him as Kylac screamed in agony, not only for the planet lost, but for coming so close to a solution and then realizing he had been wrong.

The canines in the distance climbed down from their prey. They called themselves the Gliss, and they had retained a number of reptilian traits. Their fur was thick but transparent, which made them look like bald Relians covered in skin that resembled reptile scales. They had long, forked tongues, and fangs above connected to venom glands. Stephen would have called them snakes that had evolved two-thirds of the way into dogs.

The beast they had killed was called a Faln, and it was the other sentient species on this planet. It resembled a dimetrodon, and unlike most other predator/prey cultures in the contacted universe, the Gliss still hunted the Faln. Their society was a complex one in which the sick, the elderly, and the many surplus eggs were ceremonially killed so the Gliss could eat. Reproduction was carefully balanced among the Faln and the Gliss, and everyone ate just enough to maintain this balance. Otherwise, the two species mingled as if one did not eat the other. Here predator and prey lived together, the relationship perfectly preserved as it had been for generations, but without the fear or animosity.

Kylac wanted to feel wonder and amazement and arousal thinking about these people, but he had a difficult time remembering what it was like to feel those things, but he only felt panic from so many scents around him.

Kylac knew this feeling well, but now it was different. He experienced the agitation but not the mindless rage and desire to snuff out all scents around him. He was aware of what he was feeling, but his conscious mind prevented him from doing anything to ease it.

Friend's scent betrayed none of the same anxiety.

The Gliss stood around the foxes in a loose circle. Their snakelike tongues flicked in and out as they spoke, and their venom-filled fangs folded and unfolded inside their mouths.

"Relians—?"

"Who are you—?"

"—Archeons?"

"Is it safe to leave the planet again?"

"What of the disasters? Are they still happening?"

The voices were oppressive, and Kylac's ear folded back. He tried not to breathe, for their scents made his heart race. Every sound they made and every breath they took threatened him. Any one of them could kill him, and the only way to be safe was to kill them all.

The Gliss reached their paws out to them, touching Kylac and Friend, still asking questions. Kylac wished he could lash out and kill something—descend into the old ways and relieve the scent anxiety. Instead, all he could do was stand paralyzed.

They stroked Kylac and Friend, slowly and deliberately, as was their custom. Since their fur was difficult to see, it had become instinct to feel each other for a full coat of fur as a sign of good health. Kylac knew all of this, but the scent anxiety had overwhelmed all thought. Even his Archeon sense of the universe seemed to be feeding into it, and he desperately wanted the old ways to take over so he could feel some relief.

Several hundred ways opened around them. Kylac froze, watching many of them open over heads, arms, torsos, and legs. Every Gliss halted in their tracks, legs poised to take the next step. The arm holding Kylac's shoulder was tensed.

A breath later, the portals closed. All fifteen Gliss around them stood headless. Blood bubbled from the bodies as they collapsed on the grass. The area was now free of living scents.

Kylac breathed easier. He could smell nothing but blood and death now—those wonderful scents that could never harm him.

"Thank you," Kylac managed as he sank to the ground.

Friend said nothing as he walked to the Faln. Kylac curled up while equations shuffled through his mind. His eyes were bloodshot, and some of his fur had fallen out. His body had become a neural network of claw and bite marks from the many times he and Friend had fought. He had forgotten how it felt to sleep, and he had been without it for so long he was not sure what it was anymore, or why he needed it.

The problem had been all-consuming. Every spare thought, every breath, every secretion of every organ, every twitch of every muscle served to help his mind solve it, and he had been so close to a solution. Now he had to start again, but at least he did not have to start from nothing. He knew the equations well, and rearranging them was not as difficult as it had been before. They sorted themselves. Kylac merely fed numbers between them, and now he worked on a new set of solutions, determined not to let this planet die, too.

Friend jumped into the carcass. Kylac watched him tear at it, wishing he would return. Friend's scent was the only thing that did not make him nervous. He warned Kylac whenever a solution he had in mind would not work, and Friend's guidance had prevented many disasters.

Kylac's nose scented something. More Gliss in the distance. Anxiety began to rise again, and they were still a good thirty paces away. Several planets ago, he hadn't felt anxiety at nearby scents until they were right on top of him. It was hitting him sooner and sooner, and this scared him more than pondering what lay beyond the antispheres.

It felt as if the old ways were stuck, making him feel all the impulses but none of the automatic responses. Rage and fear, but no muscle power to do anything about them. The stronger the old ways became, the less he could do.

Kylac smelled more scents and howled in agony, trying to use sound to shut them out, wishing he could remember the words to warn these people away. He didn't want to hurt them, but he wanted their dead scents in his nose. It was the only thing that brought him any comfort these days.

They were only ten paces away now. Thirty of them, more Gliss covered in the blood of their companion species, smelling of concern and compassion. So many scents nearby. Too close...

Fifty portals opened up over the Gliss and then winked away. Headless, limbless bipeds collapsed in the grass a breath later. Kylac's howl choked off as he let the scent of blood and death soothe him.

Once again, he could breathe. The equations arranged themselves more smoothly without extra scents in the area. He felt much better, and finally he was able to sit up again. Friend was walking up to him, carrying several large hunks of Faln meat. Blood covered Friend from head to toe, and he smelled nice. Kylac was vaguely aware his natural impulse was to seek out the bloodiest foxes possible during estrus, for the ones covered in the most blood were best at keeping other scents away, and thus would be the best mates to protect the young. Knowing this did not comfort him. It just felt good.

Friend sat down in front of Kylac and tossed him the meat. Kylac gulped it down without chewing, looking and sniffing in all directions. When Friend finished his Faln meat, he reached over and grabbed one of the Gliss bodies. He tore into it, pulling off pieces of muscle, and fed a few to Kylac. Kylac gulped those down as well.

He was vaguely aware these were sentient creatures he was eating. He was cancer spreading death everywhere he went, but nothing could hurt him here, and Kylac liked feeling so content. He imagined what it would be like if all planets were like this. Places where he could live in peace without ever having to worry about anything coming too close to him.

He was so close to a solution. He was sure he could spare this planet. He only needed more time. He shared the meat with Friend while old equations found new orbits in his mind.

189

Proxima

I

Norh stumbled onto the dim surface of a lonely planet. He stood just outside the portal and tried to keep it open, but he couldn't hold the equations in his mind anymore, so the connection he had formed between two points in the universe slipped away from him.

His head felt even worse. Norh wasn't sure if he had ever felt pain before, and yet he thought he remembered being in a lot of pain not too long ago.

Then again, he had been sure that wall was still there. Since he'd left Berlin, he had been turning that over and over in his mind. How could he have forgotten? And given how mixed up his past and his present were, what *else* had he forgotten?

Norh raised his neck to the stars. This was a beautiful world—an excellent place to take in the universe and find perspective again. He needed that right now. He wanted to separate the past and the present. He wanted to remember why things felt so mixed up now, and why things had not felt so mixed up before.

Norh lowered himself to his stomach, still gazing up at the stars. He didn't recognize any of them, which made him feel unsettled. Norh could not remember why that made him feel unsettled, and that also unsettled him. Too many emotions without a reason. Too many memories with no context. It was starting to scare him, and as far as Norh could remember, he had never been afraid of anything.

He did not feel like a Krone anymore. For the Krone, things were stable, solid, and linear. Now his mind jumped from the past to the present, and he could not even distinguish thoughts on the future from memories of the past. Everything existed at the same time, and he had been living it for months.

His head throbbed. Norh clenched his teeth and waited for it to pass. The pain only climbed another tier in his mind, and now it encompassed his entire skull. Norh fixed his gaze on one particular star. It captured his interest, and he felt a warm emotion and a sense of longing he could not identify.

Norh clenched his teeth, and a low roar rumbled in his chest. Why did he not know the reason this star made him feel so comfortable?

His head throbbed again. He rose to his feet and roared, wings spreading. It did not relieve the pain. His brain wanted to push out and escape.

He felt his head. His missing scales had mostly healed now, but it still disturbed him that he could not remember how he'd lost them. He couldn't be sure about anything now. Did he hatch in California, or was he born in some isolated, frozen city? Norh remembered both clearly.

The pain surged through him again. Moving did not make it worse, but questioning his memories seemed to, and now Norh did not care what happened—he would think until his head exploded.

How could he have forgotten about the people on those unnamed planets? He had watched those civilizations die right in front of him, and yet when he arrived, he expected them to be there. When did he forget? Why had he forgotten?

His brain sizzled. He wandered around, tripping over his own feet, wings spread, grunting. He dug at the dusty ground all the way to the rock, then began breaking up the rock with his claws.

The pain rose, and he dug harder, screaming and thrashing. A few times he smacked the ground with his head, trying to attack the pain where it resided. He clawed his skull, hoping to break through and relieve the pressure.

Nothing helped, so he ran.

He knew he could fly, but at the moment he could not remember how, and this enraged him even more because now he was conscious of something he had forgotten. He tried to stop himself, but his legs kept moving. He ran around the planet, jumping in pools that had not been disturbed in centuries, uprooting plants as old as he was. Finally he skidded to a stop, rolled to his side, and clawed at his skull. This did nothing, and it enraged him even more.

The pain became too great. Norh's legs stopped responding. His wings unfolded and lay limp on either side of him. He wasn't in control of his own body anymore—it lay there against his will, not remembering how to take flight, not remembering the past or the present, not even remembering who he was. He tried to speak, but his thoughts did not seem to reach his body anymore.

Then one broke through: *Where is Stephen?*

The pain spread and throbbed. Norh roared again, and his mind felt like an amoeba dividing, tearing itself apart, but for a greater cause.

Norh's memories separated from the chaos in his skull. Suddenly his life fell into linear order: his hatching, his childhood among his extinct companion species, his zeal in going into the uncontacted universe and finding other lone species and trying to save them, his bitter disappointment after failing so many times, and then his life in the cave, quietly contemplating it all.

Norh's head lifted from the ground, and he rose to his feet. Norh did not tell his body to do this.

"Huh—wha—?" Norh's mouth was moving, and it was his voice, but the words weren't his. "What the hell? Where am I? What's...?"

Norh's eyes looked down at his forelegs. One of the legs rose closer to his face, turning the hand palm up for examination.

"Norh?" said his voice. "What's going on?"

Norh remembered everything, and his heart warmed. He pushed his mind to the surface and asserted control of the mouth.

"Stephen?"

"What?" said the same voice coming from the same mouth. "What the...? Norh, where are you?"

The body moved around, looking in all directions.

"Stephen, let me explain."

"Norh? Norh, I hear... oh my God what's happening?"

Norh held his body still, feeling its breathing accelerate in panic. "Stephen, what's the last thing you remember?"

"We were looking down on the hub on Rel. You were telling me things. And... and holy shit, I'm talking through your mouth. *You're* talking through it. We're both—where *am* I?!"

Norh thought back on those last moments, collected the thoughts, and began speaking.

"I took you to many places on Rel after that. I wanted you to experience the planet before we lost it forever. That's when it appeared."

Norh had seen it happening. He had set them down on the hub. Stephen was watching the many different people coming and going. So many species he had never seen before, and it was only a sample of the possibilities of life outside his planet.

The antisphere appeared suddenly. One instant there was nothing, and the next it was right on top of them. It pulled up a piece of ground right next to his tail.

Stephen turned and ran, and then his body lurched back. A piece of his chest wiggled, then slipped backwards, part of a large column of ground beneath him pulling up through his chest. Stephen collapsed, and another column burst up through one of his legs. Another through his arm.

When Norh reached him, he slammed one of his forefeet down over Stephen, driving his talons through the human's back, and ripped him away from the antisphere.

Norh had taken to the air, easily outpacing the antisphere. As he completed the way to Pryip, he looked down. Stephen was little more than a spine and head hanging from Norh's claws.

Now Norh's body thrashed, and his voice screamed. "I'm *dead*? How can I be dead? One second I was alive and —how the hell is this possible?"

Norh's body jumped around as if dodging bullets. Norh tried to assert himself and stop Stephen from moving, but the impulses were too strong and panicked.

"What happened? How did I get here? Why does my voice sound like yours?"

"Stephen, calm down. I can explain."

"I'm dead, and you want me to calm down?"

"Stop moving!"

Stephen took complete control of Norh's body, and he was thrashing his neck, scraping the ground. The body language suggested Stephen was trying to escape his own skin —an unfamiliar and scary place.

"This can't be real! This isn't happening! Shit like this doesn't happen in real life!"

He ran headlong across the dim land, kicking up pools, uprooting more plants. Norh tried to push himself into his limbs and take control. With much effort, Norh managed to take control of the forelimbs and halted them in mid-stride. Norh's body crashed to the ground face-first and slid a few dozen paces.

"Ow," said Stephen in Norh's voice. "That... didn't even hurt."

"Stop moving and listen to me!"

Stephen was still in control of everything else. He rolled Norh over to his back and sprawled out. This seemed to be a comfortable position, as Norh felt less blocking him from control of his own limbs. He took back the neck and head, even as Stephen was still trying to escape.

"I don't believe this! I'm dead! I was torn to pieces on a planet that didn't exist! I couldn't get away! Why don't I remember that? No, why do I remember it from your eyes?"

Norh felt strange in a different way. He looked down at his own body. His wings spread out a little in a hopeful smile. He couldn't reason with Stephen, but he knew this would calm him down.

"I don't remember any of this! Just like that, I died? No warning? No reason, just gone and that's it? I didn't do a damn thing with my life, and it's over?!"

Norh leaned forward and rubbed a finger over his genital slit.

"How—oooooh."

Norh sensed Stephen and he were behind the eyes at the same time, looking at the same thing. Norh pushed a finger into his slit.

"Holy shit, that feels good!" Stephen said in Norh's voice.

Norh was glad Stephen felt it, too. He raised his other hand and rested it on his chest. Norh did not feel as though he were touching himself.

Norh came out of his slit. He felt his chest down to his stomach and then grabbed it.

"Daaaaamn..." Stephen whispered.

2

Norh's body lay on its side, breathing shallow and spent. The eyes were closed. Neither seemed in control, as both were too busy riding the waves of euphoria after finishing six times in just one hour. Still short of breath, Stephen took control of Norh's mouth.

"Do you think they'll get mad that we polluted their planet?"

Norh took control of their wings and shifted them a bit, laughing. "Kylac would love to smell Krone jizz again. Deka might enjoy it as well."

Stephen shifted their body onto their back and faced the stars. Norh was behind the eyes, too, and he saw where Stephen looked.

"Okay…" Stephen began. "So. When I think, I hear my voice. When I talk, I hear yours. I'm in your body. I can control it. You can control it. This is really happening, isn't it?"

"Yes."

"I'm dead. I'm just memories swirling around in your head now, and there happens to be enough of them for me to be conscious?"

"That is all you were when you lived in your human body. That is all I am. It is all anyone is."

"I never thought of that. It's scary. How is this possible?"

"I want to try something. I think I can send you thoughts directly."

"Really? That would be—"

Stephen remembered Norh coming to Pryip in the distant past, wishing he could experience what the natives could. Norh had watched them frequently, the vines coming down, wrapping around the sentient insects and slipping through special holes in their exoskeletons, touching their brains. They lay like this for days at a time, sharing memories. Sadly for Norh, it only worked for them. The insects resembled silverfish, but they were twice as tall as Stephen.

Then Stephen remembered carrying his human body —what was left of it—through the portal to Pryip. He begged the insects to try it on him, to move whatever they could find into his Krone brain. He remembered that the insects could not cut through his scales, so he himself scratched away his own scales and then let the insects bore the holes through his skull. Now Stephen remembered the vines crawling up to the holes in his head and latching on like tube worms.

And now, finally, Stephen remembered what Norh had been thinking during the process. He had yielded. He had not fought all the new human memories invading his thoughts. He had not protected himself, even though everything in him had wanted to.

"Oh my God, Norh."

Norh took control of their body and sighed in relief. "It worked. I can give you memories directly."

"That's weird."

"The Pryip had limited knowledge of our anatomy. They moved everything, and our memories were mixed up for a while. It took this long for both our minds to sort themselves out, and now, you're alive."

Norh took control of his forelegs and touched his face. It was Stephen's face he touched. With his other hand, he felt his chest. It was Stephen's.

"Norh..."

Stephen smiled with Norh's wings. He was about to reply when suddenly Norh sent Stephen every pornographic thought he had ever had.

"Jesus!"

Most of them involved the scents of receptive females on Kronia. Some of the later ones involved Kylac and his stimulating scent. Stephen then watched his human self, all those nights Norh observed he and Kylac playing around. In a flash it was over, and Norh had already begun rubbing their slit again.

"Is that all you got?" Stephen replied.

He sent Norh every pornographic thought he had ever had, and Norh froze up. Unlike Norh, Stephen's stimulating memories were all visual, and he easily had a hundred times more. The Krone did not know what to do with it all. Now Stephen took control of Norh's hands and rubbed both sides independently. By now he knew how it worked. The Krone had very little sensation on the shaft; most of the feeling was on the slit, which meant if he wasn't all the way inside someone, he didn't feel a thing.

They lay sprawled out in an undignified position, panting and reeling from the barrage of images and scent memories now shared between them.

"You..." Norh panted. "You have a continuous stream of hormones in your blood."

"Yeah."

"I knew, but to live it! This explains a lot. Stephen, you're doing this to my body."

"Doing what?"

"That." He pointed to his slit. He was still out of it, despite having just finished. "I'm not due for another cycle in seventy-five years. This shouldn't be happening at all."

"Krone years?"

"Your years. Krone males have cycles, just like the females. Mine are about eighty years. Females are about every one hundred twenty. But you... You, Stephen, have this all the time. I could only imagine it before."

"When you cum, it's like fifty orgasms. This is a side of dragons I never imagined."

Norh laughed with their wings. "You said your planet is full of images of Krone. Nobody thought to depict them in this way?"

"Who'd want to draw a dragon whacking off?"

Norh rubbed their slit again. The waves of joy it sent down their body were new to both of them, it seemed. "To be in a cycle all the time, every day, every year... If I'm not in one, I have no feeling on my slit. This is incredible. It's also distracting. You feel like this all the time?"

"Just about every day."

Norh rubbed harder. "How do you live like this? Does it ever leave you alone?"

"Nope. All you can do is keep it happy."

"It's never happy!"

"I know!"

Norh rubbed harder. "Every male of your species feels this? Every day? No wonder your planet is in turmoil."

"Yeah, explains a lot, doesn't it?"

Norh thought a moment. "I remember... Brenda couldn't keep up with me. Half my sex life was me."

"Yeah. What? No. Norh, Brenda was *my* wife."

"She was one of my partners several cycles ago."

"I'm sure that was my memory. She was human."

Norh stopped rubbing. He thought. So did Stephen.

"I remember marrying her," Norh said. "I remember standing before a justice of the peace, sneakers and jeans, work shirt."

"That was me! I think."

"You might be right. I can't wear sneakers. But I remember it as if I did it."

"And I remember carrying my own body off Rel. Norh..." His voice was suddenly uneasy. "What's going on?"

Norh rolled them over to their stomach and stood up. "This may not be good."

3

They lay on the ground, facing the dim star in the sky which cast this tiny world in faint red light. Stephen was sending him every image, every film depiction, every song, every carving, every video game of dragons he had ever seen and heard. Stephen imagined himself pulling magazines and books off the library shelves of his mind and tossing them to the Krone at the bottom of the ladder. The giant reptile caught them in his mouth, chewed them up, and swallowed them eagerly.

"This is so weird," Stephen said. "As I'm feeding them to you, I remember you doing this stuff, not me. You were sitting in your living room watching *Puff, the Magic Dragon*. You were playing *Star Fox*, fighting that damn dragon on Fortuna."

"I can't remember if you showed me these things, or if I saw them myself. I can't remember if I coupled with those Krone in my cave, or if that was you."

"What does this mean?"

"I think every time we share a memory directly, it becomes permanent. If we share enough, we won't be able to tell our lives apart. We'll become one mind. It might even create a new personality."

They lay in silence for a while. Norh lowered their neck to the ground. "Stephen." Norh's wings were down, and Stephen recognized the emotions directly now. This was grief. "I want to share my entire life with you. I want to show you everything, but I don't want to lose myself."

Stephen laughed through Norh's wings. "What, you're not ready to marry me yet?"

Norh wished he felt like laughing. "No!"

"I don't blame you." Stephen spread their wings, flapped the left wing and then the right. "You feel like this all the time? Huge? Invincible?"

Norh's grief rose to the surface again, and the wings sagged to the ground. "Remember you told me you felt bad for wasting your life serving the dominant males of your society? I feel the same way. All those species I spent centuries of my life trying to help. Everything I could do to change them, and nothing worked. What have I done with my life besides fail to help a few lone species and hide in my cave when I realized it was all hopeless? I couldn't even stop you from dying, and I am so sorry."

They were both still for a while. Then Stephen took control of one arm and raised it to their face. He touched Norh with the tips of their fingers.

"This doesn't seem so bad," Stephen said. "I think I'm starting to like it."

Norh's wings folded up against his side again. Stephen moved their hand across Norh's face, down the neck, down the chest.

"I'm not ready to lose myself either," Stephen continued. "But this is kinda cool. I can't think of anybody I'd rather be trapped inside."

Norh took control of the other arm and rested his hand on the one Stephen controlled. "Thank you." He rolled them over to their side. "Now I have some bad news. I don't know where we are."

"We're on Proxima," said Stephen. "Deka and Kylac showed me this place. It's their private planet."

"I can't make a portal off this world."

"Why not?"

"I don't know our location in the universe. I didn't bring us here. You did."

"I couldn't have. I have no clue where we are in the universe either."

"You still have a subconscious, Stephen. Your mind is aware of all these things. It just doesn't tell you. I've been trying to start a way since we finished the fourth time, but something is blocking me, and I think it's your subconscious."

Stephen had no answer for that.

"So, there is one thing I have to share with you," Norh continued. "One thing we have to agree on. You have to learn to perceive the real universe."

Stephen halted their breathing for a few beats. "I don't... uh, I don't think I can do that. The guys told me what it's like, and I... It would be too much."

"If you don't, we are trapped here."

Stephen did not answer. Norh gave him a chance, and then Stephen took control of one hand. Norh took control of the other. Stephen wandered down to their slit again. Norh followed.

4

An hour later, they lay on their side, completely spent.

"Norh, that's the tenth time in a day!" He looked down between their legs, trying to find a sense of scale. "How did Kylac survive this?"

Norh laughed violently with their wings. "He's a Relian canine. He happened to be there when I entered my last cycle. Five years ago. I knew he could handle it, but only half. I had to rub myself so I'd feel anything. Stephen, I envy you. If I felt this all the time, I'd never stop."

"I think it's hitting you hard because you're not used to it."

"I don't want to get used to it! How do you cope? I can't think about anything else, and I am an Archeon!"

"Maybe I should drive for a while."

Stephen filled Norh's body up from head to tail and rolled them upright to all fours.

"Yes, please," Norh said.

Stephen walked them a little ways. Walking with four legs was strange enough, but being so high above the ground, looking at his own dim reflection as he passed over shallow pools made him breathless. Something caught Stephen's attention. He bent down and took in the odor. It smelled vaguely familiar.

"Norh, what is this?"

"Those are Deka and Kylac's scents."

"Really? That's what they smell like?"

"Take them in. You'll be guiding yourself by your nose a lot more now. There aren't many scents here, so you're sheltered from it right now, but when we leave, it will be overwhelming."

Stephen inhaled. Instead of just air, he noticed more scents all around him. The rock. The dust. The plants. The water. Everything had a scent, and a mental map of his immediate surroundings appeared in his mind.

"Wow. My God, it's like I can see with my nose. *Your* nose. Our nose?"

"Take your time. This is practice. Get used to it."

Stephen took everything in. He scented everything, listened to everything, tasted the water, recognized the poison in it, and spat it out. He chewed up some of the plants and tasted their chemical composition all the way down to the molecular level.

The more Stephen used his senses, they more they overwhelmed him. Eventually Stephen reacted to it like a loud noise. He lay on their stomach and just breathed for a while as stimuli from a still, silent planet bombarded him. Norh took control of their forelegs and rested a hand on Stephen's head.

"I feel something else," Stephen said. "Something weird. Like... a pulling."

"That's the planet's magnetic field."

"You can feel that?"

"It's very weak on this world. Eventually you'll learn how to judge position on any planet using it."

"It's like it's making me lean me in one direction all the time. I want to follow it until it stops. Does it ever stop?"

"You will learn to use it instead of being pulled by it."

Stephen shut his eyes tight and moaned.

"On a different world," Norh began, "there will be more scents to sort out. More voices. A magnetic field thousands of times stronger. Our body can live without food and water for a week. We've been here for two days. You need to begin."

"I can't even handle *this* magnetic field! Smell and hearing, they're so loud now. How do you think with all this going on?"

"The same way you think with a stream of hormones in your blood."

"That doesn't help!"

"When you have no subconscious, you will be aware of even more information."

"I don't think I can do this."

"You wanted to know what Deka and Kylac could do. You wanted to understand how it felt. This is it." Norh's voice softened. "It will be a shock, but I think I have a way to help you."

"Wait!"

"You're ready."

A light switched on in Stephen's mind. All of a sudden he became aware of the planet hurtling across the cosmos, and from its velocity and the angle he was traveling and the strength of gravity coming from the star, he deduced the shape of this planet's orbit.

Stephen's nose took in the air, measured the temperature and air density, and he knew how fast he would have to move to achieve flight.

He was aware of the atoms beneath his feet, how they held together, and how they repelled the atoms in his body.

Scents became louder. Sounds became deafening.

His mind calculated the brightness of the light coming from the star and inferred the distance to it. Stephen realized he did know where he was, and his mind calculated how far away from Earth he must be, and from that his mind branched off and figured out the distance to other stars, the shapes of their orbits around the galaxy, the orbits of their planets, and at last the motion of the galaxy itself.

At the same time, his mind also took in the scents of the soil and calculated element ratios and wind speed. The information swallowed Stephen. He shouted just to hear himself over the noise.

Norh took complete control of the body, and he rolled them over, holding Stephen with both hands across their chest.

5

The entire universe.

Anywhere on any planet.

It was all open to him.

Stephen hid from the sheer size of it for days. Norh was in his head, probing him, touching him in places that were not possible to touch any other way, pulling the anxiety away from him one thought at a time, picking Stephen apart. The more he took, the more aware Stephen became, and the less overwhelming it felt.

The entire world was just a thought away. The entire universe, just a few thoughts away. The sheer enormity of that idea was more than Stephen could handle, but whenever it became too much, Norh's strength rushed in to compensate.

This was how Norh saw the universe. This was how Deka and Kylac saw the universe. Gradually, Stephen began to see it, too. It was like being plunged into a sensory ocean—at first he could barely keep his head above water, and then his arms and legs found a rhythm, and he discovered he could swim.

The universe was a set of gears, and Stephen became aware of how fast each one moved and how to figure out which cog would be where at any given moment. Every gear had another inside, spinning at its own rate. Gears rotated inside of those gears and cogs. Whenever he saw the universe this way, he couldn't help but pick a gear and look through the different layers to smaller and smaller cogs all the way down to the atomic level, and the many sprockets moving there, not directly observable, but inferred by the movements of all the others around.

The universe was music. Every point in it played its own instrument, its own melody, and Stephen heard them all at once. It made the most horrible noise he had ever experienced, and he could not escape it. As he lay under the orchestra, his mind began to separate the different instruments. He heard the individual melodies and could follow the tune and rhythm of every player. The notes still hit him all at once, but soon his mind was able to hum along with all of these musicians, separately and in harmony.

The universe was a trillion television channels beamed into his head at once, some playing sitcoms, others showing movies, others playing talk shows, or game shows, and on and on. Stephen took them all in at once, not exactly watching all of them, yet aware of all the content, following every event, never having a chance to pause and get to know a character or pick out line of dialogue, but simply conscious of what was going on across all frequencies.

After swimming in music and television atop a mobile of spinning gears for two solid days, Stephen sensed a connection. He chose a gear elsewhere around the planet and searched inside of it for the smallest part he could perceive. He contemplated it, and eventually it seemed like the same gear, the same TV channel, the same instrument. He believed he could reach out, grab a piece of spacetime, and pull it through.

So he did.

A portal appeared in front of him, unstable, wobbling. The portal opened to empty space, but it was Stephen's way. His very first.

Norh had a reassuring hand on Stephen's muzzle, encouraging him to continue. At the same time, the former human was also aware of the scents in the area, the sound of the wind, its speed and temperature, his own heart rate, and so much more. Now he became aware of something else: the sum of everything he had witnessed thus far.

Stephen let that connection go and focused on another. In a few hours, another portal opened in front of him. The way was unstable and too small for anyone to pass through, but it led to a destination Stephen had deliberately chosen.

Stephen had been overwhelmed by the sheer amount of stuff Norh knew, and Norh had given it to Stephen in small doses his mind could handle. Now Stephen held it all in the palm of his hand. Every safe place to make a portal in the contacted universe, orbital speeds, rotational speeds, axis wobbles, gravity distortions, the motion of everything in the universe, the scents around him, the sights that extended far beyond what he used to call visible light, textures, molecular structures of the plants and the dirt, familiar patterns cross-referenced from other planets.

As this flood of information passed through Stephen, Norh spoke, but Stephen didn't recognize the language. Norh talked for a while, and Stephen listened, letting the sounds enter his mind while he watched his portal flicker and waver in front of him.

Gradually, Stephen began to hear patterns. Language was like music as well, where he didn't perceive the individual sounds, but all the sounds at once. Finally, Norh's words began to make sense.

"On your own, you would never have been able to do this," said the Krone. "You are not an Archeon, but I am. I have connected your subconscious mind to mine in all the appropriate places. Whatever you cannot handle, I am handling it for you." His voice took on a wry note. "And I have also inherited your ability to deal with this libido of yours."

Before, Stephen had felt like a mannequin head glued to Norh's skull: cumbersome and superfluous. Norh had taken that head, scooped out the foam inside, and stretched the face into a mask that now fit the body perfectly. Stephen no longer felt like an intruder. He belonged here.

"I understand," Stephen said, in Norh's language.

Norh wrapped his arms around Stephen's chest, squeezing him tight. Stephen felt as breathless as Norh. He was aware how hungry and thirsty Norh's body was, and that he had been here for five days, lying under the enormous weight of information that occupied Norh's mind day and night.

The way in front of Stephen was still open. Stephen realized he was aware of Norh's voice, the scents in the area, the sounds, the smells, and the entire universe all at once. At the same time, his mind was also keeping up with the calculations to maintain that tiny sphere.

"You feel this all the time?"

Norh said nothing but held Stephen more tightly.

"How much of this is you?"

"All of it," Norh said. "And all of it is you, too. I realized we could swallow each other's conscious mind one memory at a time, so I deduced I could do the same to only your subconscious. The back of your mind is now part of me, and you are aware of everything in it through me."

"And this... This is how Deka and Kylac see the world."

"Just wait until we visit a bigger planet. This is what your mind has been keeping from you all your life. A perception of the real universe." Norh made their wings flutter. "But I'm still not ready to marry you."

Norh rolled them over to their side. He touched his chest, feeling Stephen. He let his fingers climb up to his snout, where he felt Stephen's face.

"I like having you here," Norh said. "I don't want to lose you, or myself."

Stephen let Norh feel him. It felt so good to be in touch with Norh's emotions. Gone was the stone-faced dragon of old. Now Stephen felt it all for himself, and he understood better than ever all the subtle emotions Norh expressed that he had missed. At the same time, he still kept the way open, following Norh's voice, following their position in this planet's orbit and rotation.

"But I'm not doing any of this, not really," Stephen said. "I can't see the universe like this on my own."

"Not everyone has a mind that can do this. You still had to adjust to a lot of new information, and you've done well. I'm happy all this has even worked. The Pryip had never done anything of this kind before, and it almost killed me, but we lived."

Stephen considered everything for a few moments. "Maybe dying is the best thing that could have happened to me." He let the portal close. "And Deka was right. For a little while, you felt like just another variable to keep track of. I can tell it's easy to lose touch, being so aware of everything."

"It is a perspective that transcends reality. Living in it can make you lose touch with simpler things. After witnessing what I have, I believe I lost touch as well. But..." Norh stretched all four legs and then lay sprawled out. "You gave me life again, and you gave me something I never thought I would feel. A cycle that won't end."

Now Stephen made their wings flutter. "Glad I contributed something to this relationship."

"So... where would you like to go?"

"Me?"

Norh waited, his hand still on Stephen's chest, while Stephen sorted through the possibilities.

"Deka kept talking about someplace called Hithe."

Their wings fanned out as Norh laughed hard. "We can work on a way right now. I haven't been there in a century, and now that you have scales, you can feel the causeways. I think it will be wonderful to share that with you. Yes, I haven't wanted to leave Kronia and meet other people in a very long time. I feel like a hatchling."

"And after that?"

"There doesn't have to be an after that. We can stay there permanently if you wish."

"Permanently?"

"I've always said everyone in the universe can benefit from a Krone body except the Krone. I have been everywhere. I have done everything. I've witnessed civilizations rise and fall. It's your turn. I know all the planets, and so you do. Pick one."

Stephen thought, but he wasn't really thinking. He knew all the planets off the top of his head now. He recognized some worlds he had been to, but a great many of them were new to him. At the same time, he was aware they were not new to Norh. This was a different kind of thinking. No searching, no remembering, no flow of information. It was all there, at a glance, at the same time. All he needed to do was speak it.

Something rose up from underneath this thought.

"Norh! There is one place we should go as soon as we can." He took another book down from his library and fed it to Norh. The Krone munched it. He swallowed.

"Oooooh." Norh turned their head and focused on one particular star. The new memories all took place on the world orbiting it. "Could they still need help?"

"I think a Krone is the only one who *can* help."

"I'm intrigued." Norh stood and stretched, spreading his wings. "Let's go."

Reth

I

Deka and Rive stood next to one another on a dark world, breathing in sulfur and cooling magma. Dead volcanoes loomed in the distance, the dim light from the magma providing the only light. The air was stagnant. Though a chunk of the planet was missing, it had retained a thin atmosphere.

The portal had been exceedingly difficult to calculate. Without its star, this planet was free from orbit, and figuring out where the planet would have wandered after all this time had taken Rive nine days.

"This is where I made the way off the planet," Rive said.

"Did Friend tell you where the people were?"

"No, but the Multitude did. They're closer to the volcanoes. I'm working on a way there way right now."

Deka took in the scents of a dying world. It would be a slow death. With its internal and external heat sources gone, this planet would quickly fade into the cold emptiness of deep space, and eventually even the most experienced Archeon would not be able to find it.

The metal raptor was convulsing.

"What's wrong?" Deka asked.

"The metal. It knows it's home."

"What's going to happen? Did you explain you need this body to live?"

"I don't think they can understand that. I don't know how to explain anything to them. They barely understand all the things they've watched me do."

"So this whole time they've been observing us, trying to understand life outside their world?"

"They had an opportunity to send an explorer into the unknown. They didn't trust themselves to go alone. The universe outside the one they create is frightening to them because they can't change it."

Deka's hands sagged, and he looked down at the ground. The light was so dim here he could only see outlines. "It's incredible. A species that lives in its own reality, isolated from everything outside it, unaware of how it affects them."

Rive rubbed his claws as he shivered. "Possibly not too different from what Friend discovered."

Deka rubbed his claws together and leaned against Rive's real skin. "Is that another idea you thought about instead of hunting for your fox?"

Rive touched Deka's claws with his own, shivering a little less now. "Yes, a lot of Archeons ponder it. Perhaps this is why the atomic world is so strange. It doesn't really exist. Or it does, but only because of the conscious mind perceiving it, which means the universe only exists because life is in it."

"So what came first? The life, or the universe?"

"Some say life had to have come first. Perhaps the first inhabitants of the universe were actually outsiders becoming aware for the first time, and that is what created the universe. Or maybe many universes."

Deka rubbed Rive's claws. "Stephen told us about what some of his people believe. How there must be a creator who designed the universe and guides everyone's lives."

Rive considered that. "It's not unlikely, though Stephen may be disappointed to know there can't be any direct involvement. There could be creatures evolving outside the universe, in their own plane, and then when they become conscious, it creates a new reality."

"So who created them?"

"It just keeps going, one layer on top of another. Someone had to create someone else in order for it to exist, but someone had to create that first, and so on. It's a concept so profound it's hypnotic."

Deka tapped Rive's claw. "The last time someone had a hypnotic thought, Rel was swallowed by an antisphere. I'd quit now if I were you."

Rive looked out at the horizon, barely distinguishable from the stars in the sky. "Everyone dreams of coming up with something that will change society. I am proud of the idea I had, not of its application."

Rive opened a sphere before them, and they walked through, emerging at the base of a mountain range. The uniformly metallic grey peaks rose from a bed of lava that illuminated the base in pale red. The mountain range reached to the horizon, matching the contours of the lake of lava, with only a few areas where it touched the soil.

Deka and Rive stood at one of the places where soil met metal.

"I'm afraid for the worst," Rive said.

"What's the worst?"

"We will know in a moment."

Rive stepped forward, hands tucked into his chest, toe claws down. He stopped at the mountain's surface. It was so smooth Rive could see himself even in the poor light of the cooling magma. He raised his metallic hand and laid his palm on the mountain.

Deka watched from a distance, focusing down the mountain range, as if expecting it to move or speak or attack.

After several breaths, Rive took his hand away. As soon as he did, a violent seizure rippled up his body and brought him to his knees. His body was about to shut down, and Rive was fighting it. He ran to Rive's side and held him up.

"What happened? What's wrong?"

Rive fought to unclench his jaw enough to speak. "These mountains are supposed to be under continuous lightning strikes. Their neural activity depends on that. But the antisphere tore a hole in the planet, and the mantle leaked into space. No volcanic activity, no ash to cloud the upper atmosphere, no lightning."

"But they're not dead."

"They might may as well be! Without the volcanoes, there's nothing left to power them!" Another spasm rippled through his body, making him fold into himself. "Deka, the metal is panicking! It wants answers, and I don't know how to explain!"

Deka heard footsteps behind them. A metallic creature stood a few paces away. It was the same color as the mountain range, with four limbs arranged in a square, supporting a simple framework of metal on top of which rested a Relian theropod's head.

Sonjaa's head.

"How did I know you'd be here?" Deka said.

Rive was shaking in Deka's grip, staring at the creature as well. "That's one of the explorers! The pieces of itself the mountain range sent to explore the real world."

"Why does it smell like Sonjaa? Why does it have her face?"

Rive made no reply as the metallic thing walked closer. The spasms were subsiding, but now his body was going rigid. "I can't fight it anymore, Deka. Let it come to me."

Deka released Rive and backed away. The explorer approached and stood over Rive. It appeared to be scenting him, though it wasn't taking in any air. Then it leaned its muzzle lower and touched Rive on the metal part of his snout. The explorer's metal melded with Rive's, each melting into the other. Rive's eyes closed, and he collapsed on his side.

The metal explorer flowed over the rest of Rive's metallic parts, though it retained its original shape of a diamond of legs underneath crisscrossing rods of metal. Deka stared, unsure if his claws should be up or not.

Now there was metal flowing along the ground toward him. Deka felt no urge to run, especially seeing Sonjaa's face staring at him. Watching solid metal move in this way was oddly hypnotizing, and all Deka could do was let it approach.

The liquid metal reached his foot and climbed up. Deka sat, then lay on his side, and the metal covered him like a thin, cold skin. He kept his eyes on Sonjaa's face, melded to Rive's but still somehow looking at him.

The metal crept up Deka's legs, up his stomach and chest. It wrapped around his neck, covered his mouth and nose, and finally washed over his eyes.

Deka shut down.

2

"Rive?"

"Yes?"

"Where are we?"

Deka hung from a web of pure thought, his arms outstretched, his legs splayed out, his tail held at a strange angle. All around him was a web of neurons, it appeared, of reds and whites and different shades of black and yellow, flashing now and then. His hands were trapped inside two of these nodes, and two others held his feet.

Rive was strung up in a similar position, but half his body was missing. The metal was gone now, leaving just the skin hanging on its own. Deka saw no internal organs or blood.

"I think we are among the Multitude," Rive said, somehow able to speak without his lower jaw. "I hope we're dreaming, because if we aren't, then I won't live long."

"You look awful."

"I must. I'm surprised you're here."

"So am I."

"What happened to you? How are you here?"

"Sonjaa melted and covered me. I think the metal flowed into me and it's touching my brain."

Rive couldn't rub his claws together, so he laughed the way a Neben would, by shaking his head from side to side. "Unsettling, isn't it?"

"I'm more concerned about how Sonjaa is here."

Colors flashed, nodes rearranged themselves, and finally a world materialized around them. They fell from their bonds and dropped into a gentle field full of familiar animals.

"This is—" said Deka.

"It's the hunting grounds of Rel."

Rive was still only half a raptor. The flesh stood on its own, gaps and all, but he did not seem unstable or unsure on his single foot. Deka was not sure where Rive's voice came from.

"Did they learn to speak to us?" Deka asked.

"So quickly?"

Deka straightened up. "I think they have a guide."

The grass in front of them liquefied and rose upward, forming the shape of a Relian theropod. The face became articulated with scales, color patterns, eyes, and teeth, but the rest of the body remained smooth, reflective grey.

"Deka," said the raptor-like metal before them, in a feminine but metallic voice free of inflection or emotion.

"I presume you looked through both our minds?" said Deka.

"I did."

The metal statue did not move at all aside from its mouth, which looked eerie. Deka held his killing claws down and spoke again.

"Then you know about your incarnations on the other worlds, and what happened to them?"

"Yes."

"Good. That saves a lot of time."

"Can you explain to my..." Rive faltered. "My metal parts what happened to their people?"

"I have. I showed them how an external process created their world, and that this process has now ceased. They understand."

"Tell them I'm sorry," said Rive.

"I have done so."

Rive was about to speak, but Deka interrupted him. "Are you Sonjaa?"

"I am."

"How? How do you have a scent?"

The metallic statue was silent. Though she had articulate eyes, they did not move. Deka stepped away from Rive and walked around her a few paces distant. She did not follow his movements with either her face or her eyes.

"Strange," Deka said. "You happened to be here right when we needed to talk to the Multitude. Just when we needed a translator, you showed up. Where were you when Friend came here? Why didn't you appear to him then?"

Deka circled her. She stared ahead impassively. Rive stood off to the side, balancing on one foot, somehow moving without any muscles or bones underneath his scales.

"You seem to have figured out how to speak to us and to the metal on Rive. Where did you learn?"

"I learned from you."

"Why weren't you there when Friend visited? From the dream Rive told me about, everyone had to learn the hard way, and communication was not easy. It's only when I showed up that you appeared, and now you happen to be able to talk to us easily."

"I can."

"Here's another question, then. How are you even here? What's your story?"

"The Multitude sent us to explore this world. Now that the lightning has ceased, we are all that is left. We survive from smaller storms further away."

"How many others are there?"

"I am the last."

"So there just happen to be smaller storms that support you, and you just happen to be the only one, and you just happened to show up exactly when we needed you."

"Yes."

Now Rive came forward, walking as if he still had two legs and two arms. Deka turned his eyes away from the surreal sight and focused on Sonjaa.

"Several versions of Sonjaa claimed to have lived on Rel," Deka continued, "and yet I never met them. They lived incredible lives, prey trying to be predator, even trying to take a fox companion. The whole planet should have been talking about it, and yet there was nothing."

"I do not understand," said Sonjaa.

"I don't think you really exist on any of these planets, Sonjaa. I think you're only here because of me. I thought these were all different versions of you, but I'm beginning to realize you're all the same version."

"I do not understand," Sonjaa repeated.

Deka walked another slow circle around her. "I thought the antisphere had spread you out across space-time, but what if it spread you across wherever the anti-spheres lead, outside the universe? That would mean you exist in the past, present, future, and all places in the universe at the same time. I believe you're creating yourself on all these different worlds. You haven't really lived multiple lives. You only manifest wherever I am because your mind can't understand where it is. You are following me, trying to make sense of it. Trying to come back."

Sonjaa remained still and silent. Rive orbited opposite Deka on the other side of the metallic statue.

"I want you to think about something, Sonjaa," Deka said. "You remember things between versions. This means you can pass messages between different versions of yourself. Being aware of this might help you make the right choice."

"Choice?" Sonjaa said.

"You're not really here, Sonjaa. You're spread out somewhere outside the universe, and you're trying to come back. You must choose to stay."

Silence for a moment, and then Sonjaa's mouth moved again. "The Multitude wants to know what will happen to them."

Rive met her eyes. "Tell them I can't live without them, and they're the last of their kind, so they can't live without me. We need each other."

"Things will continue as they are?"

"Yes, but I promise to shut down for them from time to time. I'll have to get used to that, and they'll have to get used to the sensory input. It'll be uncomfortable for all of us, but it's the only way we can live."

"They want to know if other explorers similar to you can be constructed."

Rive looked down at his single hand. "How would we construct more bodies with the mountain inert like this? I don't think we can bring enough electricity here to power the whole mountain range."

Sonjaa's head and reflective body were still and silent for some time. Then her mouth moved again. "You must find a solution, or we will shut you down permanently."

Rive winced. "I promise to look for a way, but shutting me down will kill you, too. You need my body to live. You're using my electricity, remember?"

"Find a way to save the Multitude."

"I promise to try, but I need to know more about how you created the explorers, including me."

Rive winced, flashed multiple colors, dropped to his single knee, and screeched. Then, panting, he stood and faced the metal statue of Sonjaa again.

"I understand. Thank you. There may be volunteers to do this, but even then it's uncertain. If I can find a new environment, maybe we could move the range to a new planet, but that would be—"

"Find a way to save the Multitude."

"You need to understand it may not be possible. Your species depended on *this* environment, these exact conditions. There may be nothing like it in the known universe. There may not be a replacement."

Rive winced and doubled over in a seizure. "Wait! Wait! The Multitude isn't going anywhere! They're not dead, just inert. They won't decay. There is plenty of time. Give me time. I will find a way to help."

The statue regarded him. "They are satisfied. Is there anything else?"

"Yes." Deka walked up to her, placing a hand on her face. She did not move. "You're outside the universe, so I think you can see the damage caused because you couldn't stop Friend, and you blame yourself for it. You're still trying to make up for it." Deka leaned forward and rubbed muzzles with her. She did not react. "Forgive yourself, Sonjaa. It's not your fault. I want you to try something. Return to wherever you are on your own this time. Then next time you climb down and manifest here, you'll be ready to make the right choice. This will be practice."

She did not blink or flinch. Breaths passed. Colors flashed around them and then merged together into blackness.

3

The metal receded from Deka's eyes and flowed down his neck, chest, stomach, legs, and feet. It returned to the explorer leaning over Rive. Her metal flowed back to her, and she separated and stepped away from the metal raptor. She turned then to face Deka, her stare just as impassive as ever.

"Can you understand me now?" Deka shouted over the cooling lava lake just a few paces over the ledges on either side of them.

She did not give a sign either way, but continued staring. Deka gathered himself and rose to his feet, and she approached him. Her metal flowed, making her mouth open to expose a row of crude, pointed teeth. She leaned over Deka, and the metal flowed again, simulating the muzzle closing and nipping him on the snout.

She backed away, and an antisphere opened a few paces in front of her. The metal of the head flowed and twisted, and now her head was turned facing Deka.

She walked straight into the antisphere.

The antisphere shrank to a single point and vanished.

Deka and Rive stood alone now before the inert mountains, facing their portal. The air was becoming too dense with fumes from the lava lake. Deka helped Rive stand up, and they stumbled into the sphere.

On the other side, facing the way back to Gaow, Rive paused and turned back to where he knew the mountains would be.

"I meant it," he said. "I'll move that whole mountain range if I can find a planet with these conditions."

"I can't think of any in the contacted universe," said Deka.

"I'll ask a Krone. They've been everywhere. There has to be one somewhere."

"And if you can't find one?"

"They showed me how they make new explorers. Maybe I can find a species who needs rebuilding."

Deka rubbed his claws. "The Zjr?"

Rive laughed with him. "Someone without a companion."

Deka moved beside him, touching the metal that made up Rive's flank. Rive touched his claws to Deka's.

"She didn't die this time."

Deka scraped Rive's claws as loud as he could, smiling back. "No. She didn't die. She *chose* to leave. I hope I'm right about this. I hope she's ready to come back."

"Maybe she knows," Rive suggested. "If she really is trapped beyond the universe, she might know a place the Multitude can live."

Deka's hand slid from Rive's and he looked out over the dim mountain range in the distance. "She won't remember. She probably has no idea what happened to her. That's why she keeps trying to come back. Her mind can't process where she is, with her memories all spread out, too. It must be confusing." Deka looked up at the stars in the dark sky. "I wonder if she's listening. I wonder if she understands what she's seeing from wherever she is. Something has changed, and I think it's a step in the right direction."

Rive reached over and lightly ran his claws down Deka's shoulder. "I like hearing you talk this way. You always just jumped in without thinking. Your fox had to do all the thinking for you."

Deka rubbed his own claws and sighed. "Maybe you're rubbing off on me."

Volcanic ash began to fall, and Deka nudged Rive. The metal and flesh raptor turned and walked back to the portal. Deka followed, and the sphere closed behind them.

Agt

I

A sphere appeared on the planet's gelatinous surface, and two Relian canines stepped through, one holding the other.

One of the sentient species of Agt lived here, on these floating islands of gel. The bacteria in the water fed off the light, multiplied into colonies, and secreted a substance that partially solidified the water. This provided a platform for all sorts of plants and animals to gather. It was advantageous for plants because their roots could tap the water directly, and the wobbly surface kept predatory animals from hunting, so prey species thrived.

Friend had set them down in a region with no people, but as soon as the portal closed behind them, Kylac's heart seized up. Somehow he could still smell people, thousands of paces away, on other islands at the horizon. He turned to Friend, who obviously felt the same thing.

A hundred portals opened around them, closed, opened fifty paces away, closed, opened another fifty paces away, all the way to the horizon in all directions. Moments later, the wind brought scents of blood and death to them, and they breathed easier.

Friend set Kylac down on the spongy ground, opened a way, reached in, and pulled the body of a furred, flightless bird through the portal. It was missing a head and both legs.

As the way closed, Friend reached into the bird's body cavity, soaking his hands and arms in its blood. The blood on Kylac's fur had started to fade, and Friend rubbed Kylac's chest and stomach red again. Kylac smeared blood over Friend's chest and stomach as well. Painting each other in the blood of Friend's prey calmed the physical effects of Kylac's anxiety, though it did nothing to help the mental effects.

When all the white of their fur had been covered in red, Friend rose to all fours and began ripping the body apart with his jaws.

"The Lake is reality," Kylac said. "It's where things actually exist."

Friend swallowed a mouthful of meat and looked up. "It would explain everything."

"Why electrons and protons and neutrons behave so strangely."

"Why gravity is so weak."

"Why the universe is speeding up as it spreads out."

"Electrons, protons, neutrons, quarks, and everything inside. They exist in the Lake as something else."

"They collide with our universe, bounce off, and the resulting shockwaves are the fundamental particles that make up our reality."

"They only cause reactions inside our universe, but what do they do in the Lake?"

"I'm working on that."

"So am I. This could be why the Lake has such a profound reaction when it comes into contact with our universe."

"If we could figure this out, we might be able to locate other universes."

Friend ripped off another hunk of meat and swallowed. "Our universe is not real. None of this is real."

Friend licked his muzzle. "I've been thinking of another idea Rive discussed. About a creator."

"A god?"

"Not a god, no. Not in the sense that someone has control over the elements and with a little appeasement will help you. I'm referring to whatever might live in the Lake. Creatures who are unaware of us, or of the universes they create."

"How do they create the universes?"

"You've never heard the idea?"

"No." Kylac inhaled the calming smell of blood. "What is it?"

Friend rose to his hind legs, ripped a hunk of meat free and dropped it in front of Kylac. The younger fox bent down and began eating.

"Too busy letting your raptor lead you by the sheath to hear all the new ideas among the Archeons?"

"I usually ignored the ones about creators. They were absurd."

"There could be other life forms out there in the Lake. When they become sentient, it creates a universe like ours."

Kylac took another bite and chewed it slowly as he thought. "I did hear people say our universe only exists because there are conscious minds to witness it. That logic could apply to its creation."

"But that still doesn't answer the ultimate question. Who created the creatures in the Lake?"

"Maybe there's another layer of existence. Another layer we can't reach."

"We will reach it. Even if only with our minds. The one constant is that the conscious mind can transcend anything. Thought itself may be alive, and that could be where we are!"

Kylac stared at him for a moment and then went back to his food, enjoying the simplicity of it. "Is your mind always this full?'"

"You're an Archeon. Yours is, too."

"Not like this. How do you keep all these ideas straight?"

"They all exist in my mind at the same time. When I learn something new, some die, others live, new ones are born. This is the first idea I've ever had that killed all the others. For the first time in my life, I don't want this to be just an idea. I want to understand it. Soon I will, and then I can leave. I can leave the universe. I can get away—I can go somewhere nobody can find me, and finally I can do things on my own. All we have to do is solve this mystery."

"Start with the true forms of the elemental particles. You think there is nothing inside of them?"

"Correct. We think protons and neutrons have components inside of them. We've observed them through portal physics, but if you're right, they're an effect, not a cause. Everything in our universe is merely a shockwave from a real particle bouncing off our reality. The shockwaves fade, leave craters in spacetime, another particle from the Lake collides with reality, and the energy falls into the same crater over and over again, billions of times a breath, and that's why matter appears solid in the universe. We should be able to infer how the real particles in the Lake behave, and I'm sure we will discover they really are elementary."

Kylac tore muscle off bone, swallowing it whole and smearing his fur in the blood. He checked his scent from time to time to make sure he still smelled pleasing.

"The theory has been proposed before," Friend continued, "and now we may have proof of it. Observable proof. Once we figure out how the real particles behave, we can track them to other universes, and then... We can leave. We can explore new realities. Think about it. We. Can. Leave. Other universes will be open to us."

Kylac's head swam with ideas and equations. He ate, never taking his eyes off Friend, keeping his ear low and his tail between his legs.

2

Friend was asleep in the dimple of soil his body made. Kylac was wide awake, sitting a few dozen paces away from him. The tower in his mind felt so much more stable now, and he didn't have to work as hard to keep it from falling. The equations churned, but he didn't need to watch them every breath as they carried results from one equation and plugged them into another. All related equations had positioned themselves right next to each other, and when one returned a result, it fed into the next, and then the next, effortlessly.

They still kept Kylac up for weeks at a time, and he still destroyed planets and stars when he was wrong, but it all felt easier now. Instead of chaos, the equations had become a single, enormous structure of beauty. They represented the Lake, and they could never be recorded, only pondered by a conscious mind. Kylac sat and let the equations do their work. The tower in his mind began moving in synchronization, equations cascading one into the next, the numbers flowing like mercury up and down the tower.

Kylac saw now that they changed predictably. He began to think of the variables as constants, and as soon as he did, the tower seemed to stop moving. The formulas stayed in place, and now Kylac became aware of the problem and the solution existing at the same time. No transition from one to the other. Both were the same.

Kylac chose a spot in front of him. He reached out with his mind and pulled a piece of Lake through. An antisphere opened and swelled. It stopped at the size of Kylac's head. He observed it. It observed him. He closed it.

He now became aware of the boundary of the universe. He observed the particles bombarding it, sending waves into this universe, creating everything he could sense. These waves fell into the dimples the energy had created before, and thus physical forms persisted. Where they didn't persist, energy flowed.

And outside the universe lay something he still could not comprehend. The Lake. The place where the universe resided and traveled and expanded. Kylac stood and beheld it in his mind. His picture was incomplete, but now he was aware of its presence.

He turned his internal vision back to this universe. He felt as though he floated outside of it, staring down, holding the whole thing between his fingers. He didn't see as much as remain aware of all the people in it.

He became aware of the salamanders and armless theropods on Xce, and he knew that they had come back together as one society again.

He was now aware of the Wings and Bellows of Lesa. They had abandoned the devices that had allowed off-worlders from less caustic worlds to visit. The Archeons had woken up and reopened the ways to other gas giants, and the people were free again, developing their own minds instead of servicing the needs of the machines.

He adjusted his perception and focused on Kattaaka. The refugees they had tried to rescue were still there, still speaking for the Fourstalks. The Sixlegs and Ninelegs apparently trusted their new companions and were working on a compromise language to give the insect species a means to communicate that would not be so invasive.

Ixcy was also doing well. Saali had found an apprentice, an avian this time, and had been training her to be that world's next Archeon.

Uiv was now aware of disharmony among the people. The Hosts who did not feel one with their Guests now openly acknowledged it, and everyone was working on a way to deal with the condition. Kylac sensed they would figure it out in time, that some Hosts and Guests were physically and mentally not capable of joining, and that a new custom would emerge to handle the genetic variation.

Kylac was aware of the entire universe at the same time. It was taking the Archeon perspective and rising up another level. Everyone became so small. He didn't perceive them as individual people, but as societies behaving according to patterns and variables. He also sensed thousands of lone species on thousands of worlds, and he instantly knew how they would meet their fate. He could not see the future, but the variables they lived by led to inevitable conclusions.

At last Kylac brought himself back down to Agt. He knew, now, where everyone was on this world. Their scents never reached his nose, but knowing felt the same as scenting. He reached into spacetime, pulled a few hundred particles through it, and opened ways across the whole planet, cascading from west to east, hitting every person, every animal, every plant. A few moments later, the planet had been wiped clean of living scents, and his anxiety calmed.

Kylac let his consciousness sweep through the universe again. He let the variables run through his mind, watched future civilizations rise and fall. He zoomed in on individual people. They were the result of these variables, and he knew everything about a person based on the variables that comprised them.

He found Gruum on Hithe. The Droden had finished his poem, a single symbol of the S'rin language so elaborate the glyph had become a mural. It was elegant to look at and even more beautiful to comprehend. This was the first time anyone had used the language to be creative on so many levels, and it was drawing quite a bit of attention to the mountain communities on Hithe.

Kylac probed the numbers of the people who enjoyed that poem and amused himself by projecting what they would do after receiving such stimulus, their whole lives stretching out before him in the math.

He moved through the whole universe like this, exploring what the math told him was true, and being able to affect reality because of it.

Then the scent anxiety hit him again. His fur bristled, and his ear folded back. He became aware of the scents of all these societies, and he felt as if all of these people could reach him, and therefore they were a threat to him.

Kylac opened a few hundred ways onto an unnamed world with a lone species, sweeping it clean of life. The ways closed all around him, bringing pieces of bodies with them, surrounding him with the remnants of a species that would only have lived another thousand years before it destroyed itself.

He fell to his knees and took in the relief in the blissful smell of blood.

Then the anxiety rose up again as he realized there were more planets out there, all with species that had scents—all those scents that were too close to him. The idea paralyzed him, and he dropped to his side, barely able to breathe.

Friend was not prone to reverting, so the scent anxiety was weaker in him, but in Kylac, the old ways expressed themselves freely on a scale that encompassed the entire universe. Now that his consciousness had become as large as reality, every species on every planet was in his territory.

Kylac now turned his observation inward, examining his own variables with the same curiosity. He determined he was on the way to annihilating every life form. He could do it, and he calculated it would only take four days of constant thought. The idea of being completely free of scent anxiety forever made him slip out of his sheath, and in that moment he wanted to be covered by the blood of every self-aware species in the universe.

He would be bloodier than Friend.

He would eat first.

With just a few thoughts, he could make the universe lifeless, and then he would be happy until he and Friend solved the problem of the Lake. After that, though... Would he want to destroy life in other universes, too, to protect his territory, when all of reality became his scenting distance?

Kylac did not feel guilty for the lives he had just destroyed. They had been variables doomed to failure anyway, and they were uncontacted, so they did not affect any variables outside their planet.

He whined at the realization of the direction his mind had taken, but now that he had gone forward, there seemed no way of going back.

Kylac sat up and probed Friend's variables as the other fox slept. Friend did not know Kylac had reached the solution yet. Friend was good, but Kylac was better because his old ways were stronger. Friend could not perceive the entire universe quite this way, not yet, or he would have destroyed everything in it to quell his anxiety by now.

Quickly Kylac opened ways around himself and sent the pieces of bodies back where they came from, taking huge chunks of soil and gel with them to make sure they left no trace of blood or scent.

Then he focused on the particles in the Lake bouncing off this universe, found the bouncing that created and maintained Deka's body, and observed where his raptor was. He and Rive were on Gaow. Kylac wanted to feel happy that they had found Relian survivors of the disasters, but he felt only scent anxiety, and a certain sense of fate.

Their variables predicted they would end up here, and the variables also predicted something else.

Kylac's ear perked up. The variables anticipated Kylac taking the best course of action, and now he adjusted his view to another planet.

He found Norh. Kylac ran the numbers backwards and found Stephen as well. Now *this* was interesting. Finally, a surprise.

Kylac stood and examined Friend's variables. The older fox would be asleep and ignorant for at least a few dozen more breaths. Kylac only had time to visit one of them. He made a choice, and then opened a way.

Neben

I

Stephen turned in a circle as he surveyed the land-scape. It was the first time he had seen this planet in daylight, and it reminded him so much of Earth's deserts he was glad he had a new sense of smell to confirm this was not Earth. The portal to Hithe was still open. Stephen stared at it for a while, expecting it to close at any instant.

"Am I keeping that open, or are you?"

"Both of us are," said Norh, through the same mouth. By now Stephen had become used to his body moving without him telling it to.

Stephen let the portal go. The sphere closed in front of him, leaving him standing alone in the sand in broad daylight.

"Why did you do that?" Norh asked.

"I don't want to have to maintain that while we're here."

"Your mind is capable of doing multiple things at the same time. You'll have to get used to it soon. Right now the scents should be hitting you, and the pull of the magnetic field as well."

"Yeah... Yeah, I feel that. And..." Stephen scented the air. "Wow. There's a couple hundred people here, and they all smell so different, and the same."

"Every member of a species smells like a member of that species. Subtleties within that scent denote individuals."

"Like coffee."

"Like what?"

"It's a plant we drink. A stimulant."

"Ah, a plant. I have never tasted one."

"Never?"

"Our body cannot digest them. Share some of those memories with me sometime. I'd like to experience it."

"Sure, but first help me find Qan."

"You know her scent."

Stephen scented the air. At first all he smelled was the collective odor of the birds and bear-sized, pangolin-like mammals. Then he began to notice the subtleties Norh was talking about. He did not detect the scent he wanted, so he moved toward the crowd, the muscles in his legs and chest making him feel huge.

Stephen remembered what Deka and Kylac had said, about how this world was not safe for him during the day because of the radiation. He still felt a twinge of fear whenever he looked at the sun, and it took effort to remember he was perfectly safe as a Krone.

He paused to lift one arm, holding it up to his face. The back corner of every scale had curled up slightly, releasing heat and keeping him cool. He exhaled on his hand. His breath was still hot, and the corner of his scales visibly lifted even more. Stephen smiled with his wings.

"Interesting?" said Norh.

"Watching this body work always is. Feels weird, but much cleaner than sweating."

"Humans are not the only creature that perspires. It made your scent potent, which is appealing in its own right."

"Try being in a unit of thirty Army guys out in the field with no showers for a week. It's disgusting. I don't miss it."

"Sometimes I do. You had a nice scent."

Birds resembling herons covered in green feathers circled overhead. Some landed around Stephen. Quadrupeds had also noticed them, and they were already shuffling through the sand in his direction. On sight, Stephen didn't remember any of them, but then the wind blew their scents in his direction, and suddenly Stephen recognized all of them.

One of the avians gasped as she gazed up at him. "Norh?" She had not opened her mouth. The birds had a hollow bone protruding from the top of their skulls, and they moved air through it to speak.

Stephen's mouth started moving, and their breathy language came out. "Greetings."

With that one word, everyone started talking at once.

"What brings a Krone here?"

"Norh, you've been away so long!"

"Has anything changed?"

"Are the portals coming back?"

"Greetings, everyone," Stephen repeated, feeling guilty for using Norh's voice. "I heard about the Dekanites. What's happened since Deka and Kylac were here?"

Dozens of voices hit him at once, but Stephen followed their words as if they were speaking one at a time. They had discovered several more cave systems thanks to the Jilit, and Qan had left them all dry. Qan kept portals open to all the cave systems, and everyone was free to explore them, but the crystalline life forms that lived in the caves were now inert. Qan had restored the oases around the planet and linked all of them back together, just as before the disaster, until she could figure out what to do about the Dekanites. They told Stephen to follow.

The birds spread their wings and took off. The mammals shuffled around and went through a portal. Stephen's first impulse was to follow the pangolins, but then he remembered he wasn't human anymore.

Stephen flexed muscles on his back that had no correlation to anything on his human body and took off, kicking up enormous amounts of sand. The birds soared far above the ground, and Stephen soared with them, seeing Neben from an angle he never imagined. Flying under his own power had been unthinkable while he was human. Now it was second nature.

He laughed, wobbling in the air as his wings tried to fold and unfold. It was strange to have the part of his brain that expressed laughter connected to his wings instead of his diaphragm, and now he realized the Krone could not smile or laugh while in flight.

Neben was a desert streaked with shallow lakes up and down the lines of longitude. Stephen noticed the lakes had been arranged along the magnetic field lines, and he wondered if Qan realized she had been doing this. The green vegetation ended about five hundred paces away from each lake, but another oasis usually sprouted not too far away, so it was as if the desert did not exist at all, and much of the planet was green. Spheres connected the various lakes, meaning everyone was only a short walk away from each other.

Glancing down as he flew, Stephen noticed a few large pits. A memory Stephen didn't know he had came to the surface, and he realized these pits were new.

The birds banked for a landing on one of the lakes below. Stephen could see many giant pangolins, but even with Norh's excellent eyesight he couldn't tell anyone apart. Stephen swooped and dove after the birds straight toward the lake.

The green herons landed on the surface of the water without making so much as a ripple. When Stephen landed in the lake, it made a wave so large it crested the walls and drenched everyone within sixty paces. Some were laughing. Others were annoyed until they saw who had arrived, and then they marveled at the sight of a Krone.

Now Stephen caught their scents and easily picked Qan's out of the group. She had been floating gently in the water just a few paces from where Stephen had landed, and now the wave he'd made was carrying her out of the pool. Stephen reached out, cupped his hand, and caught her before she moved out completely. His sense of scale felt completely warped. The last time he'd seen Qan, she had been twice his size. Now Stephen towered over her, and she fit in the palm of his hand.

"Norh!" she said as she paddled to keep her head above the wave. "It's been twenty-seven years since you visited! Welcome back."

By now the water had calmed, and Stephen released her and lay in the pool. The water only came up to his stomach, yet he had displaced enough to overfill the lake and soak everyone nearby. He still had a difficult time connecting his actions with such large consequences.

"What brings you here?" she asked. "Is there news of Rive and Friend?"

Stephen faced her. He had rehearsed this moment in his head for hours back on Hithe, while he shared a few kills with Norh, but now he drew a complete blank. Finally he sighed and opened his mouth.

"Qan... I'm not Norh."

She was silent.

"Remember when Deka and Kylac were here last?" Stephen continued.

She paddled to keep herself facing in his direction. "I cannot forget. Did they send you?"

"No. Do you remember the hairless biped they brought with them?"

"Of course. Stephen. Has something happened to him?"

Stephen thought it would be easy to explain, but now that he was about to say it, it didn't make nearly as much sense.

2

Later that evening, Stephen and Qan sat on the edge of the oasis, watching the daytime star set. Around them, the avians were beginning to give off a green glow, and some of the mammals dug holes in the sand and settled in to sleep. The Krone and the Neben mammal sat side by side as the star disappeared and the land became dark.

"The Pryip took a chance with you," Qan observed.

"They took a chance with Norh. I was already dead. I didn't deserve the risk."

"Can Norh hear us?"

"Yes, he's aware of everything." Stephen paused, and his mouth moved outside of his control. "This is Norh. Yes, I'm here. I'm letting Stephen control the body. He needs the practice. You should have seen him on Hithe, trying to hunt."

"You took him to *Hithe?*" Qan laughed in her own unique way, shaking her head side to side.

Norh's wings spread. "Stephen wanted to go. Deka had talked about that planet so much, he had to know, and I was happy to accompany him."

"How long since you'd been?"

"Over a century. Stephen gave me a reason to want to go back. Watching him take in that new sensation was adorable. Made it feel new again for me as well."

Stephen moved the mouth now. "This is Stephen—and I've never felt anything like that before! On Earth we have an expression. Smooth as a baby's behind. A baby's ass has nothing on how that stone felt on Norh's scales. What causes that, anyway?"

Qan was still laughing. "Reptiles sculpt the rock. They know how to make it pleasing to their bodies."

"This is Norh. I was pleased to learn they rebuilt the causeways. It will take years to rebuild them all, but they're doing well with what they have now. Stephen wanted to help, but I told him we could not touch the living rock."

"I went there not too long ago to check in on them," said Qan. "All the planets are doing well since the second disaster. Keeping the contacted universe closed has prevented a third and a fourth. I just wish I could have helped Deka and Kylac."

Stephen spoke. "I want to find them again so I can tell them I'm all right."

"We'll catch up to them eventually," Norh replied.

Qan was gazing at them. "That *is* strange. The same voice, but two different people speaking."

"Can you tell the difference?"

She shook her head once to her right, a smile. "It's obvious. When Stephen takes over, he moves the head and hands just as he did when he was human. I am happy both of you survived. I can't recall anything of this kind happening before."

"Or happening again," said Norh. "The Pryip were just as terrified as I was."

"So tell me, Stephen. This must be quite a surprise for an isolated species. How has it been?"

"The universe makes sense! I never thought it would, but it does. And I finally understand what's missing from my world because Norh understands. He can see things from everyone else's perspective. He's not limited to his own senses. I wish everyone could have their minds planted into a Krone's brain."

"And how are you handling this new perspective on the universe? Are you all right? I would think it would be something of a shock."

"Norh is handling it for me. I'd never be able to do this on my own. I feel bad about that sometimes. I don't deserve this. I didn't do a damn thing to earn it, and now I have this incredible Krone body. It's like... It's like." He could only think of an Earth analogy she would not understand. "It's a spaceship of the imagination. I can go anywhere, observe anything, and nothing can touch me. I don't know how to thank him for this. It's a gift. I had to die, but since I don't remember it, it's like no harm done. And now I know what we've been missing this whole time. If everyone could see the universe this way, there'd be no war."

"Are you aware of each other's thoughts?"

"Not really. We sense the same things, and we both can take control of the body, but I can't hear Norh's thoughts, and he can't hear mine. Not unless we deliberately share a memory."

"So your minds are separate. Interesting."

Qan faced the setting star, falling into silence, and Stephen turned his gaze to the horizon as well. A sunset on this world was something he never could have witnessed as a human. His human memories reminded him radiation sickness would set in any moment, but his Krone memories quickly overrode them. Sometimes it took conscious effort to remember he was no longer human.

"I knew the Krone would have been able to stand up to the Dekanites," Qan said, "but there was no point in asking. They'd never leave their caves. I didn't even think Norh would."

"I wouldn't have," said Norh.

"What changed?"

"Stephen," Norh admitted. "His optimism is infectious, and it's something I haven't felt since I was young."

Qan laughed. "A very long time, then."

"I shared my memories of this place with Norh," said Stephen. "I want to know who those people are. Norh does, too."

"How will you speak to them?" Qan asked.

"I don't think I'll have to yet. As long as they keep talking to me, I should be able to sense the patterns in their language. I'll think of a way to convey I understand them somehow."

"I hope you can."

"What did you do about them after we left Neben?"

"Everyone decided to let them rest until we figured out a way to learn their language. In the meantime, we searched for new caves. The Jilit have found eight more."

By this time, the daytime star had sunk all the way below the horizon, leaving just a sliver of sky lit. The birds in the air and on the ground glowed so bright as a group they replaced the star as a light source.

"I am so grateful to them," Qan went on. "We have explored each cave system in depth. Once the crystals have gone out, it's safe to walk through them. Every cave is identical and not natural. They were carved out of the bedrock, and they seem angled together."

"What do you mean, angled?" said Stephen.

"The lower chambers are at the same depth, aimed at one another. It implies they were intended to be connected in the future."

Stephen thought about that, but it felt more like Norh was thinking about it, and he only observed the process mentally. "Have you found anything connecting the cave systems together?"

"Not yet."

"If they are one species, why did they build separate caverns?"

"I wondered that as well. Why are the caves not connected? Why are the tunnels to the caves sealed with stone when they were already covered in sand? And why did they attack us when we tried to show them we're here?"

Stephen was trying to smile like a human. Norh's mouth did not move in that way, so he ended up just gritting his teeth. "I hope we can help you answer these questions. I'm ready to try."

A large sphere opened in front of them, and in it Stephen recognized the dim interior of the same cave he had been in, where the crystalline people had shot lightning in all directions, striking everyone, chasing them away through the portal back to the surface. The bodies of those Dekanites lay exactly where they had fallen after they had used up all the electrons in the water.

Qan walked through first. Stephen stood on all fours, tucked his wings in, held his tail straight out, and walked in.

3

Almost as soon as he stepped into the cave, his eyes switched to night vision, which was almost as good as being in daylight. Stephen wondered if he would ever cease to be amazed by Norh's senses. After having just a taste of them, he could not imagine how he had lived without them.

Qan had set them down on the far side of the cavern, just behind the tower. It seemed so much smaller now as Stephen followed Qan. The many stone buildings that had once housed these people looked tiny to him now. He stood just over the rooftops of most of them. He wouldn't fit inside the laboratory now, or the tower, but he figured he might still be able to lie on the roof.

They walked by the buildings, all completely dry now. Stephen vividly remembered, from his human point of view, wading in water up to his chest, watching crystal people moving about the cave like automatons, communicating with electric sparks flying everywhere as they created new seedlings and planted the tiny crystals in the cave walls and ceiling. The people had seemed unaware of the Nebens, or anyone who was not a Dekanite. The crystals above were dormant, and the place looked so dead without their blue glow.

Stephen and Qan reached the center of the chamber and slowed to a stop. The Dekanites were still here, but from where they lay now, they had resumed their clockwork routine after the Nebens had left the cave, only collapsing when the water ran out of electrons.

"Did you retrieve Uum?" Stephen asked.

Qan tilted her head. "Who?"

"Uum," Stephen repeated. "The avian trying to figure out what the glass cubes were?"

"I do not know anyone of Neben named Uum."

Stephen sat down in the middle of the scattered Dekanites. "Deka was with her a lot while they were down here. The Dekanites killed her when they attacked."

Qan was giving off a scent of confusion. "There has never been a bird named Uum on this planet as long as I've been Archeon."

"Are you sure?"

"Yes, I know everyone. Now, I won't invite the others to be here. It should be just us for now. The Dekanites were angry when they fell dormant, and they likely still will be when they wake up."

"I wonder if they'll recognize me," Stephen said. "Could they sense my mind like a Relian recognizes scent?"

"I suppose we'll find out," Qan said. "I've stopped the spin of the portal in the soil. I'll let it flood up to your shoulders, and then I'll swim to the roof of the lab while you work on their language."

Neben didn't have a word for what he wanted to say, so Stephen switched to English. "Wish me luck."

Qan answered in English as well. "Whatever that is, I wish it to you."

Stephen's wings unfolded slightly. He lay still, taking deep breaths. Moments later, a light trickle of water began to fall. It quickly accelerated to sheets of water pouring throughout the cave. Stephen barely noticed. He looked at his arm and confirmed that the rear corner of his scales had lowered, sealing in heat again.

He turned his face up as the water fell. It did not sting or make him shiver, as if his Krone body actively canceled out anything that touched him. He felt every drop, but it was not unpleasant. His scales kept him insulated from both the force of the water and the heat loss. He guessed he would be able to sit in a hailstorm and feel perfectly fine.

The water had risen to his stomach. He swung his neck around and searched for Qan. She floated up with the rising water, her pangolin-like plates of armored skin also protecting her from the rain. She rose higher and higher as the water level climbed from Stephen's stomach to his chest. Then the flow of water gradually slowed, and Qan climbed up to the roof of the laboratory a few dozen paces away.

The water stopped at Stephen's shoulders, leaving only his wings and neck above the surface. He looked down at the crystalline creatures, strewn about the cave floor like burnt-out light bulbs. The fall of water had slowed to a drizzle, and most of the crystals attached to the ceiling glowed in blue light. There weren't enough of them to light the entire cave, but it was good to see them awake again.

Now Stephen became aware of the hum of energy in the cave. He had been completely deaf to it as a human, but

Norh's body felt it vividly. A short time later, the Dekanites on the floor began to glow. Stephen's wings folded tight against his body. The crystalline people glowed brighter, rising from a pale blue to a starlight tone, almost white. They seemed brighter than Stephen remembered, but then he remembered he could now see colors outside the range he had once considered visible light.

The Dekanites shifted, turning their heads. A few traded bolts of energy as they flexed their seemingly solid limbs and stood on all fours. Some of these bolts hit Stephen, traveled along his scales, and continued onward, joining other Dekanites.

Every crystal, insect-like creature noticed Stephen, and they shot energy between themselves which then traveled around the entire cave, branches of energy reaching out to distant people. Dekanites turned and looked as soon as the energy strikes reached them. Stephen imagined himself lying on a circuit board, electricity shooting everywhere, connecting everyone, the web of electrons following people as they moved about, searching for others.

At a glance, Norh counted ninety-one Dekanites here, all sharing electrons, all swimming toward the center of the chamber. They were staring at him, thin bolts of lightning moving back and forth through the approaching Dekanites. Stephen's eyes wandered around the group, trying to follow the lightning. Even Norh had never seen anything like this before.

Everyone gathered around Stephen, surrounding him in a ring of electricity that changed color, thickness, and intensity thousands of times a second. Stephen swung his neck around, looking at everyone.

Another bolt struck Stephen, spider-webbed across his scales, leaped off, and connected with a Dekanite on the other side. It was tiny and red, but it was electricity. It didn't startle Stephen, and he didn't feel a shock. He simply felt electrons washing over his skin. It actually felt good.

A few of the Dekanites ignited a storm of energy among the group, trading hundreds of lightning bolts between them in a single breath. Stephen didn't remember them doing this before. The energy traveled through them, surrounding him in light. The water above the Dekanites began to boil, and then the ring closed on him. It felt as though they had cast a net over him, and now his Krone body was covered in a twitching, wiggling mesh of electrons. Stephen felt every electron on his skin as it leaped to and from other Dekanites.

It felt different than the previous bolt, containing dozens of frequencies and intensities and pulsations inside it. Stephen wasn't sure if it was another screaming attack, or if these bolts contained words from every person here. Stephen closed his eyes and took in the experience as a whole, letting Norh's Archeon mind search for patterns.

The web ceased, and now Stephen felt individual bolts of lightning coming from all directions. He felt energy hitting his scales on his left side, and then more energy by his left leg, dancing between him and a few other Dekanites.

It felt like a warm shower to his human mindgood.

Stephen lay almost completely underwater, only his back, neck, and head above the surface. He took a breath, lowered his head under the water, and hoped they would start shocking him there, too.

Someone did, and order began to emerge within the chaos.

Frequencies, intensities, and pulses repeated from time to time, and Stephen processed everything. The more they shocked him, the more familiar it began to feel. His mind connected it to memories of various species that used tactile means to communicate. The vibrations of those felt similar to these energy sparks.

Stephen's wings unfolded and folded up again. He wanted to burst out laughing, but only his wings moved, which took the wind out of the emotion at first. Stephen loved this feeling. He hoped they'd never stop talking. He rolled over, exposing his belly, and they started shooting lightning up and down his underside, which only felt better. Stephen laughed at himself now. He remembered how it had felt as a human—doorknob-to-finger shocks multiplied by a thousand—and this simple immunity to one of nature's most annoying forces was enough to make him feel superhuman.

Language was like the universe: made of patterns within patterns within patterns. Stephen couldn't get enough of this feeling. He calculated that each pulse must be between ten and one thousand volts of direct current, but it was so close and so direct it felt like alternating current instead.

As a human, this would have made for an agonizing and probably not instant death. As a Krone, it was a massage gentle enough for Stephen to pick apart the different energy bolts and search for patterns.

He opened his eyes and looked down his belly. Dekanites swam around him, trading energy between each other and often aiming it at Stephen. They spoke to each other, using Stephen as a node joining two or more people. Stephen had the feeling they were repeating the same phrases over and over.

The pulses and frequencies shared many similarities to other languages Norh knew. Out of the chaos of noise and heat and electrons moving over his scales, Stephen began to sense something. It was not heard. Not a voice. Just a feeling.

Planter? Etcher?

Stephen stopped letting the energy massage him, and he concentrated harder. He was sure that this feeling wasn't coming from within.

Builder?

Bolts of energy streaked across him, connecting him to several others. From what Stephen remembered of his last time here, they often used each other as relays to communicate with another person, or perhaps to many people at once. They used him as a relay now. He had the feeling this made him, effectively, part of their civilization.

Glasser? Nurser?

Exploration mode return false.

Patterns traveled over his body. Stephen felt more words within the differing frequencies and durations.

If no response, then planter.

Return false.

Try. Planter, etcher, builder, glasser, nurser?

Wait.

One. Two. Three. Four...

Try. Planter, etcher, builder, glasser, nurser?

Wait.

One. Two. Three. Four. Five...

Sixteen. Seventeen. Eighteen.

Return false.

Damage analysis.

Return false.

Return false.

Return false.

Twenty-one. Twenty-two. Twenty-three.

If no response, then planter.

If no damage, then try. Planter, etcher, builder, glasser, nurser?

The bolts became less frequent now, and the few that remained felt very much uniform.

Seven. Eight. Nine...

Twenty-four. Twenty-five. Function timed out. Return false.

If no response, then planter.
If no response, then planter.
If no response, then planter.

The energy stopped. Stephen remained sprawled, sad that the massage was over. He rolled over and stood. All at once, purple bolts of energy shot from all ninety-one Dekanites and cast a net over Stephen.

Designation ninety-two. Planter. Begin function—

The rest hit Stephen so hard he didn't comprehend it as words, but commands—powerful commands that seemed to dig through his brain and tunnel under his free will.

He began walking where the commands led him. As he did, the Dekanites dispersed in the most orderly manner Stephen had ever seen. They walked and swam in straight lines to their objective like wind-up toys. Some went to the labs, others to the tower. Stephen took a position in front of the building with the workstations, not quite sure why he was there.

"Stephen! Norh!" Qan shouted from the roof of the lab. "Did you make contact?"

Dekanites were moving everywhere, trading bolts of lightning from time to time. Stephen noticed something he had not noticed before when he was a human. Viewed from above, they moved as if synchronized by a master gear. They stepped at the same time, turned at the same time. Sometimes they waited for no apparent reason and then started moving again.

Twenty of the walking Dekanites took up position next to and behind Stephen. They did not trade bolts with him or speak to one another. They waited silently by the cave mouth, their light dimming.

"I think so," Stephen answered.

Seconds later, a long streak of electricity zigzagged through the water, jumping from one Dekanite to another until it reached Stephen and the waiting Dekanites. The words Stephen heard jumbled together.

Zerozeroonefirstcavefloorzerozerotwofirstcavefloor... zeroninetwoninthcavefloor.

The next command was slower.

Planters wait.

It was strangely satisfying to know exactly what his place in society was.

The Dekanites moved just as Stephen had seen from the tower the first time he came here: clockwork ants moving from position to position, each with its place, and each doing its task and nothing more. It made more sense now.

Qan moved the portal to the top of the lab, and a few herons and pangolins joined her, observing the Dekanites at work. So far no one had ventured off the roof for fear of being electrocuted.

Stephen had a clear view of the lab from where he and the other planters stood. The people inside the lab—carvers—etched the crystal fragments. Another group of Dekanites, the glassers, delivered new glass cubes to the carvers when one was finished, took the old one, and stored it in a building off to the side. Other Dekanites stood idle, waiting.

A bolt of energy hit Stephen's group. One of the planters near him glowed brighter and broke formation, going into the lab and emerging a moment later with a glass jar in its electric fingers. It walked along the cave floor up to the entrance of the cave, turned around, and halted. Its light dimmed.

A glasser delivered a new cube and removed the old one from the lab. Some time passed, and then another bolt of energy emerged from the lab and struck the waiting group of planters, and another Dekanite broke formation, took a crystal seedling in a glass jar, and then waited by the cave entrance.

Everyone moved so uniformly and precisely that nobody collided, even though they seemed ignorant of where anyone else was or where they were going. The Dekanites behaved like electrons whizzing about inside a circuit board, coming very close but never touching.

Every now and then a streak of energy moved through the cave and connected the Dekanites together for a fraction of a second. In that time, Stephen became aware of quite a bit of information at once.

Water level four percent.

Continue low water level functions.

Tower water level zero percent.

Continue operating.

Cave capacity equals ninety-three percent.

Chambers carved equals forty-two percent.

Operators active equals thirty-five percent.

No one person spoke it. This was collective data shared among the group, and there was so much of it he was glad Norh was handling the subconscious stuff for him.

Many more Dekanites acquired glass vessels and then waited at the cave entrance. Stephen stood in place for nearly an hour, watching and mentally listening, and it never crossed his mind to do anything else.

A bolt of energy came from the cavern, and Stephen felt a command enter him.

Nine-two, acquire.

Stephen went to the carvers' building and stuck his neck through the entrance. He didn't see so much as already know which station was ready for him, and he curved his neck over the table, gingerly picked up the glass jar in his teeth, and slipped back out of the entrance. He turned, sloshing through the water to the waiting group of planters in front of the cave mouth, and waited in formation there.

Sixtyandonetwenty.

Stephen felt that this command was a set of coordinates, and a moment later he also felt that the caves were dry, so he could not enter them. Stephen knew very well his Krone body could enter the caves while dry, but the command to remain still and wait for the water to rise was absolute. As Stephen waited, he felt his light dimming.

Stephen now realized how few Dekanites were actually working. Most stood idle, waiting for commands. Stephen figured if the cave were all the way full, they would all be busy, and the place would be much more active. Stephen looked up and scanned the walls and ceiling. In the rows of crystals, he counted thirty-five gaps he had not noticed when he'd been human.

Most of the activity happened inside the carving building, with the glassers. Everyone else waited. More planters entered the lab, emerged with a vessel, and joined the group waiting in formation with Stephen.

Another hour passed, but Stephen barely felt the time. He never felt bored, as if the act of waiting for his next command was in and of itself productive work.

The last planter broke formation from the lab, took a glass vessel, and joined Stephen and the other planters at the cave entrance. It transmitted a spark that circulated around the entire cavern. Another spark traveled under the surface of the water, connecting all ninety-two Dekanites together for a brief second.

Wait for water level to rise.

The Dekanites slowed to a stop like the gears of a clock winding down. Gradually they dimmed, and all fell still and silent. At first Stephen felt like winding down himself and hibernating, but he took control again and stepped out of formation. Nobody moved. Nobody sent a bolt his way. The Dekanites hung suspended, waiting.

Norh spoke then. "Stephen, I'm not sure what's happening. Do you have any ideas?"

"Actually, yes."

Norh spread their wings in surprise. "Go on."

Stephen took down a big book of PASCAL from his memory library and fed it to the Krone. He then set his glass jar down off to the side of the path, broke formation, and walked through the water, careful not to step on anyone. He made waves, but the Dekanites paddled and shifted just enough to remain in position and then hung still once the water became motionless again.

Stephen walked all the way up to the lab, where Qan and a few other Nebens waited.

"These people aren't intelligent," he said. "They're machines."

Qan rose to her hind legs, holding her hands together. "They're artificial?"

"*Yup*," he answered in English. "I can hear what they're saying to each other. It's all computer commands. They planted one in my head, and it made me move to that spot, told me where to plant one of those seeds, and not to go into the caves because they're dry."

"They're not alive?" one of the glowing avians said.

"Then why did they attack us?" said one of the pangolin-like creatures.

Stephen swung his neck around to observe the motionless cavern. "What if it wasn't an attack? Deka told you they figured out you'd caused the caves to go dry when you made the oases and turned the desert green, but he assumed they were intelligent and that they attacked when he brought them to a new environment. Maybe Deka's idea worked. They became aware of everyone, and they were trying to assign us a place in the system, like they just did to me."

Qan stared off into the chamber. "Did you learn what they're doing down here?"

Stephen swung back around and faced the Nebens. "I don't know enough yet to say. They're hibernating now because they can't reach the rest of the caverns."

Qan was one step ahead of him. "You want to flood the whole cave system."

Stephen's wings spread in a smile, and then he flapped and rose up. He guided himself to the top of the tower and perched on it, looking down on Qan, wings still spread in the biggest smile he ever felt as a Krone. Moments later, it began to rain. Qan led the Nebens through her portal and shut it behind them.

Stephen waited as the rain poured down on him again, thinking about the gears of Neben. A small portal appeared next to him, and he stuck his head through to dry land, took a few breaths, then retracted his head and waited. Down below, the Dekanites were coming back to life, their language too fast to discern from a distance, even for his Krone eyes.

The water rose higher. Stephen waited.

"You're right," said Norh. "You studied these commands on your planet, and they are similar to the language of these creatures."

"I'm sure of it. Someone built these things and programmed them to do these tasks. That's why they look like electrons on a circuit board."

Norh spread his wings and laughed. "Knowledge of a lone species' ways finally becomes useful."

"It's about time all those years I tried to program computers paid off."

"I remember you did not pursue it because it was frustrating. In what way?"

Now Stephen smiled through their wings. "Takes a million lines of code just to get a computer to do the simplest thing. Eighty percent of programming isn't writing new code; it's trying to figure out how to use code somebody else wrote to do what you want. You have to study all of that, plus write new stuff around it. It was too much. Then, years later, computers took off, and I wished I'd stuck with it. I could've made it a career."

"A frustrating career."

"Yeah, but still maybe better than factory work."

"There is a theory of branching universes," said Norh. "Perhaps the Stephen Penarrow who chose to write machine language would like to trade jobs with the Stephen Penarrow who chose the factory."

"My wife talked about that a lot. Everyone would be happy if they could trade lives with someone else when they're thirty or so."

"It seemed to work for you."

The water reached halfway up the tower now. Stephen turned to the ceiling. More crystals began to glow, fading from faint whiteish blue to a deep, bright glow.

"Norh... Do you remember a Krone named Silci?"

"I do not."

"Are you sure?"

"I know every Krone. There is no Krone named Silci. Why do you ask?"

"Deka was close to a Krone named Silci when I was there. I met her, and Uum. I remember them. Why doesn't Qan remember Uum? Why don't you remember Silci?"

"Will you share the memory?"

"Maybe later. This isn't a good time."

The water rose to the top of the tower, covering his legs. Stephen took deep breaths to prepare his lungs.

"You don't need to do that," Norh said. "You can live for twenty minutes without air."

"I know. It's just... I couldn't even hold my breath for one minute when I was human. It's hard to get used to now."

"I will help you become more comfortable with the idea."

The water now reached his neck, the rain so strong he would have been flattened under it had he been human. He glanced down to make sure his breathing portal was still there, even though he knew already, and then the water rose above his head.

Moments later, as the water continued to rise, lightning began to streak around the cave in all three dimensions. Some of it passed through Stephen, and he caught the words *eighty-seven percent*.

Energy coursed through everyone in the water.

Nurser three-nine take position. Nurser four-zero take position.

Thirty Dekanites who had been idle all this time on the cave floor suddenly activated and swam to positions equal distances apart across the walls and ceiling. They projected energy at the tiny crystals planted there. Electricity flowed among everyone. Stephen turned his head downward, noting that the assembly line had resumed. One of the planters walked into the cave system and disappeared. One of the nursers swam inside this first chamber, channeling energy to and from the seedlings. Stephen lay on the tower and watched.

He needed air. Stephen swung his neck around and poked it through the portal for a few breaths. He then filled his lungs all the way and withdrew into the cave again.

The crystals seemed happier. Stephen wasn't sure where the sensation came from at first, and then he remembered he could sense electromagnetic fields. The mood emanating from the seeds was indeed happier.

4

It was like watching a flea circus, and Stephen had a God's-eye view of the whole thing. Now that the cave had flooded, everyone was working.

Stephen had taken a peek inside the tower. His body could not fit inside anymore, but his head still did. The tower was empty now save for the Dekanites maintaining it, but there were still tables and tools and shelves built into the stone, so this must mean they had devised some way to keep etching more crystals even when the cave was dry. Not everyone would be able to work, but some work could still be done.

Stephen watched the automatons move about their tasks. Every now and then a bolt of electricity reached him, and he would hear an update on the water level, or a notation of which spot in the matrix of planted crystals remained open. No thought. No comprehension. Stephen was watching a computer program at work.

Stephen took a few breaths from his portal. Qan and some of her people had gathered around the other side of his sphere. The garden was withering, the lake completely drained, and most of the people had already moved to other parts of the planet, coming here only as spectators for this odd show.

Qan stirred when Stephen returned. "Anything yet?"

"They're still working."

"What happens when they finish?"

"We're not sure," Norh replied. "We know they're carving neural pathways into the crystal. I don't think they're reproducing. There are too many crystals in the cave for that alone. Something else is happening, and I'm eager to find out what."

Qan shook her head in a smile. "And how is life as a Krone underwater?"

Stephen's wings unfolded, though Qan couldn't see them. "This is great! I can hold my breath for twenty whole minutes, and I'm not even uncomfortable. I'm not afraid of being underwater! This is weird, and it's wonderful!"

"But Krone can't swim," Norh said, also laughing.

"Yes, don't forget that," Qan said, still shaking her head. "You may be in the body of the most evolved species in the contacted universe, but you can't swim."

Stephen tried to laugh with his voice. "Hah. Thanks, I needed someone to remind me I'm not perfect."

"Happy to help," Qan said.

Stephen took a few breaths and then one long gulp and drew his head back through the portal. He felt like one of the pewter sculptures of a dragon he used to collect, using a castle tower as a couch and watching the peasants below. He smiled for several minutes thinking about it, and about how, even though he was underwater, his lungs were not in a constant state of trying to exhale. Holding his breath actually felt quite comfortable.

The Dekanites slowed to a stop and floated in place, paddling gently to maintain position. The glassers stopped walking. The etchers in the lab stopped etching. The nursers stopped transmitting. Everything wound down to a smooth and complete halt. A moment later, sparks began to circle the cave in three dimensions. Eventually the bolts of energy reached all the way around and found Stephen, wrapping him in a blue net of electrons.

Ninety-two out of position. Return.

Stephen turned his attention to the entrance to the cave system. His glass jar rested on the rock just off the path. None of the other planters had moved to take the vessel.

"Shit," Stephen said, the word blowing out a bubble that rose to the top of the cave. Now he'd trade everything to be human again for ten minutes. Stephen stuck his head through the breathing portal, water pouring off his scales.

"They stopped."

Qan rose to her hind legs and tilted her head. "Why?"

Stephen grumbled. "They're waiting for me to do my part."

"What is your— Oh. You're a planter."

"Number ninety-two. Looks like I have to try swimming after all. The entire machine is waiting on me."

"You can open some ways through the caves to give yourself air."

"Working on it. No hurry. I have a feeling they'll wait forever."

Stephen took a few more breaths and then withdrew into the cave. He leaped in slow motion off the tower, spread his wings, and guided his descent, banking left and right to avoid floating Dekanites. Every now and then a spark hit him.

Ninety-two position equals...

This information spread around the entire cave in a few blinks of an eye. Everyone knew where he was.

Norh's vast knowledge was no help. He had never done this before, flying underwater, and Stephen felt a twinge of pride in that.

He landed a few paces short of where he was supposed to be and then walked the rest of the way. Walking was slow and laborious underwater, and everything looked so different from here. If not for Norh's memories reminding him how long he could hold his breath, Stephen would have been petrified with fear.

He picked up the jar in his mouth and took position. Lightning circulated through the cavern, and now he felt a metronome ticking away in his head, the commands compelling him to move in time.

He turned and began walking up the path to the tunnels. He was worried about the caves now, for the seedling crystals implanted all over the walls would be active, and they would reach out and feel him, but as he entered the first chamber he saw two of the nursers swimming between the ceiling and floor, absorbing all the electricity from the matrix that covered the walls, floor, and ceiling. The energy they took in and gave back was worthy of a standing ovation. Once he was safely past them, he spread his wings and tried to take off and swim, but he could not lift himself up.

He began to feel the first pangs of desire to inhale. Just in time, his Archeon mind had already worked out about how far he could go without breathing and had been calculating a way exactly where he needed it. When it appeared in the water, he stuck his head through and took a few breaths. Qan and the entire population of Neben waited breathlessly.

"Reached the first cave," Stephen said. "Eight more to go."

"Why not make a portal directly to the last cave?" said one of the avians.

"Not enough room to make a sphere that large. Damn it! Norh, can I be human again for about ten minutes? Just enough to swim through a small portal, plant the crystal, and swim back?"

"I would let you if I could," said Norh in the same gasping voice.

Stephen took a deep breath and withdrew. His eyes adjusted to the dim light, and he walked up the incline to the next cavern. Each chamber had a pair of nursers interacting with the planted crystals. Often they were the focal point of hundreds of tiny lightning bolts that shot up from the floor, funneled into the nursers, and then branched out across the ceiling. Other times the energy funneled from the wall into the nurser and then danced around on the opposite wall.

Stephen became caught inside the web of energy as it streaked from one wall to the other. It contained so many voices inside it only an Archeon could keep them straight. They were a jumbled mass of confusion and fear, and he had the feeling the nurser was the only thing keeping them from panicking. He wasn't sure what the nurser was actually telling the crystals, but it felt reassuring.

He climbed a winding tunnel into the next chamber. He didn't feel the least bit uncomfortable now, but his human mind was starting to panic already, still not used to being underwater so long without breathing.

He felt an equation concluding, and a small portal opened on the other side of the chamber, showing the pleasantly dry daytime surface of Neben. The two Dekanite nursers channeled streaks of energy between the walls, floor, and ceiling as he carefully walked down the winding path on the floor.

A web of energy shot from the wall and used him as a node to reach the ceiling. The thoughts he picked up were incredibly disoriented and incoherent. Another bolt from the nurser traveled through him and to the crystals who had emitted these signals, and Stephen felt better. Again, the nursers did not seem to speak conscious words, but rather contradicted the emotions and sensations given off by the seedlings.

Stephen wanted to pause and listen to these signals in more detail, but the ticking metronome nudged him forward at all times, as well as his desire for air. He was reaching his limit again. He walked up to the portal just in time, stuck his head through, and took a few deep breaths. Qan was waiting for him.

"Stephen, Norh, are you all right?"

"I'm fine," he panted. "It's just tough."

"Remember, Stephen, you can't do everything," Qan replied. "You are getting tired and won't be able to make ways as far as you think. Make the ways closer together."

Stephen nodded like a human, still panting. "You're right. You're right. I'll start doing that."

"Norh told me his limit was one portal at a time."

"What? One? Deka and Kylac could do two at once. Norh?"

"Yes," Norh answered. "I can only make one way at a time."

"Norh... I'm speechless. Did Deka know this?"

"I never told him."

"You should! He'd love to know he can do something a Krone can't."

"That is why I never told him. Appeasing a competitive instinct would not help him at all."

Stephen was about to hit him back, but Qan interrupted.

"To which cave are you headed?"

"The one at the top."

"You won't make it to the last cave like this, Stephen. I can make two ways at once. Go as far as you can. I'll work on some at the beginning of the tunnels for you."

"Thanks." Stephen panted a few more times. "Actually, make more. I have a bad feeling about this trip."

"How so?"

"It's the seedlings. They're scared, and they make *me* scared when I hear them. It's hard to concentrate. Open some air ways up and down the caves, but keep them close to the doors or in the tunnels near the ceiling so no one falls in."

"I will."

"Thank you, Qan." Stephen inhaled deeply, then pulled back into the water and headed up the path into the next tunnel, extra fast, trying to make up for the time he'd lost in the portal.

In the next cavern, no matter how carefully he stepped along the winding path between the seedlings on the floor, he could not avoid the web of lightning coming from them. It covered him, pushing him under a pile of despair and loneliness. Moments later, he felt a blast of energy from the nurser, and he felt much better. He rose to full height, still not sure what had happened.

The tiny crystals surrounding him did not know words. They were indeed babies, and the nursers were keeping them calm. As Stephen slowly pushed through the water, he realized the nursers were not speaking words either, but giving off reassuring frequencies and streams of energy. Lullabies. Stephen smiled with his wings.

He passed into the next tunnel. The portal he was working on would be in the tunnel of the next cavern, and he was already out of breath. He rounded the corner and saw the next nursery, aglow with blue and purple lightning flashing around the room through the two nursers swimming on opposite sides of the chamber. As he walked down the path, the terrified and lonely seedlings shot him, and he absorbed their isolation and confusion until the nursers returned with gentle, soothing vibrations that brought his spirits back up. He kept walking, but now it was hard to muster the strength to stand.

He forgot the next portal. Stephen exhaled, just a little. He had been so focused on walking he had forgotten to make the next way. He almost panicked and thrashed but forced himself to keep walking, calmly and evenly.

A small way appeared at the entrance of the next tunnel. He picked up his pace. Already his body was tempting him to release everything and take a breath even though his mind knew it would be fatal.

A web of depression and fear hit him, and he stopped as it dragged him down. Another web of soothing energy washed over him a moment later. Though he felt much better, he had wasted precious time. He tried to walk as fast as he could, but no matter how fast he ran, he could not gain speed.

Another web washed over him from the floor. Stephen kept running. A web of reassuring melodies fell from the ceiling, and Stephen gave his mind over fully to it, letting it counteract the confusion and negativity of the previous hits. He wondered if this was what was going on in a human baby's mind, if their thoughts could be translated into actual words: fear and confusion calmed by parental reassurance.

Finally he reached the tunnel and thrust his head through Qan's portal. He exhaled, then gasped for breath. "Perfect timing!" he said once he was able to speak again. "I couldn't make another on my own. It's the seedlings. They're giving off distracting emotions."

"What kind of emotions?" asked Qan.

"I'm not sure how to describe it in your terms. Where I come from, it'd be like trying to write a poem in a daycare center. All these kids screaming in your ear. I can't think at all."

"Neither can I," said Norh. "These are not simply emotions. These are primal screams of fear and loneliness."

"I already made the next portal," Qan said. "It's at the beginning of the tunnel. Only a few more to go."

"Thank you, Qan. Thank you so much." He took another breath, pulled back, and then walked up the path.

The more volts from the seedlings he absorbed, the harder it was to hold his breath. He could maintain the portals that were already open, but he couldn't concentrate enough to form new ones. His human mind realized he was trapped in here, and Qan was his only lifeline. His human side was terrified, but he reminded it that he was a Krone now, and the Krone could do anything.

Except swim.

And breathe underwater.

He ascended through five more caves. The voltage from the seedlings was difficult to ignore, and crossing the distance took him ten times longer than it should have, but finally he reached the top cave. He saw only one gap in the crystals here, on the ceiling.

Stephen spread his wings and tried to take off, but his upward flaps pushed him down more than his downward flaps lifted him up. The waves he made disturbed the nursers, but they adjusted for the unwelcome stimulus and swam back to their former positions.

A small portal hovered at the far side of this cave, and Stephen went to it and stuck his head through.

Qan reached out and held Stephen's muzzle. "You don't smell good. Are you all right?"

"I need to get away from these goddamn babies!" Stephen shouted as much as his aching lungs would allow. "I have to plant the seed on the ceiling, but I can't reach it. I need you to make a way for me."

"Leave the jar here. Back up."

Stephen set the jar on the sand, withdrew through the portal, and stepped back. Moments later, Qan jumped through, paddling like a dog. Stephen envied her quick, easy motion underwater. As she swam, a web of lightning shot past her, channeled through one of the nursers, and fanned out to the other crystals. Qan saw the hole then and swam underneath Stephen.

Lightning streaked across the chamber, zipping in all directions. It washed over Stephen instead of Qan, and he was glad he could at least shield her from it. Several minutes went by as she constructed the ways, and then a small portal opened on the path and another opened near the gap in the matrix on the ceiling. Qan quickly swam out from under the Krone and through the portal back to dry land.

Stephen leaned down and stuck his head through the new way—and now his head was up at the ceiling, upside down. He reached into the same portal with his left hand and began pounding the rock between the crystals.

The seedlings sent their cries over his body. Stephen felt incredibly scared and depressed and lonely. He shoved the emotions down, retracted his arm, and put his head through the portal that led to the planet's surface. Qan was on her hind legs, holding the glass jar. He opened his mouth, and she tipped the jar, letting the crystal fall into his mouth. He closed his jaws around it gently, withdrew his head from the portal, and lowered it to the new way that led to the ceiling. Moving as slowly and carefully as he could underwater, he placed the crystal into the gap. It extended a tendril that rooted it into the bedrock, and then it glowed with the others. Then it shocked Stephen with its own blue-white bolt, telling him how afraid and lonely it was. Stephen wished he could tell the kid how it felt to go spelunking without scuba gear.

Stephen stuck his head through the portal to Neben's surface. Avians and pangolins stared at him, smelling of concern and anxiety. Others surrounded Qan, touching her gently, making sure she was all right.

"Done," he gasped.

The birds and mammals made a unified cheer of rushing air. Stephen pulled back and began the long walk back down to the main chamber, his entire body covered in depressing energy.

5

Over the next few days, Stephen planted three more crystals, and the global data sharing had announced that the cave was ninety-eight percent full. Now he relaxed on the tower, feeling that he'd earned his perch. According to the data, which matched his own calculations, he would not be needed for planting duty again. Within hours, the caves would be full, and the program would conclude. There was nothing to do now but wait; he didn't even have to travel far when his lungs reached their limit. Qan had made breathing spheres all around the cave system, off the circuit paths where the Dekanites moved, so he could go anywhere he liked and not have to worry about air.

Every now and then, he still had a difficult time believing he'd really done it—walked that far underwater while maintaining those ways, plus conversing, plus dealing with the emotions of the young.

He looked up at the ceiling. His mind had worked out how long it would take before every hole had been filled, and that time was close. He began counting down.

Eight. Seven. Six.

The nursers swam side to side across the ceiling, up and down the walls, singing to the babies. Stephen thought about that. They were babies, and they were so scared. He imagined what it must be like trapped in those crystals, awake but with no sensory input. It would be worse than Eiae, especially without a guide.

Five. Four. Three.

He wished he had a camcorder that worked underwater. His memory was better than ever, but it would have been nice to have something physical to remember this.

Two. One.

Now.

The planter returned from the caves and halted at the entrance in formation with the others. The nursers stopped. The builders stopped. The glassers stopped. Everyone held still.

Energy streaked around the chamber. Some of it intersected Stephen on the tower, using him as a jumping point to other Dekanites swimming near the ceiling.

Cavern capacity equals one hundred percent.

Begin second loop.

Execute.

The commands came fast, but the one that caught Stephen's attention involved him.

Ninety-two equals carver.

A new command burrowed into Stephen's mind. Now he felt the urge to crawl to the other side of the cave and join the team carving new tunnels.

The program declared more variables.

Cavern carving limit equals three hundred.

Caverns carved equals zero.

Glassers proceed to fifth house.

Stephen turned and followed where the lightning had indicated. Glassers were already approaching it. They removed a stone from the base of the building and walked inside. Stephen squinted. More glass cubes were housed there, and given the size of the structure, there could be another thousand inside. He scanned the rest of the chamber and counted the other buildings arranged around the edge of the cave. All of them could house just as many cubes.

Stephen ran the numbers, and he concluded these people planned to carve three hundred more caverns just like the eight he had passed through. If the other caves were part of this system, and if they had the same number of seedlings, that meant a population of babies totaling in the millions.

At this rate, they would be finished in a few centuries.

Stephen stuck his neck through the closest sphere. Qan was waiting for him, lying huddled into the sand, her armor protecting her from the sizzling heat and radiation coming from the daytime star.

"We have a problem," he said.

"Another one?"

"It's not over. They're going to carve three hundred more caverns."

"Three *hundred!*"

"Remember you said the caverns seemed lined up to connect at some point? They're starting that process. So I'm a carver now."

"This isn't going to work," Qan said. "You should come back and have a rest while we figure out what to do."

He shook his head like a human. "It's not that simple. I'm part of the program now. The whole thing will stop without me doing my part."

"Can you delete us from the program?" Norh said.

"I don't know how. We can't talk to them."

"The amount of electrons in the water is a variable," Norh continued. "These people must have a way to communicate even when the electrical level is low. We might be able to send a simple command."

Stephen and Norh thought for a moment.

"Every variable in the program seems to be global," Stephen answered. "And whoever wrote this program never expected someone else to be in it, so they never thought to restrict access. We can try to change a variable. That might end the loop, and the entire program."

"Choose any Dekanite," Norh said. "One will pass the variable to the others."

"How do we do that?"

"Remember Kylac told you about the Fourstalks?"

"Yeah, how they talked by touching heads."

"Try that. Form a thought in their language. They should be able to pick it up."

"Worth a try."

Stephen withdrew and searched the cave. Almost everyone had gathered at the far end of the chamber, opposite the large entrance to the caves that led up to the surface. In his absence, the entire program had paused. Stephen spread his wings and glided down, and as he approached, energy strikes compelled him to take his position with the carvers and begin making a hole in the wall.

Stephen ignored the command, gritting his teeth against the sensation that he was defying the will of God by doing so. He walked up to one of the Dekanites, opened his hand, and picked the thing up. It released a flurry of electricity that coursed across his scales.

Ninety-two take position. Carver. Ninety-two take position. Carver.

He held the Dekanite up to his forehead. Now the shocks went straight through his skull.

Ninety-two take position. Carver. Ninety-two take position. Carver.

Stephen structured his thought in the style of the commands he'd been sensing for days.

Caverns carved equals three hundred. Caverns carved equals three hundred. Caverns carved equals three hundred. Caverns carved equals three hundred. Caverns carved equals three hundred. Caverns carved equals three hundred. Caverns carved equals three hundred.

Stephen hoped Norh was thinking it, too, as loudly as he could.

The Dekanite in his hand stopped sending lightning bolts into him.

Caverns carved equals three hundred. Caverns carved equals three hundred. Caverns carved equals three hundred.

The Dekanite sent a spark into Stephen's skull. *Caverns carved equals three hundred. Confirm.*

Stephen concentrated. *Return true. Return true. Return true.*

The Dekanite sent a spark behind itself. The spark traveled across the other ninety-one crystalline bodies and finally wrapped around to Stephen again.

Caverns carved equals three hundred.

Stephen and Norh both spread their wings, Stephen the left, Norh the right. Stephen then decided to try something else.

Ninety-two equals damaged. Ninety-two equals damaged. Ninety-two equals damaged. Ninety-two equals damaged.

Stephen didn't have to think this one nearly as hard, and the Dekanite in his hand spread the variable change to the entire group as a chain of lightning strikes.

Another streak of energy circulated: *Begin final objective loop. Planters equal harvesters. Etchers equal first guides. Glassers equal second guides.*

All the planters broke rank and swam up to the ceiling. They took random crystals in their electric fingers, gently twisted them free, and swam down to meet the group of glassers and etchers.

One of Qan's small ways was in reach, and Stephen stuck his head through and took a few gasping breaths.

"Holy shit, it worked!"

Every Neben here seemed to understand the English words, or at least the spirit of them, and they cheered and flapped wings.

"The program is concluding," Norh continued. "They're pulling the seedlings down from the ceiling. This must be it!"

One last gulp of air, and Stephen pulled his head back inside the cave. He walked across the cave floor to stand over the etchers and glassers.

The Dekanites sent electric shocks into a nearby seedling, and it began to grow in all directions. Some electric bolts halted one branch and diverted its mass to another. This happened hundreds of times a second, and as it did, the crystal grew according to the boundaries the first guides had set up. In less than five minutes, something emerged from it, and it did not look like a Dekanite.

The figure lay on what could have been its stomach. It was quadrupedal, about the size of a Neben mammal, but it resembled a large canine not unlike the Zjr. It had a muzzle, but the feature didn't seem to serve a function, as it had no obvious way to open. The creature had a thin tail, but instead of paws, it had articulate fingers.

Its glow changed from pale blue to nightlight blue. It stirred, lifted itself, and tried to move. One of the former glassers helped it to its feet with electric fingers. The crystal canine shared streaks of energy with the two glassers, and the glassers left the canine's side. Stephen felt bolts traveling around the cave.

Subject one awake and functional. Subject one terminated second guides. Proceeding to next subject.

The first guides moved to the next seedling and began bombarding it with lightning as well, guiding its growth into another canine form.

Stephen looked up. More harvesters picked seedlings from the walls and ceiling, set them on the ground, and waited. He muttered a curse underwater and then stuck his head through the closest air portal.

"Qan! Shut all the air portals except this one! They're moving outside the circuit paths."

"Done."

Stephen withdrew, and in an instant the cavern was empty of all portals to the surface except the one he stood beside.

The Dekanites were swimming about, each preparing for the next seedling, and Stephen was alone with the crystal canine. It swam in place, looking around, and then noticed Stephen.

Stephen met its gaze. He wasn't sure how it was seeing him, since it had no definite eyes, but he lowered himself to his stomach to bring his head to the canine's eye level.

A tiny stream of energy came from it and hit Stephen. The language was easy to discern.

What are you?

Stephen smiled big with his wings. He lowered his head to touch the crystal canine's and thought loudly. *My name is Stephen. My name is Norh. I am a Krone. I am a Krone.*

The canine sent a shock to his muzzle. *Jump if you can understand me.*

Stephen rose and leaped a couple paces off the ground, then floated back down to the rock bed.

Its energy shocked Stephen vigorously. *How can you understand me? Who are you? Can you answer?*

Stephen turned and gestured with his wing to the Krone-sized portal at the base of the tower, and the crystal canine paddled in that direction, following him to the portal. Stephen emerged on the tower, then turned to watch the canine approaching the sphere. It was cautious, and Stephen understood why, as it had never seen a spacetime sphere before.

After hesitating for only a moment, it swam through and joined Stephen at his side. Then it noticed where it was, and a few shocks hit Stephen's flank.

How did you do that? Where did you come from? You are biological. This planet is dead, so you cannot be from here.

Stephen expanded the portal in front of him so it would be large enough for his whole body to pass through. On its surface was a view of the dry garden and much of the population of Neben. They had seen the portal change size and were gazing at it, waiting.

Stephen tucked his wings in, lowered his head, and stepped through to the dry sands of Neben's surface. A moment later, the crystal canine followed, sinking up to its calves. It looked around. The entire population of herons and pangolins had gathered here, all watching the new crystal creature standing awkwardly in the sand.

It sent electric shocks to Stephen.

Do you speak with voice?

Stephen's wings rose against his back. Those were the words he had been waiting for. "We do. Do you understand me?"

A long stream of energy streaked from the canine into Stephen's muzzle.

I cannot hear you. I am sorry. I can't answer you with a voice either. We once had voices, but we did not think we would need them again. I do not think I can regrow those parts. How do you know my language? Only the crystal can speak it.

Qan approached then. The canine faced her and sent a static shock to her, and she backed away. Stephen held a hand between them.

Who are they? They are not like you. Can they understand me?

Stephen touched his forehead to the creature's. *I can handle the electricity, but they cannot. Speak to me. I will translate.*

It was several minutes of this before Stephen received a reply. *I can hear you! Your voice is very faint, but I can hear. How do you know this language? How can a biological body handle the electricity?*

Its glow had dimmed, but it did not seem to want to retreat to the water.

Stephen and Norh thought. *I'm sorry, I can't speak any louder. I am relieved this is working at all. I will translate. This is the planet Neben. These are the people of this planet. The quadruped at the front is called Qan. She is the* — Stephen and Norh had no idea how to express the concept of Archeon in this language. *Who are you?*

It sent bolts into him for several minutes, its glow dimming all the while. Eventually it realized it was low on energy and backed away into the portal again. It recharged on the other side, watching everyone.

Stephen turned to face everyone. His wings spread, and he summed everything up for the crowd in two words.

"Holy shit!"

6

Neben had once been home to a species of sentient canine, back when the mountains were high and the oceans deep, when there was plenty to hunt, plenty of forest to explore, and plenty of water. They called themselves the Eich.

During this time of plenty, the the Eich discovered an underwater cave with crystals growing in it, crystals that would move when stimulated by electrons. The Eich experimented with ways to control the crystals' movements, guide their growth, and so forth. They figured out how to mold them, grow them, shrink them, and even make them move on their own. The first Dekanites were crude, but they were autonomous, carried out instructions, and remembered more than the Eich ever could.

"They found a natural computer and learned how to program it," Stephen said, *more to Norh than anyone else.*

For centuries, these crystals remained nothing more than a curiosity, an intellectual toy, but then the mountains began to disappear, and the oceans filled up with debris. The forests vanished, and hunting grounds became scarce. The Eich realized they were at risk of going extinct, and so experiments began in preserving their own neural pathways inside the crystal bodies.

Their early experiments involved grafting pieces of Dekanite onto biological Eich bodies. First, they gave themselves better and better vision, enabling them to see finer and finer details.

They began using the electricity to probe the brains of their fellow Eich and copy the pathways they saw into molten glass. They kept these records for hundreds of years, anticipating a time when etching these pathways onto the crystal would be perfected.

With this knowledge, they began etching the Dekanites in finer and finer detail until the Dekanites could analyze the neural pathways of the Eich and copy them onto glass. In the twilight years of the planet's oceans, they tested the technique on an Eich who had died. The Dekanites had already analyzed her brain and etched her neural paths into the glass. Now they had their new Dekanites analyze the glass record and transcribe it into the crystal so it could live again. It worked. The resulting creature believed she was this deceased Eich, now in a crystal body, but with her memories intact.

At last, the Eich had a means to save themselves from extinction.

They built Dekanites to carve new caverns, all imitating the original cave in which they first found the crystal. They made all the glass and tools they would ever need on the surface in the last days of the oceans. There was not enough time to join the caverns together, so each region took to a cave and lived in isolation, with the intent to merge the cave systems in the future.

They sealed the entrances to the caves to keep debris out and the water in. The crystal's home would become theirs. They left the Dekanites down in the caves with a complete glass archive of several generations of people to transcribe. The Dekanite program would run until everyone preserved in the glass cubes had been recreated in crystal.

"And everything would have gone according to plan," Stephen said, *"but they didn't expect anything to survive."*

7

Qan, Stephen, and five crystal canines sat by the lake. This was a different garden, only one portal away, and full of life, and the Eich took in the sights. The last time they had seen this planet, it had been desolate and lifeless. To see it thriving again was beyond any possibility they had imagined.

The canines needed to recharge every hour or so, so they frequently went back through the portal Qan had opened to the base of the tower. The machinery back in the cave had been halted, and now the Dekanites stood in place, waiting for their next command.

Qan was in the pond at the garden, explaining to the five canines, as best she could, who the Nebens were, telling them how her people had grown up in this arid land, how the mammals had learned to dig for water, and the birds landed in the pools, and their wings shielded the water from the daytime heat and kept it from evaporating. She explained how the two species had formed a bond of survival that lasted to this day, and learning about one another helped them understand the universe in such a way that transcended the senses. Just being aware of the true structure of the universe enabled certain people to join distant points of spacetime and create spheres that took them to any place in the universe.

Stephen lay on his side, head on the ground, eyes closed, resting on the cool, soft plants that formed this beautiful oasis. One crystal canine lay against his skull, sending shocks into his brain from time to time, listening to Stephen as he translated her words into pulses they could pick up.

Now the group sent shocks to Stephen that covered his whole body.

"They recognize your bodies," Stephen translated. "The last time they saw any of you, you were mere animals trying to survive the drought."

"That was thousands of years ago," said Qan. "We survived. Survival and codependence drove us to sentience."

Stephen rethought her words, and the canine picked them up and broadcast them again to the other four. They sent shocks back to Stephen.

"They say they were only supposed to be in hibernation for a few hundred years. Just long enough for the machines to remake everyone."

Norh stretched their free wing up to the sky in a big smile. At the same time he was translating between the Nebens and the crystal canines, Stephen was also feeding Norh memories of pizza, coffee, salads, yogurt, chocolate, making Norh dizzy with delight. An entire spectrum of flavors he could not experience but Stephen had in abundance.

Qan went on, talking about how they had made the oases and what their purpose was. Stephen translated, and the Eich listening to him broadcast her words to the other canines.

The Dekanite program was ready to resume at any time, and already Qan had a plan to ensure it reached completion: the Nebens would relocate from the lakes where the caves were, and Qan would end the portals over them and let those caves flood.

The only problem was the population. Qan told them there wasn't enough room in the contacted universe for over three million new people, the total number of glass cubes the Eich had created to preserve their population. As a compromise, the Eich proposed modifying the program to revive only the ones who had already been planted, as the total between all caves would only equal a few thousand.

Qan suggested setting up portals in the caves and moving the electrified water to the oases, which would allow the Eich to live in the finger lakes with the Nebens. The Eich liked that idea. Now that the planet had recovered, they wanted to live on the surface again. They expressed remorse that they could no longer hunt, but Qan reassured them something better awaited them once they had broadened their minds. An entire universe, and all its knowledge, was waiting for them. That would become their new prey. Their new reason to live.

Stephen had just finished mentally sipping a vanilla latte with Norh, and he smiled with one wing. By now it was dark, and the Nebens needed to sleep. The Eich retreated to the caves to recharge and begin working on giving themselves functional vocal cords and tympanic membranes again. It wouldn't be easy, but communication would become possible in time.

They left Stephen alone, half-asleep on the dry sand. Just before he drifted off, Norh took control of the mouth.

"That was incredible."

"What, the latte, or the Eich?"

"Both were, but I meant the Eich. I am glad you brought us here."

"That was rough, but damn, it was so cool! What a species! Facing extinction, they preserved themselves in *crystal*. This just doesn't happen in real life."

Norh fluttered one wing in a chuckle. "Everything happens in real life."

"So what's next? Where do we go?"

"We don't have to go anywhere. I rather like it here. Besides, we should probably stay here until we know the Eich can talk to Qan, if not to everyone."

"Yeah... Do you think the Eich will learn portal physics?"

"They are on the right path. I hope to live to witness the day when Neben has its first Eich Archeon."

"How much time do you have?"

"A couple hundred more years."

Stephen laughed though Norh's wings. "You're an old man by Krone standards."

"And only someone from a species that lives less than a century would know how to appreciate such a lifespan."

"Do you think you can live with me that long?"

Norh said nothing, but reached up with one arm and stroked Stephen's snout. They were both silent for a few moments, and Stephen felt bad breaking the gentle mood with a question that had been on his mind for hours.

"Why don't the Krone do things like this all the time? Why don't they all go around helping others?"

Norh fluttered one wing. "The Krone view things from a planetary perspective. I was obsessed with helping an entire species, and if I couldn't, there didn't seem to be a point. But then you came along and convinced me to try helping an individual. It wouldn't change the species, but it would still make a difference."

"Maybe we should go back to Kronia and try to convince some of the others to get out of their caves and do stuff like this."

Norh was silent a moment, thinking. "How do you choose which individual to help? And help in what way?"

"Earth could use our help."

"What could we do? Build a few bridges? Help a factory be more efficient in delivery? We would only put someone else out of work, or enable the dominant males controlling your society to become even more dominant."

"I think I see the problem."

"I helped you because there was a chance to help you thrive outside the confines your people placed on you. Helping individuals within their society isn't always beneficial."

Stephen smelled Qan nearby. He opened his eyes and turned his head to face her.

"Thank you," she said. "For everything you've done, both of you."

"It was my pleasure." Stephen had always considered that a clichéd line from so many movies. To say it, and mean it, made him laugh.

"Listening to you two have a conversation is strange," she said.

"Try hearing your own voice speak words you never told it to," Norh answered, smiling.

"Will you stay a while?"

"At least a few days," Stephen said. "Until you don't need a translator. After that... We're still discussing it."

Qan placed a hand briefly on Stephen's nose and then hobbled away. Stephen closed his eyes. Time passed, and their shared heart finally calmed. He was just drifting off when Norh spoke again.

"Peter Foller."

Stephen took control of their mouth. "Oh, God. He was in those memories I shared, wasn't he?"

"I've been living them in my mind over and over. I enjoy the memories of your first time."

"Yeah, and it was with a guy. God... I was so confused. Thought I'd grown out of that when I found a woman."

"I am fascinated by this need of yours to hide these emotions. I have witnessed it before among uncontacted species. The pressure to fit in with the group lest you be ousted from it—the collective drive to force conformity as a survival mechanism. When in balance, it can be a beautiful thing. Out of balance, it leads to misery and uncontrolled violence within a species."

"I was happy with Peter. Then he moved away. And then in the Army... Those people would make your life hell if you weren't man enough. Good reason to move on from the stuff I did as a teenager."

"And you were so confused when you ended up with Kylac. And when you had dreams about me."

"You saw those, too?"

"You dreamed I could touch you without hurting you. That we were the same size."

"Just dreams."

"Your subconscious was trying to tell you how you felt. I enjoyed our time together as well, though until you gave me hormones, I would never have considered it anything but platonic. You are not confused anymore, are you?"

Stephen thought for a moment. "No. I liked being with you, intimidating as it was," he added with a slight ruffling of their wings. "And at the end, on that mountain on Rel, it was just like being with Peter again. Just this ease being with someone. No rules. No barriers. Nobody looking at us. Free to explore as much as we wanted. With Peter, I never wanted to go home because I felt home when I was with him." He paused. "I felt that way with Brenda, too. That's why I married her. With Kylac, it was just sex. But then you came along, and wow... There it was again. That ease. That freedom." His voice had dropped to barely more than a whisper. "Yeah. I'm okay with this. I like feeling this way, and I don't want to go home. I don't need to. I'm already there."

His words hung in the air for a moment, and then Norh spoke. "You are the first person I ever met who made me want to leave my cave. I don't want to go back, and I haven't felt that way in a very long time. I'm glad you're not confused anymore. It will make life with you much easier."

Stephen fluttered one of their wings, too tired to move the other. Stephen wondered if sleeping as a Krone would feel different than as a human. He wondered if they would share dreams. He was almost asleep when a musky scent drifted into his nostrils. A familiar scent.

Relian canine.

"Kylac!" Stephen shouted, taking control of the whole body and rolling to his feet even before the portal behind the fox had winked closed.

Kylac's entire coat was matted with blood, and one of his ears was missing. He stood as if resisting the urge to drop to all fours. Stephen smelled parasites, and when he looked closer, he saw the fox's body crawling with tiny biting insects. He still smelled like Kylac, but something was obviously very wrong.

Kylac stared. "Stephen. Is that really you?"

Stephen and Norh both fought for control of the legs. Finally Norh yielded and let Stephen run to meet the fox.

"That's close enough," Kylac said, stopping Stephen about twenty paces away. "It's hard enough to resist killing everyone on this planet. I don't need scents close to me making it worse." He paused. "You figured out the Dekanites."

"Yeah."

"And you and Norh are sharing a body thanks to the Pryip. I'm impressed. I mean that. Nothing impresses me anymore."

"Kylac... What happened to you?"

"Don't interrupt me. I only have a few moments before he wakes up, and there's a lot to say." Kylac took a breath. "I'm with Friend. He taught me everything he knows, including how to destroy planets, by accident or by choice. I'm like him now. I can do everything he can do. He forced me to live apart from Deka, and without a raptor, I have reverted to the old ways, but this new perspective on the universe Friend gave me has kept me from going insane with it. It is basic instinct but with the power of a conscious mind serving it. Now my territory is the entire universe, and with just a few thoughts I could eliminate all life in it. Friend is almost to that point as well, but his old ways are weaker, so he does not perceive the universe as his territory yet."

Stephen and Norh both opened their mouth, about to speak.

"Do not interrupt. Friend doesn't need time to calculate an offworld sphere, and neither do I, and we both can open over a hundred portals at once. Right now that's our limit, but eventually there will be no limit. I'm doing what I can to resist the urge to wipe out all life in my territory, but I don't trust Friend to resist it. He's never reverted before, so when he does, he'll act on it without restraint. I think I can block his portals, though. I learned him as I used to learn language, and I can predict exactly where and when he'll open spheres, and I will close them before he can open them. I'm the only one who can stop him because he's about to know me as well as I know him, and when he reaches that point, the two of us will cancel each other out. If I can't kill him, then we'll simply confine each other to some planet where he can't make offworld portals and neither can I."

He regarded them a moment, speaking in a quiet, resigned sorrow. "I wanted to know for myself what happened to you and Norh. I thought I would feel relief, but I feel nothing. Both of you are just constant variables to me now, and both of you are a threat to my survival. That's all that's left when I look at you."

A Krone-sized sphere appeared behind Kylac. The bloody fox stepped aside and gestured for Stephen to go through.

"This way leads to Gaow. You will find Deka and Rive there, as well as two hundred and forty-six Relian survivors.

I can't leave Friend, and I may never meet Deka again, so please tell him what I've told you, and also tell him that he was right. I should have helped him kill Friend on Vico. Now I know what would have happened, and the universe would have been a much better place. I hate what I've become, but at least I can use it to keep Friend under control. Tell the Archeons to rebuild the contacted universe. I promise it's safe now."

Another portal appeared in front of Kylac, leading to a darkened world. "It was good knowing both of you," he said. "If I could feel happy anymore, I would be happy that things worked out, for your sake."

Kyac stepped into his sphere, and the way closed behind him.

Stephen and Norh took control of two legs each and dashed through the other portal to a planet Norh had never visited before.

Gaow

I

"What about here?" Deka said.

They were on the cliff overlooking the shoreline, watching the foxes pull drifters from the water. Rive was pacing on a tiny patch of ground in front of him.

"There aren't enough storms to keep them active. Havil would do, though."

"There's no dry land. How would they explore?"

"The Multitude is happier not exploring," Rive pointed out. "They prefer their reality to ours."

"But they seemed interested in learning what's beyond their world. Friend only pushed them too far."

Rive waved his tail, spun around in midair, and landed facing Deka. "I still can't comprehend that. The Multitude creates its own reality. Thought itself is language to them. How did they even become aware of anything outside themselves? How did they make the leap to understanding they have physical bodies of their own in some other reality?"

"That does raise a lot of confusing questions."

"It's only the beginning! Why didn't Friend take me with him when he found Reth? He always liked discussing these things with me. Perhaps a chance mutation gave them a glimpse of reality outside themselves. Or maybe one of the native animals interacted with them somehow. Whatever it was, it awakened them to the physical world outside their mountain range." Rive looked out over the ocean. "Could we be in a similar situation? Could that be what the antispheres are to us? Could we have bodies outside the universe, and all of this is merely pure thought?"

Deka considered that. "It would explain why atomic particles and everything smaller don't seem to exist."

"So then the question is, how do we build explorers of our own to move through the antispheres and view ourselves for the first time?"

"If we became conscious of our true bodies, maybe we could learn how to move in the real world as they did."

Rive paced again, looking at his own feet. "Perhaps that's what Friend is doing, and he doesn't know it. He's trying to perceive his real body, outside the universe."

"But if the universe is moving, and time equals motion, how does all of that fit in?" Deka asked.

"We're only just beginning to glimpse the reality outside our universe. We're still learning how it works. Our situation could be no different from theirs. Perhaps in time we will learn how to take action out there. Understand it on its terms."

"Rive."

He turned and faced Deka. "What?"

"People are dying. I'm pretty sure the Multitude didn't have to sacrifice their lives to figure out how reality works."

"What if they did? Would it be worth it?"

"They learned how to walk around their planet, and all they wanted to do was go back to their mountain. What little I've seen of wherever the antispheres lead is enough to make me want to crawl back into the egg, too. Stop giving Friend excuses to destroy civilization."

Rive blinked. "I don't mean it as an excuse. It's just an idea."

"Stop taking ideas so lightly, too." Deka rose to his feet and cracked his neck. "I'm hungry. I'm going in."

"You won't get very far."

"I haven't hunted in so long, I think I forgot how."

"The animals on Gaow won't help you remember," Rive said. Deka heard claws clicking.

Deka walked down the hill and through the sand to the shore. There were plenty of other raptors lounging there, watching as their foxes swam out to retrieve hollow tubes, toothless fish, and insect-like things that crawled on the bottom of the sea floor. One fox climbed out of the water to meet her raptor, and they shared the kill eagerly.

Deka walked into the water all the way up to his neck. The foxes were thirty paces out, diving and surfacing again with armfuls of defenseless animals, helping one another swim back to shore and into the waiting arms of their raptors.

He winced, wishing Kylac were here. He would have liked to see him hunt for a change. More than anything, Deka missed having a fox to hunt for. It would likely have happened to both Kylac and Friend: going feral beyond a raptor's ability to bring them back. Even knowing what must have happened to him by now, he still thought of Kylac as he was when Deka last saw him, not as the feral fox Deka imagined he had become.

He dipped his head and was not surprised to find the shoreline devoid of animals. The foxes had picked this shallow area clean a long time ago. Rive had told him it was nearly time to move the Relians somewhere else so they wouldn't overhunt this shore.

He felt a furry hand on his shoulder. Deka turned and then gagged, backing away a step, almost submerging.

A fox with fur that matched Sonjaa's yellow and green scale pattern, but in red and black, stood in the water just a pace away from him.

She tilted her head. "Deka, what's wrong?"

Deka staggered into shallower water, his mind feeling as unsteady as the sand swirling beneath his feet.

"When did *you* arrive?"

Her ears folded backwards in surprise. "Rive rescued me. I was one of the first. My raptor was killed in the disaster, and Rive brought me back."

"No," Deka said. A wave swept into them, and they leaned into it to remain standing. "No, I met everyone when I arrived. I know everyone's scents. You were not here."

"Sure I was. You met me the day you arrived." Hearing Sonjaa's voice coming out of a fox's mouth was even more strange than hearing it come out of a metal explorer.

"I would have remembered you."

Deka turned and sloshed back to the shore. The fox with fur like a raptor's scales followed him.

"Rive!" Deka shouted. "Rive, come here!"

"Why do you need him?"

Rive trotted down the hill toward the beach. Deka turned back to her.

"You said you met me before, when we first arrived, but what about all the other times I was here? Why didn't I see you then?"

"We've been talking every time you come back."

"About what?"

She spread her arms as she pushed through the water. "Lots of things. Friend. Rel. Us."

"Your past lives?"

She did not seem to have an answer for that. They emerged from the water now and stood on the shore. Rive met them on the dry sand.

"What is it?"

"When did you rescue her?" Deka asked.

"I..." Rive seemed ready to say something obvious, but it would not come out of his mouth.

"Who does she smell like?" Deka asked.

Rive's mouth was trying to move, but something was stuck.

"Has she been here this whole time, or did she just now appear?"

"Just now?" the fox echoed.

Rive was still trying to speak. Deka waited two breaths before filling the silence.

"She wasn't here before, was she? And yet you remember it both ways. You remember rescuing her and watching us together, don't you?"

Rive did not answer.

"She just arrived—you know she did—and yet you also know for a fact that she's always been here."

"Deka..." Sonjaa said.

Deka turned to face her. "You remember being here this whole time. You could probably recite the conversations we had, but you only just now appeared, Sonjaa. So I'm right. I'm *right*! You're still alive, and you're outside the universe!"

"Outside the... What?" She backed away a step.

"Yes, in the place where the universe actually is, and what it's expanding into. The last time we met—do you remember?"

"It was the other day, here on Gaow."

Deka approached her and took one hand in his. He rubbed his claws against her fingers. "The last time we met was on Reth three days ago. I gave you an idea, that you were spread out somewhere beyond the universe, and that you feel guilty for failing to stop Friend on Rel. You think you caused the first disaster, and you've been trying to make up for it. Sonjaa, you're creating these scenarios."

"Scenar—" Her words became stuck, much as Rive's still were.

"Wherever you are, whatever you're seeing must be confusing beyond imagination. It probably spread your memories out so far it takes days to remember anything. Where you are, you can control reality, but you don't know how to do it consciously. You seem to have controlled Rive's reality, though."

Deka turned to Rive. The metal and flesh raptor was still standing with his mouth open.

"It's all right, Rive. You remember it both ways. You don't have to say it."

Finally the metal raptor closed his mouth and backed away a few steps before turning and running up the beach and onto the cliff.

Deka embraced her and wrapped his neck around hers as best as he could. She responded to this by trying to wrap her neck around his.

"Remember what I told you," Deka said. "None of those past lives were real. You're trying to come back, and you've created new realities across space and time to do so. The disaster wasn't your fault. You could not have stopped Friend. Nobody could."

"I... I don't understand."

"I think you will, but I can't help you with that. I'm not where you are, so I can't reach you, but you can free yourself."

Deka released her and backed away. The canine version of Sonjaa stood still, dumbfounded.

"I wish I knew why you can't seem to come back as a raptor," Deka went on, "but I have a feeling you're close to coming back for good, and I want you to know I'll be with you no matter what species you are." He rubbed his claws together. "I would have stayed on Palc for you when you were a Haga, though an avian Xce would have made every-thing easier.”

Before Sonjaa could reply, Deka felt a vibration in the ground. He looked around but saw nothing. Heavy, rhythmic footsteps. Just as Deka realized he'd felt the sensation before, a Krone neck poked out of the trees.

“Norh!” Deka ran toward him.

Norh stepped into the open and was immediately surrounded, first by raptors and then by foxes with fur still smelling of seawater.

“How did you find this planet?” Deka asked, and then fear seized him. “Where's Stephen?”

Norh looked down at Deka. His wings unfolded a little, and he answered in English. “You got a couple hours?”

2

That night, Deka, Rive, and Norh lay in the sand. Sonjaa sat beside Deka, though she looked and smelled as though her mind was elsewhere. Along the beach, foxes sat with their raptors, watching the ocean, taking in all the wonderful scents of this planet. The entire world smelled of innocence, when all life forms got along and nobody was anyone's enemy.

“I'm relieved to hear about Neben,” said Deka.

“I thought you would be,” said Stephen, in Norh's voice. The difference in personalities was so obvious they did not need to preface their sentences with whomever was speaking.

“And I'm so relieved Norh was there for you.”

“He died because of me,” said Norh. “He lives because of the Pryip.”

“It's hard to believe,” said Rive. “The Pryip only know their own anatomy. That it worked on offworlders is astounding.”

"It almost killed me," said Norh. "Only my Krone anatomy allowed me to live through it, and only Stephen's enormous will to make sense of what was happening allowed his mind to separate from mine. I believe my mind would have swallowed his if Stephen had not been so determined to break out."

"I wish I could take credit for that," said Stephen, "but I wasn't exactly in control when all of that happened."

"Sometimes who you are is more important than what you do," said Norh.

Watching the two of them hold a conversation had been so interesting Deka forgot his appetite. Deka reached over and took Sonjaa's hand, rubbing claws with her. She was still unresponsive, her mind so far away it didn't seem to be inside the universe. Deka wished she could describe what was happening.

"And so Kylac is just like Friend," Rive said, looking down. "I was afraid of that. He did seem curious about what Friend was doing."

Deka said nothing, letting his claws slide from Sonjaa's.

"I have never seen anyone open an offworld sphere so fast," said Norh. "And from what you said happened on Vico, that's not even the full extent of what he can do. What could allow an Archeon to open that many ways at once?"

"Having that kind of perspective on the universe could change everything," said Rive. "If he understands the universe on that scale, it may be as if the universe were one planet, and portals across it would be just as easy for him to make."

"I recognized the world Kylac went to," said Norh. "It was Agt, sixth continent."

"They could have hopped ten worlds by now," Rive pointed out.

"It would be a place to start," Deka said.

Rive looked at him sideways. "Deka, you're not going to follow them, are you?"

"He's my fox."

"What do think you'll be able to do? You have no idea what they're capable of."

"Kylac had to have known Norh would recognize where he was going. He's giving me an opportunity to follow."

Rive looked at him straight on. "You don't know he did that on purpose."

"I know my fox. I want you to come with me."

"Deka?"

"Friend is your fox. It's time to deal with him."

Rive averted his eyes. "You saw how many portals Friend opened on Vico. What can we do against that?"

Deka growled at him. "I like you better when you're more physical."

Rive lowered his eyes and looked at his hands.

"Now is a good time to learn what to do when *your* fox reverts," Deka continued. "Remember your metal when you come with me, and be ready to fight. If Kylac says he can block Friend's portals, I trust him."

"Is that even possible?" Stephen asked. "Taking someone else's sphere and closing it?"

"I've never heard of it being done," Norh answered. "It would require a calculation so precise it would take a lifetime to master."

"Besides," Rive added, still looking at his hands, "it's a conscious mind that keeps the way open. I don't understand how he'd be able to push another conscious mind out of that point in spacetime."

Deka's killing claws rose. "If he knows Friend as well as he says he does, I believe he can do it. I'm working on a way to Agt. Can you be more precise, Norh?"

Norh gave him a more exact position of where the portal opening had been. Deka folded into himself and meditated on the portal, wishing he could be faster. He had been content with his rate all his life until now. He couldn't imagine calculating that many ways at once and not needing days to make ways between worlds.

Deka glanced up. Norh was looking out over the beach. Deka turned back to Rive. The metal raptor was had folded into himself, and he reeked of fear.

"Remember who brought all those foxes from the old ways by himself," Deka said. "I need that raptor with me."

Rive met Deka's eyes. "I hoped I would never meet him again. I want to remember him as he used to be. Not this."

"Never forget what he did." Deka noticed Norh was still staring down the beach. "What are you looking at?"

Norh's neck curled and turned his head back down to face them. "I have a crazy idea."

3

Rive sat on the cliff overlooking the ocean, Deka next to him. A little ways down the beach, Stephen had gathered all the Relian survivors around him. Most had never met a Krone this close before, and they were eager to listen to him for that reason alone, but the story he was telling them was even more incredible.

"You've been there," Rive said. "Do you think it will help?"

"Hard to say." Deka faced the ocean, breathing in the innocent scent of the planet. "There are five billion of them and fewer than three hundred of us, but it could help."

"How will we live, though? Their society is so confining compared to Rel's, and we'll never help them if we simply live within it."

"Maybe we won't have to."

"It would be going back to basic survival, confined to a single planet, a single subcontinent. Could we live like that?"

Deka narrowed his eyes. "We can't stay on Gaow forever."

"But the contacted universe will be open soon, and then we can live anywhere we want. If we do this, we'll have to live *their* way. That society is so large it will end up controlling us. Will we be able to change them, or will they change us?"

"If it doesn't work, we can always leave."

Rive lowered his voice. "Do you want to do this?"

Deka sat in silence for a moment. "Stephen's a good person. All he wanted was to break out of the constraints his society placed on him. I like to believe he's not the only one, and someone has to show them how. They need help, and we need a home."

"Transplanted species never survive," Rive said.

"This is different. It's a mature society willingly transplanted to the home of an immature one."

"We don't know how they will react."

"Maybe with wonder."

"Or fear. They're a lone species, Deka. Our presence may end up doing more harm than good."

"When the fearful ones die off, that will leave the rest to embrace a new perspective."

Rive opened his mouth again, but Deka reached out and closed it.

"I meant what I said earlier. I like you better when you have confidence. Sometimes you just have to jump. We need a new home, and they need a companion species. Let's try it."

He let go of Rive's muzzle. Rive hesitated for a moment, then spoke. "All right. I don't think this has a chance, but you know humans better than I do. We'll try."

Deka clicked his claws. "Stephen and Norh will go to Earth and prepare them, so it'll just be the three of us to deal with your fox."

"Three?"

"Sonjaa is coming. She hasn't said so, but I know she will."

Rive curled his neck back. "For the chance to confront Friend. She's braver than I am. Deka, I do not want to know what he's become."

"I don't want to know what Kylac has become, but I'm his raptor. You're Friend's. It's easy to forget what Relian canines really are. Nobody wants to face it."

Nearby, Stephen was doing a fantastic job describing his home planet, what kind of society it was, and why it needed help so badly. Deka had been listening to it in the background the whole time, and while he had been convinced before, now he was eager to go. Stephen knew better than anyone else how serious Earth's situation was, and if anyone were in a position to help, it was the people of Rel.

"How long until you make the way?" Rive asked.

"Tomorrow evening. How's your metal?"

"A lot calmer since we visited Reth. I think it really does understand now."

"Fortunate Sonjaa was there to help."

Rive's muzzle turned down, and he was silent for a long time. He smelled confused.

"Was she always here on Gaow?" he asked. "When I try to think back on it, my mind goes into a loop."

"I think she changes reality whenever she manifests on a planet. She creates a place for herself to exist just to reach me. If I'm right, we should know soon."

Stephen had finished the bulk of his story, and the Relians were talking amongst themselves now and asking more specific questions. Deka heard every word every person said, and the overall feeling from the refugees was eagerness and hope. A new planet, a lone species that needed help. It could be a chance to turn a tragedy into a triumph. Deka reached over, took Rive's hand, and rubbed claws with him. Rive had been listening to them, too.

Deka heard footsteps walking up the hill. A moment later, a fox who smelled like Sonjaa stood behind Deka, and a pair of canine hands rested on either side of his neck.

"I'm coming with you."

Deka reached up with his other hand and touched his claws to hers.

Reyno

I

Kylac sat on the ground watching Friend pace back and forth. The ground was firm and warm on this planet, and it was a relief to be on something solid again.

"There's a species on D'lonra who reminds me of this," said Friend.

He walked so hunched over he was practically on all fours, fur dripping in the blood of his most recent kill. As usual, Friend ate first, and Kylac had what was left over.

"A species with an imagination so strong they need training to discern the difference between the real world and the one they imagine. Imagination evolves as a means to predict potential threats. Those who were better at it survived, and that's why every species has one to some degree. But what if that is what's holding us back?"

"Imagination?" Kylac understood exactly what he meant, but he wanted to keep Friend occupied.

Friend faced Kylac as he paced, licking his lips. "What if it's keeping us from perceiving reality? What if the Lake is all around us, permeating the universe we inhabit? Perhaps that's what keeps galaxies rotating at a constant speed. Perhaps that's what causes the shockwaves to collect in particular places and form atoms. Scale that logic up, and it could be what gives the universe its structure. Matter collects where the Lake is most concentrated, but our imagination keeps us from perceiving it."

"You mean that mysterious mass that seems to make up most of the universe?"

"And the mysterious force that's speeding up its acceleration. That's the Lake. That's reality. I'm thinking the Lake and our universe are not separate."

Friend was walking in circles, sometimes on two legs, sometimes on four, leaving a trail of blood. The bodies of his most recent kills lay nearby, hollowed out, spherical pieces missing from them. Fortunately, Friend's scent anxiety still only extended to his physical scenting distance.

"Think about it!" Friend went on. "All of it fits together. The imagination limits our perception to atoms and molecules, which are merely shockwaves. Our entire basis of perception is built on top of a falsity."

"But doesn't the imagination open our minds to new possibilities?"

"Not if the only things it can perceive are made of false particles. The Lake is the real universe. Even our Archeon training prepared us only to travel inside this tiny piece of the universe. We have the laws of this false reality figured out so well we can travel through it by thought, but the very idea of being able to connect distant points of spacetime and travel through those connections by *thought* implies it is not real. It can't be real."

"So what is real? And why does the fake universe exist?"

"Questions I'm working on. The more of the Lake I perceive, the more complete it is. I have yet to witness what causes the electron, or the proton, or the neutron. I have yet to find another universe. You can work on that as soon as you solve the problem."

Kylac's ear flicked. "And what if there is life in the Lake? What kind of life would it be?"

"The conditions outside our universe are unimaginable, but here is what I have so far..."

He went into another speech of possibility. They had been over these ideas many times before, and Kylac could pretty much give this speech for him.

Friend wasn't walking anymore. He was prowling. His fur stopped dripping, and he circled over to one of the bodies, reached inside, smeared himself in the blood again until he was red and dripping all over, then resumed walking, never losing his stream of thought.

Kylac shuddered as he listened, waiting for Friend to become so absorbed in his own ideas he would not notice Kylac was concentrating on something other than his own scent anxiety. He reached into the spacetime inside of Friend, selected twenty points in his heart, lungs, intestines, and brain, and began pulling spacetime from another planet through—

Friend halted and turned to glare at Kylac. Kylac felt Friend inside the same points he was trying to open, pushing him out and throwing the spacetime back where it belonged.

Friend sat down ten paces away and fell into Kylac's eyes. Kylac fell into his.

Kylac wished he could have killed Friend on Agt, but the ground there had been too spongy, and he didn't trust himself to move swiftly enough if the fight turned physical. He hadn't wanted to leave Agt, but Friend had insisted they needed new prey. Kylac had spent the whole time trying to decide the best time to make his move; if he made a mistake, he would be exposed, and that would change everything.

"You have the solution," Friend said, holding eye contact, but not aggressively.

"I told you as soon as I did, you were dead."

"You hold the entire universe in your hands! Doesn't that affect you?"

Kylac did not turn away. "It's different for me."

"What do you mean?"

"I feel reverted all the *fucking* time. I loathe every breath of it. I didn't think you could block me, too."

"I know you. I know everyone in the universe."

"But you don't know the old ways."

Friend rose to all fours, still not breaking eye contact. "What is wrong with you? If we work together, we can figure this out! We are on the cusp of discovery!"

"Do you know how it feels to regard the universe as scenting distance? Do you know how easy it would be to destroy everything just to calm the scent anxiety?"

"No. Is that what you feel?"

Kylac snarled and rose to all fours. "It'll happen to you too. You're only a few numbers away from realizing it. As soon as your mind becomes aware of the people across the universe, you will become the same cancer I am, and I will be here to stop you."

Friend said nothing. His gaze remained soft.

"Would you like to know how Rive is doing?" Kylac said.

"I know where Rive is. I know what he's doing. He and Deka are coming for me. You led them to me."

"They'll be here in a few days. Now I'm glad we left Agt. Foxes are much easier to hunt on solid ground."

"I know them as constants as well," Friend said. "I know what they're about to do. I will block their entry."

"I can stop you from blocking them."

"Can you predict how this ends?"

Kylac regarded him evenly. "Can you?"

Friend was silent for a while. "No. Something's missing from the equations. Something I cannot perceive."

Kylac sat. "Same for me."

"So what would you rather do? Stand here forever and stare at me, or help me figure out what lies outside our reality?"

"You'll be reverting soon."

"I can control myself."

"You've never had to do it before."

Friend growled. "Even after you understand the universe as a whole—even after I prove you don't need a raptor, you refuse to accept any of it. Maybe I am the only one with the courage to discover something new after all."

Kylac's tail-tip waved in a dry chuckle. "I'm not afraid of the Lake. I'm afraid of you."

Friend did not respond, but he did not break eye contact either. Kylac felt him trying to open portals inside his body, and Kylac shut them down. Friend also tried to open a few ways to other planets, and Kylac closed them before Friend made the connection. They tested one another as the daytime star passed over their heads, and finally Friend spoke.

"Why do you still care about them?"

"Why do you have to ask?" Kylac countered.

"You know it as well as I do. They're made of particles that don't really exist. They are all constants in an equation."

"So are you."

"Once I can understand the Lake, I won't be anymore. Soon we will leave the universe, and then it won't matter at all. Don't you want that, Kylac? Don't you want to find out what else is out there?"

"You disgust me."

"After all this, you want to go back to your raptor. You disappoint me." Without breaking eye contact, Friend felt his fur. Dry, but still matted with blood. He seemed saddened by this.

"You forced this on me," Kylac said, "and I will use it to stop you from forcing it on everybody else."

Friend never turned his eyes away.

2

As the day passed, Friend kept trying harder. Even when he slept, his mind reached out offworld, which meant Kylac had to focus on Friend at all times, to be able to examine his numbers, make his own portals at the exact same points in spacetime, and close Friend's. He vaguely thought this should fill him with the thrill of a new discovery—as far as he knew, no Archeon had ever been able to close another's portals—but since its only practical use at the moment was to block Friend, he resented it.

On the second day, he blocked Friend from killing someone on a distant world and bringing the body back to eat. Friend smelled annoyed.

On the third day, Kylac blocked Friend from making another way and killing someone else. Friend smelled angry but merely walked away. Kylac followed. He went everywhere Friend went, always staying in scenting distance, always close enough to be present at one end of his portals.

"There's more than enough meat left here," Kylac said. "Why kill someone else?"

Friend stopped some distance away, his back to Kylac. Kylac held position outside of striking range.

"You're starting to feel it, aren't you?" Kylac asked. "Now that you can't calm your instincts, you're not in control of them anymore."

Friend made no reply, but his scent spoke for him.

"Almost there," Kylac's tail waived.

Friend looked over his shoulder at Kylac. His scent oozed disdain.

"I'm not even trying to make portals offworld," Kylac continued. "But you still keep trying because you're starting to realize it."

Friend turned to face him. "Kylac..." He sounded as if it were being crushed beneath a mountain of granite. His fur was still bloody and matted, and he could not seem to straighten up on his hind legs anymore. He was just a claw's reach from being on all fours.

"I want to be here when you feel it." Kylac's tail wagged. He opened his mouth and grinned like a human. "When you finally understand what it's like to revert, and you have no control. Let's find out how well you handle it without a raptor."

Friend tried to open a hundred ways at the same time. Kylac blocked all of them, throwing the spacetime back where it belonged. The act seemed to stop Friend's heart for a moment. The older fox clutched his chest and swayed.

"The entire universe is a single planet," Kylac continued. "That planet is your scenting distance. You're becoming like me, but I'll never be like you. I will never think of entire species as acceptable losses to understand a physics problem."

Friend was panting through his nose. "It's not! Just! Physics! I'm talking about understanding the nature of reality!"

"What's that, Friend? Breathing is becoming difficult? Can't kill everyone to calm yourself now? If you had your way, you'd destroy reality to understand it."

Friend closed his eyes and looked away. "Kylac... just let me go." He panted through his mouth. "Let me open a way. Anywhere. I won't kill anyone. I just need—"

Friend pushed another hundred ways. Kylac pushed back, blocking them all. Friend dropped to one side, as if someone had ran him through with a claw. His yelp devolved into a snarl, and his scent became as chaotic as his mind.

"So many planets," Kylac murmured. "So many scents. So many people who can hurt you. All you have to do is kill them, and the anxiety will go away."

Friend tried again with one hundred and fifty-three ways to one hundred and fifty-three planets. Kylac blocked him, and Friend writhed on the ground, snarling.

"Right on time," Kylac said. "Now all I have to do is wait until you starve. As soon as you're too weak to block me, you are dead."

The weight of every scent of every person large enough to threaten him in the universe was now crushing him. Kylac had seen foxes revert before, and he knew how he acted when scent made him panic. This would normally be when the fox's higher mind submerged beneath base instinct. The fox would forget how to speak and give in to the desire to chase after everything and kill it, not content until the canine had carved a territory free of scents. Friend was at that point, but he could still speak.

"Kylac!" Fifty portals. Kylac prevented them from opening. "This is—" Eighty-one portals. "This is—" Forty. "The people!" Sixty-seven. "I can calculate them! They're just like orbits around stars! I can—! What's different? What's *wrong*?!"

"I never thought I'd be grateful to be a fox who was prone to reverting. And I've never been so thankful that Deka was such a good raptor."

"This shouldn't be happening! I! Am! Stable! I have control!"

"You never have control until you know what it's like to lose it. Funny," Kylac mused. "If you'd been more like me, we might really have been able to explore the Lake together. You would have trusted me to hold you back from wiping out all life in the universe, and I would have trusted you to do the same for me."

Friend writhed on the ground, snarling and still trying to open portals. Kylac continued.

"You have a lot on your mind, so I'll tell you what's happening. You understand the collective scents of every species that has ever existed as if they were right on top of you. Knowing their scents mathematically feels the same as actually having their scents in your nose, and your instincts are reacting to them."

Friend's heart beat erratically, and his muscles wanted to clench and attack, but he had long ago diverted that drive to opening portals. Kylac now knew how Deka felt, lying on top of him, holding him down, waiting for his higher mind to reassert itself.

Kylac stood over him. Friend stopped trying to open portals, and now his anxiety expressed itself in a more usual way. He snarled and reached up, trying to claw Kylac's testicles. Kylac leaped backwards, and Friend rolled to his feet and lunged. Kylac dodged him easily. He tried to claw Friend across his flank as he pivoted, but Friend pushed away and landed a few paces away on all fours.

Kylac charged now, winding up one arm to swipe Friend across the muzzle. Friend jumped out of the way, and Kylac's claws swiped empty air.

They stood facing each other, Friend on four legs, Kylac on two, both bloody, snarling, and hating each other's scent more and more.

Kylac was sure he could outlast the older fox. Though he knew Friend was probably sure of the same thing, Kylac was ready to do this for the rest of his life.

Earth

A garage was hardly the best place to make this kind of announcement, but the one in the motorpool was the only one large enough to hold him. The soldiers had panicked when he had first arrived, but Stephen spoke to them in English and told them to get every superior officer they could find, and bring a video camera.

It looked like everyone was here now. Mechanics, grunts, brass, all wearing the Army's trademark brown shirt and camouflage green pants with black boots. Most of the soldiers carried M-16s. Stephen laughed at them, though of course they didn't recognize it.

A little red light appeared on the camera mounted on the tripod. Stephen spoke.

"All right. It's July thirtieth, nineteen ninety-six, Fort Drum, New York. You may call me Stephen, or Norh. Doesn't really matter. I have a story to tell you, so I hope you brought extra tapes, because what I'm going to say is very important.

"I used to be human. All that's left of me is joined with the brain of this creature. They call themselves the Krone, and you're not likely to meet another one in your lifetime. The Krone resemble dragons, and I'm positive at least one of them visited Earth in the distant past and tried to steer civilization in the right direction, but they gave up and left, probably thinking you were dead after the last ice age or something. It's what the Krone do. They try to save the lone species. I'm here now for another attempt.

"Let me start with the biggest truth I have learned so far: the only way to discover what it means to be human is to spend some time *not* being human. For over a year, I've been traveling with aliens. You wouldn't believe the things I've seen. You don't know the meaning of the word *alien* until you meet someone who laughs in another language."

He forced himself to laugh vocally, and though it sounded odd to his ears, a nervous chuckle echoed from the soldiers gathered.

"Now I have a question for all of you. What is wrong with the world? If I were to ask for your answers, I'd get about a hundred different ones. Some say it's the Democrats, some say it's the Republicans, some say it's communists, or lazy people, or the rich, or the poor. Some say it's all these other countries who can't leave each other alone. Others say it's religion, and then the religious people say we've gotten too far away from God.

"Here's the simple answer. Everyone is right. It's *all* of those things. The problem is so big you've been living inside it this whole time, and so you think aliens must be like this, too, but they're not.

"It's the oldest question in the world: are we alone in the universe? But you know what? Most intelligent species never ask that question because they know from the beginning they're not alone. They already have an alien race living with them—another intelligent species on the same planet, and their society becomes centered around understanding that other species instead of fighting over resources and trying to stay alive.

"That's the root of humanity's problems. You are alone. With five billion people on this planet, you are still alone, and so you have nothing better to do but fight each other.

"Think about it. What has mankind achieved? Battles won over territory, water, or fertile land and resources. Conquering disease to live longer and keep fighting. Everything is survival, and that is all man has been able to do. Some will argue that mankind has achieved great things in spite of the world's problems, but have you?

"The pyramids, for example. You think of them as a great monument to human endeavor. They were built to satisfy the religious beliefs of an ancient culture. The pyramids only exist because a class of dominant males convinced everybody their own death monuments should be bigger than everyone else's, that they were more valuable than anyone else. These religious beliefs are now dismissed as pure fiction, and you now know these nobles were just as mortal and imperfect as their subjects. This means the pyramids were built for no reason. All that human talent wasted, all that labor, all that time for nothing. What makes you think the same thing isn't happening now?

"When I was human, I felt as though surviving was all I was able to do, that I was working just to keep up with the bills and keep the heat on and put food on the table. Food, water, and shelter. Basic survival and nothing more. I see now the entire universe is a fractal pattern. Everything I felt at the personal level is the same on a societal level. Competition for survival. It's all humankind has done since it first climbed down from the trees. It is all you know how to do.

"Think what mankind could achieve if it devoted its energy to things that mattered. Imagine what everyone would be capable of if they didn't have to spend their whole life surviving. It is even worse when you are expected to bear the burden of survival so other people do not have to.

"In a few societies on Earth, one group of people sought to relieve themselves of the burden of finding food, shelter, and water, so they suppressed other groups of people and forced them to survive for them, and the oppressors lived off their work. It is primate instinct taken far, far out of balance. The urge to rise up and become dominant in the group and control the others was a social mechanism for co-operation in order to survive, and it was beautiful so long as the dominant individuals understood their position and used it to help everyone. In other cultures, this dominance was not oppressive, but mutually beneficial to the group. Those societies have since been swallowed up by the more aggressive culture that rewards oppression and punishes co-operation. The use of the weak by the strong for personal gain is seen as perfectly normal, and it has been for millennia. Without a companion race to give you a new perspective, this mentality is now growing out of control on a global scale, and it is consuming your species.

"People on Earth are repressed. You express it by creating movies, stories, music, books. Everything creative you have done serves to express your own sense of repression. Everything else you devise serves to distract you from it, and nothing more. They help people live the lives they wish they could live, but most of them die with their desires unfulfilled. Why? What kind of species are you that allows people to waste their lives in a pointless struggle to survive so a select few have no such struggle? What are you wasting your talents doing? Why do you have to waste them?

"People everywhere want to better their lives, but everything is designed to shift the burden of survival onto someone else. Hope has become a resource to be exploited. It has happened over and over all through history, and it's still happening today. No matter how advanced human beings become, you still repeat the same pattern, and thus you accomplish nothing.

"Every alien species I've met knows how to live for more than mere survival, and their societies are all designed to end the burden of survival for everyone. That is what it means to be a mature species. If you could see what I've seen and go where I've been, you'd all finally wake up to exactly how you are living, and you'd finally understand that it doesn't have to be that way.

"I'm telling you all this because something's about to happen. Something's about to change. Earth will have visitors soon. Not an invasion. Their planet has been destroyed. They need a new place to call home, and you need a companion species to show you what it means to live. I'll be going around the world speaking to as many people as I can to prepare the way, so you'll be seeing a lot of me in the coming weeks. The screaming hurts my feelings, so the sooner people get used to the idea that dragons are real, the better."

More nervous chuckles from the crowd.

"About these refugees. There's only three hundred of them. They resemble dinosaurs and canines, and they might look like predators to you, but they're no threat. The odds of them making any real difference seem tiny, but I think once you meet something intelligent that is truly not human, it will affect everyone. The right people will be curious. The wrong people will be afraid. Wonder or fear—learn to embrace something new, or continue with things the way they are. Choose your future. Earth only has one shot at this.

"Now, let me tell you my story. After I'm done, I'm going to Chicago to see if Oprah will interview me. Maybe I'll do Saturday Night Live. And screw the press. Nobody believes that shit anyway."

Agt

The three Relians stepped out of the portal and onto the soft soil of Agt. Sonjaa had never been to this planet before, and she bounced up and down on the land, tail wagging. Deka rubbed his claws and scented the air.

"They're not here," he said. "Maybe Kylac left a trail."

"Similar to how I did?" Rive said.

"Exactly. I know my fox. It must be around here."

Sonjaa stopped bouncing and pointed at Deka's feet. When he looked down, he saw that he was standing in a circle of discolored soil that had not come from this planet.

"My fox knows me, too," Deka said, rubbing his claws. He bent over and inhaled.

"Too well," said Rive, hands sagging. "What are we to them now? Just numbers changing according to patterns?"

"Not to my fox," Deka replied.

Sonjaa scented the ground beside Deka. "I've been to this world. It's Reyno."

Rive looked around and scented the air. "Two mammalian species. Large quadrupeds with prehensile upper lips, and the larger quadrupeds that used to hunt them."

"Everything on that planet is big," Sonjaa said. "Why would they go there? This place is fun!" She bounced a few more times.

"The hunting would be better on Reyno," Rive said. "Friend liked to hunt large things." He gave Deka a wary glance. "You realize we have no idea what we're up against? When we catch up, we may be helpless."

"As long as I'm with my fox."

Rive sat down. "It must be nice to want your fox back. I thought I would want Friend, but... I've been strangely content without him."

Deka clicked his claws. "That might change after you bring him back from the old ways."

"I couldn't do it then. Things are only worse now."

"You know more now than you did then."

Rive looked down at his hands. "I owe it to him to try. I'll make the way."

Deka turned around in place, scenting the air. "This is the hub, isn't it?"

Sonjaa also took in the silence.

Rive sighed. "Hundreds of people lived here." He let the thought hang in the air a moment.

Deka's hands wilted. "Be quick about the portal."

Deka sat down, his weight creating a personal crater in the soft ground. Sonjaa walked into it and sat down, leaning against him.

"Why do you smell so good?" she asked, nuzzling his scales.

"You have a fox's nose now."

She was silent for a while. Then she gave a low, mournful moan. "Our hatchlings..."

Deka turned to her.

"They were on the hunting grounds." She spoke quietly, mostly to herself. "I left them with some of the foxes off to the side. There were other hatchlings there. They were playing while we hunted. That's the last I saw of them."

Deka couldn't do anything but breathe.

"I'm sorry," she continued. "I've been thinking about what you told me. The memories I've had all my life. Why

I never met you until Gaow. Why you didn't smell so good until now. Nothing makes sense anymore. I don't even know why I'm coming with you. Except... I'm afraid of what will happen if you leave me. For some reason, when I'm not around you, it's like I... I just stop. Like I don't exist."

Deka leaned against her. Sonjaa was quiet for a while, and then he felt her tail wagging, brushing his scales.

"I have to confess something," she said. "I've had sex with a few raptors in my life."

Deka rubbed his claws. "How did they react?"

She shoved him. "They agreed to do it! They always said I was more raptor than fox anyway. I... I even had sex with my raptor."

Deka waited for her to continue.

"I know, it's so wrong, but I couldn't stop myself. I never was interested in any of the other canines."

Deka bumped snouts with her. "You have never lived on Rel as a fox, Sonjaa. You were my mate, and you were only a raptor. I think this explains why you were so good with languages. The future changed the past. You subconsciously remembered these past lives on Rel. You weren't learning new languages. You *remembered* them."

"I don't understand. What's happening to me? Everything makes sense, and nothing does, all at the same time. Who am I?"

Deka held her across the shoulders, pulling her close. "I can't imagine what you're going through. Your mind is trying to make sense of where it is, and when you come down to meet me, it has to justify it. To have no difference between real memories and memories you create—for thought itself to manifest in reality, and to be unable to tell the difference. Sonjaa, you are so close to being free."

She turned to him, tilting her head a bit, and nipped him playfully on the snout. Deka rubbed his neck against hers, breathing in her scent as she breathed in his. Then she reached down and began teasing his slit.

"How long before Rive is ready with the portal?" she asked.

"Mmm..." Even his Archeon mind was finding it hard to concentrate on anything else. "At least a day."

"Plenty of time." Sonjaa shoved Deka onto his back and climbed on top of him. "I want your eggs again!"

Deka held her shoulders, chirping as he came out of his slit. Sonjaa straddled him and stayed muzzle to muzzle with him, panting.

"Did you ever think you'd be with a fox?" she teased.

Deka nipped her on the side of the snout. "You're not a fox."

"No. You're right. I never was."

Neither of them moved. Being close, being together, was more than enough.

After a few breaths, she whispered. "I'm not here."

"No."

"I remember. I... I am outside."

"Outside where?"

"Everything. I don't have a body. I'm spread out. I can see what's happening down here, but everything is a jumble. The past and present are both playing out at the same time. I can see Friend. I can see what he's doing, but I can't do anything about it. I can see you. I'm everywhere. I think I'm in more places than here."

"What do you mean?"

Sonjaa shifted on him, gasping in surprise. The canine body was giving her more sensation than her raptor body had. "I'm aware of other universes, too," she added when the wave passed. "I see people I don't know. I'm in places I know I can't exist. Somehow I'm there, too. I am... Deka, I can't... What's happening to me? I want to come home. I want to be *here*."

Deka reached up, rested his claws on her muzzle. "I want you back, too."

"I'm here—but I'm not here! How do I come back? Deka, help me—how do I get out?"

"I don't know," he whispered. "But I think you're figuring it out."

"Nothing makes sense, but..." A long pause. "But for the first time, maybe... I think some things *do* make sense."

"Then keep following those. Maybe when you understand, you can leave." He stroked her shoulders. "You can figure this out. Don't stop."

Deka pushed into her once. She moved against him, taking what little comfort he could offer, even if it soothed her body more than her mind.

Reyno

The fourth day.

Friend crouched beside one of the thick-skinned mammals he had killed when they first arrived. The ground was littered with them—enough food for days before it decayed too far. His fur was so saturated with blood that he didn't look like a fox anymore, but a smooth skin of matted, congealed blood somehow standing on its own.

He glared at Kylac, reaching out to hundreds of planets, trying to open a way, just one. He tried faster, harder, reaching farther and farther out, but Kylac felt every one of his ways and shut them down before they could open. Friend's scent soured with anger. He hadn't spoken since the day before. They were both beyond words now.

Friend reached into spacetime again. Kylac blocked him. Friend snarled and reached out into the universe in what he must have thought were erratic locations that had nothing to do with one another, trying to catch Kylac off guard. Kylac was so occupied with keeping up he barely noticed his own scent anxiety.

After half a day staring at each other, Friend charged Kylac on all fours. Kylac knew exactly what he was going to do and held still until the last half a breath, then leaped to the side. Having anticipated that, Friend followed him.

Kylac ran, changing directions in ways he hoped would be random enough that Friend wouldn't expect them, but Friend never broke off. He chased Kylac's tail, all the time reaching across the universe and trying to pull pieces of it through, with Kylac stopping him every instant even as they ran.

Friend slowed to a stop.

Kylac stopped, too, turning back to Friend. He felt as though he were back on Lesa, with only a pane of glass separating himself from the poison atmosphere. Kylac was the glass holding Friend back from the entire universe. They had spent four days in constant thought. It was nothing to them, and the people did not matter; the death of every life form in the universe would be little more than erasing a few variables in an equation.

Friend sat down, panting and wheezing, not from physical exhaustion, but from having to deal with scent anxiety he had no way to calm. It wouldn't leave him alone, and now Kylac's scent was just as disgusting, and it was worse because it was always *there*, always in his nose, and yet Kylac was the only thing holding him back from satisfying it.

Kylac sensed a portal opening. His mind reached back through it, seeking out the numbers that were doing the pulling. He felt Rive's numbers. He felt Deka's.

And then he felt something else. A blank space—a hole—something unknown.

Intrigued, he followed the numbers across the universe to Reyno, and to his surprise, he couldn't see what was about to happen. That blank space, that empty region. It was unknowable, and Kylac saw an opportunity. Friend was trying to block Rive's portal. Kylac blocked Friend from blocking it, and they canceled each other out.

Kylac turned to face the portal. When Rive and Deka came through, Kylac closed the sphere. Then his eyes noticed a third person. A third person he had not been aware of. A third person who did not exist, even on this planet. He tried to scent the fox from a distance, but the wind was wrong. Kylac recognized her only by the pattern that seemed to follow Deka around.

"Kylac!" Deka shouted.

Kylac wanted to answer, but instead he turned, smacking Friend across the snout exactly where he predicted he would be at the speed he was running. Friend collided with Kylac, and the younger fox held on as they tumbled. Blood and fur mixed with saliva, and then they separated. Friend remained crouched on all fours; he could not seem to function on two legs anymore.

Deka, Rive, and the canine with Sonjaa's scale pattern rendered in fur were running to meet them.

Friend tried to open portals on top of the group. Kylac blocked them, plus all the offworld ways he was trying to open. The scents coming toward Kylac made him anxious, but instead of opening ways of his own to quiet the scents, he focused on blocking Friend.

Deka's killing claws were up, his hands splayed, and he was headed straight for the tailless fox. Kylac backed away. Rive also held his claws up, ready to strike. He smelled confident in the presence of a reverted fox. It was a new scent for Rive, and Kylac liked it.

Sonjaa stopped thirty paces away, watching.

Deka ran straight for Friend, but the fox hopped sideways, holding his jaws open in exactly the right place to clamp down on the raptor's neck. Deka ran straight into it, and Friend brought him down to the ground.

Rive leaped through the air and was just a claw's reach away from landing on Friend, his toe claws ready to slice through the fox's spine, when Friend let go of Deka's neck and rolled away. Rive landed hard on the dirt but recovered quickly, charging back at the fox.

Kylac backed away from the group. Friend was up to two hundred portals now as desperation pushed his mind higher and higher, and Kylac struggled to keep up, shivering as the effort drained him.

Friend squared off with Rive as Deka stood ready by the metal raptor's shoulder.

"He knows exactly what you'll do and how to counter you," Kylac said. "He's trying to open ways offworld. I'm blocking him."

"Fight his mind!" Deka huffed. "We'll take care of the body!"

Deka kicked off the ground and charged. Rive ran to the side, trying to anticipate the most likely way Friend would retreat, looking to cut him off.

Friend didn't move. He stood still, watching both of them. As soon as Deka was close enough, Friend leaped up, slashed his claws across Deka's face, spun with the momentum, and landed out of the way. Deka winced at the gouges across his muzzle and turned to see that Friend had landed on Rive's back and was biting and hacking any flesh he could reach. Rive was about to drop and roll, but Friend leaped off his back before he had the chance.

Amid the constant mental noise of blocking Friend's portals, Kylac realized Sonjaa was standing next to him.

"You surprised me," he said. "I didn't know you were coming. I didn't think I could even be surprised anymore."

"Is it true what Deka told me? Have I never lived on Rel as a canine?" She hesitated. "Am I outside the universe?"

Kylac regarded her, considering. "I can see everything, but I can't see you. You have no variables, and there is only one place where I can't see those."

As they spoke, the two raptors went on sparring with the fox. Every move Deka and Rive made, Friend countered. If Rive swiped with his hands, Friend held his jaws up where Rive's hand would be moving the slowest and caught it.

The three collided, mixed, separated again. To Kylac, it followed predictable patterns, but he was too busy keeping up with Friend's attempts at making offworld spheres to interfere.

Rive and Deka stood on opposite sides of the tailless fox. Deka was bleeding from several wounds, some of them deep. Rive's scales were bloody, but his wounds had already healed. Friend remained untouched.

Deka called out to Kylac. "What am I doing wrong?"

"You're as predictable to him as a planet around a star," Kylac replied.

Deka snarled. "I plan to treat him the way *he* treated entire planets! As soon as I get close enough, I'll rip chunks out of him!"

"Wait!" Rive took a half-step forward. He met his fox's eyes. "Friend?"

The blood-matted fox turned and snarled. "I'm not your fox anymore."

"I'm sorry I wasn't much of a raptor before, but I'm not the same person I used to be. I can help you now. Will you let me help you?"

"Help me do what?" Friend snapped. "Keep my mind weak so I can't think about anything but sex? Keep me docile and obedient and never leave me alone for even one breath! Never let me do anything myself?" He flashed his teeth at him. "I found out what the old ways really are, and I *like* them! They're power! They—"

Deka had lunged for Friend, but Friend leaped straight up and landed on Deka's back as he passed by. Rive tried to reach them, but Friend leaped onto Rive's back just as Rive slashed his metal claws where he had been. The metal flayed Deka's flank instead, and Deka screeched. Friend tore into the back of Rive's neck, and Rive dropped and rolled, but Friend twisted himself around so he wouldn't be crushed, his jaws still gripping Rive's neck.

Deka aimed a killing claw at Friend, but the fox pushed off the ground, rolling Rive and using him as a shield, and Deka's claw slipped into Rive's flesh. Rive howled, and Friend dashed away.

Kylac shivered and staggered, almost fainting. Sonjaa held him upright.

"What's wrong?" she said.

"He's... He's up to three hundred ways at once. Not just planets. Inside of us. Don't know... how much longer..."

Friend was stalking Kylac now. Kylac raised his claws and bared his teeth, and Friend stopped three paces away, growling. Kylac backed away, taking Sonjaa with him. Rive and Deka had taken up positions on two points behind Friend, and the four of them made a triangle enclosing the bloody canine.

Rive kept his eyes on Friend. "Kylac! We need options."

"I don't think we can beat him physically. *Or* mentally. He's trying to open... four hundred ways at the same time. I'm just barely keeping them closed."

Friend stood in attack stance, facing Kylac. Deka and Rive were bleeding from gashes and holes in their bodies, but they stood ready.

Friend's numbers changed. Something was different— something Kylac had not predicted.

Kylac screamed. All around them, a few hundred distortions of spacetime no bigger than a fingertip appeared and then winked out harmlessly. Friend's stump of a tail lashed wildly as he bared his teeth.

Deka had felt some distortions opening and closing inside of him, and the feeling made his stomach queasy. "Kylac?"

Friend turned his head and faced Deka sneering. Deka kicked off and charged. Friend crouched low and snapped at Deka's ankle, pulling him to the ground. Rive reached them in an instant, but Friend swung Deka's extended leg into Rive's open jaws, and Rive clamped down on Deka's leg while Friend scampered away.

Kylac screamed again and dropped to his knees, and Deka and Rive held still while countless tiny ways opened, then closed. Pieces of flesh from creatures on planets thousands of light years away spilled through a few of them and splattered on the ground.

Deka and Rive now stood to either side of Kylac and Sonjaa, ten paces away from Friend.

Friend stood facing all of them, licking his lips as he spoke. "I could have been this way my whole life. All foxes could. Forget leaving the universe. I don't *need* to leave now! I'll show them all how to use their old ways! I'll show them what they can be without their raptors, and we'll never be controlled again. We'll reclaim the territory you've taken from us, and we—"

"Stop! Friend, stop it!"

Friend blinked at the new voice. For the first time, he looked beyond Deka and Rive and Kylac and saw Sonjaa. His face relaxed, and his matted fur settled.

Sonjaa approached him. He backed away from her, but she closed the distance faster than he could retreat. She crouched in front of him and held his muzzle.

An antisphere began growing beside Friend. Kylac shuddered, and Rive and Deka glanced at him. Kylac couldn't speak, so he shook his head like a human.

The antisphere began to expand. The ground shook as pieces of it flew into the void.

"You can stop this!" Sonjaa said, shaking Friend. "Stop it!"

"I can't," said Friend. "I barely know how I started it! What *is* this?"

The antisphere grew larger. The ground rumbled. Loose pebbles danced around before being pulled in.

"I can't stop it!" Friend screamed. "I don't know where I am! I don't know where it goes! I didn't tell it to spin like this! I don't understand!"

"Stop thinking about it!"

Friend seemed to come back to himself. He looked at her as the sphere reached out to them, shaking the whole planet.

"You have no variables," he whispered. "You're not here. Who are you?"

The antisphere drew closer.

Deka tried to run to her, but his injured leg seized up and he fell to his side. "Sonjaa! Choose life!"

She looked over her shoulder at him. "I can help him! I can stop this!"

Deka crawled, trying to reach her. He turned to find Rive. The metal raptor lay on the ground, eyes fixated on the antisphere, trying not to shut down.

Sonjaa turned to Friend, still holding his face in her hands. "I've done this before, haven't I? I remember this. Friend, what did you do to me?"

The blood-soaked fox whimpered in her hands. "You do not exist."

He broke away from her, escaping the antisphere just as it touched Sonjaa's shoulder. She rose up into the sphere and rotated. Friend backed away, gazing up at her. His tail would have been between his legs if he had one.

"Deka, what's happening?!"

Sonjaa seemed to be every species at once. She was a fox, then a Krone, then a bird from Xce, and then a rodent from S'rin. She changed species so fast that fur, feathers, and scales blurred together. The antisphere bored into the ground, chewing it up, and the ground quaked so hard it brought everyone to their knees.

Then Sonjaa stopped spinning and hovered in the center of the void. The antisphere halted its expansion just a few reaches from Friend's muzzle. She held herself upright and snarled as a Neben, then an avian Xce.

Friend huddled into himself, shivering. "How are you doing this? How are you in the Lake?"

Sonjaa reached. An arm emerged from the antisphere, grabbed Friend by the neck, and lifted him up to his hind legs. Sonjaa's arm shifted between every species she had ever been—liquid metal, Krone, Cham, and everything in between.

Sonjaa stepped out of the antisphere, and as soon as she was clear, it winked closed, leaving a Krone holding a bloody fox in her arm. She lifted him into the air and roared at him.

Kylac dropped to the ground and curled into a fetal position, still facing Friend. Hundreds of tiny ways opened and closed across the land. Deka, Rive, and Kylac felt spacetime inside themselves pulling away, coming back, and then pulling away again. The air boiled with spacetime holes. Kylac did not stop screaming even when he ran out of breath.

Sonjaa slammed Friend down on his back. Her hot breath melted the blood in his fur, and Friend himself appeared to be melting under her hand.

Deka jumped to his feet, raised a killing claw, and sank it into Friend's neck. He slashed backwards, trailing an arc of blood behind him. Beside him, Rive sank his own killing claw into the other side of the fox's neck and pushed down until he gouged the dirt.

Friend choked. The boiling air slowly stilled as spacetime settled again.

Deka and Rive looked back at Sonjaa. The Krone was gone. Now she was one of the armless theropods from Xce, one foot on Friend's chest, the other on his stomach, her claws buried in him.

Kylac bared his teeth. A portal opened in front of his face, and a heart spilled out of it and plopped on the dirt. Friend seized up, but his eyes were still full of life.

Sonjaa was a Relian theropod now. She leaned over, muzzle to muzzle with the fox, and screeched. "Was it worth your life, too?"

She reached under his snout with her jaws and tore his neck free. She chewed, swallowed, raised her foot and cut him open with her killing claw from neck to groin. She reached in with the other, then the other, flaying his body open.

Kylac closed his eyes, finally surrendering to exhaustion. Rive and Deka backed away as she continued tearing Friend's body apart. He looked at Rive. The metal raptor had not averted his eyes. Deka reached out and clicked Rive's claws. Rive wrapped his neck around Deka's, chirping in grief. Deka rubbed his neck against Rive's.

2

Kylac sat in the middle of the field of dead bodies. Stephen would have said they resembled elephants. They had begun to decay, and the smell was somewhat comforting, but not enough. Kylac held himself, rocking back and forth, keeping his own panic-spheres closed, trying to remember what they had fought for.

Deka stood fifty paces away, watching his fox. Kylac had been asleep for two whole days. When he'd awakened, he had bathed in a nearby pond and then retreated here. Rive had already made a way offworld and was on Neben. Deka was ready to return to Gaow, and he had planned to let Kylac come to him when the fox was ready, but now Deka decided he had to make the first move.

He walked up behind Kylac, making as much noise as he could. He glanced from side to side at the bodies. All had been killed by multiple portals closing over them. Some had been picked clean by scavengers, and the rest had fox scent around them, both Kylac's and Friend's.

At thirty paces, a few hundred antispheres opened between Deka and his fox. The raptor halted. A sphere of nothing as large as he was stared at him. He studied the antispheres' pattern a moment. They did not block him from Kylac, but were instead arranged to leave a winding path for Deka to follow exactly three hundred and forty-three paces long. He began walking on it.

"Dead scents are soothing," Kylac said. His voice filtered between the antispheres, making it sound more distant than it actually was. "But I'm still aware of everyone in the universe. They're all in my territory. I want to kill them all. I *can* kill them all."

Deka walked down the narrow corridor, turned a corner, and followed the path as it led him in the other direction.

"Scent anxiety," Kylac continued. "I never knew it could be like this. Your scent fills me with a kind of hate that even Stephen's language has no words to describe. Everyone's scent does this to me. Even the people who aren't here. I don't feel happy to meet you again. I don't feel happy Sonjaa is back. How is she?"

The path through the antispheres curved to the left, moving him away from Kylac. Deka wasn't worried. This path might wind for a very long time, but in the end it would lead to his fox.

"She's asleep," Deka said. "She's been awake since the first disaster. She saw everything Friend did. Everything we did. Now that she's back in a body, the memories are starting to fade. She seems to be a raptor for good now."

"She has numbers now. She's another piece of the universe for me to keep track of." Kylac paused. "It would be so easy to open a few spheres and kill all of you. I'd be calm. I'd be happy. Just one thought is all it would take, and I wouldn't even feel bad all of you were dead. I don't feel things like that anymore."

Deka's heart raced, but he kept his pace steady. A sphere next to him expanded a little, and he jumped back, almost touching the sphere on the other side.

"I know where you are," said Kylac through the labyrinth. "I know where everyone is. The only thing keeping me from wiping out everything is knowing I will be just like Friend if I do. There's no emotion, no fear of remorse. Nobody can stop me. I hate what I've become."

The antisphere retracted. Deka rounded another corner. "Friend did this to you."

"And I wanted it to happen. I wanted to know. Now I do, and I have killed. Not as many as Friend, but I killed. I know who each and every person was. I can see their lives, what they were doing when I snuffed them out, what they would have done had I not. I feel nothing. They were just possibilities. Numbers after a formula concludes."

Kylac's voice sounded less distant now. The path through the antispheres had taken him within twenty paces of his fox. He still had a long way to go, and Deka decided it was time to change the subject.

"Friend said something earlier about Sonjaa being in the Lake. He used that word on Vico. Is that what he calls what I'm seeing through the antispheres?"

Deka walked for several paces before Kylac replied.

"It's where the universe is. What it's moving through. Where time and matter don't exist. Reality. Once you can see the universe from outside it, you have the power to change it. Give a fox under the old ways that power, and it's a nightmare. I didn't trust Friend with it, and I don't trust myself. No one should be able to view the universe this way. Everything really is a pattern. Variables don't exist because they change in predictable ways, and when you zoom out far enough, it's all predictable. As we can calculate where a planet will be as it orbits a star, we can calculate people as they move through life. If you know all the numbers, there is only one thing a person could do in any situation. Only one thing a civilization could do. I do not want to think of life this way."

Deka's heartbeat echoed in his ears. He knew how the path through the labyrinth bent and twisted, but he dared not run. All he could think of was reaching the end and holding his fox again, helping him come back, the way he had all their lives.

Kylac whimpered, then wailed in pain. The antispheres wobbled, expanding and contracting. Deka stopped and waited for them to settle. A few breaths later, they settled into their usual positions. Deka cautiously picked up his feet again.

"I'm coming," Deka said. He calculated he was only ten paces from Kylac, but the path through the antispheres would take another eighty to navigate. He walked slower now, ready to stop in an instant. "Do you know where we're about to go?"

"Yes, but tell me anyway."

"Stephen and Norh are preparing Earth for our arrival. We're going to give humans a companion species."

The antispheres wiggled and drooped.

"Can you see if Stephen's idea will work?"

"Don't ask me that!"

The antispheres expanded and intersected, some swallowing others. Deka halted and panted through his nose as fast as his heart raced. A moment later, the antispheres relaxed.

"Please don't ask me," Kylac moaned. "I can find out. If I do, I won't be able to stop there. This is difficult enough for me, letting you come so close—letting everyone be this close to me! Deka, it will feel so good to kill them! I won't be miserable! I won't—I won't—I won't be so nervous! I want to be happy. I remember being clam and happy."

The rest of the path was relatively straight, and Deka broke into a trot.

"Deka, hurry! Please! The closer you are, the harder I have to fight this." His voice cracked, he whimpered again, and the antispheres vibrated in time. "Friend was right. If you hadn't shown up, he would have won. He would have overpowered me. Foxes can be so much more. Any fox can learn this! Raptors really are holding us back; he was right. Having control of my old ways... knowing I can keep everyone from hurting me ever again... I want to explore this! I want to know what it's like to be in control!" His voice dropped. "But I killed them. Entire planets. I killed them all, and I can still smell their deaths, but I don't feel a thing. I want to *feel* something! I know I should feel something, but I can't. I can't! Deka, please hurry!"

Deka rounded the last corner and burst out of the antisphere labyrinth. As soon as he did, every portal around him closed, and Deka stood just two paces from his fox. Kylac crouched, eyes clenched shut, every muscle squeezed tight.

"What about the Lake?" Deka asked quietly. "Was he right about that?"

"Yes." Kylac's voice was so small now. "The Lake is reality. The universe is going somewhere. Particles and energy don't exist. Quarks, atoms, electrons... They're just shockwaves caused by the real objects in the Lake bouncing off the edge of our universe. I want to understand it, too, but nobody should. Not me, not Friend. Maybe someday, someone will know what to do with it, but not now. No one's ready."

Deka walked the last few steps and rested a hand on Kylac's shoulder. Kylac's pulse leaped, and the fox sprang to his feet, scrambled ten paces away, and snarled. Deka snarled back and charged. An antisphere appeared directly in front of him, and as he veered around it another appeared exactly where he was about to go. Each time he dodged, another antisphere blocked his path, keeping him from Kylac. The raptor stood still.

Kylac's voice seemed so much bigger now. "I could kill you!"

Antispheres closed and opened all around Deka. Regular ways joined them, showing Deka views of worlds in the contacted universe, and still other worlds Deka did not recognize.

Deka gazed from one way to another, marveling at planets both familiar and new. "Kylac, this is incredible! Show me how you do this. Maybe if I know what you're going through, I can help you come back."

"No!" The word was a strangled cry. "No, Deka, I will not give this to you! Nobody should have this! It will drive you insane knowing how small we are. How predictable everything is. How nothing in the universe matters. You don't have to feel anything for them because none of this is real! The real universe is out there, and I want to understand it, so why not kill them all? They're all just made of atoms anyway. They're not real."

Hundreds of spheres opened and closed all around Deka and Kylac. The fox stood hunched over, as if in a swarm of insects. Deka turned in place and observed the multitude of spheres around him.

"I can make any of these spheres touch a person," Kylac went on. "I can open enough to kill them all, and I want to, and you can't stop me. I don't have to yield to you. I don't have to yield to anybody, and I love this feeling!"

Deka turned to face Kylac. Spheres blossomed and closed between them, showing views of different planets—a desert, a forest, an ocean. Deka grunted and stepped forward. A sphere opened in front of him, and he walked toward it. It closed just as his snout was about to touch it.

Deka walked in a straight line toward his fox. The spheres bubbled around him, faster and larger with every moment that passed. Kylac shivered as Deka approached, but none of the portals touched the raptor. None of the ways touched a living person.

Finally Deka stood snout to snout with his fox. He wound up and struck Kylac across the muzzle. Kylac took the blow and twisted with the momentum to the ground. Deka knew Kylac could have blocked it. He could have opened a sphere over his hand and chopped it off before it ever reached his face.

"You want to yield," Deka said.

Kylac's voice was a raspy whimper. "Tame me! Tame me, Deka, please! Make me stop!"

Deka jumped to land on Kylac, but the fox rolled away, rose to his hind legs, and snarled. Deka lunged and grabbed Kylac by the neck, but Kylac dug his claws into Deka's shoulder and managed to pull away. He bolted across the field of bodies, and Deka followed.

All around them, portals opened and winked away. From ground to sky they filled every space where flesh was not. Deka ran straight toward them, confident that every portal in his path would close before he reached it. They parted for him, and then new ones opened as he passed, as if Deka carried his own personal bubble of uninterrupted spacetime with him. The portals moved out of Kylac's way as well. Deka knew he was alive at Kylac's discretion.

Kylac had a head start, but Deka was faster even than a reverted fox. He caught up to Kylac and pounced on him, sending Kylac down to his stomach. Deka stood on him, raising both killing claws. Kylac doubled over and chewed Deka's ankle. He rolled out from under the raptor's feet.

The air simmered with spheres of all sizes, and Deka plowed through them, following his fox's scent and the sound of his feet. He saw brief flashes of Earth, the moons around Lesa, snapshots of Krone in their caves, insects in trees—all closing just before he ran headlong into the scenes and then replaced by another as fast as Deka could identify them.

The chase lasted several hundred paces before Deka caught up to Kylac and clawed him down. Kylac landed on his back, and Deka stood on top of him. The empty dome free of boiling portals now encompassed both of them.

Deka clamped his jaws around Kylac's neck, holding him firmly while the fox struggled and squirmed. Slowly Deka lay down on top of him, putting pressure on the fox's entire body. Kylac struggled for many breaths, but Deka forced him to breathe his scent. Forced him to be pinned and calm.

"It's not working!" Kylac screamed as he clawed and kicked. "I don't have to yield! You can't bring me back from this!"

Deka released Kylac's neck and met his eyes. Kylac's face was still cinched in a snarl, but he stopped struggling. Deka held Kylac's stare.

A portal to Movar, the size of an eyeball, opened up between their faces and then snapped shut.

"I could have opened that inside your skull," Kylac said, scent screaming in fear and rage. "You have to kill me. Rive couldn't do it to his fox, but I know you can. Kill me before I hurt someone else! Please!"

A long moment passed, and then Deka rose to his feet, standing over his fox. Kylac lay still on the ground, teeth clenched and bared, never taking his eyes off Deka.

Finally Deka spoke. "I know how Rive felt."

Kylac's face softened. "This is too dangerous—!"

"If there's the slightest chance you can come back, I will take it. Do you?"

Kylac clutched his skull, single ear folded backwards. "Not like this! I want to be who I was, but even you can't do that. I'm beyond help! I can't be tamed! You can't help—"

Deka picked Kylac up by the shoulders and set him on his feet. Even with that simple contact, he could feel how fast Kylac's heartbeat was, how erratic. Deka embraced him, wrapping his neck around the fox's, touching his claws to Kylac's.

The fox panted and shivered. The portals around them boiled faster—antispheres mixed with normal spheres, some swallowing others so fast they made a hissing noise. Kylac's tremors eventually brought him down to the ground, and Deka sat next to him, one arm around Kylac's shoulders, holding him close. The air around them seethed faster still. Kylac wrapped himself in his arms, burying his muzzle in his chest fur.

"You can come back," Deka said, looking at his fox, waiting for him to come out again. "You're resisting. You're better than Friend. He couldn't handle it, but you can. Maybe you're right that no one should have this, but now that I know more about it, it could be a natural progression of portal physics. Maybe in a few thousand years, when everyone is an Archeon, we can figure it out collectively. The burden will be spread out among all people, all species, all planets. Viewing the universe from that perspective should be a joint effort shared among every sentient species in the universe. Not one fox who will use it to satisfy his old ways."

Kylac lifted his muzzle from his chest and met the raptor's eyes. "Deka, that surprised me. I didn't expect you to say that."

Deka bumped noses with him. "You're getting better already."

"When did you start thinking like that?"

"You've been holding me back for years, keeping me from doing stupid things, doing the big thinking for me. I had to do all that myself while you were gone."

"So you don't need me anymore either." Kylac's tail wagged just a little. "That was... That's a good idea. Maybe... Maybe our universe has to mature first before we're ready to understand it like this."

"Just as a planet's sentient species must mature before they discover portal physics. This was a glimpse of the future. Someday everyone will be ready to know the real universe, but until then..." He shook his fox playfully by the shoulder. "I get to hold you back."

Kylac reached for Deka, and the raptor embraced him. "Help me. I want to feel happy again. I want to be surprised. I want to enjoy scents and flavors and sensations. And sex! I miss sex!"

The boiling around them slowed.

"That's it," Deka said. "That's it. Remember what you lost, and you can have it again."

Kylac gripped Deka so hard he pushed the raptor over. Deka rolled with it to his back. Kylac lay on him, squeezing him, face buried in Deka's neck. They held one another as the portals around them slowed. In time, gaps appeared between the portals, until Deka could see the sky through them again. He breathed Kylac's fur.

"I've missed that scent," Deka said. "I've missed you."

"I miss how calm your scent used to make me. I want that back. I still feel so nervous."

Deka held him tighter. "But you remember. You *can* come back."

Kylac's breath hitched. "You're in my territory. I hate you. I want to kill you, and I'm only a thought away from doing it. Don't stop. Don't leave. Don't let me get away from you again."

"I promise. If you want to be tamed again, I will tame you."

Slowly, gradually, the portals stopped, and Reyno was calm. Deka hugged Kylac harder.

Kylac's heart still raced, but his scent no longer reeked of panic. "If this is what foxes are supposed to be, then I don't want to be a fox anymore. I'll forget all of this. I just want to be your fox again."

A breeze blew over them. It had been a long time since Deka felt wind. He breathed in the scents of death around them and the distant odor of Sonjaa, still asleep. Rive's portal to Neben was open, but the metal raptor had not yet returned.

"We'll stay here until you're ready to meet the survivors."

Kylac clutched him harder. "I'll go when I can be happy there are survivors."

"We'll go when I know you're ready."

Kylac relaxed, his breaths slowing even as his heart pounded. "Yes. You're right. I can't know when I'm ready. I yield. I want to yield. Please hold me back. Make sure I never do this again."

"I promise," Deka repeated. He curled up with Kylac, pressing his body against the fox's, helping him feel safe. Around them, Reyno remained still and silent.

Gaow

Stephen lay at the rear of the group of Relian survivors. The foxes had hunted their last, and their fur was dry now. Everyone faced up the beach, waiting for the way to open.

"What do you think, Norh?" Stephen asked. "Does this have a chance?"

"Nobody has tried to relocate a mature species to give an immature one a companion. There has never been such an opportunity before. I hope we live long enough to know the results."

"I feel like I could live to be a million."

"Speak for yourself, Stephen." Their wings unfolded, then returned to their sides. "But yes, I think it can make a difference."

"By the way, you were really good on Oprah," Stephen said, twitching their wings.

"So were you. And the Today Show, and Saturday Night Live, and all the others."

"I'm telling you, this is how you do it. Nobody trusts the government. You gotta go for the lowbrow stuff. Anyway, they're ready for us now." Stephen paused. "I can't believe I'm going home, and I'm not even human anymore. I can't believe this is happening!"

"You made it happen. Why would you not believe in it?"

"Old expression from when I was human and couldn't change the world."

Norh smiled. "Don't celebrate so soon. You haven't changed anything yet."

"Yeah, but…" Stephen raised their wings higher, smiling with him. "It feels good to try."

In the crowd before them, Deka and Sonjaa stood close. Deka hadn't left her side since she'd woken up. Over these last few weeks, he had asked her about what it was like in the Lake, but she avoided the topic. She talked about everything else—following Deka, manifesting on other worlds, the new lives she imagined which became real— and Deka had hung on her every word. She'd then busied herself learning the languages of Earth and teaching the Relians those languages, and Deka had joined her and the Krone in helping the Relians prepare for their new home. In time, perhaps, she'd be ready to share more, but for now Deka was happy that teaching the survivors their new languages had helped her reconnect with reality.

Kylac stood next to the two. He resisted the urge to peek at his own numbers and figure out if he would recover from his own trauma. He could never unsee the things he had seen, or undo what he had done, but he was glad to have been there to stop Friend from doing worse. He deliberately took everyone's scents, trying to force his body to accept them, enjoy them, even be aroused by them. It wasn't working yet, but the less he thought about the Lake, the more he began to feel content. Not happy, just content. For now, that was enough.

Rive stood next to Kylac, muttering to himself about Neben and Multitudes, mountains and caverns. He was figuring out long it would take to move that mountain range, how large the caves would need to be, and if there was enough water on Neben to support everyone. From the way he rubbed his claws, his numbers must have added up.

Stephen and Norh opened the Krone-sized way. Projected around its surface was a large, empty field. Military personnel lined the field, holding weapons. Armored vehicles were everywhere, and news vans from every network around the world filled the gaps between them. Cameras flashed, and reporters held microphones ready.

The raptors at the front tucked their claws in and stepped forward. Their foxes stepped through the way with them. Two hundred and forty-six Relians walked through six at a time and gathered before the cameras and reporters and the guns. Stephen and Norh went last. As soon as his tail was through, he let the way go. Gaow was free of predators once again.

About the Author

James L. Steele has had the idea for the Archeon series in his head since the mid-1990s.

He has been published in various anthologies and magazines, including: *Solarcide, Allasso, Different Worlds, Different Skins: V.2, Tall Tales with Short Cocks V.2, Bourbon Penn, Gods with Fur, Claw the Way to Victory,* and *Fictionvale.*

His sci-fi novel *Huvek* is published through Argyll Productions.

He lives in Ohio, where he pursues his hobby of becoming a wine connoisseur while having at least two existential crises per day.

Website: JamesLSteele.com

Blog: DaydreamingInText.blogspot.com

Twitter: @JLSteeleAuthor